ONCE UPON A WISH

16 DREAMY FAERIE TALES

C. GOCKEL ✧ COLLEEN GLEASON ✧ KASEY MACKENZIE
SHAWNTELLE MADISON ✧ ALEXIA PURDY ✧ PHAEDRA WELDON
RACHEL MORGAN ✧ ALETHEA KONTIS ✧ DEVON MONK
JAMIE FERGUSON ✧ KAY MCSPADDEN ✧ JULIA CRANE
JENNA ELIZABETH JOHNSON ✧ CHRISTINE POPE
NIKKI JEFFORD ✧ ANTHEA SHARP

Fiddlehead Press

Read more fabulous fairytale retellings from these authors - available in print and digital at all online retailers!

ONCE UPON A CURSE - 17 Dark Faerie Tales

ONCE UPON A KISS - 17 Romantic Faerie Tales

ONCE UPON A QUEST - 15 Tales of Adventure

ONCE UPON A STAR - 14 SF-Inspired Faerie Tales

ONCE UPON A GHOST - 20 Eerie Faerie Tales

Join our FB group Urban Fantasy Fiends to keep up with all the news from these authors!

CONTENTS

ABOUT THE STORIES

The Dust Wish - Alethea Kontis
A prince attempting to win the hand of a princess is helped by an enthusiastic boy, a snarky maid, and a wish-granting dust bunny.

Ashes to Ashes - Phaedra Weldon
Bounty Hunter Cynder's latest job is to hunt down a Djinn who refuses to fulfill his third wish. Not quite believing in such things as Wish Givers (especially Fairy Godmothers), Cynder's world capsizes when she discovers what that third wish is all about.

Wallina - Nikki Jefford
A beautiful orphan is adopted then imprisoned by marriage-minded trolls, sorcerers, and faeries in this magical adventure.

Wicked Winds - Kasey Mackenzie
Dorrie Gale's been a ball of anxiety since her mother was ripped away from her arms by a Kansas twister, never to be seen again. When wicked winds return over a decade later only to sweep *her* away, Dorrie's forced to believe that her mother's storybook tales are actually true.

The Fairest Shop of Them All - Shawntelle Madison
A tyrannical duchess makes a dark wish, for her to have the fairest hat shop of them all, but an orphan shopkeeper with mystical goods stands in her way.

Immortal Wish - Colleen Gleason
Lyla Harris lives at the bottom of the Sea in the city of Atlantis…but she knows there's something else up there. When she makes a wish to learn more, a whole new world opens up for her.

Unseen - Christine Pope

After the end of the world, an invisible benefactor comes to Janna Sayers' aid. But will her curiosity about her mysterious guardian be her undoing?

First Snow - Alexia Purdy

In the dead of winter, Jonna is saved from the cold by an unlikely ally. She's determined to rescue her family from the clutches of an ancient witch who rules the desolate frost lands and turns trespassers into statues of ice.

The Dreamer's Curse - Rachel Morgan

When a wish bargain with the Godmother goes wrong, Cress winds up cursed to an eternal slumber. But a potion that gives her the ability to travel through dreams may be the key to her escape.

The Lady of the Lake - Julia Crane

What would an otherworldly creature want more than anything? To be mortal, of course. The Lady of the Lake might have bitten off more than she could chew.

The Wishing Thorn - Jamie Ferguson

Leah never believed in her Irish grandmother's stories about trees granting wishes, but after having her life turned upside-down, she decided to see if the stories were real after all. She chose to make her wish of a blackthorn: the tree of warfare and ill omens, and the keeper of dark secrets...

Woven from Pure Starlight - Jenna Elizabeth Johnson

Caitlin's glamour-infused hair has kept her from living a life of her own since the death of her mother. When a stranger arrives in the magical forest near her home, Caitlin gets a chance at friendship, love, and the most important thing of all: freedom.

Last Wish - C. Gockel

Once upon a time there was no death. Spirits walked among humans, and giant game sustained them. But as the world changed, something worse than death came to the world.

Heart of the Forest - Anthea Sharp

Pursuing an enchanted creature into a magical forest, a prince discovers that his heart's desire isn't what he thought…

Pin Oak's Wish - Kay McSpadden

Pin Oaks knows her Grandmother Blue can grant wishes, but she's never needed one until now. It's 1952, and the young mountain healer wants her grandmother to help her become a real city woman —and to find her true love before he ships out for Korea.

Wish Upon a Straw - Devon Monk

One magical gold spinner, one kingdom full of dragons…

Read more fabulous fairytale retellings from these authors - available in print and digital at all online retailers!

ONCE UPON A CURSE - 17 Dark Faerie Tales

ONCE UPON A KISS - 17 Romantic Faerie Tales

ONCE UPON A QUEST - 15 Tales of Adventure

ONCE UPON A STAR - 14 SF-Inspired Faerie Tales

ONCE UPON A GHOST - 20 Eerie Faerie Tales

Join our FB group Urban Fantasy Fiends to keep up with all the news from these authors!

THE DUST WISH

ALETHEA KONTIS

Once upon a time, in the days when humans, fairies and trolls were scattered across the world, there was a great mountain. Now, there had been a good many great mountains before this time, and there have been a good many great mountains since, but this great mountain in particular was of such great quality indeed that the humans called it Magnus.

(The fairies who lived inside the mountain called it something else, but that's beside the point.)

A Young Man of No Land grew up hearing the stories that surrounded Magnus, legends of magical waters and mythical beasts and powers beyond all comprehension that dwelled in the stone. This young man journeyed across the world and claimed the great mountain for his kingdom. He built a castle upon its slopes and took the most beautiful woman in the world for his bride. He dubbed himself Great King Swordspoint; his wife, Great Queen Lark.

(The fairies who lived inside the mountain had other names for them, but that's neither here nor there.)

Between them, their great majesties had a great many children blessed with beauty and long life. Each son was righteous, handsome, and named after some implement that drew blood. They fought in great battles, conquered great foes, married well, and brought much wealth to the kingdom. Each daughter was headstrong, as beautiful as the dawn, and named after a bird. They, too, fought in great battles, conquered great foes, married well, and brought much wealth to the kingdom.

For generations the family ruled peacefully over their great kingdom. The trolls didn't trouble them, as Magnus was too far out of the way to be of consequence, and the fairies were said to only threaten anyone who ventured out into the woods after dark and young children who did not clean their rooms.

(The fairies said differently, but I digress.)

Years passed, and trolls ravaged more and more of the countryside until the High King called upon the human kingdoms to aid him in assembling an army to fight them. Great King Paper did not want to send his only son Pen into the fray, but the recalcitrant young buck took up arms and joined his brethren at the battlefront regardless.

The human army held back the trolls, but at great cost. Prince Pen did not turn out to be mightier than the sword that brought him down, and Great King Paper was left with his only daughter, Princess Pallua, to inherit the kingdom.

After the loss of his beloved Great Queen (a non-troll-related virus), the king had been remiss about betrothing his daughter to anyone. Thanks to his prolific ancestors, the princess was directly related to every noble within riding distance, and Great King Paper had never relished the thought of shipping his dearest daughter so far away that they'd have to cross troll country just to visit on holiday. Unfortunately, Princess Pallua was of marriageable age and the kingdom's fate was yet to be decided. The king's hands were tied.

So messengers were sent far and wide to every nook and cranny of the habitable earth, announcing a contest to win the hand of the fair Princess Pallua and a seat beside her in the castle on Magnus. The only stipulation was that the contestant must not be a ruler of his own kingdom, as he would be expected to step into the shoes of Great King Paper and rule over Magnus whenever His Majesty took it upon himself to pass away. (Which the contestant should not expect to happen for a very long time.)

Dozens of messengers returned to the slopes of the great mountain bearing applications for the contest. The ones who had crossed through troll country were quite worse for wear. Some came back wounded, without purse, without clothes, without a head, and sometimes without a horse. A few steeds showed up without a rider. One response even managed to be delivered sans human or beast, though none could make heads or tails of the strange foreign scrawl. Rumors spread that the missive had come from the fairies who lived inside the mountain.

The fairies said nothing.

By the next full moon, the great castle on the great mountain was swarming with eligible gentlemen (and a handful who were neither). The last among them was Ardian of Ilir.

Ardian was a prince of little consequence—the third son of a healthy king, sixth of ten siblings in total. His hair and eyes were black as a night without stars, and his skin was the color of sunset on warm sand. He was tall, but not overly so, good-looking but not distracting. Ilir was a country of similar consequence: a small, pretty swath of land to the south and west.

Prince Ardian entered the bustling courtyard like a dusty vagabond. He had journeyed to Magnus mostly on foot, so as not to draw the attention of any nearby trolls. He was dazzled by the bright colors surrounding him and tempted by the smell of sumptuous food…though he was distracted by the distinct odor of his own tired body.

He kept an eye out for the smallest page he could find—few men had the patience for the enthusiasm of youth, but Ardian had brothers. His gaze alit on a timid boy. The boy examined each towering man in the room but seemed too frightened to approach anyone. He looked as overwhelmed as Ardian felt.

"Pardon me, good squire," Ardian said, giving the youngster a promotion. "Would you know where I might acquire a cup of water?"

Ardian waited for the boy to realize he was the one being spoken to. Finally, the page looked up. "Me, sir? Sire? My lord? You're talking to me? Your Majesty? Your Royal…no? You're not talking to me?"

Ardian was smiling and shaking his head. "There are too many Highnesses here already. One more would just confuse matters."

The boy's wide eyes were a color somewhere between dry grass and blue sky—his inquisitiveness reminded Ardian of Merkush, his youngest brother. Slowly, the boy nodded.

The prince leaned down. "What say for now you call me Ardian? And I shall call you…?"

The boy snapped to attention. "Rabbit."

Ardian arched a dark eyebrow. "Rabbit?"

"My friends call me Rabbit, sir. Sire. Your…Ardian. Sir."

Ardian chuckled. "Then I am honored to be counted among your friends. Well met, Squire Rabbit." He bowed his head, loosing a slight shower of dust to the floor. He desperately needed to clean up before meeting the princess.

"Shall I show you to your room?" Rabbit asked insightfully.

"If you know which room in this great castle is mine, then I have discovered quite the treasure in you, Squire."

Rabbit grinned widely. One of his bottom teeth was missing, and his top two overly large incisors had already grown in. Ardian quickly guessed the origin of the boy's nickname.

The boy darted through the crowd of men as quickly as his animal namesake. Luckily, Ardian had enough troll-dodging energy left in him to keep up. Rabbit led the prince to a corridor behind the left-hand-most staircase, and then down a Very Long Hall.

Just when Ardian thought the hall would never end, it opened up into what looked like an older wing of the castle. There were no colorful tapestries on these walls, no sumptuous rugs, and no windows whatsoever. As far as Ardian's eye could see was nothing but gray and brown stone.

"Are you leading me to the dungeon, Squire?"

"This is the best room." Rabbit skipped ahead. "You'll see."

By the time they reached the large wooden door, Ardian's feet were sore, his lower back ached mightily, and if he'd been in possession of his family's best horse he would have traded it without pause for a thimbleful of palatable liquid.

Rabbit pushed the heavy door open with gusto. He hopped into the chamber and threw his arms wide. "We have arrived!"

Before them, a maid sat in what once must have been a very valuable chair. Her feet were propped up on the matching desk. Unlike Rabbit, her clothes and slippers were almost rags, and her messy mane reminded Ardian of a matted brown bear's pelt. She paused the examination of her ragged fingernails and took in the pair of them.

"Raaaaaa-bbit," she groaned. "Don't you know the difference between a beggar and a prince?"

"He does," Ardian answered in his most princely voice.

The maid cocked her head, examining Ardian from head to toe and back again. Slowly she slid her feet from the desk to the floor, but she remained dubious.

If Ardian had been more like Ylli, his eldest brother, he would have instantly taken this maid to task and reminded her of her place, or removed her from it. Ardian, however, was more like his mother. He found his efforts better spent forging allies instead of enemies. If he had started this journey on the wrong foot, he needed to take another step forward and set it right.

He bowed formally to the maid, as low as he might have bowed to a queen. "I am Prince Ardian of Ilir."

When he straightened, he saw that the maid was now on her feet, knees bent deep into her own curtsey. He could not see her face, but he could imagine the embarrassed blush across her cheeks. "Your Royal Highness," she said meekly.

"Told you," Rabbit jeered.

"Shut up," hissed the maid. Her head remained bowed as she straightened. "If you desire a new maid to service your quarters, Highness, I will fetch one immediately."

Energy finally spent, Ardian dropped his rucksack. It fell gracelessly to the stone floor in a plume of dust. "What I truly desire is a large cup of water."

"I'll get it! We have good water here!" With that, Rabbit scurried through one of the chamber's many inner doors.

Ardian collapsed into the chair on the opposite side of the old desk. "What is your name?"

"Zelya, Highness."

"Oh, don't stand on ceremony now." Ardian stretched out his tired legs. "That ship has sailed. Good riddance to it."

One corner of her lips turned up ever so slightly. "And my fate?"

At that moment, Rabbit returned with a goblet filled with water. Ardian thanked every god he knew for its presence and tried not to curse the enthusiastic boy for every beautiful, shining drop that spilled over the side.

It tasted stale.

Ardian wondered then if what he'd detected wasn't from the water, but from his own lips. Or the goblet itself. Or both. The chamber he sat in looked as if it hadn't been touched in years. Possibly decades. What did this maid do, if not…maidstuff? Perhaps her current appointment in the furthest reaches of the castle was a reflection of her lackluster abilities.

Don't be so quick to judge, umbabi. Mother's voice echoed in his head as he set the goblet on the desk. *She has other strengths. Find them.*

"As I'm sure you've guessed," said Ardian, "I've come to win the hand of the princess."

"And you need our help," said Rabbit. It was not a question.

"Why?" asked the maid.

This time, it was Ardian's turn to look confused. "Why do I need your help?"

"Why do you want to marry the princess?"

Ardian took in the expressions on both of their faces. "Do we not like the princess?"

Rabbit's nose crinkled in what could only be described as disgust. "She's selfish and mean and horrible and…what's the thing when you only care about yourself? Not selfish. The other one." He preened in pantomime.

"Vain," Zelya supplied helpfully.

Ardian sighed. He had no answer to give them but the truth. "Ilir is a small country. We have always lived on what we grow, but the last few years have not been kind to our soil. It was a dry winter. Rain is still scarce and the crops are weak. Even a tiny fraction of this kingdom's wealth would go a long way toward irrigation systems and heartier seeds and more…" Ardian let the explanation fade into the ether. He was tired of giving it, tired of being constantly reminded how helpless he was to change it. He waved his hand in the air instead. If only he could erase all Ilir's problems with such a simple gesture.

"Don't you have a family?" Rabbit asked.

"Yes." Ardian's heart ached to think of home, loud and full of love.

"Don't you like them?"

"Of course I do." Ardian turned to the boy. "I love them. That's why I'm here. That's why I will try my very best to marry this princess, even if she…has the head of a lion and the tail of a scorpion!"

Rabbit burst into giggles.

Zelya remained serious. "Your competition is mighty."

"I know," said Ardian. "Which is why I am willing to accept all the help I can get." *Even from a page and a maid in a wing of the castle that time forgot.* The voice in his head now was Gezim's, Ardian's second eldest brother, the clever one who would have had a good night's sleep before selecting far more strategic allies.

But Ardian was the third son, and Mother always said that third sons had luck on their side. If this was his lot, and these were to be his companions, then he would make the most of them. Who was he to argue with the gods? "So? Will you help me?"

Rabbit glanced at Zelya, obviously deferring to her judgment. Ardian wondered if the two of them were siblings. He understood siblings.

"You may not succeed," said the maid. "Even with our help."

"Do I have a chance without it?" Ardian asked.

"Nope," said Rabbit.

"Not even a little," added the maid.

"Then it's settled." Ardian extended his hand to Zelya.

Zelya stared at his dirty fingers. "You need to bathe, posthaste. And you," she said to Rabbit, "need to find His Highness something suitable to wear to dinner."

"How do you know I don't already have something? You haven't seen what's in my pack."

Zelya looked down her nose at the limp rucksack. "Wild guess."

"Aye-aye!" Rabbit saluted the maid. He was halfway out the door when he turned back. "Hey, what about swords and stuff?"

Zelya turned to the significantly unarmed Ardian and waited for him to shake his head. The little curved troll-dagger in his possession was currently as dull as a paving stone. Even sharp, it certainly wouldn't impress a princess.

"Swords and stuff too. Just don't overdo it!" she called after him, but the door had already closed in his wake. "He's going to overdo it."

"Dare I ask where our Rabbit is going to procure said items?"

"Nope." Zelya made her way to one of the chamber doors—the one from behind which Rabbit had fetched Ardian's goblet of water —and opened it. "Into the bath with you, Your Dirtiness."

Ardian wasn't sure what he expected to see on the other side of that door, but it was not the impressive sight that greeted him. This water closet had ceilings as high as the chamber he'd just left, and the stonework on every wall was intricately carved in painstaking detail. There were two pumps on opposite sides of the room: one that emptied into a small basin, and one that emptied into a large tub.

Ardian removed his shoes, thankful for the small plush rug leading to the tub that matched the stack of similarly plush towels beside it. "I suppose it's too much to hope for warm water," he muttered dejectedly.

Zelya placed a hand on the larger pump. "We do have good water here."

As water streamed into the tub, Ardian watched in awe as steam rose from it. "Blessed gods," he breathed.

"The benefit to being on this end of the castle is access to the mountain's hot springs," the maid said proudly. "Some of us feel it worth the sparser accommodations."

"I would happily sleep on a slab after a bath like this." Ardian paused in the middle of unwrapping his traveling scarves. "I don't have to sleep on a slab, do I?"

"Just a boring old feather mattress, I'm afraid." Zelya stopped pumping when the tub had filled to an acceptable level. "Do the best you can with the grime. I'll send Rabbit in when he returns. Call out if you need anything."

"Thank you," the prince whispered in reverence as she shut the door. He quickly divested himself of the rest of his filthy clothing and stepped into the steaming water.

It took his sore feet and muscles a moment to adjust to the heat —after so many nights sleeping under the stars without a fire, he didn't think his bones would be warm again until summer. Unlike the cool water that had been in his cup, this warm water smelled slightly metallic, with a hint of natural brimstone. It wasn't entirely unpleasant. It could have smelled like fresh dung for all his body cared. (Ardian thanked the gods it didn't smell like fresh dung.)

He easily could have soaked all night, even slept in the bath, but he had work to do. He reached for one of the smaller towels on top of the fluffy stack and contorted himself crossways to scrub every inch of his body that he could reach. After his third rinse, he reluctantly stepped out of the warm bath and toweled off.

When Rabbit reappeared, his arms were piled high with rich, colorful fabrics. There was a long-sleeved fitted shirt, hose, a tunic, a belt, even shoes. Ardian's young squire had quite the eye—somehow all of it fit perfectly.

"I do need one thing…" The prince exited the water closet and retrieved a long silk scarf from his rucksack. He wound the purple and blue wave of it around his neck, then secured it at one shoulder with a bronze pin that had belonged to his grandfather.

He looked up to find Zelya staring at him as if he'd suddenly grown a third eye.

"It's from my home," Ardian explained of the decoration. "I'm afraid I must insist on being allowed this small concession."

"You look splendiferous," Rabbit declared.

"Thank you, Squire."

"Your hair wants a comb," Zelya said brusquely. "I'll fetch it. Sit."

Ardian was but a moment away from scolding the maid for addressing him in such a tone when that disapproving look of hers stirred a memory. It brought to mind his eldest sister Pranvera, and a certain countenance he'd witnessed many times in the days before she'd married.

Silently, the prince obeyed Zelya's command and sank into the chair with a satisfied grin. Yes, his attire would do just fine.

"I don't envy you," said Rabbit. "She's a monster when it comes to untangling hair."

"And I'll continue to be, for as long as you continue sleeping in barns and burrows," the maid called from the other room.

"I don't sleep in burrows!" Rabbit hollered back.

"The nest on your head says otherwise." Zelya pointed at the prince with her comb as if it were a magic wand. "Scoot back and sit up straight."

"Aye-aye." Ardian took Rabbit's lead and saluted the maid. Then he rested back in the chair and scratched his jawline. "Is there time to shave as well, do you think?"

"No." Zelya's comb sank into the hair at his crown. "The princess won't want a beau who's prettier than she is."

"You think I'm handsome?" Ardian winked at Rabbit right before his head snapped backward. Zelya's comb had caught a knot.

"You better be." She yanked the comb through. "You're not going to impress Princess Pallua with the size of your country."

"Ouch," Ardian said as she repositioned his head.

"Told you she was a monster." Rabbit held up a gleaming longsword almost taller than he was. "What about this one?"

"How in the gods' names…would I make that work at a royal feast?" Ardian recalled his promise not to ask from whence Rabbit had purloined these items, never mind how.

"He needs something tiny and pretty," Zelya said as she pulled the comb through the prince's locks. He was beginning to wish Mother had shaved his head before starting this journey. As Zelya ran her strong fingers through his hair to check for stray snarls, however, he changed his mind.

"Did you bother scrounging up anything smaller than a seax? Baselard, kirpan, dirk…anything."

Ardian found it interesting that a maid knew so much about armament. "I do have a…" the prince began, but neither the maid nor the boy paid him any mind.

"I got this knife," Rabbit said reluctantly, pulling an ornate hilt out of his own belt.

Zelya snatched the knife out of the boy's hands and pushed it at Ardian. "Here." She pointed at the rucksack. "Now, show me what you have for a gift."

Ardian spread his hands wide. "My winning personality?"

Zelya smirked.

Rabbit held up the shiny longsword again.

"Eh?" Ardian pointed at the weapon.

Zelya bent her head and sighed.

"I don't actually have a chance here, do I?" Ardian sank into the chair. "I never should have come."

"Oh, no," said Zelya. "You don't get to give up until you've actually tried first. You've come all this way. We're going to see it through."

"We?" Ardian asked.

"We're in this together now," Rabbit chirped. "We will find a way!" The boy dropped the longsword with a clang. He darted in and out of the doors of the chamber, presumably looking for this "way."

Ardian met the maid's eyes and she nodded, though he wasn't sure what they'd be able to come up with in these almost empty rooms. A bath towel? Ardian ran his fingers along the edge of his silk scarf, dyed to match his family's crest. He would sacrifice it if he must, though he suspected the princess had a thousand scarves, spun from moon moths or somesuch.

"Found it!" Rabbit cried from across the chamber.

"That was fast," muttered Ardian.

The boy hopped back to them, arm outstretched, fist closed. The prince and the maid bent their heads together as Rabbit slowly opened his fingers to reveal…

"A clump of dust," said Zelya.

"And you say I'm unimpressive," Ardian told the sorry excuse for a maid.

"It's a hav," said Rabbit.

The prince furrowed his brow. "I've heard of a dev before, but never a hav." Ardian hoped the two weren't related. He certainly didn't have the energy to deal with a dev right now.

"It's a dust mouse," Zelya said, as if that clarified anything.

"Hooray?" said the prince.

"It's a *wishing* dust mouse!" Rabbit waved the fluffy lump of dirt, hair, and debris emphatically under the prince's nose. "Just make a wish and our problems are solved!"

Ardian pursed his lips. He'd grown up with nine siblings; he'd certainly done stranger things. With a shrug, he held his hand out flat over Rabbit's, enclosing the so-called hav between their palms. "I wish for the Princess Pallua to fall madly in love with me."

Rabbit and Zelya both groaned.

"What?"

"Everybody knows you can't wish for someone to love you," said Rabbit.

"He's right," said Zelya. "Free will and all that. It's a rule even the gods obey."

Ardian thought back to the stories Mother had told him as a boy. He couldn't remember any specifics, but he did remember that wishes usually went terribly wrong. Good thing he had nothing to lose.

"All right then." Ardian closed his eyes. "I wish for a gift fit for a princess."

"Much better," said Zelya.

The prince removed his hand, but the only thing in Rabbit's palm was the dust mouse.

"I think this hav is broken," said Ardian.

"Are you sure?" Zelya asked.

Ardian poked the ball of dust and…encountered something solid. He pinched whatever it was between his fingers and slowly pulled.

"Your wish has been granted!" Rabbit clapped his hands together, filling the air with the remnants of the hav.

Ardian examined the depressingly limp item. "How is a length of twine supposed to be a gift fit for a princess?"

"Only you can know that. It was your wish. Now hurry up, so you can get a good spot at dinner!" The maid shooed them out of the chamber.

Rabbit led Ardian back into the heart of the castle at a steady clip. They slowed as they entered the main area. Ardian racked his brain all the way down the long corridor wondering how a bit of twine could impress a princess, but nothing came to him.

The dining hall was already filled with men—short men and tall men, thin men and wide men, light men and dark men—all bedecked in their finest finery. Gold, silver and furs abounded; shining crowns and shinier swords sparkled by lamplight (perhaps Rabbit had been right to suggest the longsword). Even in the bright colors of his stolen clothes, Ardian appeared underdressed.

Rabbit secured a seat for Ardian right out from under someone who'd made the age-old mistake of turning to greet an old friend *before* sitting down as opposed to *after*. Rabbit gently nudged the chatting man away from the table, and Ardian slid into the chair as if he'd always been there. Casually, he looked around the dining hall. This spot afforded a perfect view of the royal dais and their royal majesties, when they entered.

The assembly stood and bowed as Princess Pallua took her seat, a smaller throne situated at Great King Paper's left hand. She was the picture perfect image of a princess stepped from the pages of a storybook: as petite as her skirts were large, with long golden hair bound by a silver, jewel-encrusted circlet. In her beaded reticule she carried a miniature dog, which she sat on the table next to her golden plate. The mass of curly ginger fur was no bigger than the king's wine goblet.

"Great King Paper, the Great Princess Pallua, and her Great Royal Hound, Master Snoggins!" the Herald of Magnus announced with an absolutely straight face. The other men in the room were not so well disciplined, and a wave of random coughing quickly swept through the dining hall.

Great King Paper stood and gave a brief speech, complimenting the contestants assembled and welcoming them to his great mountain. Personal introductions would be made following the feast where, presumably, Ardian would make his offering.

He considered the dilemma throughout the meal. Suddenly, dinner was over. He still had no answer.

"You should hurry if you want to get near the front of the introduction line," Rabbit whispered.

"Let them go first," said Ardian. "I need more time."

But time to do what? What did he think would magically spring to his exhausted mind? There was the option of not giving the princess anything, but that idea vanished as one man after another presented gifts from around the world. They ran the gamut from agriculture (including a giant wheel of cheese and the largest tomato Ardian had ever seen) to gilt-edged books and golden chamber pots. Everyone brought something, and each gift came with its own story. The more involved the story, the more time the potential suitor had to make an impression on the princess.

This initial meeting was everything. This time together would set the tone of Ardian's relationship with the princess for the rest of his life. Did he dare risk presenting her with…

Question yourself, but never question the gods. Mother's words echoed inside his mind. Perhaps *that* is what the twine was: a test from the gods. A leap of faith.

Leaving it up to the gods, Ardian took his place at the end of a line that was over far too quickly. He bowed low before the dais. "Prince Ardian of Ilir, Your Great Majesties. It is an honor to—"

Princess Pallua made no attempt to hide her yawn. (Indeed, judging by the high windows in the dining hall, it was full dark. The Great Royal Hound had long since fallen asleep in his mistress's lap.) "What have you brought me?"

Right to it, then. Ardian took a deep breath and slowly pulled the twine from his pocket.

The handful of suitors left in the room murmured in consternation. Ardian glanced over to Rabbit. Even after hours on his feet, the boy stood to attention, an enthusiastic grin plastered across his face. He nodded in encouragement.

"If I may, Your Highness. Your wrist, please."

Stupefied, Princess Pallua extended one pale wrist. The prince knelt before her and made a show of tying the twine into a perfect ribbon.

"What?" The princess's exclamation startled Master Snoggins, who woke with a growl (as well as her father, who huffed instead of growling). She turned up her pert nose at the rough-hewn bow. "What is this rubbish? I thought perhaps I had fallen asleep and started dreaming, but no, here I am, awake and wearing a pauper's bracelet."

"Explain yourself, young man!" the king bellowed.

Ardian remained on one knee. "There exists no bauble on this earth that would not dim in comparison to your beauty, Princess Pallua. This simple length of rope has no fear of being humbled by your awesome presence. And in comparison, your true magnificence is thus brought forth for all the world to see."

For a moment Princess Pallua was charmed by his pretty face and pretty words, and that moment was enough for Ardian.

"It is true, I am far more beautiful than this plain ornament," the princess replied as she examined her wrist. But then her face fell, and Ardian's hopes with it. "But wouldn't I also be far more beautiful than…a bracelet of pink diamonds? Those are my favorite."

There was a hum in the air as soon as she spoke the words. In a bright flash, the twine on the princess's wrist changed into a sparkling row of pink diamonds. Ardian hid his shock in a deeper bow.

The princess's shriek of surprise was like a stiletto in Ardian's ear. Fortunately, it was of short duration. "What a wonderful trick! I confess, you had me fooled at the start. What was your name again?"

This time, everyone but Rabbit leaned in to hear it. "Ardian of Ilir, Highness. It has been my pleasure to make you smile."

"Daddy," the princess said to her father, "I want them all to make me smile!"

"So be it," proclaimed the king. "In lieu of tomorrow's shows of strength, all suitors are now instructed to find an extraordinary gift that will make my daughter smile."

"So be it." The Great Herald banged his staff upon the floor. (Master Snoggins simply barked.) "This assembly is hereby dismissed," the herald said to the almost empty room.

Ardian stood with a flourish, turned his back to the dais, and walked regally away.

"Well done, sir! Ardian! Sire!" Rabbit said when they were far enough down the long hall to be out of ear shot. "Did you know that was going to happen?"

"No idea! If I had, I might have stood in line sooner."

"But then everything might not have happened exactly the way it did."

"Too true, Squire. Oh, I can't wait to tell Zelya! How she will laugh!"

"She'll be asleep," Rabbit pointed out. "Like the rest of the castle."

"Right," Ardian realized.

Rabbit yawned. "We'll tell her in the morning."

Ardian fell into the musty sheets of the bed in his rooms. This night had gone excessively well…but what about tomorrow? What extraordinary item could Ardian find better than a magical twine-to-diamond bracelet? He couldn't even conceive of such a thing. So he left it up to the gods and fell asleep thinking about the fantastic tale he and Rabbit were going to tell Zelya.

As soon as he woke, he bounded into the main chamber. The maid was slowly sweeping and the boy was sharpening Ardian's troll-dagger.

"Good morning!" the prince said cheerfully.

The maid scowled as she swept. "It's afternoon, genius."

Rabbit sighed over the whetstone. "You slept foreeeeeeveeeeeer."

"How was I supposed to know the hour? There are no windows in this godsforsaken wing of the castle." Ardian put his hands on his hips. "I haven't slept the day away, have I?"

"It's just past lunch." The maid pointed to a tray on the desk. "We brought food."

The tray overflowed with roasted meat, fresh fruit, several types of breads and cheeses, and at least a dozen pastries Ardian didn't recognize. He immediately tore off an end of bread and a chunk of cheese and tucked in.

"Go easy," the maid warned. "That needs to last the rest of the night."

"Immna goina dinner?" Ardian swallowed the food he'd been chewing and repeated the question. "Won't I need to present Pallua with a new gift?"

"The princess will pester you the second you appear," Zelya pointed out. "You wouldn't have time to eat even if you did show up early. Better to keep her distracted all evening looking for you, and then make a grand appearance at the very end, like you did last night."

"You told her!" Ardian made a face at Rabbit.

Rabbit made a face in response. "I was awake first."

Ardian picked up an apple from the tray and threw it at the boy. Rabbit caught the fruit and sank his large front teeth into it with impressive vigor.

Zelya stepped between the two of them. "Rabbit will find new clothes for you today, but we have a more pressing order of business to attend to first."

"Breakfast." Ardian shoved another bit of bread and cheese into his mouth. Rabbit agreed by taking another bite of his apple.

"*The gift*," said Zelya. "You might have noticed, there doesn't seem to be another dust mouse lying around."

"Are you sure?" asked Ardian. "That broom of yours doesn't seem to do much."

Zelya thrust the broom at the prince. "You're welcome to see for yourself."

"That's it!" Rabbit snapped his fingers. "If we don't have a hav, we'll make one!"

"Can we do that?" Ardian asked.

"Only one way to find out," said the boy.

Zelya tried to retrieve her broom, but the prince wouldn't relinquish it. He and Rabbit sought out every bit of dust in those rooms. They made a game of it, shouting jests back and forth as they tackled each section. Zelya, meanwhile, wrapped a cloth around the end of a long stick and gathered every cobweb she could reach in the high ceilings. After that, she emptied Ardian's rucksack and beat a journey's worth of dust out of it.

In the end, the trio stood proudly over the result of their efforts.

"That is quite the pile of dust, my friends," said Ardian.

"Yes, but…" Rabbit peered intently. "Is it ever going to look like anything more than a pile of dust?"

"Maybe it needs time to think about itself," said Zelya. "Which works for us, because Rabbit has errands to run. And if you'll follow me, Your Highness, there is something I think you'd like to see."

Even though it had only been a day, it felt like ages since Zelya had addressed him as royalty. This friendship with his co-conspirators had come so easily it was almost second nature. Ardian stepped back, reminded of his place. Even if his was a small country and hers was a great castle, he was still a prince and she was still a maid. It was his job to be noticed; it was her job to disappear into the stonework. Perhaps when he became King of Magnus, he would find a way to care for her and Rabbit.

Ardian laughed silently at his delusions of grandeur. *If* he became king of this place.

He dressed in the plain clothes he'd brought from home, tunic and trousers as drab and gray as the castle's stone. He pulled his mass of hair back into a rough queue and hoped it was enough to keep him from being recognized.

Thankfully, it was. Staying in the shadows, Ardian and Zelya made their way down the long hallway and through the great castle. It occurred to Ardian that he probably should take more notice of the architecture, but there would be time enough for that when he became king. And if he didn't become king, there was no need to care. So he kept his eyes on Zelya and stayed close. For safety, he told himself. And when she took his hand to guide him around a particularly sharp corner, he did not let go.

The place she led him to was a cavernous greenhouse with an opening to the sky far overhead, and a garden the likes of which he had never seen before. Greenery towered above and around him. Flowers blossomed in every color imaginable. There were petals as tiny as the nail on Ardian's smallest finger and leaves as tall as his entire body.

"Can you believe a place like this exists on the side of a mountain?" she asked.

Ardian had heard legends of the forests inside great old mountains like Magnus. "You could tell me that every plant here grew from a seed kissed by a fairy the size of a walnut and I would believe you."

Zelya laughed at that, and in this place her laughter sparkled more than the diamonds on Princess Pallua's magic bracelet. "You said your family grows things, so I thought you might appreciate it."

"You thought right. This place is more beautiful than…" Ardian stopped before trapping himself in a false comparison. Instead, he squeezed her hand and said in earnest, "Thank you."

They stayed in the garden as long as they dared before slipping back to his rooms. At the end of the very long hallway, Ardian finally released Zelya's hand and opened the door to an excitedly jumping Rabbit.

"Itworkeditworkeditworkeditworked!" Rabbit pointed to the corner where they had gathered their dirt and debris. Curled there now was a hav far larger than yesterday's.

"That's no dust mouse," said Ardian.

This collection of hair and cobweb detritus *breathed*. It stood, stretched itself out, and yawned a magnificent, tongue-rolling yawn.

"It's a dust *cat*," Rabbit said triumphantly.

Ardian was glad their work had only been able to produce a breadbox's worth of dirt. What chaos would there have been if they'd returned to a hav the size of a dust sheep? Or a dust elephant?

The dust cat wound itself lazily around Ardian's legs. All three of them sneezed. Ardian reached down to gently pet the hav. It nuzzled his fingers. Ardian could have sworn he felt whiskers on his skin.

"Is it…purring?" Zelya asked.

"Quick!" Rabbit urged. "Make a wish!"

"I wish for the gift that will make Princess Pallua the happiest of all," Ardian said as he trailed his hand along the hav's back.

In a flash, the hav began seizing.

"What's happening?" Rabbit yelled. The dust cat continued to back away from Ardian, choking. "He can't breathe!"

"Havs don't breathe," said Zelya. "Do they?"

Ardian realized he knew what was happening. "He's coughing up a hairball."

Rabbit wrinkled his nose. "Ewwwwwww."

Sure enough, the hav continued seizing until he vomited up a separate chunk of filth. Then, like the dust mouse, the cat crumbled into nothingness. They stared at the hairball.

"I don't want to touch it." Ardian looked at Zelya. "You're the maid."

Zelya folded her arms. "It's *your* wish."

With a sigh and a groan, Ardian stuck his fingers in the hairball. He pulled out the solid thing inside and held it up to examine.

"Well, you were just talking about walnuts," said Zelya.

And that's exactly what the hav's gift seemed to be: a simple walnut. No more, no less.

"What are you going to do with it?" Rabbit asked.

"The same thing I did last night," said Ardian. "Give it to the princess and leave the rest up to the gods."

"But not before you wash your hands," said Zelya. "And the rest of you, too, for that matter. I'll clean up." She reached for the broom leaning against the wall, and then paused. "Should I dispose of the dirt or keep it?"

"Keep it," Rabbit and Ardian said at the same time.

"Just in case we need it again," Ardian added.

"But I hope we don't," said Rabbit. "I hope that tonight, you win."

Zelya did not voice her hopes, only nodded at the pile. "I'll find something to put it in. You both go get ready."

Ardian's clothes that night were all black: shirt, hose, tunic, and shoes all as black as his hair and eyes. The only color upon him was the purple and blue wave of his family scarf. The prince stood steady as Zelya affixed the bronze pin to his shoulder.

"Your appearance will show them that you have nothing to prove," she said. "Your gift will do the talking."

"I just hope it says what we need it to say."

"It will." There was no doubt in her words.

Ardian caught Zelya's hand before she could step away. "Wait up for us," he said. "I want to be the one to recount tonight's story to you, whatever happens." If he was to be King of Magnus, he wanted her to be the first (besides Rabbit) to know. If he wasn't...then perhaps Ardian could convince the two of them to accompany him back to Ilir. No one at home knew they were a maid and a page. In Ilir, they could be anyone.

"I will," she said. "Meet me in the garden after your audience."

Ardian bowed over her hand, kissing it quickly before releasing it. "Until then, my lady."

Ardian and Rabbit did not rush to the packed dining hall. A hush fell over the assembly when they entered the room. This time, there was no line to get to the dais.

Princess Pallua's face lit up when she saw Ardian approach. She wore a delicately hammered silver headpiece, a mantle of the finest ermine, and a ruff that could only have been made of dragonskin. Beneath the ruff was a necklace in which each gemstone echoed the vibrant colors of the sunset. Her cup and plate were bejeweled, as was the Great Hound's bowl. Master Snoggins also wore a dragon-skin collar. Beside them was a chest filled with rings and more jewelry, plus a polished sphere of solid gold and what looked like a unicorn's horn.

Ardian felt sorry for the unicorn.

He lowered his head as he approached the princess. "Forgive me, Highness. Your brilliance shines so amidst these magnificent gifts that I cannot look directly upon you."

"Oh no!" The princess feigned surprise. "I beg you shield your eyes a bit longer, sir. For I am sure your gift will put all those before you to shame."

The men groaned. Ardian tried not to grin too broadly at that— Zelya had been absolutely right about his timing.

"No, Highness. I dare not present my humble gift in such luxurious company."

"Oh, please." This time, the princess's begging was real. "Is the necklace too bright? The crown? I will take them off. Please don't go." She removed the opulent finery piece by piece and dropped them onto the chest beside her chair.

The sight of such discarded wealth made Ardian want to gag. Just one of those rings she cared nothing about would take care of his kingdom for months. He placed his hand over the pocket in his tunic, felt the lump of the walnut there. He was too deep into this farce to back out now.

"I should not have come." Ardian stepped back from the dais. "I am but a humble man, unworthy of your grace."

This time, it was Great King Paper who spoke. "You applied to court my daughter, sir. I demand you adhere to that contract!"

"Yes, Your Great Majesty." It was time. Ardian pulled the walnut out of his pocket and got down on one knee.

Curiously, Princess Pallua reached forward to pluck the walnut from Ardian's hand. She stared at it: front and back, top and bottom. Finally, she set it down on her bejeweled plate.

"I don't understand," she said. "I truly thought, of all the men in this room, that you would be the one to make me the happiest. But I—"

A *crack* interrupted the princess's speech as the walnut split open. Only Ardian, Rabbit, the princess and the king were close enough to see the exquisite tiny black puppy nudge his way from beneath the shell. He sat like an errant puff of midnight sky in the middle of the plate, wagging his tail and panting prettily. No one moved. No one breathed. And then the puppy barked.

At that crisp, crystalline "yip," the princess squealed so mightily that Ardian temporarily lost the use of his left ear. She leapt from her chair into Ardian's arms and proceeded to hug the breath right out of him.

"Seize him!"

Ardian simultaneously felt his arms grasped on either side and the princess bodily removed from his person.

"Magistrate!" Great King Paper bellowed. "What is the meaning of this?"

A stodgy man with a salt and pepper beard stepped into Ardian's line of sight. The Magistrate. The one man on Magnus with the gall (and authority) to stand up to His Great Majesty.

"It was reported to me earlier today that this man is not what he seems."

Ardian shot a glance at Rabbit. The boy stood to one side, eyes like saucers. Ardian prayed he did not say anything that might give him and Zelya away.

"Prince"—the magistrate checked his papers—"Ardian has been accused of using magics not his own to unfairly win the hand of the princess."

"They're just mad that he won," said the princess.

Ardian's heart caught somewhere between soaring and sinking. *He'd won.*

"But he didn't!" The accusation came from a large towheaded man in a dragonskin collar that matched the one still affixed around the princess's throat. "The girl did it. I saw her!"

"How dare you!" cried the princess. I am no mere *girl!*"

"You saw someone—not the princess—create this walnut?" asked the magistrate.

The blond man shook his head. "No, but I saw them together, in the greenhouse. She made the garden grow."

Ardian's head shot up. It was one thing to accuse Zelya of creating the walnut, when he'd seen the hav spit it out with his own two eyes. But the garden…he hadn't been paying attention to the garden when they'd entered. The lush foliage had been there the whole time. Hadn't it?

This time when he stole a glance at Rabbit, the boy was looking at his feet. What in the gods' names…?

"If anyone made my sad cave-garden grow, I want to see it," demanded the princess. "Right now."

The princess scooped up her miniature dogs and led the king, the magistrate, the guards, Ardian, Rabbit, and half the dining hall all the way to the greenhouse. Where Ardian had asked Zelya to wait for him. If he cried out, would he be able to warn—

Princess Pallua's squeal echoed down the corridor. She had seen the cave-garden, in all its magnificent glory.

"What…? How…?" Great King Paper's face was so red, it could have been a flower.

The guards dragged Ardian forward. On a bench there, surrounded by weeping willows, was Zelya. Her face was washed free of dirt and dust, her long brown hair was brushed, and the plain sheath dress she wore looked new. Ardian couldn't help but smile at the precious sight of her. She'd done all this for him. And maybe more.

"Young woman," said the magistrate, "are you responsible for the state of this garden?"

"Yes." Her eyes did not meet Ardian's.

"Are you also responsible for the magical items given to the princess by Ardian of Ilir?"

"Yes."

"Then by right of contract, Prince Ardian is forfeit!" the blond man hollered. "The contest is back on!"

Zelya held up a finger. "No, it is not."

"Is that so?" asked the magistrate. "Pray tell."

"Explain yourself this instant!" demanded Great King Paper.

"My gifts obtained the favor of the princess," said Zelya. "The winner of the contest for her hand, therefore, must be me."

The blond man pointed at Zelya. "Only you didn't have a contract."

"On the contrary." In her hand appeared a scroll. She unrolled it to reveal the response that had been sent to Great King Paper, written in unintelligible script. The signature below it, while also unintelligible, definitely began with a Z. "Just because none of you can read the language of the fairies doesn't make the contract any less binding. As I'm sure the magistrate will agree."

"I will," agreed the magistrate, without so much as a hem or a haw.

"You're a fairy?" asked Great King Paper.

"I am queen of the fairies that live in this mountain," Zelya replied. "It is we who harness the magic here."

Ardian would have fallen to the ground had it not been for the guards holding him. Oh, what a fool he was. Oh, what a total, utter, human fool!

Ardian scanned the garden, but Rabbit was nowhere to be found. The prince began to wonder if maybe the boy was actually a rabbit. He recalled their first encounter and Rabbit's utter surprise at being spoken to. Yes. It was entirely possible that the boy Ardian had grown so fond of in such a short time was not really a human boy at all.

With each word Zelya spoke, her hair grew longer and thicker, her skin smoother and darker. Vines slid up her wrists and arms and settled on her brow in a tiara of leaf and stone. Her presence became so awesome that a few of Pallua's suitors began to tremble.

"You built your castle upon our home, profited off our good fortune, and gave us nothing in return. So we hid underground, waiting for the time when we could rightfully claim this kingdom once again for our own. And so we have."

Princess Pallua stomped her foot, crushing an innocent violet beneath her heel. "Daddy, I don't want to marry *her*!"

"I don't think you have a choice, dearest," said the king. "You will marry this fairy, and together you will rule over Magnus after I am gone."

"Just a moment," said the magistrate. "If this young woman is the fairy queen of this great mountain, as she appears to be, then I believe *she* is the true ruler here, sire. Not you."

Great King Paper blustered. "But...but...my family has ruled this mountain for generations!"

The magistrate didn't even blink. "In light of new facts, sire, that information seems to be neither here nor there."

This time, Princess Pallua's shrill wail pierced Ardian's brain. The guards released the prince so they could cover their ears. Thus freed, he approached Zelya.

"If this was your plan the whole time, why involve me at all?" he asked into the din.

The look of pain upon her face now was something Ardian had never seen on his sisters before. If he had, he would have killed the soul who put it there. "You were the one element I could not conjure."

She reached for him with an ivy-wreathed wrist, but Ardian stepped back. "I have to go."

He escaped under cover of the princess's deafening screams. He raced back through the castle, turned behind the grand stair, and…stopped.

There was no very long hallway. Ardian pounded his fist against the solid gray stone.

"Can I help you?" asked a guard.

"There was a hallway here." Ardian knew it sounded ridiculous even as he said the words. "It led to a chamber of rooms. There was a desk, and a few old chairs, and a water closet…"

The guard shook his head. "Nothing back there, mate. Never has been. Nothing but solid mountain."

Ardian slapped the wall again and screamed a growl through his teeth. A full day he had spent there, deep in the mountain, inside the fairies' lair, and he had never realized. Never wanted to realize. The clothing, the swords, the armor, the food…all fairy magic. All mountain dust. All one great lie.

When he spotted the urn sitting neatly against the wall, full of dirt and hair and filth, the prince upended it onto the floor.

"Hey now! What do you think you're doing?"

Ardian bent over the debris and stuck his hand inside the pile. "I wish to go home," he said.

"I can fetch you a carriage, if—"

Ardian ignored the guard and closed his eyes. "I wish to go home!" Tears slid down his cheeks and fell into the pile. "I wish to go home!"

At once the dirt rose up in a whirlwind until it was taller than a sheep, taller than Ardian. Finally, the dust fashioned itself into the shape of a horse. The hav pawed at the stone floor and whinnied. Ardian leapt upon the dust horse's back. Somehow, it stayed solid.

It stayed solid all the way back to Ilir.

The first two days at home, Ardian slept. On the third day, he went to work in the fields. On the seventh day, the carriage arrived.

The rains had returned while Ardian was away, and the crops

were improving. The prince should have been glad that Ilir was no longer in dire straits, but his mood remained black. His family hadn't needed him to marry the Great Princess of Magnus after all, in the end—a good thing, considering his spectacular failure.

Ardian didn't tell his siblings the details of what happened at Magnus. He told his parents more, but not everything. Mother, however, was quite skilled at wheedling information out of her children. She had been there when the dust horse delivered Ardian safely home, and then crumbled at her feet. She had been the one to nurse her son back to health when he would not leave his room. By week's end, she had pieced together most of what transpired on that mountain, including the maid and boy to whom her trusting, loyal son had lost his heart.

So when the carriage drawn by two gray stallions came to a stop in front of the house, Ardian and his mother were the only ones not surprised. They continued to sip coffee at the table while the others raced to see the arrivals. His brothers and sisters promptly hurried back into the room brimming with details and questions.

"Those horses!" Samira exclaimed.

"They look like they're made of stone," said young Merkush, eyes as wide as another rambunctious boy Ardian knew.

"The carriage is empty," Ylli reported. "There's no one driving, and no one inside. That doesn't make any sense!"

"Is it lost?" Tirana asked. "Maybe the owners were beset by thieves."

"Then why would they leave one massive trunk behind?" asked Gezim.

"Maybe because it's locked," said Era, "Abba, do you have some keys we can try?"

"Maybe there was never anyone inside," Gezim said in a spooky voice.

"Why would anyone send an empty carriage here?" Adriel wondered.

Ardian knew the answer. "It's an invitation." There was silence as his family took in the weight of the quiet prince's words. But only for a moment.

"This carriage is for *Ardian?*" Samira laughed. "Well, lah-dee-dah."

"Someone on that mountain likes you," said Ylli.

Mina, the youngest sister, pulled up a chair beside him. Mina had always been as sensitive as she was beautiful. "If it's an invitation, brother, will you accept?"

"I don't know." Truly, Ardian wasn't sure what his heart wanted. But it had started pounding at the carriage's arrival and it wouldn't stop.

"Who sent it?" Ylli asked.

"The Queen of Magnus," said Ardian.

"I thought there was only a king and a princess," said Merkush.

"Things changed," said Ardian.

"That must be why you came back," guessed Gezim.

"Does she love you?" Mina asked. "The queen, I mean."

"Judging by that carriage, I'd say yes," said Ylli.

"Do you love her?" Mina asked.

"I don't know," Ardian said again.

"I think maybe you do," said Mother.

"Of course he does," said Father. "The Queen of Magnus is a witch, and Ardian is still under her spell."

"No," Ardian said with sudden certainty. "Magic can't make you love someone."

"Why?" asked Merkush.

"Free will is a rule even the gods obey." It hurt to remember the first time Ardian had heard those words, but it also brought him joy. What fun they'd had. He'd fallen in love with Zelya and Rabbit around the magic spells, not because of them.

"That gods obey…and queens," said the mother who had first told Ardian those legends.

"But, Amma, she lied to me. She used me and betrayed me."

"I'll set fire to the carriage," Ylli offered. The rest of Ardian's siblings quickly agreed, but their mother held up a hand.

"What was your purpose on the great mountain?" Mother asked Ardian.

"To win the hand of the princess and save Ilir."

"Fat lot of good that did," said Samira.

"We saved ourselves anyway," said Tirana.

"Hush," said Father.

"And what was her purpose on the great mountain?" Mother asked gently.

She did not need to clarify who "her" was. Ardian knew well enough. "To trick some worthless, gullible prince into wooing the princess on her behalf," he spat.

"…so that she might win the hand of the princess and save her people," Mother finished.

"Wait. Is that true?" Adriel asked.

Ardian nodded.

"Those two things sound the same," said Mina.

"What it sounds like is two decent, honorable people who fell in love with each other despite all else," said Mother.

"But she used magic on me," Ardian fought back.

Mother raised her eyebrows. "That same magic you used to woo the princess?"

"Hold on, Ardian used magic?" Tirana asked.

"We *really* need to hear this whole story, brother," said Ylli.

"You will, umbabi," said Mother. "But I don't think the story is finished yet."

"How can I forgive her?" Ardian's head hurt and his heart ached. Even if he did find a way to forgive Zelya, how would he let her know? But the answer to that question sat outside the door, drawn by two gray horses.

"Find a way." Father put his hand on Ardian's shoulder. "Son, when a beautiful and powerful woman loves you and wants to be with you, don't argue." He put his other hand on his beloved wife's shoulder and gazed longingly into her eyes. "Trust me."

Ardian nodded. He stood, hugged Mina, and then hugged his mother. His family followed him out to greet the carriage. And when he opened the door of the carriage, Zelya was sitting there. He saw her for the fairy queen she was, with her shining hair and frightening beauty, but he also saw the maid he loved who leaped into his arms.

"Please forgive me," she whispered into his neck. "I love you so much."

"I forgive you." There were tears in his eyes. "And I love you, too."

"And I love you, too!" This time it was Rabbit who launched himself out of the carriage and hugged both of them tightly. Ardian patted the boy's head, so happy he was to see him again. Rabbit peered up at the prince with those eyes of dry grass and blue sky. "And Pallua loves you, too, but we didn't bring her. She's so screechy."

Confused, Ardian looked to Zelya. "Somehow she and the king got turned into peacocks," she said innocently. "They and the dogs have the run of the garden. I assure you, the princess is happier now than she's ever been."

But Rabbit wasn't finished. "And the mountain loves you, too, but she couldn't come with us for obvious reasons."

"The mountain?" Ardian asked the woman he never wanted to let go.

"Of course," said Zelya. "I wasn't responsible for everything that happened up there. You and the mountain made a great deal of magic on your own. She would have no other soul rule by my side." The fairy queen hesitated. "Assuming you still want to."

"Say yes!" Rabbit cried out, refusing to release either of them from his embrace. "If you say yes, then the trunk will open and be full of new clothes for your family to wear to the celebration!"

"And if I say no?" Ardian quietly asked his queen.

"Then the trunk will be full of seeds kissed by fairies the size of walnuts," said Zelya. "Ilir's crops will never wane again. And we will take our leave."

Ardian pretended to mull over the decision. "Is there any way I can negotiate for the seeds *and* the clothes?"

Zelya smiled mischievously. "If you play your cards right."

"Then yes," Ardian said, because it was the word he needed to say, and because every other word left his mind as he kissed his dearest love.

And that, gentle reader, is how a fairy and a farmer came to rule the great mountain once known as Magnus. Their reign lasted centuries, marked by ease, grace, and love above all else. The kingdom prospered, and their subjects remained loyal. There was as much green on the mountain as stone, a pile of dust in every corner of the castle, and every wish they made for the rest of their days came true.

When Casey called to help me brainstorm this story, I was balancing on the loveseat, dusting the grimy air return vent in my ceiling. (I have very high ceilings.) Casey has been my best friend since we were eleven. She was my first writing partner and collaborator. Now she's my content editor—and Chair of English at Winthrop University. When Casey gives me notes, I pay attention. And when I'm stuck, she is the BEST at helping to shake things loose.

"All I know at this moment is that I want to write something *fun*," I told her. "The world needs fun right now. The more absurd the better. Like"—I glanced at my Swiffer—"a dust bunny that grants wishes."

Casey laughed. "What about 'The White Cat' from *The Blue Fairy Book*? That's always been my favorite. The prince has to perform all those tasks…the little dog in the acorn, and the muslin in the walnut…maybe the dust bunny could help with that?"

"Ooh! That would work." As I'd hoped, Casey's magic made sparks in my brain. "Only I want my heroine to be proud and cocky, like Peri-Banu, from *1001 Nights*. She manipulated the tasks and chose the prince because she *wanted* to marry him, not because he had to marry her."

"Absolutely."

"The Greeks had super powerful fairies like that, too. Shoot, I could just *set* it in the Middle East! Give it an Eastern Mediterranean flavor and landscape, anyway. I feel so much more comfortable writing about areas of the world that my family's actually from."

"Sounds amazing!"

The fire of inspiration thus lit, we began discussing the role of the dust bunny in the story. Because of course it couldn't stay a bunny forever. Besides, depending on one's country of origin, the expression might be "dust mouse" or "dust poodle" or even a "dust sheep." We talked for about an hour, and I thanked her for her time.

"I may call you and ask for help again later," I said. And then I paused. "No…no I won't."

"You won't?" Casey asked sadly.

"Nope. I'm going to write this story *for* you. Like a present. You won't get it until I'm completely finished. You will be my motivation. I will write you a story that will make you smile!"

And, gentle reader, she did.

ABOUT THE AUTHOR

New York Times bestselling author Alethea Kontis is a princess, storm chaser, and Saturday Songwriter. Author of over 20 books and 40 short stories, Alethea is the recipient of the Jane Yolen Mid-List Author Grant, the Scribe Award, the Garden State Teen Book Award, and two-time winner of the Gelett Burgess Children's Book Award. She has been twice nominated for both the Andre Norton Nebula and the Dragon Award. She was an active contributor to *The Fireside Sessions*, a benefit EP created by Snow Patrol and her fellow Saturday Songwriters during lockdown 2020. Alethea also narrates stories for multiple award-winning online magazines, contributes regular YA book reviews to NPR, and hosts Princess Alethea's Traveling Sideshow every year at Dragon Con. Born in Vermont, she currently resides on the Space Coast of Florida with her teddy bear, Charlie. Find out more about Princess Alethea and her wonderful world at aletheakontis.com.

ASHES TO ASHES

PHAEDRA WELDON

"You want me to hunt down a what?"

"A Djinn."

I stared at my boss as he sat behind his cluttered desk. He looked like a troll—if trolls were real. Thinning hair, combed from the left to the right, two chins, a round, gin-blossom nose, a body like piled pillows and a permanently inserted cigar between his thin lips. He wasn't really a kidder, if you know what I mean. No sense of humor.

"What the hell is a Djinn?"

He pushed a few papers around until he came to a gold file and opened it. That color file meant high dollar pay out. And I needed the money. He scanned and muttered for a few seconds. "Its a legendary wish giver, confined by contracts." He closed the file and tossed it across the desk at me. "In other words, the thing broke a contract and now it's wanted."

I picked up the very thin file. "I don't think Djinns exist." I opened the file, which contained one page of carefully typed out instructions. Basic requirements. But nothing else. "This guy's got no priors."

"Not in *our* legal system." He looked up at me. "Look, I don't ask. But this broad threw a wad of cash at me, claiming this guy broke a contract with her and she wants him. So you got twenty-four hours."

"Why the time limit?"

"Because apparently," and his voice became very sarcastic. "The contract will dissolve and he'll be a free Djinn again." And in twenty-four hours, I was going to be twenty-five. "So," he gestured for me to leave. "I don't care if you catch it or not. She gave me my non-refundable retainer. You wanna get paid, you find him."

In case it isn't clear, I'm a Bounty Hunter and work for *Kingdom Bounty*. No questions asked. This job lived up to the by-line.

Hunting down criminals wasn't exactly my dream job. As a child, in a house full of love, my mother was murdered in a home invasion when I was fifteen. They stole not only my childhood, but my mother's favorite piece of jewelry, something she promised to me.

An opal necklace.

My father remarried and I tried to accept my new step sisters and my stepmother. I worked hard at graduating with honors and prepared my transcripts for entrance into law school. My father wasn't a rich man, but he'd put his faith in me, and his inheritance into my education when he died on my eighteenth birthday.

A month later, I learned my stepmother contested the will and won, claiming she needed that money to raise her two children and maintain the house he left to her in the will. My dreams of being a lawyer and finding my mother's necklace popped like soap bubbles when my role as oldest daughter transformed into caretaker, servant, and housekeeper.

I decided to become a cop, and within two years, became a detective. Needing something more exciting, I became a bounty hunter by the time I was twenty-four. The money was long gone, mismanaged by my stepmother. She wanted to sell the house, but my name was on the deed and I refused. Instead, I gave her an allowance to spend while I paid the bills and renovated the house.

In the six years since dad's death, I noticed furniture, family heirlooms, and even kitchen utensils, especially the silverware, disappearing. Days later one of the sisters would have a new dress or a new purse, and my stepmother suddenly had money to attend a few parties she could drag her daughters to in society.

She desperately wanted to marry her children off to rich husbands.

I wanted to do that too so I could take the house and kick them all out. I should have done that to begin with, but in a private letter given to me by the executor, my father asked me to watch over them. I never refused him.

On my way home that day my car broke down—third time this month. I called my buddy the repair guy and he promised he'd come tow it, but it would be an hour before he could get there. I checked the bus schedule on my phone and sighed. Another hour before the bus I needed would arrive. Looking around, I spotted a few stores behind me. Maybe I could kill time in one of those. A bookstore, an antique store, and…I had no idea what the third was. Might be an organic herb place…with tea?

I chose the antique store. Maybe I could replace one of missing lamps from the living room.

I spotted a tall man by a shelf of dishes. He smiled at me and I wasn't sure if he was an employee or a customer. He was dressed in slacks, a soft blue sweater and a white collared shirt beneath it. As he turned I saw a name tag on his chest but he was too far away for me to read it. He had brownish hair and I thought for a second he had a long ponytail down the entirety of his back. "Welcome. You need any help?"

"No, I'm fine." Employee. I moved past him and went further into the maze of pretties.

"Good evening," came a voice from the plethora of antiques. The place smelled of old ghosts and memories, wood oil and dust cleaner, creating an odor that both repelled and comforted me.

"Hello," I called out, looking for the owner of the voice. "How are you today?"

"Oh fine, fine," the voice was closer and I turned to see a small, stooped gentleman as he wove his way around the furniture. "What can I help you with today?"

"Lamps."

"Ah…come this way." He turned and I followed.

The floor felt uneven, but I couldn't see the wood beneath rugs stacked over each other along the path. As we moved, I noticed a curio cabinet in a corner, the kind my mother used to have in the living room. This cabinet contained a number of shoes.

I stopped in front of it, not because I *wanted* shoes, but because on the display's center shelf was the most incredible shoe I'd laid eyes on.

"Something catch your eye?" The proprietor found his way back to me.

I pointed at the shoe. It was clear, with beautiful crystals along the edges. The contour of the base up the arch to the heel was like a waterfall of colors. "What is this shoe made of? Plastic?"

"Ah, no. That is a glass slipper."

I blinked at him. "A shoe made of glass? Really?"

"Oh yes," and he pulled out a ring of keys and unlocked the cabinet. He reached in and retrieved the shoe and held it out to me. "Please, take it."

I expected it to be cold, but the smooth surface was warm and it was even more beautiful out of the case than in. "This is…incredible."

"Yes." He looked puzzled. "I just don't remember where it came from."

"Is it really wearable?"

"I suppose so. I usually don't wear such things." He smiled.

I actually laughed. "No, I suppose not. Do you have the mate to it?"

"Alas, no. I believe that fault is the reason this shoe has languished in this cabinet for such a long time."

"You've kept it in good condition."

"Thank you. Are you interested in it?"

"I—" I needed new lamps…but this shoe had my attention.

Since losing my mother's necklace, I had not bought myself anything, save suits for work. The necessities. The longer I held the shoe, the more I wanted it.

The only justification I could come up with was…it was alone. Like me. With no mate. With no prospects of ever finding a mate like itself.

"Ma'am?"

I surprised myself. I'd not had thoughts like these in a long time. I sort of assumed I would always be alone. "I'll take it."

"Of course," He gestured for me to follow him. He packed it in a box surrounded in foam, and set it on the counter. "That will be ten dollars."

My jaw dropped. "Wot?"

"Ten dollars." He smiled at me. "Unless you've changed your mind?"

"No, no. I want it." I retrieved a ten from my wallet. "Thank you."

"Thank you for giving it a good home." He handed me a receipt. "Please, have a nice evening. Oh," he pointed to the front door. "Your car is here."

"My car?" I looked out the window and saw a limo parked in front of the shop. "I don't have a—"

"It's part of our service, to make sure you get home safely. Your car has already been towed by your friend. Good evening, Miss Ella."

I nodded, started to the door with my package and stopped. How did he know my last name? I turned to ask, but he wasn't there. In fact, I didn't see the desk and register either. I shook my head as I left the shop and stepped into the waiting limo. The driver remained invisible behind dark glass as he wove around traffic to my house.

All the while, I couldn't remember ever giving that old fellow my name. He never even saw my credit card.

Once at my house, I stepped out of the limo (the door opened on its own) and the driver's side window rolled down just a little so I could hear a voice say, "Polish the shoe. It requires care." The window rolled up and the limo pulled away.

I stood there at the edge of my driveway, holding my new single shoe…just a little freaked out.

"Where have you been?"

"I'm hungry and there are no groceries!"

"How can you do this? Just go off and leave us here to starve?"

"You know my sister and I are on workman's comp and we can't do anything that might jeopardize our compensation!"

Actually, I didn't know that. But I didn't care.

The two of them were in my face the moment I stepped inside. I set my package on a nearby table before I hung up my coat, switched out my high heels for some flats I kept by the door, and picked up my package again and headed up the stairs. I didn't bother looking at the living room or kitchen. I already knew there would be a mess of fast food boxes, dishes, food left in pots and pans where the two misfits would have attempted to cook and given up. The house smelled of burned lettuce.

"Cynder! What's in that box?"

"Is that food? Did you get yourself food and not anything for us! Wait till we tell mother!"

I really…*really*…didn't care. I continued up to the attic where I'd moved my things when the sisters took over my room and the spare room. My stepmother had the master bedroom on the ground floor and never came upstairs unless chased. The sisters never came into my room because I'd convinced them the attic was haunted.

I opened the box after sitting on my bed and took out the shoe. It hadn't lost its glitter and shine as it lit up my little room. I'd feared there was something in that odd little store that made it sparkle and shine…but it was still as lovely here as it had been there.

I knew I should put it away and get started on this Djinn case, but I think in the back of my mind, I'd convinced myself it was a waste of time.

I flipped off my shoe and hesitantly slipped the shoe on my foot. It fit!

I never even asked the size. I also thought it would be cold, but it was warm and smooth and comfortable. Standing on it was another thing, though, and I didn't want to break it. I set it on the bed and started to undress, thinking about the Djinn case—

"Oh…no. Don't go any further. I'm not here to see woman parts. But at least I now know *where* I am."

I spun around to see an elderly woman—maybe in her fifties—kinda matronly—standing in front of my mirror. She wore a beige suit dress, matching shoes and her hair was pulled into a severe bun. She clasped her hands in front of her as she stared at me. The room abruptly smelled like sandalwood.

I pursed my lips, went to my nightstand, retrieved my gun and pointed it at her. "Identify yourself and tell me how you got into my room and I promise I'll shoot you in a place that'll be painful, but won't kill you, though it will make it possible for the police to cart you off."

The woman snapped her fingers. My gun disappeared. "None of that. There's no time."

I looked around for my gun a second before I glared at her. "Who the hell are you?"

"I'm your Fairy Godmother…well," She made a face. "That's what I have to be at this moment since that derelict isn't able to take on your wishes. Once in, wishes out. OIWO and all that. My primary function is attache to the *Common Belief in Wishes*. We call ourselves CBW for short."

C…B… "What?" I shook my head. "How did you get in here and what are you talking about?"

"You put on the shoe, didn't you?" and she nodded to the bed where the shoe lay. "If the Djinn currently inhabiting this vessel wasn't derelict in fulfilling a previous wish, you would be conversing with him. Instead, you get me—and because of this inconvenience, you have an emergency wish and I'm here to grant it. Now, the bylaws state you can use this wish now, or later. But only within twenty-four hours. It does not linger into old age."

"Are you serious?"

"Always." She stared at me. "Do you have an emergency wish?"

"No," I frowned. "Yes. Maybe."

"Let's hear it—"

"Oh no you don't. I say it as a maybe, you take it as gold, and I'm out a wish." I clamped my mouth shut. I couldn't believe I'd just said that.

"I see. I'll file this wish as *To Be Used Later.* TaBUL." A tablet appeared in her left hand, a quill in the right and she scribbled something down. Then both utensils vanished. "Now, just remember you must state *I wish* before any wish or the magic won't trigger." She brushed her hands together as if wiping off chalk. "Now to the more important business of your bounty."

"My bounty…you mean this Djinn?"

"Yes. You must understand that this miscreant has caused enough trouble after actually becoming a Djinn and has been in trouble more times than you can count!" She put her hands on her wide hips. "So I will lay out our added terms to the original client's requirements. Bring him in alive and we shall grant you your unknown desire." She paused. "Not including the emergency wish. That's a separate order."

I hated to tell her I already knew my desires. I had a lot of them. Kicking the step-monsters out of the house was the big one, as well as solving my mother's murder and finding that necklace—though the necklace wasn't really a reality I clung to.

"Any questions?"

"Yeah…how is it your demands coincide with this new client I got tonight? Are you them? Are you the one my boss said threw money at him to find this guy?"

"I am certainly not. And I would suggest you get more serious now and get out there and start looking. And don't let that harridan get hold of that shoe, or his life and yours will be in grave danger."

I sat on the bed and crossed my legs and my arms. I was going to test this old biddy. "I don't have a car."

A car honked outside as if in answer. I jumped up and looked out the attic window. In my usual parking spot sat a beautiful '64 hatchback Mustang. Mint condition. I turned and pointed to the window. "You put that there?"

"It's a bonus perk. Bring him in to me, not the first client. We might actually get this fixed. We have a contract?" She said.

"Well yes but—"

She grabbed my hand, gave it a hard shake, and vanished.

I stared at the tingling in my fingers and finally thought…what the hell have I got myself into?

The local coffee shop across the plaza from the antique shop was still open so I grabbed a cup and sat with the folder—er, piece of paper. I don't know why I was staring at it. I guess with all the weird that'd happened to me in the past five hours, I figured maybe more pages would show up. But there was absolutely nothing. I didn't even have a description.

Maybe I should just look up what a Djinn was, or what it did. And after twenty minutes, I wasn't really that much more educated. Mythologies that made no sense, and nothing about contracts. So whatever CBW woman was after, wasn't readily available on the internet.

I was ready to hurl this really dumb folder at the wall and had it in my hand when a man stepped into view. He looked familiar but I couldn't quite place him. A beat later I realized I'd almost hurled the folder *at* him as he was passing by. "Oh…sorry. Didn't see you there."

He had a cup in his hand, wore a long coat, gloves, and a soft blue scarf around his neck. He had a nice face, with hair just a tad too long over his brows and the sides of his face, as if a shorter cut had grown out. "It's fine. I just didn't want to be the destination of your frustration." He cocked his head to the side. "You look familiar."

"So do you. But not sure where."

"You look more like one of Mr. Ribirosa's employees."

"Mr. who?"

He chuckled and gestured to the empty chair facing me. "May I?"

I nodded.

He sat down. This close I could see light golden eyes and long lashes. He was incredibly pretty. Probably gay. "Mr. Ribirosa runs *Kingdom Bounty*. You look like one of his bounty hunters."

Jeebers. That obvious? I shrugged. And I was mortified I didn't remember the old man's name. "You work around here?"

"I do. Just a second. This needs sugar." He held up a finger and stood and turned and that's when I spotted the long, thin ponytail hanging down over his nice coat. He walked to a condiment station and grabbed a handful of sugars before sitting back down.

"You work at that antique store."

He removed his gloves and a smile exposed perfect teeth. He started tearing the tops off the sugars and dumping them in the cup. *All* of them. "Ah…that's where I've seen you. You bought the glass shoe."

"Yes I did. So…you getting off work?"

"Yes. I was supposed to meet someone here, but I'm afraid she never showed."

"Blind date?"

"You could say that." He offered his hand. "I'm Rex. Rex Charming."

Charming? I couldn't help but laugh as I shook his hand. His palm was warm and his hands soft. "Cynder Ella. Your last name is really Charming?"

He shrugged. "Is yours really Ella?"

Touché.

Rex stirred his coffee. "What is that you were about to bean me with?"

I chuckled. "A target. One that makes no sense."

"Maybe I can help? We can put our collective brains together?" He must have sensed my hesitation. "Or not? I just want to help."

Eh. Why not? But… "Well first, how long had that shoe been in the store? The shoe I bought?"

He pursed his lips and shrugged. "It was there when I started and I've only been working there a few weeks."

"I see. Have you ever noticed anything…unusual about the shoe?"

Sitting back he seemed to ponder his answer. "Other than it's made of glass?"

"Yeeeah."

Rex stared at me with those golden eyes. "Did you put it on?"

I knew this was a question, but it had an accusatory feel to it. "Yes."

He looked relieved. "Good. That means she can't physically take it. And did something happen?"

I sat back. This dude was playing with me. "Yeah, this woman from the CBW popped out and asked me to track down the same Djinn my boss just assigned me to find." I pushed the folder to him. "So the kicker here—is this real or am I losing my mind?"

His expression softened and he opened the folder. His brows arched into his bangs. "This is all he had?"

"Yeah. And Miss CBW woman had even less. I don't know if I even believe in this crap."

Chuckling, he pushed the folder back to me. "You said you saw a woman pop out of that shoe, but you don't believe in Djinns?"

I drank half my coffee before I put my elbows on the table. "Do you believe in them?"

"Yes."

"Do you know who that CBW woman is?"

"Yes."

"Do you know who this client is that's looking for this Djinn?"

"I would have to know the Djinn's name."

I blinked. "He didn't give me a name. Neither of them did. I just know he owes the client one more wish."

"Ah," Rex sat back. "I might have an idea. But before we go down that road, I think you should know a few things about Djinns."

I leaned forward. I didn't really think this guy knew anything, but I was willing to listen.

Rex pushed his chair back and stood. He held out his still gloved hand. "Come with me."

When I hesitated he tilted his head to his shoulder. "Do you not trust me?"

"I don't *know* you."

"Then this would be a leap of faith."

Intrigued, I stood and took his hand. We headed into the cold morning. The streets were empty as we crossed the street and Rex led me into an alley. Of course my brain went into protection mode and I made sure my gun was unholstered before he let go of my hand and pulled a fire escape ladder down. I followed him up. Once on the roof, he didn't offer his hand again but I followed him to the opposite edge. Below us was the street and the coffee shop, and I could just see the light of the antique shop. "Look up," he said.

And when I did, I staggered back.

I think all of us, in our little worlds consumed with our little worries, keep our heads down too much. We live in our bubbles and never think to look around us. And we never look up. I couldn't remember the last time I look up at the night sky, especially this late at night, or early in the morning, how ever you want to think about it. There were no clouds, and the majesty of the milky-way seemed so close I wanted to touch it. Vast and infinite—

"Vast and infinite is the universe," Rex said, mirroring my thoughts. "All manner of creation lives and breathes, Cynder. They live, they think, they choose, they die. All in an endless circle. Except those in the CBW world."

"Eh?" I tore my gaze from the sky and looked at him. He stood a little apart from me, his hands shoved into his coat pockets. The wind whipped at his ponytail as well as the tails of his coat. He looked…ethereal standing there. "Common Belief in Wishes?"

Rex nodded, but he never looked away from the sky as the wind moved the hair around his face. "It's that common belief that started all of this, because mankind doesn't understand how the universe works, and that wishes are real. The CBW formed itself into a viable entity and tapped creation to give life to legends buried in the psyche and histories. Genies were the first to fulfill wishes, when the wisher didn't understand they had the power all along to make their dreams come true. They are the most common. And because of that, Genies have rules. Guidelines they must follow. They cannot resurrect, they cannot falsify love, and they cannot kill."

I sort of knew this…from something. Maybe something I read, or watched. But it made sense. "And Djinns?"

"They are different. Where Genies are the most common, the Djinn would be the most rare. Created from the stars themselves, harnessed, and brought to Earth to encapsulate the ultimate in history making." He sighed. "If a master wants to create a plague, a Djinn will do their best to devise one that will kill the most. If they want their enemies murdered, a Djinn will do their best in seeing it done. They force love. They steal hearts. They…" he finally looked down. I could see him so clearly in the light of the milky-way.

"They what?"

"Through the millennium, the Fairy Godmothers—those who lord over the Giving of Wishes—have lost Djinns and Genies to something more powerful than wishes."

I already knew this answer. "Choice."

He nodded and looked back up. "There comes a time in all sentient beings, where innocent death weighs too heavy. This happens in wish givers as well. Where an order to kill an innocent girl is too much to bear. There is disobedience, strategy, and desperation to save that one innocent life, to somehow believe there is atonement waiting in the saving." He looked forward. "Djinns have no rules. Save one. Always fulfill the contract."

Something in his voice touched me, and it alarmed me at the

same time. I felt as if he were…confessing.

He pulled his hand from his coat pocket and I went for my gun, until I saw he held something in his fingers. It dangled and caught the milky-way's light with tiny glints. "I could only steal what was not hers. She does not covet it. It is simply a silent power for her over you."

I held out my hand gasped as he set my mother's opal necklace into it. My eyes burned as I remembered my mother taking such good care of it. It wasn't a priceless jewel or an expensive chain, but it meant the world to her because dad gave it to her. I looked at Rex and he was still facing the street, but looking back at me. His eyes glowed a soft gold. "Where…who?"

"My master. The one who still holds a single wish over my head." He half smiled. "Even if she does not possess the vessel, the wish was made, and I refuse to carry it out. I hid my vessel until you bought it. And now I choose another."

"You were there to make sure it stayed in the store. You'd been hiding it there for six years, until the wish limit ran out."

"Yes. But now there are two contracts on *me*—both to be carried out by the very woman I chose to save." He turned to face me. "I can't do what she wants me to do, and for that I will be punished, unless I can survive another fifteen hours. Then I will be free. You wanted to know who killed your mother, Cynder. It was my master. And I…" he closed his eyes. "I was the instrument of that destruction."

The world stopped moving at that moment. A Djinn—because I was pretty damn sure at this point Rex Charming was indeed the Djinn I was meant to find—killed my mother. Did I blame him, or the one that commanded him? And who was the one he refused to kill?

"Who!?" I shouted at him. "Who is your master?"

He held out his hands and fell back over the street.

"NO!" shouted and looked down. But there was no body. Nothing. Just silence, and a voice on the wind.

"Your stepmother…"

I ran down the stairs and searched the area, but there was no sign of Rex. I believed in Djinns at that moment because I'd seen him fall… and he was not there. He had killed my mother…ordered to, by my step-mother—

Before she was my step-mother.

This little piece of information wasn't lost on me. That woman targeted my family. She stole my mother's necklace and kept it all these years. And she'd ordered him to kill…

Me.

I went to the new perk car and opened the trunk. Inside was the shoe I'd bought. I sat on the edge of the trunk and yanked off my boots. Carefully—because it was glass—I put on the shoe and stood.

Nothing happened.

I walked around in it, half expecting it to crack.

Nothing happened.

Finally, frustrated, angry, pissed off and in a very destructive mood, I pulled the shoe off and started to dash it onto the pavement.

"STOP!"

The voice surprised me and I almost lost hold of the shoe. I looked around and found my Fairy Godmother beside the car. "So you were here the whole time?"

"No. I was busy. Just, put that down. It's an active vessel—if you destroy that, you'll reset events and destroy the Djinn—and that means more paperwork."

"The wish Rex Charming didn't fulfill—it was to my step-mother to kill me, wasn't it?"

My Fairy Godmother blinked at me. "I'm not at liberty to acknowledge or deny that information."

"He refuses to kill me, and you want him punished?"

I thought she was going to give me the same pat answer, but instead her shoulders slumped. "I don't make the rules. I just enforce them. She commissioned your death after your mother's—but Rex

Charming disobeyed. Djinns can't disobey. It's not allowed. Any non-fulfillment wish must be executed for the Djinn to continue its existence as a Wish Giver."

"And if they don't?"

The lights of the coffee house went out. It was just she and I in the parking lot. Finally she said, "If they can remain free of their master to run out the time limit of the wish, there is no punishment. But if they are caught, and their master wishes it, the punishment is anything they can come up with. The Djinn is under their will."

"If you catch him."

"Yes."

"Do you hear yourself? You're willing to condemn a creature who refused to kill another living being!"

"Really?" Now she looked put out. "He refused to kill you right after killing your mother—" She held out her hands. "I want to save Rex, not have him caught by that scary old broad."

"He can't die."

"That's up to him. He has a choice. He can kill you and free himself, or he can continue to defy the rules, and try to survive."

"What about a third alternative?"

My Fairy Godmother sighed. "What?"

"I use my emergency wish to remove my stepmother's wish."

"Uh…"

"What?"

She shook her head. "I don't think they can be used like that. Wishes are individual and keyed to the wisher."

"What if I find a wish that's acceptable? I have to do something to stop my Stepmother from hurting him."

"Why?" My Fairy Godmother held out her hands. "You got your wish, Cynder. You know who killed your mother and you got your necklace back. Why are you still harping on a Djinn? If he can hold out a few more hours, he's free. I don't know why he revealed himself after all this time."

Why did he? He could have kept this shoe invisible, and yet it was there for me to see. Did he want me to see it? Had he chosen, after all this time, to reveal himself to me for a purpose?

He killed her, but I couldn't be mad at him because it was my stepmother who ordered it. But even knowing—there was no way of proving it nor any way of making her pay for it. But in truth—I was more worried about Rex than I was her. I knew she would never get what she wanted, which was me dead.

But—*why* did she want me dead? That was six years ago. Why would she *still* want me dead? Unless…there was a reason I didn't know about.

My Fairy Godmother took a step back. "I'm not sure I like that look on your face."

"I may have an idea."

My stepmother was home when I arrived five hours later. It was eight in the morning and she was in the kitchen, making her morning tea. I came in, half paid attention to the sisters snoring on the couch, and stood in the kitchen. She didn't turn around. She was dressed in her robe, her hair pulled into a ponytail. "What is it, Cynder?" She didn't turn to look at me.

"You hired my boss to hunt down a Djinn because he didn't fulfill a wish six years ago. And now you want that wish to happen. Why?"

My stepmother didn't flinch. She just kept making her tea and once it was finished, she held the mug in her hands and turned to face me. Her eyes narrowed as she looked at me, and when her line of sight rested on the glass shoe in my hand, then traveled to the necklace, she pursed her lips. "I see he gave it to you."

"It was my mother's. It was supposed to be mine."

"No, it was supposed to be *mine!*" she hissed at me. The venom in that declaration was harsh. "I was there when he picked it out. It was for me, but he gave it to her! He refused to divorce her. So I looked for other ways to get what I wanted and paid a ransom to get my hands on that shoe. I ordered that Djinn to kill your mother and he did. I married your father only to find out he'd left money to you. I made a second wish to get to that money and it came true—I won the petition. And then when I found out he'd squirreled away his true worth and you were the beneficiary, after his death, with me as second, and I ordered the Djinn to kill you."

"But he didn't."

"No. The bastard didn't. Instead he stole the necklace from me, along with his vessel. For six years that wish has been open, and I knew the day you turned twenty-five, you'd inherit a fortune. I didn't have any more wishes to make, not while that one was active."

"So you tried to hire my boss to find him and force him to fulfill it."

"Only because I knew he'd give *you* the case, and you'd find him. And you did." She smiled and I didn't like how it looked. "But don't worry. You and he will no longer be a problem very soon." She moved past me to the door by the fridge. The door into the basement.

I followed her down, noticing the temperature drop. Dad used to store his wines down here. But my stepmother had long ago drank that wine away and now she used the room for—

Rex was there, on the floor. His coat and shoes were gone, and he was bloody. He wasn't moving.

"What did you do?" I ran to him.

"I am punishing him, as is my right."

I didn't even look at my stepmother. I rolled Rex over and saw he'd been beaten pretty badly. But not by her. "Who beat him?"

"He's *my* Djinn," She leaned against the dryer and sipped her tea. "I have the power to punish him any way I like with a single thought. He refused to finish the job. But with you here, he has no choice. Once he wakes, he will kill you so he can be free."

"No he won't. He only has a few hours to go. If he can hold out, he's free of you."

She made *tsking* noises. "I'm afraid not. I made the wish again, the same one, using the same words. I reset the wish and he is mine to torture until he does what I command. Then he's free from his contract to me, and I inherit five million dollars."

I nearly fainted right then. "You're lying. My dad never had five million anything."

"I'm afraid he did. You and your mother saved for your future. Invested it with a reputable agency. Their initial investment of one million is now five."

Damn. Damn, damn, damn. Rex made a noise and I placed my hand against his cheek. His skin was so cold. "Rex, why are you even here?"

My stepmother laughed. "Fool showed up at the door with a deal. He asked me to choose another victim and release him from my contract on you. He pleaded with me, as if he had a soul. Djinns aren't human, they're demons. They're—"

"Wish Givers," Rex said softly.

I looked at him and he looked up at me with one eye, the other swollen shut. He smiled. "I am sorry…about your mother."

"It wasn't you. It was her. I don't blame you." I had my planned wish in my mind. All I had to do was say it.

He tried to smile and reached up with a bloody hand. He placed his fingers on the shoe beside me. "She's right…the only way to freedom…and your safety…is to kill…or reset everything."

Rex grabbed the shoe. I yelled when he raised it and smashed it against the cement floor. There was a flash, my stomach lurched, and Rex was gone. I was still on the floor in the basement, but he wasn't there. Neither was my stepmother. Beside me was a basket of laundry, half turned over. I pushed myself up on my feet and grabbed the vibrating dryer. It wasn't on before was it? Where…where was everyone?

"Cynder?" A voice called from upstairs. "Honey are you all right?"

I froze. That voice. It came from my past. But it was here. And it wasn't in my memory.

Someone descended the steps from the kitchen and I backed up, afraid of what might come around that corner.

My mother, much older than I remembered her, stood in front of me. Gray streaked hair in a soft bun at her collar. She wore soft jeans, slippers and her favorite kind of blouse; a button down long sleeve made of cotton. She frowned at me as I stared at her.

And at her throat flashed a beautiful opal necklace.

"Mom?" I launched at her and squeezed her, crying as I inhaled her smell, felt her warmth. She was here. Alive. And in my arms.

And she was also a bit weirded out at me. She pushed me away but I refused to let go entirely. "Oh for heaven's sake child, you're just moving across town. I'm still here. And I'm pretty sure you're going to keep coming back to do your laundry. Just remember I'm not doing it for you. You're nearly twenty five, so it's about time you left home."

Wait…I got my mother back and I'm leaving?

I didn't know what happened. I remembered Rex's words, reset everything. And my Fairy Godmother *had* warned me not to smash that shoe or I'd reset—

That's what Rex did.

He smashed the shoe and erased what happened.

I stared at the necklace.

She put her hand to her throat. "Oh…that's right. I did tell you that you could have this. Funny, I feel the need to give it to you now." She unhooked it from the back and handed it to me.

I put it around my neck and felt its weight there, comforting. But not as much as knowing my mother was alive, and I'd missed ten years of living with her.

We spent the afternoon together and I managed to learn most of what had happened in the now reset decade. My mother hadn't been killed, but my dad had died as he had before. But this time, it was mom and I who got by with the life insurance and the money he left for my education. I still hadn't gone into law school, even without the stepsisters. I was still a bounty hunter. I still worked for Kingdom Bounty. And I still drove a piece of shit. Apparently the nice '64 Mustang didn't exist for me anymore. I didn't have a glass slipper in my room or in my car.

But I was moving out and mom was thinking of moving into one of those Senior Living places across town near the lake. Several of her friends lived there now and I felt she was pretty excited about the idea. The money Dad had put away until I was twenty-five could pay for it. And that made me happy.

I had to get my new address from my mom, who was pretty sure I was coming down with something because I was acting funny. It was a nice loft, in the same building Rex and I had climbed that night to look at the sky. I moved the rest of my laundry in and took a walk down the street. The coffee shop was still there, as was the antique store. But there was no glass slipper in the case.

After the sun went down, I climbed onto the roof and looked up at the stars. They were just as brilliant as they had been that night when Rex Charming had looked upon them with what I would call envy.

Had that really been just last night?

I took the necklace off and held it in my hand. I took a deep breath and said, "I wish Rex Charming was here with me now, alive and well, and he was my Djinn—if he chooses to do so."

Did I expect my emergency wish to work? Not really. I figured when Rex reset my life by destroying his vessel, he'd reset my encounter with my Fairy Godmother.

I'd closed my eyes when I made that wish. When I opened them. I wasn't expecting to see him standing beside me, dressed once again in his coat, scarf, and gloves. The wind whipped his ponytail about as he spoke.

"Are you sure Cynder? There is a grace period where you can rescind the wish."

I grabbed him and held him to me. And to my surprise, he wrapped his arms around me. I felt his chin resting on the top of my head and realized just how tall he was.

"You didn't answer me," he said.

"I am sure. You gave me back my mother."

"Minus a few years."

"You think I care about that?" I moved back from him and looked into his golden eyes. "You're here."

"You don't know me."

"That's true."

"I don't know you."

"I think you do. You refused to kill me when I was fifteen, and you still refused to kill me nine years later. I think you know me pretty well."

He smiled at me. "So where do we go from here?"

"I just moved into this building. Do you need a room to sleep in?"

"That would be better than a closet."

I laughed. He did as well, but he looked sad. "What's wrong?"

"Cynder…I'm still a Djinn."

"With no vessel," came another voice.

We turned to see my Fairy Godmother standing there. She looked at the two of us. "I guess it could work. Given you two don't kill each other."

"I'm afraid you're wrong there, Beatrice."

Beatrice? That was her name?

"I am never wrong, you overgrown child. Wait, wrong about what?"

"I do have a vessel." He reached down and touched the necklace.

"Are you sure?" my Fairy Godmother said and I realized she was talking to me.

I nodded.

"Just remember, three wishes. That's it. After the third wish is fulfilled, Rex is free."

I smiled at him. He smiled at me. My Fairy Godmother threw up her hands and vanished.

"Should be an interesting partnership." I had this really cool idea.

A bounty hunter and a Djinn. What could go wrong?

END

AUTHOR'S NOTE

I love Djinns. And I love Dark Fantasy. For a few years I've toyed with the idea of teaming up a female bounty hunter with a male Djinn, just to see how readers like it. A wish story based on Cinderella gave me just the vehicle I needed to test drive the idea.
 ;)

ABOUT THE AUTHOR

Phaedra grew up on ghost stories in and around the deep south, from tales of lights on the railroad tracks to the singing of hymns in the ruins of old farmhouses where only the chimney remained. She later moved this love of tales into stories and with her first traditional publication, The Zoe Martinique Investigation series, embarked on an odyssey of Science Fiction, Urban Fantasy, Dark Fantasy, and upcoming Fantasy. Her books can be found at phaedraweldon.com. Her upcoming project is a women's paranormal mystery series set in the world of Ravenwood Hills, Delaware.

WALLINA

NIKKI JEFFORD

In the town of Anderson lived the old spinster Gertrude, who had given up on marriage many decades ago. She did, however, share a home with her brother. He could be exasperating, sure, but he tended to their sheep with care, ensured the roof never leaked, and always took off his muddy boots before entering the cottage.

After the spinster's brother dropped dead while shearing the sheep one spring, her neighbor's oldest son came by six afternoons a week to see to the animals and repairs.

Being in the prime of his youth, Hagen was able to do the work of the spinster's brother in less than half the time. But he could not make up for the tales her brother once told with gusto during the evenings in front of the fire in winter or on the porch rocker in summer. Bereft of family, Gertrude would stare at the yellow floral vase on her porch that had been passed down by the women in her family and feel a sense of familiar peace. Her mother had told her the heirloom brought luck, as well as beauty, to generations of their kin. Sometimes it even granted wishes. Sighing wistfully, Gertrude mourned that she had no daughter to pass the vase on to.

She got by well enough on her own, but life was lonely and dull without her brother. Peering out the window at the boy as he finished his work and headed home each evening, she dreamed, not for the first time, that she had a child of her own.

A friend in town had just the answer. In fact, so sure was she of the arrangement that she made the decision on her friend's behalf without first consulting Gertrude. It was simple, really. A single woman of a certain age had need of a companion. The girl could help cook and clean while keeping Gertrude company. Thus, the spinster was presented with a young woman who had been taken in by the nuns and raised in the convent. She arrived on the cottage porch clutching a satchel containing her meager possessions.

The girl was a beauty with warm, hazel eyes, a slight frame, and long chestnut hair that tumbled to her waist in soft waves. Having been found abandoned in a basket in the shade of a stone wall as a babe, the nuns had named her Wallina.

The spinster was skeptical at first, but Wallina's gratitude and wonder at experiencing life beyond the convent inevitably rubbed off on all those she encountered. Wallina was dutiful and tidy. From the nuns, she'd learned humility and a healthy respect for authority. In many ways, the girl was innocent—having been sheltered all her life. The first time her face broke out in freckles from spending hours in the sun, she cried, believing she had come down with the pox. A motherly instinct kicked in as Gertrude assured the girl she was all right, and this didn't excuse her from pitting cherries for that night's pie.

Wallina's imagination ran a bit wild, but this was tolerable so long as she completed her chores and did not touch the spinster's prized vase. The old woman found the tales the girl weaved brought comfort she had not known since her brother's passing.

Wallina had a very different effect on the neighbor's son.

Hagen was smitten the moment he laid eyes on the town's new beauty.

On the spinster's land, he went about his work—same as always —but when he finished, he wasn't in such a hurry to rush home or meet up with the fawning town girls.

He'd heard Wallina chattering away through open windows and

while sweeping the porch, speaking to the spinster with a lilting voice filled with delight. She had a laugh like a song that made him want to skip across the meadows picking wildflowers. If only the young beauty would spare him a word.

Try as he might to catch her eye, Wallina avoided his company as though he was a toad.

The town girls all agreed that Hagen was by far the most handsome and good natured of Anderson's boys, but only one opinion mattered to him.

"The wool on the sheep is especially soft this time of year," he said to her one afternoon when she came out to fetch a pail of water from the well.

Rather than come over and pat the bleating animal, as he'd hoped, Wallina hurried inside without a word.

The next time she ventured out, he tried complimenting her dress. Again, the girl scurried away. Having lost patience, Hagen followed her toward the cottage.

"Hey," he said, but Wallina kept walking. "Hey," he said again. The girl picked up speed. When she reached the porch, despair, humiliation, and anger clouded Hagen's judgement. "Hey, freckles!" he yelled.

When Wallina froze in her tracks, Hagen's heart stopped right alongside her. She turned slowly, a look of rage overcoming her usual serene smile. The look she shot him would have sent the devil fleeing back into the flames of hell. But all Hagen could think at the moment was, *"Finally. She looked at me."*

"Freckles!" the word burst from her lips like lightning striking. Wallina had never known this kind of anger before. It stole her breath and sight. She felt as though a dam would break inside her if she didn't first break something else—preferably over the insolent boy's head. "How dare you!"

Grabbing the nearest object, Wallina threw it at him and had the satisfaction of hearing the thing break apart upon impact.

Hagen took a stumbling step backward. His jaw went slack.

Wallina smiled with satisfaction at having achieved such excellent aim . . . until she noticed what it was she'd thrown and destroyed.

It was then that Gertrude came outside to see what the commotion was about. The old woman's eyes took on the keen appearance of an eagle's when she noticed the broken pieces of her priceless vase.

"What in the world happened?" she shrieked, clutching her chest.

Wallina's eyes widened in horror at what she had done. Gertrude would send her back to the convent where she would have to cover her hair for the rest of her life and see nothing beyond the dreary gray walls. Tears blurred her vision as she opened her mouth to confess. Before she could, Hagen stepped forward.

"I only meant to move it into the yard so Wallina could sweep the porch." Hagen clasped his hands and bowed his head. "I am very sorry."

Wallina stood in stunned silence. From the time she learned to talk, the nuns had instilled in her the importance of telling the truth. Why would Hagen lie? For her?

"Sorry?" the spinster repeated shrilly. Gertrude stomped down the three wood stairs and barreled up to poor Hagen, who flinched. "Sorry won't replace decades of memories. Sorry won't bring back my great-grandmother's most prized possession. I'm only sorry I hired you and not the Miller boy. Now get your sorry hide out of my sight and don't ever return."

Hagen's face burned red, but he kept his head down. "Yes, ma'am."

Wallina wanted to cry at the dejection in his voice. She tried to make eye contact, but the boy turned away and skulked off.

Late that night, after Gertrude was asleep in her bed, Wallina snuck out and followed the road to the neighboring cottage Hagen shared with his five younger siblings and parents. She had heard the spinster speak of them and how sad it was they struggled more and more each year. Again, she marveled at why he would risk his position for her.

Stupid boy, she thought. *Stupid wonderful boy.*

She thought she might have to throw rocks at his window like she'd read about in some of the books she'd snuck into her chamber at the convent, poring over the words by candlelight late into the night.

There was no need to awaken the boy, though, for he stood against a tree staring distantly into a clear night's sky speckled in heavenly light.

At Wallina's approach, he lowered his head and blinked twice. A smile lit up his face.

"Freckles," he whispered.

This time when he said it, her heart melted like wax.

After that, they snuck out every evening to meet beneath the stars. Whereas Wallina had been distant before, she chattered away as though she had known Hagen her entire life. He listened with rapt attention, delighting in her company in ways he had never dreamed.

Sometimes they lay on their backs staring at the sky and, oh, the wonders they saw: shooting stars, the swirling milky way, and distant planets glowing in the night.

"I once wished on that star right there," Hagen said, pointing one evening at a bright star above Anderson.

Wallina turned on her side and propped her head on her hand, smiling through a scattering of freckles she'd collected from the sun. "And what did you wish for, Hagen?"

"I wished for you."

It was with heavy hearts that the young lovers said their sad good-byes at the end of summer. Wallina and Gertrude had made candles all season to sell to merchants in the bustling town of Montgomery Lakes. The spinster was getting too old to travel, so she arranged a carriage to transport her charge and the candles.

Feeling weepy one moment, Wallina soon recovered as her heart hammered with excitement at seeing more of the world from which she'd been sheltered her entire life.

Hagen would be waiting for her in Anderson when she returned and oh, what stories she would have to share with him and Gertrude once she returned. These would be imparted separately, of course, for the spinster still cursed Hagen's name whenever she looked at the empty spot where her vase once sat.

When the day of departure arrived, the spinster presented Wallina with a gorgeous sky-blue cloak. The old woman would've had to have been blind to miss the way Wallina admired the coat in the window of Francie's Frock Shop every time they passed on their way to pick up the post.

Tears streamed from Wallina's eyes at the spinster's generosity.

"Yes, well, don't go getting used to it," Gertrude grumbled. Wallina threw her arms around the old woman and hugged her tight. "And don't go putting on airs in Montgomery Lakes. You're there to sell our stock and fetch the highest price."

Sniffling, Wallina drew back and nodded.

As its name implied, Montgomery Lakes was a town situated along the shores of grand bodies of deep blue waters. Wallina marveled at it the moment she caught sight of the first sprawling lake from the carriage.

The trees, shedding their leaves, offered a clear view of the crystalline waters.

She did not gawk long, for she had a duty to complete. After securing a room at an inn, Wallina set out with a sampling of her wares to present to vendors.

Charmed by the young beauty from Anderson, merchants quickly bought up the candles that she and Gertrude had carefully poured and set into pillars and long sticks of smooth wax to light up homes through winter.

Wallina spoke with such excitement about the process that, even though the merchants knew very well how candles were made, they listened attentively to the energy in her voice and soaked in the radiance of her rosy cheeks.

In no time at all, the candles sold and Wallina held a purse filled with more coins than Gertrude had expected when tallying potential profit. With the extra coin, Wallina purchased a purple vase and had it wrapped carefully in paper and tied with string. It looked nothing like the one she'd so carelessly broken, but Wallina had noticed that Gertrude loved the color purple. Her deception had been weighing heavy on her and hopefully the new vase would ease the spinster's anger when she told her the truth.

The vendor who sold it to Wallina had told her it was one of his most unique pieces. "Rare and lovely, like you."

The townspeople were not the only beings to take note of Wallina's beauty. One fateful evening, an ugly troll plodded into town at dusk, having wandered in from her home beneath a stone bridge shadowing a dry creek bed beside one of the town's grand lakes. The troll caught sight of the beauty just as she was retiring for the night at a local inn. The troll, temporarily forgetting her errand of scavenging bones from trash heaps, crept after Wallina.

What a fine wife this pretty human would make for her son.

Soon after Wallina fell asleep, the troll pried her window open and slipped into her chamber. She wrapped the girl in her lovely wool cloak and carried her without disturbing the girl's slumber.

Beneath the bridge, splintered bones littered the jagged floor. This would not do for such a beautiful bride. The troll needed time to prepare an exquisite dwelling for such a fine creature to share with her son.

To prevent Wallina from leaving while arrangements were made, the troll stole two rafts and placed the still slumbering girl on one. The troll tied one end of a rope around Wallina's raft and the other to an anchor, which she tossed over the side. Once the girl floated securely above the lake's depth, the troll rowed back to shore in her raft.

Most villagers, especially women and girls, knew naught how to swim. Having never stepped toe in so much as a pond, Wallina could swim as well as she could fly. When she awoke, she was dismayed to find herself trapped upon the raft. She might as well have been trapped on an island.

Seeing her awake, the troll and her son rowed over in their own raft.

"This is my son. You will marry him," the female troll said.

Her son stared at Wallina and made guttural noises that might as well have been a toad croaking for all Wallina could understand him.

"I will fetch you once your home beneath the bridge is ready. Then you and my son will have a place to live after you are wed," the female said.

Then mother and son rowed away.

Wallina pulled her legs against her chest and wept. She did not want to marry an ugly troll or live under the damp shade of a bridge. Pulling her cloak around her shuddering body, she cried bitterly as the sun began to rise above her watery prison.

As it turned out, Corgis, the local lake monster, overheard everything the troll had said and took issue with her perverse plans for Wallina. So, Corgis bit through the rope, setting the raft free.

The craft, however, drifted farther from shore. But Wallina's heart was filled with relief at escaping the horrid troll and her hideous son.

Off she floated across a vast lake that stretched on as far as her eyes could see. The wind picked up with high gusts and she held on as the raft was pitched over great swells. The craft rounded a bend between mountains and eased into a narrow channel sheltered from the gale. She floated past thick forested land. Along the banks, Wallina observed no signs of human habitation. A deer paused in her drinking to watch the girl float by.

Her stomach rumbling with hunger, Wallina crouched at the edge of the raft and attempted to paddle to shore using her hands. It was slow going, but she kept at it. When a butterfly fluttered past her, she smiled and said, "I wish you could help me return to land, my winged friend."

The butterfly flitted away while Wallina dipped one hand after another in the cool water and pushed. Light glinted off the rippling surface. Suddenly, Wallina could see through to the sandy bottom where small fish darted between stones.

Crying out with joy, she balled up her cloak, held it above her head, and slid over the raft's edge, waist deep in water. Wallina walked the remaining way to a sandbar, where she wrung out her skirts and let the light breeze slowly dry out her damp shoes, socks, and dress.

"That's better," Wallina said to the nearby trees. Straightening her shoulders, she made her way along the lake, determined to follow the water's edge to the town of Montgomery Lakes then back home to Anderson.

But Wallina had drifted far. Her feet grew weary and her empty belly ached as day turned to dusk. With the sun, the temperature dropped and Wallina marveled at how quickly the air turned from warm to cold.

Pulling her cloak tight around her, she made her way along the lake with shivering steps. The smell of woodsmoke made her pause and look around. In the twilight, she could just make out the puffs of gray rising above the trees.

She glanced between the chilly shoreline and the thicket of trees. A sudden chill blew over the water and wracked her bones. That did it; into the sheltered woods she went.

Wallina picked her way through moss-covered trunks and over rotting logs, coming at last upon a small stone cottage from which the smoke drifted from a chimney atop the roof.

Grateful that she would not freeze her bones overnight, Wallina knocked on the arched wooden door.

As luck would have it, the owner of the cottage turned out to be a medicine woman who welcomed her in at once. The healer ushered Wallina to the hearth while she added more ingredients to a large pot to share her evening stew.

"What fine timing you have," the woman said, clutching her breastbone. "My neighbor, Mr. Magus, is coming over after supper for herbal tea. You must entertain him with stories, for he is blind. Do you know any tales?"

"I do, indeed," Wallina said, eager to pay back the healer's kindness.

"Very good," the woman said, clapping her hands together. "Make sure they are not frightening or romantic. Use humor sparingly—best not use it at all unless it is suitably subtle. Mr. Magus enjoys tales of voyage and discovery. Oh, dear. I hope you are able to please him. He is a sorcerer of great wealth. Oh, but you should see his house built into the mountainside. It is filled with wonders and four times the size of my cottage. The sorcerer has a magical staff inlaid with rubies the likes no king or queen has ever possessed. A girl would be lucky to marry a man such as he."

When Mr. Magus arrived for tea, Wallina did her best to entertain the sorcerer with her story of escaping the trolls and finding herself on the other side of a lake as large as an ocean.

The sorcerer sat on the healer's upholstered chair, taking occasional sips of tea from a mug. His expression gave nothing away of the enrapture he felt at the sound of the girl's voice. Being blind had taught him to tread with care.

"What a captivating story," he said, imagining the girl beamed with delight. "The two of you must pay me a visit tomorrow afternoon."

"Oh! We would be delighted," the healer exclaimed.

The following morning, Wallina was dismayed to find the cottage windows frosted over. The chill outside leaked through the walls and into her bones, reducing her to shivers.

"Hot porridge is just what you need," the healer said, setting a pot atop the hearth. "Don't you worry, girl. I won't turn you out in the cold. You'd catch your death within hours in that thin frock. You can stay here through winter."

"Th-Thank you." Wallina's teeth chattered. She felt relief and anguish, two emotions that did not mix well. Her stomach churned.

Gertrude and Hagen would worry. At least she wouldn't freeze to death. Better to return home in the spring than not to return at all.

Wallina fell into a routine of helping the healer prepare tinctures and teas, steaming and grinding herbs the woman had grown and dried over the summer. She took over preparing their daily meals and cleaning dishes after they ate.

Every afternoon, they paid Mr. Magus a social call. The home that he had built into the side of the mountain did not contain a single window. The large space within was dark, the way the blind sorcerer preferred it. The healer would light a candle when they came over so that Wallina could see the large cavern filled with wonders. There was an extravagant armchair that looked like a throne upon which the sorcerer would sit during their stay. Stone masks with monstrous faces stared vacantly from the wall alongside the skulls of tusked beasts. Leather tomes were piled on low dark wooden tables. Creatures made of bronze and marble stood obediently in corners forever frozen in place.

"What a great and powerful sorcerer," the healer gushed whenever they walked to or from Mr. Magus's domain. "Have you ever seen such wonders?"

Wallina was always polite. Whenever Mr. Magus pointed out a book, he wished her to read from, she did as he requested. By candlelight, Wallina would squint at the pages and speak in the good-natured voice everyone found so pleasing. It was fortunate the nuns had taught her to read, though the sorcerer's collection was not the sort of divine material she had grown up with.

If Mr. Magus was the one doing the talking, he asked the healer to blow out the candle, which the woman did with a gust of breath that pitched them into darkness.

"A waste of wax," the sorcerer grumbled.

"Indeed," the healer agreed.

The light bothered Mr. Magus most of all. He detested summer and daytime, fires and lanterns. Even the single glow of a candle irritated him like the buzzing of a fly. His living space was warmed by a cast-iron stove in which heat radiated without the offense of firelight.

When Wallina stubbed her toe on the leg of a petrified wood

stool leaving the sorcerer's lair, the healer rubbed ointment over the bruised skin back at her cottage.

"Do not worry, love. Soon, you will know your way around Mr. Magus's abode without requiring the use of light or sight."

The winter dragged on, but Wallina did not go hungry or cold. With the approach of spring, her heart lifted at the prospect of returning home. She had only to make her way through the forest, back to the lake, and follow the water's edge.

The healer hummed with excitement, as well. What good news she had. An exceedingly auspicious turn of events was to transpire for her young charge. Mr. Magus had proposed to marry Wallina.

There was no question of consulting the girl. The healer had accepted on her behalf with the humble appreciation expected from such a fortunate offer. They would be married at the beginning of summer then hole up for the remainder of the season inside Mr. Magus's home, shutting out the glaring light until fall.

In the meantime, there was much to be done. Wallina had only the clothes on her back to offer the sorcerer. This would not do for a man such as he, the healer fretted. She set Wallina to work weaving baskets and making charms for her dowry. Wallina's fingers bled and stung from hours and days of crafting a suitable offering for Mr. Magus to take her in.

Being blind, the sorcerer could not keep an eye on his bride. Instead, he took to escorting the women from the cottage to his home on their daily visits. Along the way, he recounted times when trespassers had tried stealing from him only to end up transformed into frogs.

The healer clapped her hands gleefully before patting Wallina's arm. "You need never worry about theft in your household with Mr. Magus around."

While the healer grinned, Wallina took the sorcerer's tale for what it really was. A warning. Attempt to run away or leave him, and he would turn her into a frog.

She would never return to Anderson. Never see the dear old spinster who was the closest thing she'd ever had to a mother. Never again see her beloved Hagen. And it was so much worse because the sorcerer intended to take away the very sun from her life. She would spend her days in darkness, as forlorn as the stone masks bound to the walls, and as inert as the monstrous statues with their lifeless eyes.

It was that or become one of the frogs croaking from the trees.

One afternoon, staff in hand as Mr. Magus led the women to his domain, they came upon a winged white horse lying motionless on its side, halfway in the path.

"Oh! What has happened?" Wallina cried, falling to her knees beside the beautiful creature.

Mr. Magus poked at the underbelly of the Pegasus with the end of his staff. "Stupid beast was struck down by lightning last night. Landed right on my pathway."

Tears filled Wallina's eyes as she patted the animal's silken head. She felt a faint breath from its nostrils and looked up. "We must help him."

"It would be a waste of time," the sorcerer said. "Only the folk are able to tame these bothersome creatures."

"Come, dear," the healer said, pulling Wallina up. "At least it hasn't taken up the entire path. We will have to walk around it until the maggots do their work."

Wallina held back a cry as she was ushered to the sorcerer's lair where they spent the remainder of the afternoon in the dark listening to Mr. Magus speak of demons he'd reduced to ash in a distant kingdom that had repaid him by delivering trunks filled with precious artifacts. Wallina cringed in the dark. The healer was likely fanning her face. At least when they were married, the blind man would not see Wallina's disgust. The nuns had taught her to be of service and always obedient. She had been happy to assist the spinster in Anderson. She would not feel the same way attending the sorcerer in his dark lair.

That evening, after the healer snored inside her quilted bed, Wallina snuck out with a bowl of water and took it to the Pegasus.

Kneeling beside the magnificent creature, she placed the water at his lips. "Please drink."

The Pegasus's eyelids trembled then opened slowly. His tongue inched out of his mouth and took its first lap of the cool spring water. After finishing the bowl, his eyes drifted closed, his great white chest rising and falling gently.

Early every morning and late every evening, Wallina brought the winged horse food and water. He ate and drank slowly each time before again closing his eyes. It broke her heart to see such a magnificent creature brought down, though she never gave up on the Pegasus. While he ate and drank each meal she brought, she would share her woes at becoming an unhappy wife, trapped away with the sorcerer in his dark lair. The creature's ears flattened whenever she mentioned Mr. Magus.

As the forest trees budded and wildflowers blossomed with spring, Wallina came upon the Pegasus with a start one morning. He was standing!

Seeing her, he nickered and spread his wings, giving them a shake.

"Look at you! All better," Wallina exclaimed with delight. "Now you must go off to a happier place than this."

The Pegasus shook his mane.

Wallina tilted her head. "No?" she asked in confusion.

Tucking his mighty wings against his sides, he clomped up beside Wallina and knelt on his front legs.

"What—? Oh," Wallina said as understanding dawned. She looked from side to side. It was early yet, and the healer and sorcerer were still tucked snug in their beds.

Throwing caution to the wind, Wallina climbed onto the Pegasus and wrapped her arms gently around his neck. He took off at a gallop, dodging trees, boulders, and brush. Wallina held her breath, praying she would not turn into a toad on his back. When they reached a meadow, the creature's wings extended and flapped, lifting them off the ground.

The lake below became a speck of blue as the Pegasus flew into the puffy white clouds. Wallina's spirit soared with hope.

It felt like they were flying all day, though the sun still lit up the sky when the Pegasus descended into the courtyard of a faerie castle. Water sprayed from stone fountains and roses climbed up trellises arched over wide walkways. Faeries in bright-colored frocks flitted around the gardens calling out merry greetings to one another.

A handsome faerie prince in a golden crown jogged over as Wallina slipped off the Pegasus.

"Zelios, where have you been?" he cried as he ran his hand down the creature's neck. The Pegasus neighed and bobbed his head. The prince turned to Wallina, his eyes lighting up as he took in the mortal beauty. "You rescued my friend. For that, I pledge my protection and loyalty for all time."

Wallina blushed. "I am so very happy he made it home."

The prince grinned. "Your voice is as lovely as you. What is your name?"

"Wallina," she answered softly.

Grimacing for a moment, the prince's shoulders relaxed the next. "A terrible name, but names can be fixed. We shall call you Bellflower. Come, I have something to give you."

Speechless, Wallina—or rather, Bellflower if you asked the folk —followed the prince into the castle and through the grand halls to the treasury with its piles of gold and jewels.

Selecting a dainty crown of gold from a velvet pillow, the prince placed it on the young woman's head and announced that they would be married.

That night, the courtiers feasted and danced, celebrating the prince's good fortune in finding such a lovely creature with a voice as pleasing as birdsong at sunrise. She would make a fine princess, indeed.

Bellflower, they agreed, was too precious for the human world.

She belonged among the folk. So humble too. She flushed at their compliments and was ever the polite guest.

Better to be a princess, Wallina supposed, than the bride of a troll beneath a bridge or married to a sorcerer inside his dark lair. She had no idea where the Pegasus had taken her. The palace was beautiful, at least. Sunlight flowed in from large windows. The courtiers sang her praises, and the faerie prince was as handsome as could be.

That night, Wallina stood in the window of her tower, staring into the stars when something caught her eye. She blinked several times. One particular star flickered with each flutter of her lashes, brighter than the rest.

She knew that star. Her beloved Hagen, and Gertrude, and the town of Anderson lay dreaming beneath that star.

Using the constellations as guidance, Wallina set out that very night. She'd learned a great deal from the healer about foraging. Carefully selecting tubers, mushrooms, and wild berries along the way, Wallina found nourishment while avoiding habitation of any kind, keeping company with the birds and deer of the forest. When she came to a lake, her heart burst with joy. Perhaps the town of Montgomery Lakes lay on the opposite end. It was a large lake. It could be the one she'd been looking for.

She continued following the shoreline, sleeping near the water at night, using her cloak as a blanket.

When at last she came upon the familiar bustling town, she hired a carriage to transport her to Anderson with the promise that her fare would be paid on the other end.

Poor old Gertrude had despaired of ever seeing Wallina again. When a carriage trundled in front of her cottage and the girl stepped out wearing the clothes she had last been seen in, the spinster wept as she never had before.

After hugging the girl, kissing her cheeks, and inspecting her from head to toe, the old woman ushered Wallina inside. There, on the living room table, stood the purple vase. Wallina's mouth fell open.

Gertrude explained, "When you did not return from Montgomery Lakes, I sent Hagen to see what had become of you. The innkeepers where you stayed had kindly stored all the items left inside your room and wished they could offer more information about your disappearance."

"How worried you must have been," Wallina said.

"Never mind that. You are home, and you must call me Mother from this day forth."

Wallina's vision went blurry with tears.

She was not keen to recount her misadventures. They lay behind her like seasons past.

She was home with family now and reunited with her beloved Hagen, whom she married soon after he asked.

The spinster had reconciled with Hagen after Wallina told her the truth about the floral vase. It no longer mattered. Family was more precious than any possession.

In the years that followed, Wallina and Hagen gave the spinster many grandchildren. The cottage was always filled with laughter and love. It was a good life. A life that brought joy to the old woman such as she had never known. It was a life better than anything she could have dreamed.

"Wallina" is a retelling of Hans Christian Andersen's "Thumbelina" with a touch of *Anne of Green Gables*.

It had been a few decades since I last read the original telling of "Thumbelina." Reading it as an adult brought new perspective and ideas of how to update the tale. What stood out the most to me was:

1. The story begins with a woman who dreams of having a daughter and granted that wish. Then her little girl is stolen, never to return. I know it's a fairy tale, but that's a tragic ending for any mother. When I started my version, it was with the intention that mother and daughter would be reunited in the end.

2. Thumbelina is twice told whom she will marry—by other females no less—only to find "escape" by marriage. Ironic much? The fairy prince does ask her to be his wife (rather than tell her) in the original, but on my first read-through it felt more like an order. He pulled his crown off his head and stuck it on hers like a ring (or a collar). And speaking of collars…

3. The flower Thumbelina lands on doesn't like the girl's

name and renames her—like she's a pet rather than a person. What the freak berries? Different times for sure.

I did want to preserve the essence of the original in the character of Thumbelina, who was a beautiful, docile kind girl with a lovely voice. (Though it was tempting to go full-on Anne Shirley at times. Wallina got her one moment with the vase.)

Hagen is an added character not represented in the original version. (My Gilbert Blythe.) Princes and billionaire types just don't do it for me. I like my Gilberts and Mr. Darcys.

The tagline for my Royal Conquest fantasy romance saga is: Not all fairy tales end with a prince. I felt that was a good theme for Wallina as well. Returning home to loved ones is a true happy ending.

Thank you for joining us in another ONCE UPON adventure.

Keep on reading and dreaming!

ABOUT THE AUTHOR

Nikki Jefford is a lifelong daydreamer and tale-teller. Books, travel, TV series, nature walking, writing, and motorcycle riding are her favorite escapes. She loves meeting people from all walks of life, from all around the globe, and wouldn't trade in her French husband for anyone – not even Spike! Nikki is the author of the Royal Conquest Saga, Wolf Hollow Shifters, Aurora Sky: Vampire Hunter, and the Spellbound Trilogy. She also has stories in the Once Upon a Kiss, Once Upon a Quest, Once Upon a Star, and Once Upon a Ghost anthologies.

Discover more of Nikki's paranormal and fantasy worlds at NikkiJefford.com and receive a free story when you sign up for her newsletter.

WICKED WINDS

KASEY MACKENZIE

"Well, we're *definitely* not in Missouri anymore," I quip as Toto the Wonder Dog and I speed across the state line into Kansas.

The windows are down, Toto's ears are flapping in the wind, and I'm jamming out. I tap my mother's silver-sequined slippers against the floorboard and thank the Lord for cruise control. One of Mom's favorite rock albums blares as the midsummer breeze whips my hair around crazily. Too crazily for this time of year, come to think of it. Shivers dance along my skin as I realize how quickly the air has cooled since we started our drive in St. Louis. A sixth sense for weather developed during a Tornado Alley childhood inspires a frown. Extreme drops from hot to cold rarely bode well in this part of the country.

I should know. They never found my mother's body after the twister swept through Auntie Em and Uncle Henry's farm when I was a teenager.

It's to that farm nestled among the Kansas plains we're driving. I glance at Toto IV—who shares a name with the album we're listening to—and force myself to take slow, calming breaths. A panic attack while driving to spend the holiday weekend with my family is *so* not going to help. Besides, I already had one at work this week. No sense in making it two.

Freaking anxiety disorder!

Something I can also trace to that day where the storm of a century ripped me out of my mother's arms. The last time I ever saw her face, outside of pictures and dreams.

No wonder I've got issues.

Toto senses my growing unease and whuffs softly. Showing why he's my Wonder Dog, he foregoes his favorite spot at the window to snuggle close.

"That's my good boy." I scratch him on the head. That plus deep breathing helps me focus on driving the last hour before the weather becomes a spiteful witch.

I breathe a sigh of relief when we turn off the interstate onto Yellow Brick Road. Statuesque oak trees line both sides of the gravel lane. A smile cracks my lips as I breathe in the familiar scents of home. Freshly mown grass, myriad growing things, and the faintest whiff of manure. That last one may not be the most pleasant, but it does mean Gale Family Farm is just over the horizon.

My Mustang tops a rise in the road and my spirits lift further at the sight of familiar barn, sheds, and farmhouse lording it over the smaller buildings. I squint and make out the oversized porch swing where my mother spent countless hours rocking me—until her death, when the aunt and uncle who'd adopted her took on the task of raising me. They did a damned good job, considering the hell I raised in my teens.

I continue watching the swing sway in the wind as we near the farmhouse, only to frown when it begins whipping wildly. Whirling dust and debris careen across our path, and my fingers grip the steering wheel more tightly as rain begins to pound. A steady rumbling echoes in the air, so thunderous I feel it in every fiber of my being. A twister is coming.

No, it's already here!

Panic rages through my system, and I slam down the gas pedal. The car begins to shake from both the force of the wind and the sheer speed at which we're hurtling down the road, but I don't care. We're in big trouble.

Toto begins to whine loudly, and he presses even closer to me.

"I know, sweetie, but we're almost there! It'll be okay."

Or so I pray. Especially when the sky takes on a greenish tinge and the rumbling becomes the roar of a freight train. We still have a hundred feet before we reach the farmhouse, and then a flight of stairs and reinforced door to access the panic room Auntie Em and Uncle Henry installed to relieve my fears after that fateful twister.

"We're gonna make it!" I shout to reassure myself more than Toto.

But the sinking sensation sweeping across my body says otherwise. Something that's confirmed when the rearview mirror reveals an ugly black funnel cloud barreling down on us.

"We are *not* gonna make it!" I moan as sickening certainty strikes. There's nothing else to do but hunker down and keep praying.

Toto barks fiercely when I slam the Mustang to a stop and grab him before hopping out of the gyrating vehicle. Anxiety grips me tightly, but I know our best chance for survival means I must *move*. My hair becomes a tangled mess in moments, and dust chokes the air so thickly I can only cough as I squeeze Toto to my chest and throw us down into the ditch beside the road. Under ideal circumstances I would shield my head with my hands, but I'm too busy gripping my poor squirming dog. My teeth clench in determination. I won't fail Toto the way I did Mom.

I hold to that silent vow while rain and dust and rocks assault us. My skin becomes battered and bruised in moments, and I curl my body around my trembling dog to protect him. A large branch hits me in the side, and I grunt in pain. Toto, ever my fierce protector even when frightened, licks my face comfortingly. I open my mouth to reassure him, only to scream when invisible hands snatch us from the ground and hurl us straight up.

Even then I maintain a viselike grip on Toto. He barks sharply as the black funnel cloud sends us flying every which way but down.

Something I'm one part cursing and one part grateful for because there's *no* way we're going to walk away from this with a gentle landing.

A fear that proves well-founded moments later when my body smashes against the ground so hard I barely have time for a single wistful thought before everything goes black.

I clack the heels of my inherited silver slippers together three times as if my mother's storybook fancies could possibly be true. As if the adult me believes her claim that words are the most powerful magic of all. "I wish I could see my mother just one more time." A bright flash of emerald light flares and dizziness sweeps me under.

For a moment I'm back on that front porch swing curled next to my mother with Toto III in my arms. Mom's humming her catchy little tune about troubles melting like lemon drops, and I'm smiling as I stroke the dog's silky fur.

I tilt my head up when Mom's voice fades away and notice that faraway look she gets when thinking about Dad. The man I never even met. She catches my eye and shakes her head wistfully. "There really *is* no place like home, Dorrie my love. No matter *how* much you may enjoy visiting far-off lands."

"Lands like Oz?" I ask with a giggle, loving when she spins tales of the make-believe land that made her a bestselling, if anonymous, children's author.

That was always her cue to tell another story about the lands her fictional namesake visited before returning to her beloved Kansas farm. This time, however, she shoots me a serious expression and presses a kiss to my forehead.

"Yes, like Oz—and some much darker. Lands where fearsome beasts and wicked witches prowl. Lands where evil curses may be laid upon unwary farm girls who can only outrun their terrible prices for so long." She pushes back and gazes at me intensely. "That is why you must remember the true power of words; the value of brains, heart, and courage; the cleansing nature of water; but above all, that when in doubt, the rainbow will guide you home."

"And there's no place like home," I finish in a sleepy, singsong voice.

She starts to speak again, only to be ripped away by a black funnel cloud. No, that's not right. A swarm of black-furred, winged monkeys carries her away. No, wrong again. A cackling woman with flowing black robes, a strange umbrella, and glowing green skin flies her away on a magical broomstick.

I open my mouth to scream only to find myself somewhere else entirely, coughing on dust as every muscle in my body shrieks. A familiar bark has me forcing stubborn eyes open. Only when I manage to pat Toto's head does he fall silent. I rub at my eyes irritably as tears flush out what feels like a pound of dust. I push to a sitting position, at which point I blink for a completely different reason.

Brilliant sunlight floods my face. I wince but manage not to shut my eyes. A gasp escapes as I take in the stunning vista before us. It looks like a box of crayons threw up. Emerald green grass peppered with flowers of every type, size, and hue stretches in three directions. To the fourth lies something that takes my breath away. A vibrant yellow brick road that spirals out from a tiny pinprick until it becomes wider across than two highway lanes. It leads away in that fourth direction toward open farmland that shifts into rolling hills that give way to thick forest.

My gaze flies back to that golden spiral just a few feet from the hard ground where Toto and I sit. Dizziness has me swaying as realization strikes. We're sitting next to the real-life Yellow Brick Road. The one my home's gravel lane was named for, ostensibly in honor of my mother's books, and one that is most definitely *not* supposed to exist.

"Toto," I say in a daze. "We are *certainly* not in Kansas anymore."

"Are you a good witch or a bad witch?" a sweet voice asks as I push to my feet.

I glance around wildly since Toto and I are alone. Or at least we *were.*

An unfamiliar woman in a glittering pink dress—an honest-to-god ballgown—stands looking at me inquisitively. Long golden curls frame her unearthly pretty face and cerulean blue eyes. Kewpie doll lips painted a soft shade of pink purse as if I'm some puzzle to be solved. Lord knows I find this *entire* situation perplexing.

I must be dreaming. Never woke up this morning or the cyclone did *happen, but I'm laid up in a hospital somewhere.*

My brain is pulling out all the stops, showing me scenes straight from my mother's storybooks. And I have all the lines memorized.

"Who, me? I'm not a witch at all. I'm Dorrie Gale from Kansas."

My hallucinatory Glinda the Good Witch of the South tilts her head and shakes it. "I don't think that's true at all. You certainly *are* a witch, and you hail from here in Oz. *Not* Kansas. At least not originally."

"This dream is getting more absurd by the moment," I mutter and glance down at Toto, who mimics the Good Witch's head tilt down to the exact angle.

Glinda draws my attention again by tapping her scepter upon the ground. "One other visitor to this realm spoke of coming from a land called Kansas. Her name was Dorothy Gale."

That has my pulse picking up speed even though I know this is a dream. "That's my mother's name. She wrote a series of books about visiting a magical land before returning home to Kansas. That land was called…"

Glinda's lips curve in a knowing smile as we finish in tandem. "Oz."

I shake my head in denial. "What my mother wrote was fiction. Fantasy. Not real."

The other woman's expression grows rueful. "I once believed that the land of Kansas was fantasy. First when the Wizard spoke of it and again when your mother did. But then she defeated the Wicked

Witch of the West and vanished with the Silver Slippers. Only when my crystal ball finally showed me Dorothy's fate did I realize that she'd spoken true all along. Something that was confirmed again when Millicent's curse forced your mother to take her place in the West."

As impossible as all this still seems, I *did* wish to see my mother once more. And I *did* click the Silver Slippers together three times. Perhaps this is my brain's way of granting that wish before I either wake up in the hospital—or don't.

I decide to embrace the dream for now. "Millicent being…the Wicked Witch of the West?"

Glinda nods with a whimsical gesture of her scepter. "Indeed. She cast a powerful death curse when your mother felled her with your father's Trident."

That has me blinking. Mom's story says she threw a bucket of water on the witch. Not ran her through with an actual weapon. Did she just tone it down because it was a children's story or…I shake my head. *I can't believe I'm entertaining these thoughts as if they're real.* But if there's one thing that can tempt me to humor this hallucination even more surely than the thought of seeing my mother again, it's that of my father.

"Did you…did you know my father?"

The smile Glinda turns on me then is gentle. "Aye, Dorrie Gale from Kansas, I did. Your father is a great and powerful man in this realm."

The way she phrases that has me swallowing and taking an involuntary step back. "Wait. You're not trying to say that my father…my father is the…the Wiz…the Wiz…" I can't even finish that thought.

So, she does it for me. "The Wizard of Oz."

My mind reels as I take in that statement, but then something she said earlier finally registers. "Wait. You said Millicent's curse forced my mother to take her place in the West. Are you trying to say that my mother is *here?*" I gesture around us wildly. "In the Land of Oz?"

Glinda nods solemnly. "Aye. Both your parents are here in Oz, now doomed to war as mortal enemies until the child who represents both their bloodlines manages to break Millicent's curse."

I suck in my breath. "You mean me."

"The one and only."

"*I* can break the curse?"

"If you find the brains, heart, and courage to follow the path your mother once trod. If you channel the nurturing power of water and harness the rainbow as your guiding force, then yes. You just may break the curse separating your parents from each other—and from you."

Anxiety has butterflies stampeding through my stomach and me bending to pick Toto up so I can stroke his fur.

"I—I'm not anything special. Just an attorney from Kansas." And not even a very good one. A litigator who spends half her prep time before court panicking in a restroom stall? More of a joke than anything.

Glinda's expression grows for the first time stern. "You are the daughter of the Wizard of Oz and the Liberator of Oz. A Liberator who now bears the Wicked Witch of the West's mantle. Both your parents are wise and wield powerful magic. And I suspect that in Kansas as well as Oz, the apple doesn't fall far from the tree." Her lips twist wryly. "Unless a defiant farm girl uses only words to anger magical trees enough to throw their apples at her."

I envision my mother's actions and can't help but smile. "Many people say I'm the spitting image of Mom, and not just because she gave me the name she shared with her own mother before Grandma died."

"Words hold even more power in Oz than in Kansas according to both your parents. I see the physical resemblance to your mother quite clearly. I sense the magical resemblance just by standing next to you. But any other resemblance is in your own power to determine. Do you wish to follow the path she once did in hopes of breaking her curse?"

My eyes narrow as I think of how difficult the years since my mother was swept away have been. Not to mention how hard growing up without a father was. Now I have the power to rescue her and meet him for the first time? There's no longer a question in my mind whether I'm going to continue embracing this dream or vision or whatever it is. I can only hope that I at least get to see my parents *before* someone wakes me up.

"Yes." My voice echoes with determination. "I *will* follow the Yellow Brick Road."

Glinda motions with her scepter and brilliant emerald light flares. I blink rapidly. When my vision clears, a beautiful white horse tops the nearest rise and gallops toward us. My mouth drops open when the horse skids to a stop, now close enough to see that what I took for a vivid white coat is one that shimmers with a dozen—no, a *hundred* different colors.

The Good Witch notices my awe and smiles. "This is Prism, the Horse of a Hundred Colors. She will carry you wherever you need to journey while you are in Oz. She is a loyal and swift steed. Not to mention a fine warrior. You couldn't ask for a better travel companion."

I've read my mother's stories too many times to take anything for granted, and so I bow my head respectfully as I look into the horse's wise eyes. "A pleasure to meet you, Prism. My name is Dorrie Gale, daughter of Dorothy Gale from Kansas and...and the Wizard of Oz."

The horse bows her own head, and a deep feminine voice confirms my prudence in showing such deference. "I am also honored to make your acquaintance, Dorrie Gale. I had the pleasure of befriending your mother lo these many years ago upon her first visit to Oz. My condolences that Millicent's curse brought her back to our realm under such circumstances."

I shift awkwardly on my feet. Funny how the words come so easily to me sometimes and others? Not so much. "Yes, well, with your gracious assistance I hope we can right that wrong and reunite my parents."

"You have a noble steed to provide conveyance and protection. Now we must outfit you appropriately for your journey." Glinda waves her scepter one more time and emerald light flares again. When it fades, I notice a gorgeously engraved saddle loaded with several bulging bags upon Prism's back.

I can't help but frown slightly. "Those won't be too burdensome for you, will they? I could just walk."

Prism tosses her head with an amused whinny. "It speaks well of you to care for others, but never fear. I have enough strength to carry ten times the weight of these bags and you upon my back."

I give another quick bow. "Then by all means, let us be on our way." I cast an uncertain glance at Glinda. "Unless there are further preparations to be made?"

She motions her scepter from the horse to me. "All you need has been provided, both the items to sustain your body and the words to fortify your mind. Everything else is up to you. Millicent phrased her curse such that I can provide no further help."

That has me arching a brow as the attorney in me stirs. "Can you provide the actual words of her curse?"

Glinda's lips curve in approval. "I can do one better than that. I can *show* you."

Another wave of her scepter summons a shimmering bubble of light that hovers just in front of me. My eyes widen as a Technicolor battle scene begins to play, with enemy combatants locked in mortal combat inside an imposing fortress. I can't help but gasp as my mother thrusts a trident formed from shimmering water into the chest of a black-robed woman with glowing green skin and a shredded umbrella at her feet. That woman, the Wicked Witch of the West, lets out a bloodcurdling scream and sends a ball of purple energy sizzling into my mother's body.

Millicent finds the strength to cast a terrible spell even as her life begins to fade away. "I curse you to suffer in my stead as Wicked Witch of the West, to remain locked in ceaseless battle against the love you stole from me. Only the babe you now carry shall have the power to break this curse. Fight this fate all you may, love her with all your heart as you will, but wicked winds shall sweep your wretched little farm in Kansas until bringing you back to this fate you cannot escape. Your oh-so-sweet little babe shall be raised with no true knowledge of what she is or what power she holds until one of those winds carries her here in your wake—but as Wicked Witch your love will turn to hate, and you shall do everything you can to *kill* rather than help her. And *none* in Oz may give her more than physical sustenance and empty words to speed her toward you in this fortress—where one shall kill the other. Only then will this curse be broken. One shall die that the other may live."

With those words, Millicent's body crashes to the ground and Glinda's bubble pops.

I wrap my arms around myself as shivers sweep across my body. "I don't know whether to hate or pity that creature."

Prism shows a pragmatic inclination. "Why not both?"

Glinda idly taps her scepter. "Pity her as you will, we all make choices and must live with their consequences. Millicent's dark heart and evil actions drove her former love the Wizard away long before your mother ever set foot in Oz. And now, your *good* heart and *brave* actions may reunite him with his true love. Your mother." She gestures toward the Yellow Brick Road. "Now here are more of the *empty words* Millicent was too arrogant to believe are all you really need: Keep to the West, where the sun sets, and you cannot fail to find your mother. Remember the words she herself gave you and that I have reminded you, and all will be well."

I open my mouth to ask another question, but she strikes her scepter upon the ground and disappears in a final burst of emerald light. "Follow the Yellow Brick Road west. Let it and the rainbow be your guides. Now go!"

Prism lets out an encouraging whinny and prances in place. "Shall we be on our way?"

Toto barks and squirms in my arms as I step forward. "Shush,

Toto, Prism is being courteous enough to spare our poor feet a difficult journey."

One of the saddlebags catches my eye, since it's not nearly as full as the others. I transfer most of its cargo—strange but delicious-smelling fruit—to several other bags and sling the empty one across my chest. Toto falls silent as I tuck him into the bag, leaving only his head hanging out. Being mostly encapsulated in the sturdy leather bag seems to ease his anxiety as I approach Prism and easily swing us both into the saddle.

You can take the girl away from the farm, but you can't take the farm out of the girl.

The Horse of a Hundred Colors waits until I'm firmly seated before taking off. She starts with a brisk canter, allowing me to adjust to that pace before switching to a ground-eating gallop. Regular visits home have kept me in good riding shape, so she doesn't have to take it *too* easy on me. Good thing, because there's a lot of road to cover.

Something that becomes evident when we travel for what seems like hours before she pauses to catch her breath. My legs tremble as I slide out of the saddle and manage to land without falling. Toto barks insistently, so I let him out to take care of his puppy business. Trees conveniently line this side of the road. My gaze wanders to the opposite side, where the land has been cleared to make way for ripe bushes that sway in a gentle breeze. My brows raise when I recognize the same colorful fruit that Glinda provided.

Prism picks up on my interest and whinnies. "That's the farm of Oz's preeminent scholar. He restored fertility to the lands that Millicent nearly ruined thanks to his agricultural innovations. He was once a close companion of your mother's."

My pulse picks up speed. "You mean…the Scarecrow?"

A friendly voice speaks before she can respond. "The one and only. And I've waited an awfully long time to make your acquaintance, Dorrie Gale. Daughter of the Wizard of Oz and my dearest friend, Oz's Liberator."

My gaze snaps back to the bushes. A tall man formed from straw and sticks wearing loose farm clothes and an oddly shaped black hat steps onto the Yellow Brick Road.

Prism bows her head slightly. "Lord Minister Scarecrow."

Feeling awkward but not wanting to be outdone in manners by a horse, I dip a shallow curtsey. "Pleased to make your acquaintance, um, Lord Minister. My mother has told me much about you and your valiant assistance during her first visit to Oz."

His lips curve into a pleased smile. "Please, call me Scarecrow. All my friends do. And you have need of all the friends you can get if you're to break Millicent's vile curse."

I frown slightly as Toto nudges my feet, my signal to lift him back into the saddlebag. "I'd be pleased to be your friend, Lord—I mean Scarecrow. But I'm afraid the curse means nobody can offer me much in the way of aid."

His body moves in a sudden silly jig. "Wasn't I there when that Wicked Witch cursed your mother? Didn't I hear her say people could offer you all the empty words they wanted? And so, I give you this word: *Recrudescence.*"

He says the word so enthusiastically and with such an expectant air that I feel guilty it sounds only vaguely familiar. It seems Latin in origin. Perhaps I encountered it when studying such words in college, but now its meaning escapes me. Still, I don't want to crush his spirits.

"Th—thank you most kindly for the extremely impressive word."

The Scarecrow bows deeply, sending tufts of straw flying. "Most excellent. Keep that word at the top of your mind when all hope seems lost, and you'll know what to do."

"I...I'll remember that word for when the time is right. Recrudescence."

"Please *do* give my regard to your mother. And I'll expect to see you both in the Emerald City once you break that wretched curse."

He seems so confident in my success that I can't bear to disillusion him. "I will. Thank you again for your, um, word."

The Scarecrow beams a pleased smile before retreating toward his farmland. "Remember: Recrudescence!"

Toto gives a goodbye bark as our new friend vanishes from view. Prism paws the ground and nods toward a nearby stream. "Let's take a moment to refresh ourselves."

We spend the next few minutes quenching our thirst with ice-cold water that tastes better than anything back in Kansas and easing our hunger with the rainbow-colored fruit I now realize must have been cultivated by the Scarecrow. Once satisfied, we begin winding our way westward once more.

Several hours pass, and open farmland gives way to rolling hills that are low enough they don't trouble our steadfast steed. I find myself feeling none of the soreness or exhaustion I expected to by this time. Something I credit to Oz's refreshing spring and the Scarecrow's wondrous fruit. It feels like we've been journeying long enough that the sun should be setting by now. Glancing upward with a puzzled frown, however, I note the golden orb lies straight above, as if it's still high noon.

"Time passes differently in Oz than in Kansas," Prism remarks as she pauses at the top of a hill. "Or so your mother often claimed back before the curse claimed her."

"During her first visit to Oz?"

"Indeed. Oh, the fun she and I would have cantering through the Emerald City and its surrounding countryside! But then she defeated Millicent and was cursed, and your father insisted that she return to Kansas not long after your birth. He hoped it would keep you both safe while he found a way to defeat Millicent's spell, but…"

"But he never found a way."

Prism gives a horsey sigh. "Sadly not. Millicent became Wicked Witch of the West for good reason. Her spells were as powerful as her heart was evil."

A deep voice booms behind us, startling Prism into rearing and sending me crashing to the ground. "Evil as her heart may have been, those of us with love in ours will ensure her wickedness is finally defeated once and for all." I cry out when I strike hard golden bricks. Fortunately, when I gingerly push to my feet, I feel bruised rather than broken.

"Oh, please *do* beg my pardon. I didn't mean to frighten you so!"

Prism places her body protectively between mine and the man now stepping onto the rise before us. He stands even taller than the Scarecrow, and my eyes widen when I notice he's fashioned of silver metal from the top of his funnel-shaped hat to the soles of his feet. An imposing silver axe hangs upon his back.

I realize who he must be and relax. "The Tin Man, I presume? Have no fear, I'm not seriously hurt."

He sweeps an oddly elegant bow for a man made of metal. "Pleased to meet you at last, daughter of our Wizard and Liberator. One of my fondest friends, your mother is."

I sigh sadly. "I fear you mean *was.*"

The Tin Man gives a fierce smile. "No, I most certainly do *not.* Dorothy Gale of Kansas is ever my friend, whether her heart recognizes it or not. Mine will certainly never forget."

That has me giving a smile of my own. "Indeed, Sir Tin Man. My mother always spoke of the kind and unwavering heart you possess. I see just how correct she was."

"And that brings us to the *empty word* I wanted to bestow upon you before you meet your mother once more. *Adamantine.*"

"Ad…adamantine," I repeat slowly. This word seems more familiar to me than that offered by the Scarecrow. I do not see how it can help me defeat Millicent's terrible curse, and yet I've read enough of my mother's stories not to discount its power.

The Tin Man gives a gracious nod. "Yes. Adamantine. Fix that word inside your heart in the darkest hour, and you can't go wrong. I look forward to meeting you *and* your mother in the Emerald City once you liberate her like she did us."

Goosebumps break out along my flesh as fear that I can never hold a candle to my mother strikes, but I channel the skills I use in court to conceal soul-crushing anxiety. "Until we meet again, thank you for all your help. Both today and when you helped my mother."

He sweeps another stately bow before fading back into the rolling hills. Prism prances a few steps to draw my attention. I smile and swing myself into the saddle. In a flash, we're galloping along the endless lane once more.

When rolling hills give way to thick forestland on all sides of the Yellow Brick Road, a sense of expectation grows. Birds chirp, crickets sing, and leaves stir in the wind. My breath hitches now and again as some forest creature snaps a fallen branch in the distance, but the visitor I anticipate never appears. Not until we near the end of the shadowy forest.

A thunderous roar echoes in the air, sending creatures crashing away deeper into the trees. My hands clench upon Prism's mane, and I force my skittering pulse to slow. Silly to allow such fear when I've been expecting this ever since we stepped into the woods...

A large golden creature with a mane even more magnificent than Prism's leaps onto the road. "Courage, daughter of Dorothy!" an imposing voice calls out. I recognize him as the being once known as the Cowardly Lion.

Prism waits patiently as I slip off her back and dip a little curtsey. "If it isn't my mother's treasured friend, the brave and fearsome King of the Beasts!"

The Lion preens at my greeting, standing back on hind feet as he stops a few feet away. "We've been waiting ever so long for your arrival, Dorrie Gale of Kansas. And it's going to take every ounce of your bravery to liberate your mother from Millicent's curse."

Toto whines softly from the saddlebag upon my chest, and I reach down to pat him reassuringly. "I've never felt particularly brave, but I can promise that every ounce of my courage shall be dedicated to that very task."

The King of the Beasts casts me an understanding look. "A wise man taught me that courage doesn't mean you never feel fear. It means doing what needs doing despite that fear."

I smile softly. "Was that man my father?"

He gives a regal nod. "Indeed. And just like he gave me that wise counsel when I most needed it, so shall I give you a word to help in your quest. That word is *Audacious.*"

My brow arches as I repeat this much less enigmatic word. "Audacious."

"Speak that word out loud when you feel your most frightened, and you'll find every bit of bravery that you need. No witch can cast a curse that cannot be broken—it's one of magic's inescapable rules—and Millicent herself determined that you could break this one. And now I bid you a fond farewell until we see each other in the Emerald City. Remember your courage!"

He drops back onto four feet and bounds away, vanishing into the forest as suddenly as he appeared. I'm surprised to find that much of my ever-burning anxiety has also disappeared.

Prism reclaims my attention by calling for another refreshment break. Drinking from a nearby stream and eating more of the Scarecrow's rainbow fruit again washes away all exhaustion. I marvel at the renewed energy surging through my body. The Horse of a Hundred Colors also seems reenergized when I climb upon her back. In moments we return to a teeth-chattering gallop.

The Lion's forest quickly gives way to open ground once more, but this is *not* the lush land we've left behind. Eerie yellow grass creeps across the ground in sickly patches that seem starved for water. Twisted trees with jagged branches and sparse leaves dot the landscape. The few animals I spy are those traditionally associated with witches like bats, snakes, and spiders; unusually large but misshapen creatures who peer at us suspiciously before flying, slithering, or scurrying away.

Chills prick my flesh, and I shiver at the sensation that more than beastly eyes are watching us. Memories of my mother's tales pop into my mind. I shudder again, because odds are that it's *her* eyes I feel upon us, watching through the Wicked Witch of the West's crystal ball. A sense of powerlessness sweeps across me.

How can one simple farm girl from Kansas face down a Wicked

Witch and survive? Especially when fate decrees that one of us *must* die.

I force myself to think of my mother's words. Magic decrees that I *can* break the curse. Both Glinda and my mother's faithful companions stressed the importance of words rather than trying to prepare me in some other way. That must mean they are what will help me break Millicent's curse. But how?

I contemplate those words and speak each out loud as Prism continues speeding us westward. The sun finally starts lowering in the horizon, but I focus solely on the words given to me. The first is the most challenging. "Recrudescence!" My attorney brain kicks into overdrive as it puzzles out the word's meaning. Long moments pass until finally something jogs my memory. The words *does* have a Latin base, and it means the recurrence of an undesirable condition or disease.

I let my subconscious mind ponder why the Scarecrow, sage scholar that he is, would take care to share that word with me, turning my conscious brain toward the Tin Man's word. "Adamantine!" seems straightforward enough; it means rigidly firm and unyielding. Similarly, the Lion's word "Audacious!" means daring or recklessly bold.

My brow furrows as I consider all three words. My mother's second two companions seem to echo her words to use my brains and courage when danger strikes. The Scarecrow, on the other hand, seems to hint at the actual solution. Insight as to what that could be continues to elude for long moments as we canter, until finally I pair his words alongside those of my mother and Glinda—and then my anxious legal mind seizes upon the most important word of all. Not to mention the glaring loophole Millicent left in her curse. I glance down at Prism's iridescent coat and then the saddlebags laden with rainbow fruit as inspiration strikes, and a smug smile curves my lips. Just like that, I know how I'm going to save both my mother and myself.

Glinda's words that continuing westward would lead to my mother prove prophetic when Prism rounds a curve in the Yellow Brick Road and an imposing fortress looms just ahead. My breath catches as the setting sun causes its glittering black façade to shimmer with both beauty and malevolence. Several towers can be seen breaking the edifice's walls, and black-winged monkeys patrol the air above. Green-skinned soldiers line the fortress's battlements at such regular intervals it seems unlikely that anything could escape their watchful eyes.

Good thing I'm not planning on a sneak attack…

Prism draws up short and skitters a few nervous steps as she takes in the sight before us. As brave as she's been at every step of this journey, nerves at what lies ahead are only natural. We are vastly outnumbered and overmatched.

But so was my mother when she killed the original Wicked Witch.

And Glinda herself said that this proverbial apple couldn't have fallen far from the tree. I was determined to prove her right.

I throw myself out of the saddle and onto the ground, releasing Toto from his confinement. "I know what I must do now, noble Prism. But it depends on you staying outside the fortress while I allow myself to be captured and carried inside. I'll need a distraction at the right time, and you're the only one who can provide that."

Prism's ears start to flick irritably when I first mention her staying outside, but then she draws herself up proudly. "Of course I'll provide your distraction. How will I know when the time is right?"

I tell her what to look for, quickly prepare the items I need, and then carefully load them into Toto's saddlebag. I sling it across my chest and wait as Prism gallops to a safer vantage point. Once she's safe, I take Toto into my arms, careful not to crush the items in my saddlebag, and begin the terrifying march toward the fortress; where black-furred flying monkeys, green-skinned soldiers bearing sharp weapons, and my mother the Wicked Witch wait.

Furious screeches break out above once the monkeys catch sight of me, and soldiers call out an alarm. I hug Toto close as the nearby portcullis cranks open and soldiers pour out of the main gate. Anxiety claws at my belly, but I fight it back, determined to be the liberator my mother so desperately needs.

Several soldiers reach me, and the wide-eyed looks they cast make it appear they've seen a ghost. The more likely truth is they recognize a younger version of my mother, especially if any of them ever saw her here in Oz with Toto's ancestor.

The oldest-looking soldier, a man, sketches a shallow bow. "Dorrie Gale of Kansas, daughter of Dorothy Gale and the Wizard of Oz, I presume?"

Not to be outdone in manners, I give a little curtsey and nod. "The one and only. My mother expects me?"

"Indeed." He hesitates, before stepping closer and speaking so that only I can hear. "She's not the mother you knew, I'm afraid. There's nothing I can do to help you. Her magic is as powerful as Millicent's ever was. And her heart has grown just as black from the curse."

I muster my bravest smile. "Never fear. Things are not as dire as they appear."

Doubting pity crosses his face, but he merely gestures toward the open gate. "Your mother shall receive you in her throne room. It would be best if you don't try to escape."

The mechanical way he speaks make it clear he's under magical orders. The soldiers fall into step as their captain leads us through the gate, across a stone courtyard, and into the fortress. Green-skinned servants catch sight of us, and hushed whispers break out as they witness fate marching toward my mother and me.

Moments later we cross the throne room's threshold, and my knees grow weak. My mother sits upon an opulent black throne encrusted with silver scrollwork and emeralds, looking both achingly familiar and completely alien. Her face is the same lovely one I remember, her hair is as fiery red as my own, and her eyes are the same clear blue we share. But her skin is now as green as the soldiers who surround me, and her expression is harsh and foreboding where once it was loving. She is dressed much the same as Millicent in Glinda's vision, with flowing black robes and an oversized umbrella clutched in her hands.

When our eyes meet, she comes to her senses for a moment. Anguish flashes across her face, and she throws her umbrella to the ground. Shudders wrack her body as she leaps up to retrieve the umbrella, almost as if something is forcing her actions. No doubt Millicent's curse. Water is the bane of such wicked creatures. Had my mother not shredded the former witch's magical umbrella *before* striking out with my father's watery Trident, Oz would never have been liberated and I would not have been born.

It's clear the good part of my mother hidden beneath the evil wants to sacrifice herself for me; and just as clear the curse isn't going to let her.

"Hello, Mom," I finally say. "I've missed you."

Her expression is icy as she taps her umbrella upon the ground and regards me with a wrinkled lip. "Hello, misbegotten child of mine. I would say I've missed you as well, but I'd be lying. You should *not* have stepped foot inside Oz."

I pretend her words don't cut me to the quick. Foolish that they do, since I know it's the curse speaking. "If you've become the powerful Witch everyone says, you should know I had no choice in the matter. Millicent's wicked winds swept us both here."

Her lip curls again. "Yes, well, say what one might about my weaker predecessor. She *did* cast a mighty fine curse. And to be honest, I am looking forward to seeing this come to an end. The sooner you die, the sooner I can use your death to defeat your father and become the true Liberator Oz deserves."

She steps down from the dais holding her throne and approaches. I take an involuntary step backward, and the surrounding soldiers cross their long spears to impede me. My mother bares unnaturally sharp teeth in a fierce smile as she stops feet away. "And now, my pretty, I'm afraid this is where I get you and your little dog, too!"

My heart races as I give a sharp, piercing whistle that has the winged monkeys hovering outside squawking up a storm. They raise a ruckus so loud that Prism strikes, galloping around the fortress's outer wall and letting out such furious whinnies that it sounds like a small army is outside. I watch through nearby windows as most of the winged monkeys streak off toward where I can only assume Prism is cantering past the outer wall.

My mother scowls at the captain who showed me pity and gestures angrily. "Go tend to whatever foolish creatures think to save my daughter and show them just how impossible that is. I'll ensure that fate finally has its way."

The captain casts one final pitying glance before bowing and striding away. Leaving only open space between my mother and me. I bend over to drop Toto on the ground, using the motions to cover one far more vital. I withdraw the vial bearing the mixture I prepared and strike before anyone can see it coming. The glass vial shatters against my mother's face and breaks, sending a thick paste bearing every hue of the rainbow—thanks to the Scarecrow's wonderful fruit—sliding along her skin.

She screams, at first thinking I've doused her in water as she did her predecessor, but then confusion replaces fear. "What have you done, you cursed brat? Why do I feel so strange?"

I allow a smug smile to cross my face. "Why, I've used *physical sustenance and empty words* to fulfill the terms of Millicent's curse. *One shall dye that the other may live.*"

Her eyes widen as my meaning hits, and she shrieks as the curse begins to unravel. Green skin vanishes only to be replaced by a glowing peach complexion; black robes and umbrella change to the sundress and sandals I last saw her wearing; and spiteful expression smooths once more into the loving one I remember.

I reach out hesitantly, almost afraid to believe. "Mom?"

"Dorrie Gale, you amazing girl, you did it!"

We throw ourselves into each other's arms, laughing and crying at the same time, making up for the years of separation by embracing and drinking in the sight of each other's faces. Considering I was a teenager when we'd last been together, she has far more changes to get used to than I do.

An impatient whinny catches our attention, and we pull back from each other just slightly. Prism stands a few feet away, the pitying captain a healthy distance behind with dents in his armor that suspiciously resemble horse hooves and a sheepish expression.

My stalwart steed rears unexpectedly and joyfully chimes out, "The Wicked Witch is dead! Long live the Liberators of Oz!"

I blush at the realization she's added me to the same list as my mother. When Mom squeezes my hand with her own, however, I smile rather than protest. Who am I to argue with the Horse of a Hundred Colors?

Mom points to my Silver Slippers. "Remember everything I've taught you about Oz? It's way past time to introduce you to your father, my dear."

A huge smile cracks my lips as Mom tightens her grip on my hand, I lay my free arm upon Prism's coat, and Toto snuggles against my chest. The Silver Slippers make a satisfying clacking sound as I knock them together once, twice, and thrice. "There's no place like home—with my father, the Wizard of Oz!"

Vibrant green light flares as magic responds to my will and washes the last vestiges of those wicked winds away. Carrying Mom and me to the Emerald City and my father, where we all finally get our happy ending…

END

AUTHOR'S NOTE

Like many people, I've always been fascinated by the thought of an average person being transported to a magical land and facing fantastical odds to defeat an evil villain. In this Wizard of Oz retelling, it's actually Dorothy's daughter who must defeat the evil villain--who isn't quite what you might expect. If you love the Wizard of Oz (and word play) as much as I do, this one's for you!

ABOUT THE AUTHOR

Kasey Mackenzie lives with her husband and son in St. Louis, Missouri; home of the Gateway Arch, the baseball Cardinals, and the world's greatest thin-crust pizza. Kasey was one of those students who always had her nose in a book--so no big surprise when she was voted "Teacher's Pet" in her high school yearbook. Today, she is a voracious reader of fantasy, romance, science fiction, and YA. She adores her oversize dog, mischievous cat, and shaking her groove thing as a Zumba instructor. Passionate about the written word, she feels extremely lucky to make a living as an editor and writer. Now, if she could just figure out how to get paid for cleaning her own house, maybe that would happen more often....

THE FAIREST SHOP OF THEM ALL

SHAWNTELLE MADISON

CHAPTER 1

Whitley

"What a pitiful little millinery," my latest customer, a middle-aged woman with a reed-thin voice, blurted. "Not a single black ascot or Tudor beret in sight."

Two sets of footsteps entered the shop.

From my spot in the back room, embarrassment heated my cheeks, but I straightened my back. Tilted my chin upward. Clenched my skirt with one hand and my fabric shears with the other. She wouldn't be the first or the last patron to mock my designs.

Yet something about her—an ominous presence—prickled the hairs on the back of my neck. Usually, I immediately greeted my customers, but this time, my feet remained rooted to my hiding place. Mr. Chuffs, my precocious yet balding Pomeranian, feigned bravery with a flash of tiny teeth then hid behind a stack of hatboxes near me.

Even my dog thought hiding back here was a wise choice.

I dared not peek around the corner to see the woman's face, but I nevertheless caught a whiff of her horrendous perfume. The heavy, bergamot-laden scent slithered around the flowerpot hats display, jumped over the table with wide-brimmed hats, and bludgeoned the back of my head.

"Look at the subpar hat construction." She sniffed. "How is this shop two blocks from Hyde Park? I highly doubt she sold her merchandise to King Edward's court like her little sign states. What bull—"

Beeps from a Model T bounding down the cobblestone road ate away the rest of her abominable, curse-filled rant.

"This dull place cannot be the fairest of them all," she added.

Whatever did she mean by *dull*? Did she not see the eerie glow in the velvet trim on the wide-brimmed hats or the way the golden thread in the capote bonnets shimmered? One of my clients, a Miss Muffett, had stated that she favored my sunhats during her forest outings in the spring.

I glanced through the back room's doorway to see a tall woman wearing a mink stole over a teal frock coat. A matching flowerpot hat covered her gray hair. The woman glared at the bountiful white ostrich feathers poking out of a plumed hat.

"Indeed, Your Grace." Her cohort, a wasplike man wearing a wrinkled gray day suit, hovered close. "The Hammerstein Millinery down the road is far more beguiling."

She weaved around the flowerpot hats and drew closer to the back room where I stood in secret. Five steps turned to two. Her overpowering perfume practically coated my tongue with its citrus tang.

The man tsked and shook his head as his spindly fingers flicked one of my mourning hats off its perch. The hat fell to the floor with a dreadful plop. The rustle of Mr. Chuffs' trembling behind the boxes made the man pause.

"Did you hear that, Your Grace?" he whispered.

Another step and she'd see me. I held my breath.

"Let's not dawdle here any longer, Mr. Percy." Her footsteps retreated to the door. "We came to give my notice. There is no need to deliver it face to face."

"Indeed." Percy stretched out the word with an arrogant air.

The bell attached to the door jingled, and I exhaled.

Mr. Chuffs sprang from his hiding spot, raced into the shop, then gave a triumphant bark.

"That'll show 'em." I chuckled as I picked up the mourning hat. In the middle of wiping any dust off the cap, I noticed a large piece of paper attached to my store window.

Now what could that be?

I hurried out of the store. The brisk October wind rustled an errant edge of the paper, but the vibrant crimson message was all too clear.

EVICTION NOTICE

THIS SHOP, MR. HEUREUX'S FINE HATS, IS HEREBY SERVED AN EVICTION NOTICE FROM HER GRACE, THE DUCHESS OF LEINBOROUGH. PAY FIVE TIMES YOUR RENT OR VACATE IN SEVEN DAYS.

I took a step back. Maybe my eyes played a trick on me.

Did that mean my employer, Mr. Heureux, wasn't on good terms with her? I'd never seen the man's face, yet he always left the required pounds and pence on the counter for me to pay rent.

Perhaps he hadn't paid enough?

"You got the notice, too," a deep voice said behind me.

A handsome man—nearly a foot taller than me—sidestepped manure in the street to approach me. He wore a work apron over a faded cream-colored shirt and brown trousers. His shoulders were wide and his hands far too large. As Mr. Chuffs sniffed the gentleman's shoes, my gaze swept from his worn work boots to his curly black hair. He offered a small smile, revealing two dimples along his sharp cheekbones.

I sighed. "I'm absolutely perplexed as to why."

"I don't know either." The man's dark eyebrows rose and confusion touched his features. "She owns all the buildings along this road, but she chose your place and mine."

My mouth dropped open. "That is quite strange."

We stared at each other briefly before the man spoke again.

"Oh, excuse my manners. I'm Carl Princeton." The wind ruffled his hair. "It's nice to meet the lady who uses my fabric for her designs."

So this was one of the mysterious suppliers I'd never met. My employment was equally as peculiar. A year ago, a matron at the boardinghouse where I used to live informed me that a courier had left me a notice to come work at the hat shop. Unexpected as the offer was, I immediately accepted the position and was left instructions: when to open, how to greet my customers, and how to add Mr. Heureux's special price tags. All those types of things. Mr. Heureux never revealed how he acquired the materials I used—only that I should promptly carry the boxes left in front of the shop inside.

The owner also never told me why my creations appeared enchanted, but that was another story.

"The pleasure is mine, Mr. Princeton." I gave him a short nod. "My name is Whitley Snowfall."

He returned the nod, and we were left with facing what had brought us together—that horrible notice.

"I didn't want to be presumptuous, but did the owner under-pay?" he asked.

"Never. He gave me the rent every month on the first Friday."

His jaw twitched. "I've never had a problem with the Leinsbor-oughs before. Looks like we have only one recourse."

"We must have a little *chitchat* with the Duchess of Leinsbor-ough," I whispered.

Carl

Determination flared in Miss Snowfall's dark blue eyes and something else brewed in her growing frown—like a storm knocking against weather-beaten shutters. Other than her growing displeasure, her outward form appeared contained. Not a single strand strayed from her upswept black hair. Her muslin dress was impeccable, perhaps boasting a steadfast disposition.

I hoped.

With a deft turn of her wrist, she returned to her shop. She came out with her gloves and shawl. Then she locked the front door. Above the shop I observed two pairs of eyes watching us with concern. Two blonde boys. When my gaze connected with the two children, they vanished.

Miss Snowfall joined me.

"Maybe we shouldn't go see her while holding a pair of murderous-looking shears?" I pointed to her hand.

The ratlike Pomeranian at her feet barked as if in agreement.

"Good point." She gave them to me, and I slipped them into my apron pocket.

Our journey took us southward to the duchess's shop on Cromwell Road. I expected Miss Snowfall to be chatty like most of my lady customers, but she remained taciturn as she adjusted the shawl draped over her shoulders. We walked faster until we reached the finer stores that lined Claymore Road. The carriages along this road carried dignified customers wearing tailored suits and mink coats. Voluminous hats obscured many of their faces, but their perfumes saturated the air as we made our way to northward.

As a child, I'd crossed the threshold into many of these shops, where I received a piece of candy or a tap on the head from a kind shopkeeper. Now that I'd reached twenty-six years of age, I no longer had the station I'd once possessed. That was what happened to the fifth son of a Belgian duke. No property, no title, merely an education to establish a reputable trade.

Instead of becoming a merchant like my older brother, I'd escaped to London with a few coins in my pocket and an incessant desire to make my own way.

How curious that my travels brought me back here.

Finally, we reached the Leinsborough and Sons storefront.

At least no one would recognize me.

Not a single soul west of Canterbury Lane could miss the

imposing structure of the Duchess of Leinsborough's frame shop. Both royalty and the gentry often boasted of purchasing her frames for their family portraits—or as kindling for their fireplace, depending on which of her underpaid workers crafted the piece.

Mainly ornate mirrors adorned her wallpapered walls, but she also sold cheaper variations—like the one I'd used to shave this morning. The less expensive mirrors filled the back of the establishment. It was a mask to put highly decorated pieces near the front to lure in customers and give off a particular air of wealth.

Miss Snowfall and I now stood before the shop's entrance. I stuffed my hands into my pockets to gather my thoughts, but she gave a glance to Mr. Chuffs then marched through the door. I gaped for a moment before the Pomeranian barked at me.

Move it, human, he seemed to say before he turned around two times then sat.

I hurried after the milliner into the store's frigid interior.

No one greeted us while we weaved our way past a wall of round mirrors to a counter with women's hand mirrors. Through the numerous reflections, I caught all aspects of Miss Snowfall's pursed lips and her soft profile.

Halfway through the shop, we paused at an interesting sight.

"The plot thickens," Miss Snowfall murmured with a raised eyebrow.

Before us stood two displays with black mourning hats. Not a single one of them was crafted with a caring hand. Even I could make out the faults, from the poorly aligned stitches to the subpar material that made me itch just gaping at it.

"Indeed," I replied.

We strolled to the rear of the store to find a thin gentleman completing a transaction with a customer.

"Please tell His Lordship he will absolutely love his new frame," the man said.

"Good day, Mr. Percy," the customer said with a nod, and departed.

Mr. Percy should've asked us if we needed help, but he gave us a single glance, sniffed, and turned to the stack of papers at the work counter.

Miss Snowfall took a step forward with a growing frown, but I intercepted to speak first. Cooler heads would prevail.

"We both received an eviction notice this morning," I said smoothly.

"And?" Mr. Percy sniffed again, this time hard enough to shuffle the marbles that made up his brain. "Was the king's English too difficult to decipher? I thought you shop folk could at *least* read and write."

This wasn't the first time a man had mocked me. When I first opened my store back in St. John Horselydown district, many questioned why I didn't work in the docks hauling goods. Why didn't someone with my strength perform manual labor instead of spending my time with bolts of cloth, needles, and thread?

I stepped forward. "We read the notice and wanted to inquire the duchess to see if any arrangements could be made to halt the eviction. Is she available?"

Mr. Percy smirked. "Her Grace is too busy with personal affairs to deal with common folk. A suggestion? Vacate the premises and don't bother trying another day. I doubt you could afford to pay—"

"And why not?" Miss Snowfall asked.

Mr. Percy made a face as if a manure cart had rolled through. "Even if you manage to earn, steal, or grovel for the funds, your rent is impossible to pay now." He waltzed away from us, effectively ending the conversation.

With no place to go, we left to stand before the imposing shop sign. We gazed at each other, maybe hoping someone else would tell us what to do. Pedestrians passed us, each of them set on their final destination. None of them, with their finely tailored coats or high hats, would be jobless or homeless in seven days.

"Five times the amount," I said. "All the fabric in my shop and my savings could never cover the rent." I kicked a nearby rock. "I could return to St. John Horselydown and open a new place. All hope isn't lost."

Miss Snowfall stiffened and her eyes narrowed to slits. "Your odds sound far more promising, but unfortunately, mine aren't as high."

With a swirl of her skirt and Mr. Chuffs at her heels, she marched off to the west, leaving a trail of vanilla on the breeze.

CHAPTER 2

Whitley

THE WIND SCREECHED, SENDING A CHILL DOWN MY BACK. From the shop's back alley to the apartment above, I counted ten steps. At the beginning of my workday, I'd thundered down them, a smile on my lips and a hope hammering in my heartbeat.

Not so much now: in seven days, we must move.

I trudged up three steps until I stopped before a young woman perched on the fourth step. Her arms were folded, and her sun-kissed skin flushed red. Emmalyn's brow furrowed as I tried to dart past her.

Mr. Chuffs sniffed my feet, then he snuck around Em to hurry upstairs.

Where's the bravery I witnessed earlier?

"Where do you think you're going?" Even after arriving at the orphanage at five, Em still had the same spark in her hazel eyes. The breeze tugged at her dark brown corkscrew curls, but she ignored the errant strands to block my passage.

"I'm going home." I wanted to push past her, but I gripped the wooden handrail tighter. At sixteen, she had an air of authority that rivaled a general.

She snorted. "I'm not surprised one bit. You took one look at that eviction sign and you wandered off, didn't you?"

"No."

"What terms does that upper-class twit want?"

"More than we can afford."

"Have you even tried to earn the money?"

Her words stabbed my side, but I didn't deflect them. I stood there as unsaid words jumped between us. Past arguments where my faults were laid bare and I tried to defend them. Not so much anymore.

With pursed lips, she slipped around me, but I caught her arm. "Where are you going?"

"To do what needs to be done. There are five kids up there who have no idea what's about to happen to them."

"You'll do no such thing. The last hat you made couldn't even be called one."

"Fair enough." She sighed, perhaps recalling the misshapen monstrosity she'd called a flowerpot hat. "But what I said still stands. Time was never on our side. It took you five years to save all of us. Don't overthink this matter."

I will come back for all of you. I'll beg. I'll steal. But I will come back for you.

The promise echoed through my head.

I bit back a sigh. I'd wasted away a year after I left Saint Margaret's Children's Home. I'd wandered the city, lost in freedom and fresh air. All the while, my closest friends and I—the Rejects, as the other children called us—waited while no one adopted us.

I did fulfill my promise and adopted them, but Em had endured abuse the moment I left. Each time I came for a child, she'd pushed the younger ones forward.

"Take them," she always said. Each time the bruises switched places, but she never begged. She never wanted me to take her next.

So I accepted the words she said this morning.

"Go down to the store and try to get a hold of Mr. Heureux."

She clutched my shoulder, and her face softened. "He might help us. It's his bloody store. He should take care of this."

I nodded and returned to the shop. As I'd expected, not a single thing had shifted. Though Mr. Heureux had hired me, and effectively given my family a safe place to live, I had yet to meet him. Why would an eviction notice change that? For all I knew, the man galivanted through Europe and Asia to purchase exotic goods for his businesses. I imagined a short man with a curly head of hair and a mustache, chewing on dates in Istanbul, completely oblivious to our worries.

Which meant our troubles rested on me. This was my fight.

I donned my apron and straightened my shoulders. Time to find some rich folks and offload the stock. A shadow crossed the windows in front.

I glanced up to see Mr. Princeton waiting at the door.

Carl

Miss Snowfall's mouth parted in surprise. I hadn't expected to come over so soon either, but decisions needed to be made. She hurried to the door, unlocked it, and let me inside.

"Looks like you had a delivery while we were gone." I picked up one of the larger boxes right outside the door.

Her face scrunched up. "Those only come at the beginning of every season. How peculiar."

She picked up two smaller boxes with ease. I gave a nod of approval.

"We're in peculiar times," I said. None of the boxes had labels, but the parcels carried exotic scents. One had hints of nutmeg, while another reminded me of home in Belgium. After we hauled the boxes into the shop, we stood in front of each other again.

"How may I help you, Mr. Princeton?" She moved to place one of the boxes on her work counter, but I interceded and helped her.

Our bodies brushed. Her vanilla scent filled my nostrils. My heart sped up as I backed away.

"I had a similar question. Is there anything I can do to help?" I stuffed my hands into my pockets. "I took stock of my goods, and if I sell them, I can rent another place—"

"In a far less lucrative location, I guarantee," she finished.

"Unfortunately. Are you in a better position?"

She sucked in a deep breath. Many emotions flitted over her face. Despair. Resolve. Then bitterness. "No."

"I didn't want to be presumptuous, but you're welcome to join me while I search for another shopfront."

Instead of replying, she ripped off the top to the box and yanked out the contents: colorful vermillion to periwinkle bolts of silk and chiffon lay within. Those would make fine materials to craft ribbons and scarves. The container's contents seemed to sparkle under the work counter's lamp, but I had to be mistaken.

"Mr. Nemuidesu's delivery from Asia usually arrives in the summer," she whispered.

"Have you heard from the shop owner?" I asked.

"Not a peep." She opened another shipment and retrieved spools of vibrant cotton thread. "Only these things shouldn't be here. Mr. Sjenert already sent me a parcel from Norway."

"What will you do with them?"

Her reply was quick and sharp: "I'll make the hats and sell them —like I always do."

I opened my mouth to give praise, maybe even offer help, but the stark reminder of how much we needed to pay kicked my resolve off a sheer cliff.

We *both* needed fifteen pounds.

How in God's name did she believe she could earn that much in seven days? We'd need every single minute of daylight to secure another shop.

Briefly, I considered reaching out to my title-bearing cousin in York. Could I bury my pride and beg for Miss Snowfall's sake and mine? I snorted.

Returning here to reveal my ancestry and give a bailout was out of the question. That would only invite animosity. I couldn't add value to her life—or anyone's, for that matter—through money. And for some reason I wasn't sure about yet, I wanted us to be genuine acquaintances.

"I will leave you to your pursuits. Good day, Miss Snowfall." I gave her a wave, and all she did was give me a curt nod in return. We both had work to do, and it was best for me to focus on my own troubles.

CHAPTER 3

Whitley

Six days remained. Not long into that sober morning, I discovered a note on my work counter between Mr. Nemuidesu's bolts of cloth. Mr. Chuffs paused and dropped his little red ball while I read:

DEAREST MISS SNOWFALL,

MY APOLOGIES FOR MY LATE CORRESPONDENCE. MY BUSINESS DEALINGS AROUND THE COUNTRYSIDE HAVE LEFT ME FAR TOO BUSY. I TRUST YOU WILL RESOLVE THE MATTER WITH THE DUCHESS OF LEINSBOROUGH ACCORDINGLY. TO ASSIST YOU IN YOUR PURSUIT, I CONTACTED AN UNSAVORY, YET AFFLUENT CLIENT. DO NOT BE FEARFUL. THEY WILL COME IN TWO DAYS TO PURCHASE AN AUTO BONNET. AS ALWAYS, DO NOT MARK A PRICE ON THIS ITEM.

SINCERELY,

MR. HEUREUX

.   .   .

Unsavory? That didn't sound good, but an opportunity was an opportunity.

I read the letter a few more times, then pressed the paper to my face. A vivid memory flashed through my mind, like every time I smelled the hints of the past he left on the parchment. Right after I left the orphanage, I always passed a bakery on the way to the pier. To earn money to eat during that bitter winter, I'd sold newspapers weaved into flowers. One customer—a short and subdued Asian gentleman in a thick overcoat—must've taken pity on me, and gave me five shillings. Far too much money. I tried to return four. With a slow chuckle, he pushed my hand away, took his sad bouquet, and walked away.

Money in hand, I bought two decadent madeleines. I'd rarely remembered that moment until today. How the buttery dough melted in my mouth. How the delicate oval shape of the pastry fit the palm of my hand.

What a wonderful day that was.

Had Mr. Heureux enjoyed a similar treat while he wrote his letter, or was this more of his strange nature at play? As much as I wanted to contemplate the mystical dealings in the store, I had a customer coming and far too little time to craft the best hat I'd ever made in my life.

These days ladies wore wide-brimmed hats with long silk or tulle scarves that covered the face and secured the garment under their chin. I had yet to ride in an automobile, but such a grand hat made a statement: the owner had money.

Using the shimmering light blue chiffon from Mr. Nemuidesu, I used the utmost care to cut out the fabric for the bonnet. Then I sewed the bonnet's hem with Mr. Sjenert's delicate golden thread. While I toiled away, I ate the chicken soup Emmalyn had left me to eat.

Two very long days later, I completed my masterpiece. I placed it in the display and added one of Mr. Heureux's blank price tags. Golden lettering appeared on the piece of paper: 4£. My mouth fell open. If it weren't attached to my face, my lips would've tumbled to the floor.

I'd spent two days working from midnight to sunset to complete this hat, and my employer thought four pounds would be enough?

For twenty minutes I fumed, stealing glances at the pile of Mr. Heureux's price tags on the far end of the work counter. Any moment now the customer would show up and I'd be left with hefty sum pending. The chug and whine of a Model T pulling up next to the shop caught my attention. With a muffled curse, I snatched a piece of paper and scribbled a new price.

A towering lady wearing an opaque silk veil hat and forest-green riding coat entered the store. Leather boots peeked out from under her dress. I couldn't make out the features of her face, but the chill she brought into the room made me shiver. As she approached the counter, a woody yet faintly sweet scent, like plums and cinnamon, wafted from her.

"May I help you?" I crammed my nervousness into the nearest waste bin.

"I'm searching for an auto bonnet." Her voice was as deep as a grave, barely above a whisper. "A colleague recommended this establishment."

With a hint of hesitation—who wouldn't be creeped out?—I ushered her to my selection of bonnets.

Her gloved hand traveled over the pieces, briefly pausing to trace the golden stitching. "How I love this thread. Spooled on a well-made spindle, I see. Just one *prick* from one of those things can change everything."

From under her earthy odor, the stench of dead things flared. I gripped the counter but forced a full smile. What in the heavens was she talking about?

She drifted toward my latest creation but paused when her fingers ran over the eight-pound tag.

"This is lovely, but..." She put down the hat as quickly as she retrieved it.

"It's not to your taste?"

She pointed to a two-pound hat that had long sat in the case without an owner. "I'll take this one. It will make a lovely garment to wear while I conduct *business.*"

What kind of business would someone conduct smelling like they'd danced in a cemetery?

I murmured thanks—not that I wasn't grateful, but a sour feeling clenched my stomach. I'd gone from earning four pounds to two. My customer had paid the amount and even added another pound for my outstanding craftsmanship.

What an ignorant fool I was.

The money weighed heavy in my palm, but I bit my tongue for my rash decision. Why hadn't I left the price tag alone? I could've had five pounds and been closer to my goal.

Because you wanted to keep your family safe, I reminded myself.

After my disturbing customer left, I perched on a chair. Mr. Chuffs jumped into my lap for snuggles and a belly rub, but my mood had plummeted. I didn't want to go upstairs. As I ate breakfast with the children, I'd told them how I couldn't wait to earn a tidy sum from my efforts.

How I'd march up those steps and give them relief.

Not so much now.

Of course, the back door to the shop opened and Emmalyn appeared. I didn't want to face them until I had a plan. In one hand, she carried a tray of food, and she used the other hand to balance one of the children on her hip. Little Macy wiggled and squirmed to escape. Her mischievous grin made me smile.

I ignored the three-year-old's outstretched arms to snatch the loaf of bread and jar of honey on the tray. If I picked up Macy, the girl would never take an afternoon nap. I didn't know how Emmalyn minded five children through the day. Maybe her drive and patience were the fuel I needed.

"You left without breaking your fast," Em grumbled. "The boys were worried about you, so I came down to see if you were alive."

I broke the loaf in half and smothered honey on my piece. Satisfied with my drowned handiwork, I ate my meal. Licked my fingers, too. Without a customer in sight, why bother with propriety?

"Down but still kicking," I said with my mouth full.

She grabbed a stool and sat beside me. Little Macy gave up her quest when I offered her a bite of the other half of bread. For a moment I rested. The warm honey filled my empty belly, but worries settled into my bones. Emmalyn used her free had to pat my back. I wasn't a child like Macy, or even school age like the four boys upstairs, but every now and then even I needed reassurance from my younger sister.

I needed a reminder that I fought for someone other than myself.

Words that needed to be said formed at the back of my throat, but I had trouble speaking as my chest tightened. Finally, I drew a deep breath and spoke. "I never apologized for making you wait so long at Saint Margaret's, did I?"

Her hand hovered between my shoulder blades. "I never needed you to say sorry."

"But I want to do it… I need to—"

"Don't do this. I made a choice, Whit." She pressed her warm palm to my shoulder. "Nobody wanted to keep those boys together. The orphanage would've separated them. Scattered them to every borough or tossed them like trash." Her voice lowered yet grew more fervent. "Sometimes the most powerful wishes are the ones you make for others instead of yourself." She sighed. "Seeing them fight and laugh and sleep next to each other was worth every second I spent there."

She patted my back again. "I don't want to hear you mention this again, Whitley. You hear?"

We sat in silence. Her words wrapped around me and hugged me tighter than any embrace.

The bell over the door tinkled as someone new arrived.

It was Mr. Princeton.

"Oh, you have company." His gaze flicked to Emmalyn and Macy.

"These are my sisters." Neither of them resembled me in the least bit, but I didn't care. If Mr. Princeton did, he could go on his merry way.

"Pleasure to meet you, ladies." His presence filled the space. Perhaps if he stretched out his arms, he could touch both ends.

With my meal complete, Emmalyn rose from her seat. "If you don't come up for dinner, I will bring it to you."

I smiled. "I know. You're the best, Em."

Macy yelled in protest as Emmalyn gave Mr. Princeton a friendly "Good day, sir," and left.

Carl shifted from one foot to another. "I have good news, Miss Snowfall. This morning I found a favorable corner shop." His whole handsome face lit up with excitement. "There's even a living space in the rear."

"And the neighborhood?"

"Clean and safe." He stared at me a bit before he looked away. "The rent is a bit high, but we could make an arrangement. I am one of your suppliers. Why not work together?"

"Both of us." My face grew warm at the thought. What would it be like to stand side by side with a man and work together?

Mr. Princeton continued. "The owner said he had a lot of potential interest, so he'd only hold the property for me until tomorrow at noon."

I still needed to find a place for my family, but finding work came first. "Then we should go see him tomorrow. Care for a cup of warm tea, Mr. Princeton?"

He gave me a nod, and I prepared another serving.

Right as I sat to take a sip, Mr. Chuffs approached me with a piece of paper in his mouth. Had my mischievous friend gnawed on one of the receipts I'd drafted? No, it was another letter from Mr. Heureux. I nearly dropped the teacup.

. . .

DEAR MISS SNOWFALL,

I RECEIVED A MESSAGE FROM OUR CUSTOMER'S COURIER REGARDING THE HAT. SHE WAS MOST PLEASED WITH HER PURCHASE, BUT I AM DISAPPOINTED THAT YOU DIDN'T HEED MY ADVICE. I WILL GIVE YOU ANOTHER CHANCE. TOMORROW AFTER-NOON, ANOTHER SET OF DISREPUTABLE CLIENTS WILL ARRIVE TO PURCHASE FIVE OPULENT WIDE-BRIMMED HATS. IF YOU SUCCEED, MORE PROFITS AWAIT IN THE COMING MONTHS. I'M CERTAIN YOU CAN STEP UP TO THE CHALLENGE!

SINCERELY,

MR. HEUREUX

Good Lord, five opulent wide-brimmed hats in a day? And who would pick them up this time?

My head swam and the porridge I'd eaten for breakfast lurched in my stomach.

"What does it say?"

Carl repeated his question, but when I didn't reply, he grasped the paper. After he read it, he stared at his cup of tea until the steam no longer rose.

"That's an impossible order." He sighed.

"Beyond impossible. I don't have enough cloth for that many hats, let alone the time."

He scanned the goods in the store. "Could you sell them ones you already have?"

"I wish. The kind of hat he's referring to requires materials I've used already."

His forehead scrunched. "I sold most of my stock, but I've got two bolts of muslin left." The concern in his eyes made my heartbeat quicken.

"I don't have enough money to pay you."

"What you can give me doesn't matter right now. What matters is you staying here. Your whole family."

"But what about the shop you mentioned?"

He stood. "We'll consider that in the morning. We need to start cutting out the patterns out as soon as possible."

His enthusiasm set my heart aflutter. "Thank you, Mr. Princeton."

He paused at the doorway. "Call me Carl."

Carl

On my way back to the shop with my bundles, I spied another set of mysterious parcels. More deliveries from suppliers? I picked up those and entered the shop to find not only Miss Snowfall, but five eager assistants.

The shop became a hive of activity from the morning into the afternoon.

I worked at the beginning of the queue to unroll the fabric and pin the patterns. Emmalyn and another boy would cut—well, they did do the cutting until Em discovered the boy's grubby hands. Then he joined the other boys to help sort the new goods into the storage room bins.

Even Mr. Chuffs did his part and kept Macy occupied while Miss Snowfall labored at the work counter to stitch the hats together.

Customers arrived and purchased goods, but with each shilling or pound earned, the crestfallen expression on Miss Snowfall's pretty face never wavered. We needed a big sale.

The afternoon stretched out, and soon our helpers disappeared. We had too many tasks to complete. Even Miss Snowfall's hands shook while she squinted to stitch together the third hat.

I grasped the needle. Her hand was cool to the touch. "Rest a bit. I can do these and apply the ribbons—but you'll have to prepare the embellishments."

Her forehead crinkled. "Yes, I must find the adornments from Signore Scontroso and Herr Blöd—as well as the ostrich feathers from Mr. Sinirli. How ever did Mr. Heureux get these shipments all the way from Italy, Germany, and Turkey here so fast?"

"Does it matter?" I took the hat and handed her a cold cup of tea and a hard scone.

She shook her head and sat. Not long into my task, I caught her light snoring and chuckled. Her features had softened, leaving her cheekbones rosy and her lips slightly parted. Her chest slowly rose and fell. Perhaps, like me, she dreamt of work—or maybe she thought of someone special?

The familiar rhythm of working a needle and thread allowed me to drift away. Working in this quiet shop with Miss Snowfall had given me something I hadn't had in a long time: contentment.

Ten minutes later, Miss Snowfall woke up with a jerk. She rubbed her eyes and peeked in the mirror customers used.

"Your hair is perfect, as usual," I whispered. "Are you ready, Miss Snowfall?"

"Yes." A blush kissed her cheeks as strength filled her voice. "No need for formalities. Please call me Whitley."

We worked side by side at the work counter. Not even a hand span separated us as she sorted out the exotic adornments: speckled glass jewelry, pendants, and pearls. She applied the feathers and adornments in becoming spots. I stitched them into place.

Our furious pace continued until darkness descended and lamps illuminated Hyde Street outside. I hadn't noticed the passage of time until I caught someone shutting the back door. A tray with two bowls, a dessert, and bread sat off to the side. Why hadn't I heard anyone enter?

Whitley continued to construct the pieces until I gently shook her shoulder.

"Let's eat, Whitley."

Her dark eyes glazed over as her pupils shrank to pinpricks. She wet her lower lip then glanced over at the meal.

"What time is it?"

"Late." I strolled past a sleeping Mr. Chuffs. His patchy belly was on full display.

Whitley took small bites of mutton stew; her gaze often flitted to the hats.

"Are you from London?" I asked to draw her into the present.

"I was born in Scotland."

"Did you come here for work?"

She slowly shook her head, and the lamp cast a warm glow on her face. "My parents died in a train accident while coming here to find work. I ended up in an orphanage. And you?"

I paused. What should I tell her? "I was born in Belgium. I came here for work, too."

"That's a long way. Not much work where you come from?"

"There's plenty—I just don't want what they have to offer." I sighed. "I've always wished for independence. Living your life through another's efforts isn't a life at all."

"Indeed." She pushed the mutton aside, then eyed the piece of mince pie. "If you don't know how to care for yourself, what can a woman or man do when life throws its worst at them?"

"They sink and drown." I would've sunk. My education and determination had carried me here. I had to do the rest.

I slid the saucer with the pie over to her.

"You are our guest, but if you don't want it…" she said.

She grasped her fork and took a bite. I softened at seeing her bliss.

"Are you sure you don't want any? Em is a fantastic cook." She appeared thoughtful. "If I earn enough money, I want to help her open a bakery."

Whitley's sister had prepared a fine meal indeed. She'd seasoned and slow-cooked the lamb well. The pie's flaky crust and sweet filling of dried fruits and spice practically called my name. But I clamped my mouth shut until Whitley rolled her eyes, picked up her knife, and sliced the pie in half.

"If you don't eat the whole thing, I will tell on you," she whispered with a grin.

After we finished our meal, we worked late into the night. By the time five hats sat on the work counter, Whitley rested against the far wall, and I stared bleary-eyed out the window. A fog had settled along the streets. As the sun rose, the clouds dissolved, leaving growing mounds of powdery white along the street.

Was that snow?

CHAPTER 4

Whitley

I WASN'T SURE HOW LONG I'D DOZED, BUT ENOUGH TIME HAD passed for my back to stiffen and my legs to go numb. I peered across my shop to find Carl staring out the window.

"What time is it?" I groaned as my hip protested from my position on the floor. "Did I sleep through opening the millinery?"

"We have worse problems than the time of day." He jerked his chin to the outdoors.

Fat and thick snowflakes fell out of the sky to join their brethren in blocking the streets. Not a single well-to-do pedestrian braved the snowdrifts.

"Snow in October..." My breath fogged the window. "I have truly wronged someone in the heavens."

Two policemen tried to plow through at snail's pace. Another poor soul, a delivery boy carrying cake boxes, crashed face-first across the street. A delicate raspberry torte tumbled out of its box. Its gooey filling bled across the snow.

"Have faith. The weather may turn favorable."

Carl's smile should've reassured me, but as one hour passed, then two more, my faith wavered. Thick clouds obscured the sun, leaving a once vibrant street somber.

Carl donned his coat. "Let me see if I can learn when the road will be cleared." He escaped out the back door into the alley.

Time passed, and all I could do was tidy the shop. Shifting my goods a millimeter to the left or right wouldn't make them appear any more appealing. Mr. Chuffs brought me his ball again and again. Toss. Shift. Toss. Shift.

My chest grew tight as the clock on the wall reached two. Tears gathered in my eyes. I'd done everything expected of me. I'd toiled away to create this new order. I'd placed the price tags Mr. Heureux had instructed me to do.

Tomorrow, a horrible, heartless woman planned to toss my siblings into the streets. All we'd wanted—all I'd wished for—was them to feel *secure.* That old, yet familiar feeling, a hollowness in my chest and deep-set fog, smothered my senses. I was cast adrift again. Standing alone in the city with a couple pence in my pocket and no bed to rest my head.

The scrape of metal against cobblestone drew me to the window. To my surprise, I discovered Carl and the boys hard at work shoveling snow. Bit by bit, they cleared a path along the sidewalk from the end of the block to my front door.

My mouth parted and hope bubbled in my stomach. Would that be enough?

The clock ticked to two and Carl's words yesterday slammed into me: *The owner said he'd only hold the property for me until tomorrow at noon.*

Which meant he'd given up his chance at a new start.

He'd done this for me. For my family.

Once Carl and the boys reached the door, three ladies materialized behind them. Carl yanked off his cap and stepped aside.

He blurted, "Afternoon, ladies."

These highborn customers waltzed into the shop without a single snowflake on their skirts. The first young woman, by far the tallest of the three, wore a brocade-patterned, mink-lined coat. She cradled a yapping Affenpinscher that sent poor Mr. Chuffs in a hurry into the back room. The animal appeared to be a puff of curly black fur and nothing more. The flashy black beaver hat on her head was ill-fitting, but the dramatic felt fur and silk ribbons boasted of her wealth.

Right behind her, a second woman waltzed inside. Her thick mink stole swallowed her neck and chin, revealing only her spiteful, slitted eyes from under her black lace wide-brimmed hat. Enough black feathers for flight extended upward. She strode into the shop in her moss-green tailored frock coat. The final young woman peeked from behind the second. Unlike her companions, she smiled as she took in the shop. Her lavender Tudor beret was simple, as was her thick wool capelet.

My gaze swept over them, and I considered their likes and dislikes. The first two would be trouble.

"Why did you drag me here again, Drucilla?" the second woman said.

"We're here to purchase accessories so we may secure the affections of a *well-to-do* gentleman, Mary Millicent," Drucilla replied crisply. "Mr. Heureux told me *this* is the place to acquire the perfect match. Come along, Ursula. You dawdle too much."

I motioned for them to browse my wares. "Let me show you the selection we crafted personally for you."

Most clients loved personal attention. Ursula approached me, but Drucilla grabbed her shoulder.

"Mother told you to slow down," she said. "Always too zealous, sister."

Every single wide-brimmed hat, priced at 5£, should've caught any discerning shopper's eye. Mr. Sinirli's vibrant ostrich feathers appeared to flutter with a breeze. The golden thread from Mr. Sjenert glinted under the shop's lamps, and not a single wrinkle marred Mr. Nemuidesu's ribbons.

They'd given us the best materials to craft works of art.

"They are absolutely hideous." Drucilla frowned.

"What a waste of our time," Mary Millicent snapped.

"They're magnificent—" Ursula began, but shut her mouth when she caught her sisters' growing scowls.

What had I done wrong this time?

I picked up one of the hats and held it out. "You came all this way. Why not try it on?"

Mary Millicent exchanged one wide-brimmed hat for the other. Her sour face softened as she glanced in the mirror. "Now this is the one. A perfect fit."

Her taller sister peeked over the shoulder. She must've glimpsed her sibling's reflection, for she snatched away the hat.

"That doesn't suit you at all," Drucilla said. "It should be mine!"

Mary Millicent reached for the hat, but her sister held her prize out of reach with one hand while her dog barked in the other. Poor Ursula stood there. Utter chaos had leapt into my establishment.

The children upstairs had better manners.

"Miss Mary Millicent, why don't you see if this hat is far more pleasing." I added with a whisper, "This one has lovely peacock feathers from Turkey."

While Drucilla admired herself in front of one mirror, Mary Millicent attached herself to another one on the opposite side of the room. That left Ursula to browse the remaining three at her leisure. She carefully considered each before she boldly said, "I'll take all three."

Not only did Drucilla and Millicent buy the hats they now wore, but two mourning hats and berets.

"Should we buy something for Cindy?" Ursula asked.

"We told you about saying the C-word," Drucilla grumbled.

Ursula rolled her eyes.

The tallest sister turned to me. "Our footman will fetch our purchases this evening."

"They will be ready before sunset." I wanted to jump with glee, but I smiled like a fool instead.

Thank goodness this was over. And that I'd never had to fight Emmalyn over such things.

She'd win in a fair fight anyway.

As my guests departed and my coffers were filled with their pounds, my joy overflowed—until I walked into the back room to find Carl holding Mr. Chuffs.

"Sounds like it went well." He grinned at me and released my fidgety pet.

"Better than well. We made thirty-five pounds today. I've never made this much money before."

"Neither have I."

Our current circumstances, or should I say Carl's, swept through the room like a bitter December breeze. I opened my mouth to offer him half, but what good would that do? Even if he used the fifteen pounds I gave him, next month's rent had to be paid.

A month from now, he would still need to find another home.

"I couldn't have done this without you," I said, knowing what had to be done. "Mr. Heureux said if I succeeded, more profits await…us."

"Us?"

I snorted. "If all these clients are as difficult as those sisters, I won't be able to do this alone. I'll need another hat maker." I fussed with my hair—then stopped when I noticed the habit. "A tailor capable of helping me meet their demands."

"Do you now?" He slipped into an easy smile.

Was that a yes? Please?

"You'll have to sleep in the storage room. Deal with my family."

"They are a handful."

"Give my dog belly rubs." Mr. Chuffs circled twice at the mention of his name. My dog sat at Carl's feet.

He's my human now, the dog seemed to declare with a bark.

I expected Carl to refuse. Hadn't he told me he wanted to find his own way? Live his life without depending on others?

"Is that it?" he said simply.

My mouth parted as I nodded. "When can you start?"

"Yesterday appeared as good a time as any, Miss Snowfall. Yesterday."

I had an absolute blast. After watching hours of Downton Abbey, I couldn't resist returning to Edwardian England and bringing you a twist to Snow White's tale. If you enjoyed reading this tale, be sure to please join my mailing list. There are more adventures to come in the future.

Learn more about Shawntelle at shawntellemadison.com.

IMMORTAL WISH

COLLEEN GLEASON

A short story from the
Gotham Hollywood Series
by Colleen Gleason

CHAPTER 1

something more.

The Sea was powerful and ever-changing, filled with life and color, sensation and taste…but there was the Above. The Surface.

The Out There.

Atlanteans never mentioned the Above, and they usually didn't even talk about the Surface—at least, not in front of their children. As if that would keep the youngsters from wanting to know what there was "above"—where the water ended and *something else* began. Which of course it didn't, once they learned that something called the Above existed…that there was something called the Surface that was a sort of forbidden thing or place or event…

Whatever it was, it was vague and secret and never discussed if children could overhear.

Lyla was ten the first time she got close enough to the Surface to know that something was different up there—and even then, though she didn't know it, she was still far, far away from breaking through the barrier at the top of the Sea. There'd been a wild storm, filled with powerful, thrashing waves that churned the water deep below and sent seaplants and fish and even shells tossing and tumbling about.

The water was gritty with sand, minuscule shells, and even smaller creatures like water-gnats and plankton, and in the poor light and surging ocean, Lyla got separated from her older sister Renna and their brother Malento. Before she knew it, Lyla was caught up in one of the violent, churning surges of water and she felt herself being thrown about, tumbling like one of the round seaweeds that rolled along the ocean floor—but instead of bouncing along on the bottom of the Sea, Lyla was thrown up and around higher and higher from the ocean's floor.

She fought against being carried away, but the Sea had hold of her and she could do nothing but let the water's power take her. After what seemed like a long while, the swirling slowed and ceased and the buffeting quieted and the storm ebbed. And Lyla was float-ing, swimming, kicking her feet casually as she looked around her.

It was different.

The water up here, higher above the Sea floor than she'd ever been, was lighter. Lyla could see differently in this place without the help of glowing anemones and starfish…the colors were deeper and more vivid.

She'd never experienced anything like this moment of floating high above the sand and waving, weaving seagrass. The sand, the rocks and caves, were so far away down there…And above her, there was something strange…an entity of warmth and light that turned the water to something colorless…It shone through the water, brighter than any glowing fish or plant she'd ever seen.

"Lyla!"

The sound of her mother's frantic voice reverberated through the water, buffeting in little watery echoes against her. "Thank the gods we found you!"

Before Lyla could respond, could even *ask* about what the strange yellow streaks were that turned the water colorless, her mother and father were yanking her away, pulling her down, down, down…back to the floor of the Sea.

Lyla could see her mother's life crystal glowing with fear and anger from beneath the fish skin suit she wore. "What have I told you about going off by yourself?" she demanded, grasping Lyla by the arms as her legs weaved back and forth frantically. "It's too dangerous up—it's too dangerous to be out and around by yourself!"

"I'm sorry, Mother. The storm pulled me away," Lyla said, looking at Renna over her mother's shoulder. Her sister looked tense and worried as well, her long blond hair billowing around her in the water. "But what was that—"

"You'll come back home now," said Father. The crown crystal in his temple—large and colorless as a seastone and was part of his designation as an Elder—burned like a water cauldron. "It's too dangerous over here. Come now. The storm is over and we will return home."

They never allowed Lyla to ask about what she'd seen and experienced. Whenever she tried, her parents changed the subject abruptly and decisively. They kept a closer watch on her, insisting that she remain deep in the Crevice, which protected the city of Atlantis, and where the sea was dark and cold. And safe.

And even when she asked Renna about it—Renna, who was seventeen and knew so much more—she wouldn't answer her questions.

All she said was, "It's not for us, Lylie. It's not for us up there. Please don't think about it. Please don't talk about it."

And so Lyla stopped asking about what she'd seen. But she never stopped thinking about it.

She never stopped wanting to know more.

And every time she saw a sea spark arc through the ocean, she made a wish.

Seven years later, Lyla was swimming along the Marroll Passage. Tall seagrass whispered in the water on either side of the route, which had been cleared as a sort of channel between Atlantis and the crystal mines. Every so often, she could see the glow of red from deep within the sea grasses: safety crystals placed among the ocean weeds to protect the route from dangers like black sharks and green snakes. Atlanteans like Lyla and her family couldn't pass beyond the red crystals without a Passage Stone—except her father and the other Elders, of course, whose crown crystals were their own personal Passage Stones.

A group of bellyfish swam along with her, darting about and dancing in comical bursts. A trio of shiny, glittering eels slithered among the seagrass, trying to stay out of sight of Lyla while predatorily eyeing the colorful fish tumbling in the passageway. A swarm of sea-gnats burst from one side of the grassy wall and she batted it away, then shot up and over the annoying creatures. She hated the way they got tangled in her long hair.

Lyla was in a particularly fine mood because the very handsome Errell had been flirting with her at the market earlier, and because Mother had actually entrusted her with a delivery to Father at their crystal beds in the Deep Mine. Renna, who usually did that sort of thing, had recently found her mate—a partnership arranged by their parents—and was no longer available for such errands. Lyla was delighted that Renna's new status gave Lyla an opportunity to do something *fun* and exciting, and she hoped this wouldn't be the only time she was sent out on such an errand.

"Just follow the Marroll Passage—you can't get lost if you stay within the grasses," Mother had told her, looking a little nervous about sending her off. "And don't swim higher than a coral bush, do you hear me, Lylie?"

"Yes, Mama," she replied, dancing inside with excitement and impatience.

Lyla had gone out into the Passage before, but never this far—and never this distance alone. Renna had taken her to the mine several times, so Lyla knew what to expect. But to go alone—to be able to experience the journey all on her own—was the most exciting thing to ever happen to Lyla. It would be well over two hours of swimming if she hurried, and she had no desire to rush. She could take as long as she wanted.

Freedom was difficult to come by in the world of Atlantis. Especially when you were the daughter of one of the Elders. Lyla had finally received her own life crystal, which would allow her to go as far as she liked from the Yuhari crystal—the source of energy for all of Atlantis. It sat in the center of the city and illuminated the darkness of the sea floor as well as gave life and energy to all of those who lived there. The massive stone was alive—you could even see its change of color as it breathed slowly and regularly—and it constantly rejuvenated itself, shedding small translucent chunks regularly.

At age seventeen, each Atlantean was given their own piece of a discarded gem from the Yuhari crystal. The piece of translucent golden rock was embedded in the soft part of their skin just below the clavicle, where it knit itself into the body of the human by growing tiny vein-like tentacles that became one with the skin, bones, and circulatory system. The life crystal would slow their aging process significantly, keeping an Atlantean alive for centuries as long as it wasn't damaged or removed.

It was because she'd crossed that threshold into adulthood that her mother had asked Lyla to make the trip to the mines. Unfortunately, the other consequence of becoming an adult meant that it was time to make a partnership and mate. Her parents were considering several different men as a mate for Lyla, including Ren Tyroli. Lyla didn't understand why she couldn't pick her own mate, and if she could, she did not think Ren would be the one. There was something about him that put her off, despite the fact that he was charming and deferent to her parents.

But for right now, Lyla pushed away all of her concerns about her future. She was determined to enjoy her hours of freedom. She smiled at the bellyfish dancers, paused to watch a cluster of horned swirlfish as they used their tiny mouths to slurp up minuscule insects on the side of a swaying pink coral bush, and clapped her hands to startle a cluster of hovering danklefish into motion. The sea grass that created the passage rose up and up and up, so high she couldn't see the tops of the grasses.

Very high.

Up into nowhere. Up into darkness and watery shimmers.

A little shiver skittered down her spine and she felt her crystal quiver. As long as she stayed within the grasses, she would be safe...

And so Lyla swam forward, but she also swam up...and up and up...

She swam forever at an upward diagonal. Her legs were getting tired and one of her toes cramped, and still she couldn't even see the tops of the thick, sharp grass. She was growing tired and she could feel the heat of her crystal as it glowed with effort from her exertions, but Lyla pushed on.

This was her only chance to go up...to see what was Above.

As long as I stay in the grasses, I'm safe.

The ocean floor was far below her now. She could see dark shapes of coral bush, craggy rock, and patches of growth that could be seaweed, ocean flowers, or waterberries—but they were far away and she couldn't tell which was which.

A pale tentaculus streamed along beneath her, its eight legs curling and thrusting it forward in a smooth movement. There were other fish up here that were unfamiliar to Lyla, but she was still within the sea grass walls, so she felt safe from predators who might be interested in taking a bite of a non-finned, four-limbed creature.

Still, she was curious. Because now the grasses seemed thinner as she swam higher, and on occasion, she saw the actual *top* of one: its spray of feathery fronds wafting in the water, as if it hadn't grown to its full height yet...

And the water was somehow lighter.

Lyla's heart leaped and she looked up. Yes, the water above her was somehow clearer and lighter and—

She stopped suddenly, the swish of her movement sending a group of sea snails tumbling from the grasses to which they clung. There in front of her, high in the water, she saw it: the light that made the water turn colorless.

She stared at it with wonder, paused in mid-kick. A pale yellow light, a sort of glow—stronger than anything she'd ever seen before, including the energy crystals that lit the insides of their homes— beamed down from above into the darker water.

Heart thudding, Lyla swam closer, careful but inexorably drawn by curiosity. The glow melded into the blue around it, fading from a central circular shape. She reached toward it, her fingers gliding through the water to the very edge of the light...then paused.

Would it be dangerous? Would it hurt her if she touched it?

She waited, heart pounding wildly in her chest, her crystals warm with effort. As she waited, she saw a quartet of dunklefish swimming toward the circle of light and she watched as they finned their way through the sphere, seemingly unharmed and even unaware of the change of color around them.

This gave her the courage to move closer, to allow her fingers to brush through the water at the very seam of light and sea...

Nothing happened. More fish came along, swimming through—

even a posse of curly hornfish—and all passed into and out of the strange light without pause.

Lyla drew in her breath, feeling the cool, fresh water fill her lungs, and without giving it any further thought, darted into the very center of the circle of light.

It was almost anti-climactic. One moment she was in one place, and the next she was in another, and the only difference was the swirl of ocean from her sudden movement and the fact that she was surrounded by the cleanest, clearest, purest light she'd even seen.

Lyla spun in a circle within the light, her hair fluttering and twining around her like tendrils of seagrass. She felt no different, exactly the same except for the fact that what she saw within in the area was somehow cleaner and more clear than what she was used to seeing…yet she didn't understand how it could be so. The colors were brighter and stronger—and there were hues she'd never seen before.

It was like being in a little magical kingdom of light with all sorts of different creatures. Even ones with which she was familiar appeared somehow different: bolder, crisper, even bigger.

And then Lyla looked up.

The light went up and up and up…and something told her it had to come from somewhere. Somewhere Above—the place she'd only heard murmurs about.

And she began to kick herself upward, faster and harder—as if to get her breaching of the rules over with as quickly as possible. Before she could think too hard about what she was doing. She kept her face turned upward, watching ahead as she propelled herself further and further from the bottom of the sea.

As she rose, the light became stronger and even more pure and concentrated. Even the water in the sea felt different up here as well…it was more turbulent and seemed more sensitive to her move-ments. It smelled and tasted differently, too, she noticed as she drew in each breath. It was…thinner. That was the only way to describe it. *Thinner.*

And then she saw something strange.

She stopped suddenly, causing a rush of tiny bubbles to envelope her, startling a crew of brancia that flitted off using their long, silvery fins. But she hardly noticed, for Lyla was looking at the very strange sight above her.

It was like nothing she'd ever seen before: the Sea appeared so *odd*. As if it were a kind of *wall* or barrier…like a ceiling. And yet the light filtered through it. And the light was so much stronger that it now covered a broader area. As far as she could see, the ocean here was lighter and thinner and so very, very strange.

Like a delicate lugoyna attracted to the glittering, glowing stem of a crusty finger coral, Lyla was drawn to the strange texture in the water…the unusual ceiling that could only be described as shimmery and undulating.

She paused once again when she drew near, and then, carefully extending her finger, she poked it.

Nothing happened—there was no resistance. Her heart beating faster, she raised her arm up and up and—

Her finger went *through*.

She yanked her hand back down, heart in her throat, crystals burning brightly with fear and apprehension. But she couldn't stop now. She wouldn't.

She had to know.

Carefully moving up even closer to the strange, moving, water-ceiling, Lyla carefully extended her finger again, slowly pushing it up and into the strange shimmery texture…and beyond.

Her hand felt different. Warm. And…there was some other sensation she couldn't identify. She pulled her hand back and carefully examined it to ensure nothing had changed.

No…it looked the same. Her fingers still moved. Nothing had changed.

She tried it again. And again. And still nothing changed.

And then, her face tipped up, her eyes wide and her entire body vibrating with nerves and anticipation, Lyla propelled herself *up*.

She burst through the glowing, rippling, undulating barrier and found herself in another world.

Impossibly, unbelievably, she had come out of the Sea. She had actually *left* the water—her head and just the tops of her shoulders, anyway. And she was…somewhere else. Somewhere without water? How could that be? How could anyone exist without water to breathe?

And yet, she was breathing…but not easily. She could feel her body reacting to the inhalation of something strange and different. Her lungs felt tight and tense and the back of her throat had an unfamiliar sensation…a sensation of being without water. What sort of concept was that? Being without water? What was that like?

She ducked back down into the comfort of the Sea, knowing that her eyes must be wild with shock and surprise. She was able to breathe here again, and she drank in several inhalations before propelling herself up through the barrier once more.

This time, Lyla stared, looking all around her as she moved in a slow circle. What could only be described as the Top of the Sea—a concept she'd never even dreamed of—spread as far as she could see.

And there were other things too. Creatures that swam through the space—whatever it was, this place Above the Sea—making coarse *rawwwking* noises that sounded strange to her ears.

Something brushed over her face, cool and strange. It was invisible, whatever it was, and chilly, and she couldn't wipe it away. It was like…it was like someone was pushing the strange non-water area in her face in a sort of non-water surge. She didn't know how to describe it, but the sensation seemed harmless.

Lyla stared for as long as she could before she needed to breathe, propelling herself slowly in a circle. She was looking at the *tops* of waves—a concept she could hardly comprehend. They made little peaks and then flattened out, and then peaks and then flattened…

It was the most shocking, fascinating thing she'd ever experienced.

Lyla went back down, breathed again, then came back up several times before she realized she had to continue on her way to the mines before someone came out to look for her…and discovered what she'd found.

And so, reluctantly, she dove down from the Top of the Sea and began to swim in a descending, forward trajectory as quickly as she could. The sooner she delivered the small package to her father, the sooner she could be on her way back...with more opportunity to look around at the strange new world Above.

As she swam, she had so many thoughts. What was it like to be out of the Sea all the time? Did Atlanteans *live* there? Could they? She knew she couldn't breathe for very long when she broke the sea-ceiling, so it seemed unlikely that anyone could exist.

But there'd been those creatures swimming through the space above her, with their loud *rawwwwking*. Something could obviously live there.

A glimmer of light caught Lyla's attention and she turned just in time to glimpse a sea spark arcing above her, shooting into the depths of the sea grass passage.

It was the largest sea spark she'd ever seen, and its color was bright and warm. It lasted for much longer than any other spark she'd seen in her seventeen years. Lyla actually jolted to a halt when she saw it, and closed her eyes and *wished* with all of her might.

CHAPTER 3

LYLA HAD BEEN WISHING FOR YEARS TO FIND OUT MORE ABOUT the light watery area she'd first experienced at age ten. But now that she'd actually touched it, *seen* what was Above, *felt* it—she had a stronger wish.

A more specific one.

She wanted to *be* there. She wanted to explore that world, that Above.

She wanted to leave the restrictions of Atlantis and her overly protective family and *live* Up There.

As she swam back through the Marroll Passage, she held that wish strongly in her heart even as she wondered why everyone was so secretive about the Up There.

She swam near the tops of the seagrasses once more, basking in the water filled with illumination. She stopped several times to poke her head above, curious to see if anything was different from what she'd observed before.

The top of the sea—still such a strange concept—stretched as far as she could see when she came to the surface. The watery bumps splashed into her face when she was above the ocean, and Lyla learned that if she turned her face toward one of those surges of water, she could breathe it in when it crashed into her and thus keep her head above even longer.

It became a sort of rhythm for her to take a faceful of the sea, inhale it, and then turn and wait for the next surge.

But she wanted more. She wanted to be able to remain Above and—

A loud, very loud, very strange and frightening noise suddenly filled the air. It was like nothing she'd ever heard. The sound was ominous and it seemed to make the ocean quake and rumble around her, causing the splashes of water to become larger and more violent.

Lyla didn't mind that, for gulping in great nose- and mouthfuls of the Sea allowed her to breathe more easily. But the sound frightened her, and she was just about to dive back beneath the surface and go far, far away from whatever it was when she saw it: a huge *thing* moving toward her.

It was like a whale, but it wasn't. It had no eyes or mouth and it seemed to be formed from some inert material.

Her first instinct was to duck back under the water, but she didn't. Instead, Lyla remained still and calm and watched as the entity cruised through the water toward her.

As it drew near, she saw a figure moving about on the top of it— whatever it was looked like an Atlantean, but without legs…and then she realized the creature was *inside* the vessel and that was why she couldn't see the legs. The person looked like an Atlantean—and seemed to be able to breathe out of the water!

It was a female creature, with long blond hair that fell past her shoulders to her hips—a strange sight to Lyla, for under the water, everyone's hair was constantly moving about unless it was otherwise braided or confined. It looked so strange, and yet beautiful.

And the woman was wearing something that covered her body that was not fish skin or shells or woven from seagrass. It was long and loose and didn't show much of her figure.

Frozen by fascination and curiosity, Lyla didn't move as the thing coming through the water eased closer…and then another figure appeared, seemingly rising up from nowhere. She realized at that moment whatever was moving on top of the Sea must be a sort of container that was large enough to hold humans.

But then the second figure turned around and Lyla was able to see his face.

And she screamed.

Because it was her father.

CHAPTER 4

LYLA HAD NEVER HEARD THE SOUND THAT CAME FROM HER mouth before. Outside of the water, the noise was high and long and sharp and it frightened her.

But that shock was instantly overruled when her father turned and looked at her. "Lyla!" he cried, obviously shocked. His voice sounded very strange, here outside of the water, and at first she couldn't understand it. "What are you doing here?" Anger and something that might have been fear filled his eyes and tightened his expression.

"Father!" She swam closer to the vessel, uncaring that he was furious. She had to know. She had to see. "What are you doing? What is this place?"

"This is your daughter?" said the woman in the boat. She didn't have a crown crystal in her temple like Father, and Lyla couldn't tell if she even had a life crystal because whatever the woman was wearing was opaque, so the crystal's glow wouldn't shine through.

"*No*," said Father, his voice still strange but his face was tense with worry. And probably fury. "She—"

"I want to know what this is," Lyla said, gulping a mouthful of water from a large wave. "Father, what is this place? I want to—"

"She'll do," said the woman in a very calm voice. "She'll do beautifully, Locastio."

The woman knew her father's name. Who *was* she? Had her father been mating with another woman that wasn't Lyla's mother? All at once, Lyla's shock and curiosity changed to one of fear and sadness.

Surely not. Surely *not*.

"*No,*" replied Father, speaking to the woman. "No—she's too young, Wayren. She's—"

"Locastio, she's been called. Can you not see that?" The woman, whose name appeared to be Wayren and whose voice and appearance were both simply *beautiful*, came closer to the edge of the thing they were in. "And you wished upon the sea sparks, didn't you, Lyla?"

"I've been wishing for years," replied Lyla. She glanced at her parent. "Father, please don't be angry. I haven't done anything wrong.

"You came Above the Surface," he said. His expression was still thunderous. "If you had not done so, this never would have happened."

"Locastio, please," said Wayren. "You must know that if she is the one who is called, there was nothing you could do to keep it from happening. It was only because today, when she wished on the largest sea spark she'd ever seen," she gave Lyla a meaningful look, "that it happened this way—and that you were here to see it. You should be grateful for that."

"She's my youngest," Father said, desperation in his voice. Lyla had never seen her powerful parent appear so at a loss.

"She is also your most intelligent and most curious and she will do very well on Land." Wayren reached out and touched Father's hand even as she smiled over at Lyla. "Do not fear—for there is no forbidden love between your father and I. We are merely allies attempting to solve—or at least, mitigate—a problem. And you have been called to help."

Lyla could hardly believe what she was hearing. Was there something wrong with her ears, listening to their strange voices outside of the Sea? Maybe she misunderstood. Maybe she couldn't hear things as they were meant to be when she was out of the water. "What—what do you mean?"

"You have been wishing on sea sparks for many years, and there is a reason for that. Not every young Atlantean makes such a wish, and with such fervency. And today, you made the strongest of wishes —so strong that our boat"—she gestured to the vessel in which she and Father were standing—"was called here to you during our meeting."

"What were you doing in that—that boat?" Lyla asked. "Father, what does this mean?"

He gave a quiet groan, passing a hand over his face. "Wayren and I meet often. She comes from the Land, and she and I have been trying to find a way for Atlanteans to safely interact with Land-walkers."

"Land-walkers?"

He sighed again and, glancing at Wayren—who was watching them both with a pleased, beatific smile—went on. "Land is like the bottom of the Sea where the plants grow—but there is no water. Creatures like us—called humans—use their feet to move about in a manner like a crab. That is called walking."

"I want to see this Land," Lyla said without thinking. "I've *always* wanted to, Father. I've always known there was something else out there—ever since that time of the Sea storm where I got lost. I want to see it."

Wayren and her father looked at each other. And then, right before her eyes, Father's broad shoulders and powerful torso seemed to shrink. Just a little, but it was enough that Lyla could see he'd acquiesced to whatever this Wayren female wanted.

"It has long been foretold that one of my flesh will see the Land," Father said after a long moment of looking down at her. "And it appears that the chosen one will be you." Lyla was shocked to see that his eyes seemed to be filled with parts of the Sea and they were running down his cheeks. His voice sounded different again, as if he struggled to speak. He glanced at Wayren then back to Lyla. "I cannot say nay, for though I might wish to only keep you next to me and safe below the Sea…you have been called. It is clear and that I cannot contest."

"I don't understand this…*called*," Lyla said, suddenly very nervous. What problem was there between Atlanteans and Land-walkers? Why did Father look so stricken?

Wayren and her father exchanged looks once more, then when he nodded, the female spoke. "There are Land-walkers—we call them people—who want the crystals that the Atlanteans mine. They don't want them for energy or even for life…they want the grit that comes from the crystals, the very tiny pieces of gem and stone no larger than grains of sand, because of the way it makes them feel when they rub it into their skin.

"Your father and I have been working together to create an alliance to help keep unsavory—evil," she said, obviously clarifying when Lyla didn't understand the word, "people from stealing and selling this crystal grit on the land. It isn't a good thing for humans —people—to have, but there are some who want to become wealthy and powerful by selling this crystal grit."

"In turn, there are some Atlanteans who willingly trade with humans to give them the crystal grit, and we don't even know who they are. It's all done in secret," Father explained. "And it's danger-ous. Very dangerous for both humans and Atlanteans."

Lyla had taken in all of this information and began to nod as snatches of conversation she'd heard over the years—especially recently—began to make sense.

"And so," Father went on, "there is a need for Atlanteans who are willing and able to live on the Land to help find those who are endangering humans, and also potentially revealing the secrets of Atlantis to the Land-walkers. We don't want Land-walkers here." His face was stern and forbidding. "And we need to find and expel those Atlanteans who are trading with them, as well as those humans who want our crystal."

"It's dangerous work, Lyla," said Wayren. "But you have been called, and because of that, your father *will* allow you to fulfill that promise. It will be a most challenging, frightening, and amazing life."

"But how will I breathe?" Lyla asked, ignoring all of the warnings from Wayren. She already knew this was her destiny. She must have known from the time she was a youngster, the first time she caught sight of The Surface. "How are *you* breathing without water, Father?"

He heaved another sigh. "With a crown crystal I can pass through anywhere, and I can breathe in the air. But you will be given special crystals that will allow you to breathe—what is it? Oxygen?"

"Yes. Oxygen, in the air," Wayren said with a smile and a nod. "Your crystals will enable you to walk about on Land and breathe like a human…and you will also be able to return to the Sea and breathe in the water at any time."

Lyla stared at her. "This is possible?"

"Yes it is. Your father will oversee the embedding of the crystals into your torso, which will enable your lungs to take in either water or air. And then you will begin your training to be and act like a human. It won't be difficult. Humans and Atlanteans are very nearly the same; they simply live in different places."

"Is this real?" Lyla asked, looking at her father.

He shook his head, sadness sagging in his face. "How I *wish* it were not, my sweetling. But it has been foretold. You have been called. *Your* wish has been granted."

AUTHOR'S NOTE

I've always loved Hans Christian Andersen's *The Little Mermaid*, and of course the Disney version was a big hit in my household of music-loving children. Thus, when the opportunity to write a "wish" story came my way, I immediately thought of The Little Mermaid's wish to live above the ocean.

This worked particularly well for me because I could set my version of the tale in my Gotham Hollywood world (which is a combination of my Gardella Vampire Hunter, Draculia Vampire, and Heroes of New Vegas worlds, all brought to modern day LA). I decided to write the story about how DEA Agent Lyla Harris, who appears in *Immortal Glamour* (another Gotham Hollywood short) made a wish that changed her life.

—Colleen Gleason
February 2021

ABOUT THE AUTHOR

Read Colleen Gleason's *Immortal Glamour* for a short episode starring Lyla Harris, a Drug Enforcement Agent in modern-day Hollywood.

Go to this link to download the short story for free (case-sensitive URL): http://cgbks.com/ImmortalG

Find out more about Colleen Gleason's books:
http://www.colleengleason.com
http://www.facebook.com/colleengleason.author

UNSEEN

A DJINN WARS STORY

CHRISTINE POPE

JANNA SAYERS OPENED HER EYES. SHE LAY IN A ROOM WITH soft gray-blue walls and a wide window that offered a spectacular view of the San Francisco Bay, with the span of the Golden Gate Bridge centered almost perfectly within its frame.

She didn't know this room. Her own shabby little apartment was located a few blocks from Chinatown and certainly didn't have that sort of multimillion-dollar view…or any kind of view at all, actually.

As she blinked, she heard a man's voice.

"You are awake."

That seemed patently obvious, since her eyes had been open enough to take in the unfamiliar view a few yards away from the bed where she lay.

"Where am I?" she asked. A cliché, but she truly did want to know just where the hell she was. Also, where had that voice come from? It sounded as though the man had been standing close to the bed, probably no more than a few feet from where she lay, and yet she seemed to be alone in the room.

Her gaze roamed the space, looking for a speaker built into the wall or ceiling, or maybe an Alexa device or a Google Home unit. Did either of those home automation gadgets even have an option for a voice like the one she'd heard, though? The man had a very slight accent, almost British, but with just a slight singsong quality that also made her think of Omar, one of her fellow students in the pre-med program at U.C. San Francisco. He was Jordanian, and attending school on a full scholarship.

Unfortunately, thinking about Omar forced her to remember that he was dead.

Everyone was dead…except her, for some unknown reason.

"You are in the guest house of my home near Tiburon," the voice told her.

Well, he'd given her a straight answer, but Janna wasn't sure whether she liked it very much. Tiburon was across the bay from the university…from the UCSF medical center, where she'd been drafted into service. In normal times, a third-year med student wouldn't have been allowed to treat anyone unsupervised.

But the last nightmarish week hadn't been normal times. No, it had been pretty much the exact opposite.

"How did I get here?" she asked. Her tone dripped with suspicion, but she supposed she could be forgiven for that, even though she realized that she was still fully dressed under the quilt and blanket and sheet that covered her, that apparently her host had only removed the ankle boots she'd put on when she left her apartment that morning, along with the lab coat which had hidden her T-shirt and jeans. The boots now sat across the room, neatly tucked under a gorgeously simple dresser of what she thought might be tiger maple, although she saw no sign of the lab coat.

"I brought you here," the voice said. Again, it felt as though it was coming from somewhere very close by. And was that the faintest rustle of sound, something that reminded her of the silk kimono her mother used to wear as her summer robe? "You had collapsed in the hallway at the medical center."

Was that what had happened to her? Janna pushed herself up to a sitting position, figuring doing so was safe enough since she was still safely covered. Her head ached, but she resisted the urge to reach up and rub her temples. Maybe it was silly to worry about revealing even that small sign of weakness, and yet she needed to feel as though she was in control of something, even if it was only a simple movement like that.

The deadly illness had begun as just a whisper of some new disease, one that manifested as a raging fever that no medication could control. Those few whispers turned into a roar in less than forty-eight hours, with hospitals overwhelmed and people dying on the road even as they tried to drive themselves to seek treatment. Janna had gotten called into work at the medical center once it became obvious that all the doctors, nurses, and technicians were dying right along with their patients, despite all the precautions that had been taken to prevent infection. She'd been working for nearly seventy-two hours straight when everything had gone black.

A faint and nothing more, apparently. The entire time, she'd been careful to keep monitoring her own temperature, sure that soon enough, it would begin to spike and she'd suffer the same fate as everyone around her. It had remained its normal 97.8 the entire nightmarish time, however, even as she watched patient after patient succumb to the fever. The morgues should have been overwhelmed, but....

That was the part she still couldn't quite make her mind accept. It went outside all the normal laws of biology and physics and everything she'd ever learned about the human body.

Once the Heat—that was the name someone had given the deadly fever, and it went as viral as the sickness itself before the internet and the radio and the airwaves had gone black—had done its work, the body left behind simply turned to ash. Just a small pile of gray dust, a little more than you could hold in the palm of your hand.

It wasn't possible...but her horrified eyes had told her the truth of the matter.

"Was there anyone else at the medical center?" she asked.

"No," the voice said, and now it sounded almost sad. "You were the last living being in the building. There were a few survivors left in the city when I found you, I suppose, but I doubt any remain now."

Cold trickled down Janna's back, even though the last few days had been mild and beautiful, the way late September often could be in the Bay Area. It had seemed almost a mockery that the weather should be so lovely in the midst of so much death.

"Do you know why I'm still alive?" she asked. Maybe that was a silly question to ask—she had no reason to believe that the voice should possess any particular knowledge of why she had survived when so many others hadn't—but the question haunted her, even more than the identity of the hidden man with the gentle voice.

"You are immune," he said. "No disease has a hundred-percent mortality rate. You are one of the half a percent or so who survived."

Half a percent. Janna put a shaking hand up to her face and brushed away a stray strand of hair that threatened to fall into her eyes. That meant billions of people had died.

But it also meant that there must be several million survivors. Scattered across the globe, probably, scared and alone, just as she was, but....

Well, technically, she wasn't *completely* alone.

"Are you immune, too?"

A long pause, one so long that she wondered if he'd stepped away from whatever device he was using to communicate with her. Then he said, "In a manner of speaking."

"'A manner of speaking'?" she repeated, a flicker of irritation moving through her. "What's that supposed to mean? Either you're immune or you're not."

Which she knew was simplifying things. Immunity wasn't necessarily an either/or proposition, but with a disease as deadly as the Heat, partial immunity certainly wouldn't be enough to keep you alive.

When the voice replied, it spoke calmly, its tone almost cool. "My immunity derives from who I am, and not a genetic marker such as yours."

At another time, Janna would have pressed him for more information on that "genetic marker," since possessing that data might have helped to formulate a future cure. Unfortunately, there probably weren't many medical researchers who'd survived the plague, so the question seemed moot.

Besides, there'd been a lot more to unpack in his statement.

"Who are you?" she asked.

"My name is Sayid al-Hayyam," he said. "I am a djinn."

This declaration was so preposterous that she couldn't prevent a disbelieving chuckle from escaping her lips. "Right. And I'm the Queen of England."

"I assure you, that is the simple truth."

Clearly, she'd been scooped up by a madman. No doubt he had hidden cameras secreted around the room, and was getting off on watching her reactions to his wild statements.

But since he wasn't in the room with her, she figured this was probably the best time to make a break for it. The light slanting across the bay told her it was late afternoon, and the last time she'd looked at a clock the time had been a little past ten in the morning, which meant she must have been lying here for some hours. Although her head ached and she knew she needed to sleep for at least twelve hours to even start to make up for all the sleep she'd lost this week, she felt well enough to make the attempt.

"If you say so," she remarked, then pushed back the covers and climbed out of bed, intent on hurrying across the room and retrieving her boots so she could get the hell out of there.

Only something blocked her path.

A very solid something that felt like a man. Strong hands grasped her arms, holding her in place, preventing her from moving any further.

"It is not safe for you to leave," Sayid said, and this time his voice was very close.

And was that the warmth of his breath touching her cheek?

Maybe if the Heat didn't kill you, it left you insane. Madness seemed a much more likely explanation than the possibility that this Sayid person might actually be what he was claiming to be.

"Why isn't it safe?" Janna inquired. After all, if everyone in San

Francisco was dead, it wasn't as though she needed to worry about muggers or rapists or roving bands of gangbangers.

He let go of her arms, but she could tell he still stood close to her, ready to reach out and restrain her again if necessary.

"Let us just say that not all djinn are as well-intentioned as I am."

She wasn't sure how to respond to that comment. Apparently nonplussed by her silence, Sayid spoke again.

"You do know what a djinn is, don't you?"

"An entity created by God from a smokeless flame," she replied, parroting one of the texts from the comparative folklore class she'd taken during her sophomore year, figuring the class would be a good respite from all her biology and chemistry and physiology course-work. Never in her life had she imagined it would offer any kind of real-world utility.

"Precisely," Sayid said, now sounding impressed. "This world is ours now."

Janna didn't much like the sound of that. In fact, she frowned as she stared up into the region where she hoped his face was more or less located and replied, "What's that supposed to mean?"

"Humanity is done," he told her, that note of sadness returning to his voice. "This earth belongs to the djinn, since mankind's time is over."

For a few seconds, she stood there motionless, not sure what she should say or do. He'd already proven that he could easily block her movements. And while it might have been more comforting...in a way...to admit the events of the last week truly had driven her insane and she was only experiencing a massive psychotic break, Janna had a feeling it wasn't that easy.

A horrible suspicion began to rise in her mind. There had been murmured speculation among the medical center's doctors—while the place still had doctors, of course—that this disease was far too virulent, far too precise, to be anything that had occurred naturally, that it must have been cooked up in a lab somewhere. She hadn't wanted to acknowledge that possibility, mostly because while she enjoyed reading Stephen King novels, that didn't mean she wanted to be living in one.

But now with Sayid's wild talk of djinn and inheriting the earth....

Voice shaking, she asked, "Did—did you do this to us?"

"I didn't," he said. "But my people did."

It was too much. She bolted to the right, with no thought in her mind other than she needed to get away, get away *now*—but once again, he caught her. Not roughly, just enough to hold her in place, and yet the firmness of that grip and the strength of those fingers told Janna she wasn't going anywhere.

Ragged breaths tore their way out of her throat. "*Why?*"

He was silent for a long moment, strong fingers still wrapped around her biceps. Those fingers felt human enough, but because she couldn't see him, she couldn't know what he truly looked like.

"That," he said, "is a long story. Perhaps you should come with me to the main house so I can attempt to explain things to you. You have had a shock, and should eat something."

Right. When he'd first spoken, he'd said she was in his guest house. She supposed that revelation was some comfort; at least he hadn't put her in his bedroom or something equally creepy. And while she wasn't sure whether sitting down to eat a meal he provided was a very good idea, she also had to admit to herself that she was hungry. For the past few days, she'd been living on vending machine crap, and her body was just as starved for real nutrition as it was for sleep.

Maybe she'd be able to think a bit straighter with some decent food in her.

"Okay," she said, hoping she sounded casual, betraying nothing of the worry and doubt roiling within her. "Lead on."

Sayid watched Janna eat the sandwich of bread and meat he'd provided for her. While he'd visualized their first meeting many times, he'd never imagined that he would have to rescue her from the hallway of the medical center where she'd been forced to work.

No, that wasn't exactly right. Most likely, she could have refused such a call to action, if that had been her wish, but he knew such behavior would have been very unlike her. She had chosen medicine as a vocation because she wanted to help people, not because she thought she would enrich herself with such a career.

Already color had begun to return to her cheeks, and the shadows under her eyes didn't appear as dark as they had been when he first found her at the medical center. Even as weary as she had looked earlier, though, he knew he could have searched the world over and never found a woman as beautiful, no one with eyes as clear and blue, or hair as shimmering gold, or with skin as perfect as a saucer of fresh cream.

Questions crowded those blue eyes now, although she ate quietly, as if she knew it would be better to get some food inside her before she started asking questions. Some of those questions Sayid was prepared to answer. Others....

He had resolved early on to join the One Thousand, the group of djinn who objected to the decision to destroy humanity and who had been given the privilege of selecting a partner from those humans who were immune. And as soon as he had seen Janna's face and learned something of her, he had known she would be his Chosen, the woman who would be at his side for eternity.

At the same time, however, he had made an inner vow. For them to be true partners, he wanted her to come to love him for himself. There were many among the One Thousand who would not scruple to use djinn glamour to ease their partners' transitions into their new lives, to make them believe they were in love with their rescuers. The argument was that doing so would make the situation easier for their Chosen, and perhaps there was some truth to that.

But Sayid did not want Janna to fall in love with an illusion, or even with a handsome visage and nothing else. Her soul was as pure and beautiful as her face, and he wanted to make sure that their love was pure as well, a meeting of minds and hearts, and not one driven only by lusts of the flesh.

And so he kept himself shrouded, invisible. This was a trick most of his kind could manage, even though sustaining such invisibility could become wearisome if he had to maintain it for any great length of time. It would be worth the strain, however, to know that there was no question about Janna's eventual love for him.

In the meantime, though, they had a number of challenges to face.

"This world was ours once, long ago," he said as she paused to sip some of the water he'd provided for her. "It was taken from us and given to humankind, who squandered its gifts. This is the reasoning my people used for creating what became known as the Heat."

Janna set down her glass and regarded him for a moment. Except for a certain tension to the set of her delicate jaw, her face was almost blank, neutral. Was she still trying to process what he had told her, or was she only doing her best to contain the anger that must have flared inside once she learned the truth of humanity's destruction?

"Did you plan on having a certain percentage of people who were immune, or was that just an unfortunate reality?"

Her tone was cool, clipped. He reminded himself that she was a woman of science, one who occupied herself with facts and not fancy. No wonder she had not bothered to waste her energy on any emotional outbursts.

"Since I did not create the disease, I cannot say for sure," he responded. "But once it was known that some humans would survive, there were those among us who stepped forward to ensure their lives would be preserved."

For the first time, the faintest of lines appeared in the smooth skin between her brows as she frowned. The expression smoothed itself away almost immediately, making Sayid wonder if it had merely been a trick of the light.

"'Preserved'?" she repeated. "Wasn't surviving the Heat enough?"

He hesitated. But then he reminded himself that he had sworn to be truthful with her, no matter how difficult doing so might be. The only thing he would not reveal to her was the reason why he hid his face and form.

"One would like to think so," he said carefully. "But there is a bloodthirsty element among my people who have made it their mission to hunt down any immune survivors and dispatch them. That is what I meant when I said it would not be safe for you to leave this place. The djinn reavers are out in the world, and when they find a human...."

The words trailed off there, and Sayid hoped Janna would understand what he was trying to tell her. Since she gave a grim nod, he saw that the meaning of his words had sunk in.

And perhaps he was being just a bit disingenuous, since he had already made his intention of having her as his Chosen known to the universe, and therefore she should have been strictly off-limits to the reavers. The danger existed still, however, mainly because some of those bloodthirsty djinn might have been willing to take the risk of facing the elders' wrath in exchange for ridding the world of yet another hated human.

After a heavy pause, she inquired, "So...why me?"

He understood what she was asking. Her expression was still calm and thoughtful, but he noted the way her strong, slender fingers tapped against the side of her water glass, the too-rigid set of her shoulders. She had asked the question, but she was not entirely sure whether she wanted to hear the answer.

"Because I saw much in you that was of value," he replied, hoping such a response would be enough to satisfy Janna's curiosity without getting too deeply into the precise dynamics of the djinn/Chosen relationship. She was an intelligent woman and would be able to figure it out for herself soon enough, and yet he didn't want to run the risk of frightening her with the prospect of eternity with a stranger at her side.

Not that he planned for them to be strangers for long. They would spend time in one another's company and would become accustomed to each other. He had learned enough about Janna Sayers that he already knew he cared for her, admired her fierce, strong mind and the determination that had allowed the daughter of an almond farmer from California's Central Valley to attend one of the most prestigious schools in the country on a full scholarship. In truth, the only thing he truly feared was that she would find her life with him dull, would not know quite what to do with herself in a world that was vastly changed and had no need of her healing talents.

Time enough to worry about that later, however.

"And all the people who died?" she asked, a sharp note in her voice that hadn't been there a moment earlier. "My parents? My friends? My professors? The guy who made my coffee for me every morning in the place down the street from my apartment? They didn't have any value?"

The pain in those glorious blue eyes made Sayid ache. He wanted to reach out and draw her to him, hold her in a comforting embrace, but he knew this moment was far too early for that.

"I did not say that," he replied quietly. "But if someone is not immune, there is nothing even a djinn can do to save them. As for the rest...." He released a breath, and hoped Janna could not hear his sigh. "The stipulations were clear enough. The people we of the One Thousand chose to save must be no older than twenty-five, and have few connections to the world. It would have been too difficult to rescue someone whose heart was broken by the death of a spouse or a child."

"That's not the only kind of loss that can break someone's heart," Janna countered, arms now crossed as she stared in his direction. Since of course she could not see him, could only guess at his position, her gaze now seemed to be fixed on the magnificent view outside the window in the family room where they now sat.

Or perhaps she truly was looking that way. Sayid thought that such a view could do much to soothe the suffering of an aching heart.

"I know it hurts," he said, still taking care to keep his tone measured. "And I also know there is very little I can do to change that, except to tell you it will get better with time."

No response to those words, except that she lifted her glass of water and took a sip. The fine muscles in her throat moved as she swallowed, and once again he was struck by her beauty, all the more admirable because of the strength at her core, like the steel that held up a fragile-seeming tower of glass.

"I suppose we'll have to see." She broke off a piece of her sandwich and ate it, chewing deliberately as if she knew she needed the sustenance even though she had no true appetite. When she was done, she pushed the plate away and said, "I'm tired. Do you mind if I go back to the guest house and rest?"

"Not at all," Sayid replied. While he wanted to spend as much time in her company as he could, he also knew he needed to give her the space she needed to come to terms with this new life of hers. "I can bring you dinner on a tray, if you like."

He waited then, wondering what she would say in response to his offer, guessing what her answer would be even as he hoped it might be something different.

"A tray would be great," she said, and rose from her seat. "Thanks."

She left then, and he watched her go.

He would not allow himself to be too disappointed.

Janna knew if she let herself analyze the situation too closely, she'd go crazy. It truly was insane to think that humanity had been killed off by a djinn-created virus, but that not all the djinn were evil and in fact wanted to do what they could to save some part of humanity.

Just as Sayid had saved her. In exchange for what?

He hadn't said, but she hadn't fallen off the turnip truck yesterday. She somehow doubted that if she'd been a homely woman in her late sixties, he would have been quite so interested in making sure she was rescued from those supposed "reavers."

In high school, she'd been offended by the people who told her that someone as beautiful as she was didn't need to try so hard to excel in math and science. If she had a dollar for everyone who told her that she should be an actress or a model, not a doctor, she could've funded her medical degree. By the time she got to medical school, pretty much everyone around her was just as focused as she was, and so no one paid a lot of attention to her looks. Still, she thought she had a fairly good idea as to why she was here.

What she was supposed to do about it, she had no idea.

Now that she was alone in the guest house—or at least, guessed she was alone...it was hard to know for sure when you had an invisible host—Janna took closer stock of her surroundings. The property as a whole was pretty overwhelming, a warmly modern house and its guest cottage perched on a hillside lot that had to be at least an acre, all of which offered truly stupendous views of the San Francisco Bay and the Golden Gate Bridge. Back when money had meant something, the place had to have been worth millions. How Sayid had ended up here, she had no idea.

Then again, with more than ninety-nine percent of humanity effectively wiped off the map, that left a lot of prime real estate for the taking.

The guest house had to be roughly three times the size of the cramped apartment she'd shared with her roommate Charlie. The last time she'd seen him was when she made a hurried goodbye as she left for the hospital. He'd been hunched over his laptop, watching the news. Maybe he'd already been feverish at that point, although he hadn't said anything to her.

He probably hadn't wanted to do anything that would prevent her from going in to help at the hospital. Charlie was that sort of person.

When she came back, his laptop still sat on the couch, although the screen had long since gone dark. The only thing left of Charlie, though, had been one of those horrible piles of gray ash.

A shudder went through her at the memory. Forcing the image away, she checked the small, neat galley kitchen, noting that a

Keurig sat on the granite counter and that the pantry seemed to be well-stocked with a variety of K-cups. Had Sayid put them there, or were they relics from the home's previous occupants?

It probably didn't matter. What did matter was that she had a handy supply of caffeine nearby.

Not that she wanted any coffee right now. Despite her nap, exhaustion and a jangly, nervous sort of energy warred within her muscles, and she figured it was probably better to stick with water.

The bathroom was similarly nicely outfitted, with fluffy white towels and an even fluffier bathrobe hanging from the hook on the door. Shampoo and conditioner and soap in the shower, a toothbrush still in its packaging and a tube of toothpaste in one of the drawers. Moisturizers from a brand she'd never been able to afford sat inside the medicine cabinet.

Again, she wondered if Sayid had made sure to stock the place with items she would need, or whether they'd been placed there for guests the home's previous owners had been expecting.

Honestly, she didn't have any idea what sort of powers a djinn might even possess. Enough to make himself invisible…enough to create a disease deadlier than anything the military's mad geniuses had been able to concoct.

Tears burned in her eyes at that thought, but Janna knew that way lay madness. She couldn't allow herself to dwell on that loss. All she could do was try to convince herself that she was safe…for now.

But what would happen after this, she had no idea.

A tray with some truly delicious chicken and rice and vegetables had been waiting for her when she woke up from her second nap of the day. How Sayid had known exactly when she would awake, Janna didn't know. Some kind of djinn sixth sense?

She hadn't heard him come and go. Maybe he hadn't. For all she knew, all he had to do was wiggle his nose and make dinner appear, just like in that old TV show from the '60s.

Because it seemed he was living up to his promise that he wouldn't disturb her, she was able to eat with a healthy enough appetite. The guest cottage had a TV mounted to one wall and a decent selection of DVDs, but she found she didn't want to watch anything. How could she, when the whole time she'd only be reminded of a world that once was and had now disappeared?

The next morning, though, she found herself in somewhat better spirits. Maybe it was simply the effects of a good night's sleep, followed by a reviving cup of coffee and some frozen blueberry waffles, but Janna began to think she might be able to get through this after all, even as she wondered if djinn had to eat and drink the same way humans did. The shower had been glorious, with hot water that never seemed to run out, and so, after she'd gotten dressed—in her own clothes, which had been waiting for her in the closet and the dresser and which Sayid must have transported over here for her—she thought she might be ready to face him again on his home ground, so to speak.

As she paused at the French doors that opened on the patio separating the main house from the guest cottage, though, she wondered if this was such a great idea. For all she knew, he expected her to stay where she was until he specified otherwise.

When she lifted her hand to knock on the door, it opened immediately. No one there, of course; she supposed it had been kind of silly to expect Sayid to make himself visible after he'd spent the previous day hiding from her.

His voice greeted her at once, smooth and rich, like a perfect mocha java with a lot of cream swirled through it. "Good morning, Janna. Did you sleep well?"

"I did," she replied, then added boldly, "What about you?"

"Very well," he said. "I find the sound of the waves soothing."

It had been chilly enough that she'd closed the windows in the guest cottage before she went to sleep, but maybe djinn didn't have to worry about that sort of thing, being made out of flame and all. Even with them shut, however, she'd still been able to pick up the faintest murmur from the bay, only a hundred yards or so down the hill from where she'd lain in bed.

Before she could reply, he went on, "Please come in."

The door opened wider, and Janna assumed Sayid must have stepped out of the way, although of course she couldn't see him. Possibly she detected just the faintest hint of something that smelled like sandalwood as she passed by, but then, she could have been imagining the scent, wanting to believe there had to be something corporeal about him.

But then, of course there was. She'd felt his hands on her arms, knew he was solid and real, even if she couldn't see him.

The day before, they'd sat in the family room on the other side of the house, and so this was the first time Janna had seen the home's living room. It, too, had magnificent views on almost every side, but what caught her attention was the grand piano placed just behind the sectional, positioned so one could play and watch the moving waters of the bay beyond at the same time.

Some sort of sound must have escaped her throat, because Sayid asked, "Do you play?"

"I used to," she replied, even as she wondered whether she should have made that admission. The only time her hands had touched a keyboard during the last six years had been when she'd gone home for the holidays and she'd sat at the family's ancient spinet to play Christmas carols.

"'Used to'?" he echoed. "Why did you stop?"

"School, mostly," she said. "I didn't have the time. And also…."

She let the words trail off, mostly because going into further explanations felt a bit too much like bragging.

Clearly, Sayid didn't intend to let it go, because he prompted, "Also what?"

Janna pressed her lips together. Talking to someone she couldn't see was surreal at best, and off-putting at worst. Up until this point, she'd taken for granted how much she naturally picked up from a person's expression, rather than their words or even their tone of voice.

"I don't know," she said. "Why don't you tell me why you won't let me see you?"

"Because I don't feel it's necessary at the moment," he replied smoothly. "When the time is right, then you will see me."

A time that might never come. On the other hand, he'd given her that one small concession. Whatever his reasons for staying unseen, at least his words seemed to indicate that he'd never intended his invisibility to be a permanent thing.

"About your piano playing?" he asked next.

Well, he was persistent. She had to give him that. Since Janna herself possessed a good deal of that same quality, it wasn't as though she could give him too much grief for not dropping the matter.

"I started lessons when I was six years old," she said. "I took them all the way up to my freshman year of high school, when I was fourteen. That was when my piano teacher told me she couldn't teach me any more, and that I'd need to find a tutor who trained students for more of a concert track. Even then, I knew I wanted to be a doctor, and practicing six hours or more a day just so I might get a chance one day to perform with an orchestra didn't seem like a very good use of my time. So, I…stopped."

A silence. Once again, Janna wished she could see Sayid's expression. Was he impressed? Skeptical?

Amused?

Then he said, "Would you play for me?"

"I'm pretty rusty—" she protested, an understatement if there ever was one. All right, sometimes she would let Charlie cajole her into taking over the keyboard when they were out on one of their rare party nights and the manager of the bar didn't mind an amateur noodling in the background. Still, she'd fallen a long way from her peak.

"I would like to hear you," Sayid cut in. "I am a djinn, not a music critic. My people tend to consume art rather than create it, and so it is always a treat to be able to hear music live."

Any objections she might have made would have sounded churlish, so Janna gave an inner shrug and decided it probably wasn't worth arguing about.

Besides, what else did she have to do with her time?

"Okay," she said, then went over to the instrument and seated herself on the bench. The piano was a shiny black Steinway, much more intimidating than the spinet at her parents' home in Turlock. Still, she'd played on a similar instrument while performing at recitals, so she wasn't quite as intimidated as she might otherwise have been.

For a moment, she sat there, gathering herself. Her years of practice had engraved a number of pieces on her memory, and she wasn't quite sure where to start. A lively Mozart sonata? A precise Bach variation? A flashy étude by Chopin?

She thought of the soft sound of the waves in the bay, the sense of tranquility that lay over Sayid's house, even in the midst of so much death. Yes, it was a bright morning outside, the sun glittering on the water rather than shrouded in fog as it was so much of the time in the Bay Area, and yet Janna still couldn't think of a better choice.

Her hands paused for a second or two, suspended above the keyboard, and then she began to play the soft, murmuring opening notes of Beethoven's "Moonlight Sonata."

Not a sound from Sayid. Somehow, she could sense he was still there, listening, but she didn't hear a breath, or even that soft, whispery sound that she thought might be some kind of silk clothing. The notes moved out from the piano's sounding board, rich and full, perfectly in tune. Whether they'd had this magnificent instrument merely for show or because someone actually did play it, the previous owners had obviously made sure to keep it maintained.

When she was done, and the last sonorous chord had drifted off into silence, she put her hands in her lap and waited.

He didn't clap. Instead, she got a sense of him moving closer to the piano, then pausing. "That was beautiful," he said. "Beethoven?"

Janna nodded, vaguely surprised he'd recognized the piece. After all, how could a djinn know anything about human music?

But he spoke English and seemed to have some passing famil-
iarity with the human world, and so she supposed it wasn't so
strange that he might have some knowledge of music and the arts.

"It is too bad you gave it up," he went on. "I hope you will allow
yourself to play now, since there is no need for you to continue your
studies."

His tone was matter-of-fact, but Janna couldn't help wincing.
The thought of never being able to complete her medical degree, of
never putting all her hard-earned knowledge to use in saving lives,
hurt. It hurt a lot.

Her hands curled into fists, although since they were partially
obscured by the piano keyboard, she didn't know whether Sayid
could see them. "There are still survivors," she said. "I could help
them. Just because people are immune doesn't mean they won't
break a bone or have high blood pressure or whatever."

Once again, she got the sense of him moving closer to her,
although he stopped far enough away that she couldn't get a clear
idea of where he stood. "To do that, you would have to go out into
the world," he replied. "And I've already told you it isn't safe. Besides
—"

He stopped there, and Janna tilted her head in what she hoped
was his general direction. "'Besides' what?"

"There are very few survivors," Sayid said. "And fewer by the day.
You would not have anyone to help. You need to understand that
this is the beginning of a new life for you."

"A new life here," she said, her tone flat. "With you."

"Yes. I know this is all strange and will take some time to get
used to. But," he continued, and now his voice sounded almost wry,
"one can assume there are worse fates than living in a house with a
bay view and having all your needs met."

Janna lifted an eyebrow. "'All'?" she repeated.

"Yes. You have only to ask, and your wish will be granted."

Everything except a wish for her freedom. However, she didn't
bother to point that out, since she guessed that Sayid knew that as
well as she did.

"I want my laptop," she said. "My whole life was on there."

Well, and on her phone, but the iPhone's usefulness had been cut drastically once all the cell networks collapsed. She'd taken it from her purse and plugged it in to recharge it out of habit, although she couldn't think of why she might need it now.

No reply, not even a snap of his fingers. But in the next moment, her MacBook Air appeared on the piano bench next to her. Janna startled, then reached for it and opened the lid, thinking that maybe this was *a* MacBook Air, but it wasn't *her* laptop.

However, her password worked, and she was greeted with the reassuring sight of the photo she'd taken of Half Dome in Yosemite while camping with her parents a few years back as her desktop image. She couldn't begin to explain how Sayid had gotten it here, but she couldn't argue that this was definitely her laptop.

"Thank you," she said, since she really didn't know what else to say. Honestly, even though she was doing her best to come to terms with who and what Sayid was, such a casual demonstration of his powers had sent her reeling just a bit. Her entire being had been focused on science and facts for the past ten years, and seeing such a casual denial of the laws of physics made her wonder what else she might have gotten wrong.

"You're welcome," he replied politely. "Is there anything else?"

"No," Janna said. She closed the laptop and set it back down on the bench. Later, she would take it back to the guest house and indulge herself by looking at every unread email, every photo, every piece of a life that was now gone.

In the meantime, though, she might as well take advantage of this opportunity Sayid had given her.

"Would you like some Mozart?" she asked.

Janna seemed to be adapting well. Yes, Sayid could sense the sadness within her—a sadness she wouldn't allow herself to indulge, as if she feared that shedding one tear would lead to a deluge that might drown her—but she came and sat down to dinner with him that first night, and didn't appear terribly discomfited by watching the food he ate disappear into his mouth and become as invisible as the rest of him. And the next morning she appeared on his doorstep, bright hair loose on her shoulders and smelling faintly of the floral-scented shampoo he'd provided for her, obviously prepared to share her morning meal with him as well.

This pleased Sayid. Yes, there still existed far too many topics they needed to sidestep for the moment, but he told her more of his people, of how this world had once been theirs but taken away and given to humankind. Millennia of bitter resentment of their treatment had led to the creation of the disease that swept across the world, but he reassured her that she would come to no harm as long as she remained here with him.

"In fact," he added as they sat at dinner three days after he'd brought Janna to stay with him, "it is safe for you to go down into Tiburon if you feel you need a change of scenery. There are some quaint shops you might want to visit. Obviously, you can take whatever you need, as there is no one else who can lay claim to the merchandise in those stores."

She nodded, although she didn't look quite as enthused as he'd thought she might be. Then again, if her meager wardrobe was any indication, it didn't appear that she had been much of a shopper.

But she went exploring the next day anyhow, with Sayid maintaining watch from a safe distance away. All of Tiburon and Belvedere were the territory of the new djinn and Chosen community that would be established here, although he had yet to meet any of his fellow elementals. Most likely, they were doing the same thing as he—staying close to home as their Chosen adapted to their new lives. Community would come later.

Despite her apparent lack of enthusiasm about shopping, Janna nevertheless returned from her expedition with an armful of clothing and shoes. It seemed to Sayid that even she had realized her current wardrobe of jeans and T-shirts and fleece pullovers didn't quite suit the home she now inhabited. And he had to admit it pleased him to see her in pretty blouses and even the occasional dress. Her beauty would shine no matter what she wore, but now this jewel had a more appropriate setting.

She played the piano a great deal, which also pleased him. Why someone with her enormous talent would have given up the instrument to pursue medicine, he didn't quite know. While he had done his best to learn what he could about her so they would not be such strangers when she came to live with him, he hadn't known she was so musically gifted. She had abandoned the piano ten years earlier, and therefore it had no place in the life he'd studied.

But she returned to it now, as if she needed some sort of focus to keep her occupied. Sayid didn't find this so odd, considering how much time and energy she'd devoted to her medical studies. And when she encountered him trimming the trees and pruning the dead flowers from the potted plants on the patio, she'd stopped, startled by the sight of the pruning shears apparently floating by themselves in midair.

"Can't you just wave a hand and have all the trees be instantly trimmed?" she asked. By that point, she'd gotten quite good at gauging where he stood in relation to her, and so she gazed up at him as if she could actually see his face.

"I could," he replied, then moved on to the next branch of the bay laurel he was trimming. "But I am an earth elemental, and so I enjoy this sort of work. We have always cared about plants and trees, although there was little we could do with them during our exile in the otherworld."

Janna nodded. He'd explained to her how the djinn had been banished to a plane that was toxic to humans, with foul air and landscapes of barren rock, and so she absorbed his comment without question.

"There is something to be said for getting your hands dirty," she responded. "Can I help?"

The request warmed him, and he handed her a pair of pruning shears. Since she had grown up on an almond farm, he guessed that she knew quite a bit about plants and trees as well.

From then on, they spent a good deal of time together working on the garden, and also tending to the plants that grew in pots inside the house. Sayid cherished this time together, because he could tell that she was growing more comfortable in his company. While she still spent parts of her day alone in the guest cottage, she was with him more often than not, and he had to be satisfied with that.

Indeed, he began to wonder whether it was time to reveal himself to her. She had been living with him for the greater part of a week, and clearly had become accustomed to sharing his company. At dinner, their conversations were often lively, and they tended to linger there even after the meal was done and the bottle of wine finished. Surely that should be a sign that she had accepted him, even though she had never seen his face.

He couldn't quite bring himself to do such a thing, however. No, he had no reason to be ashamed of his face and form, and yet he also thought he should not rush matters. It had only been a week, after all; better to wait until a few more days had passed. More of his kind had come to this charming town on the bay, and so he knew the current situation couldn't continue indefinitely, but a bit more time could only cement the growing bond between them.

Yes, waiting a little longer seemed like a very good idea.

Janna lay in bed and stared at the ceiling. A bright moon shone down on the house, piercing the filmy curtains at the windows, although she didn't think that was the real reason why she couldn't sleep.

No, it was just the same question that had been hammering her mind for the past week.

Why wouldn't Sayid let her see his face?

Was he so hideous that he feared she'd shun him if she knew what he really looked like? She supposed that theory was plausible enough—the texts they'd used in her comparative folklore class had said that djinn often took on animal forms. Maybe he was like the minotaur or something, with the head of a bull and the body of a man.

That theory didn't feel right, though. His voice sounded as if it came from a human throat, and she'd never gotten a sense he occupied a space that was anything but man-shaped. No, there had to be something else going on here.

She just didn't know what.

Janna also couldn't say exactly why it was so important for her to see his face. Actually, scratch that. She knew damn well, even if she didn't want to admit it to herself. Although the ache of loss she carried inside her showed no sign of going away any time soon, she also realized that the week she'd spent here had been healing in a way she wouldn't have believed if she hadn't experienced it for herself. Playing the piano…taking walks on the gorgeous curved path that bordered the bay…working in the yard with Sayid…all of those pastimes had allowed her to take a breath, to understand that she could heal from this, if she allowed herself to.

And a big part of that healing was, paradoxically, the djinn who was her host. It had been easier than she thought to spend these days with him, to sit down at dinner and share a meal, to talk about all sorts of topics, from what they should have for breakfast the next day to reminiscences about growing up on her parents' almond farm. Those memories weren't as painful as she feared, but instead helped her to move on. By sharing that part of her past with Sayid, she allowed her parents to have a life beyond her own recollections.

She wouldn't be where she was, emotionally and psychologically, if it weren't for him. Now the thought of having some sort of shared future with Sayid didn't frighten her, but instead filled her with a sort of nervous anticipation.

Except that she still didn't know what he looked like. She'd tried to ask him to show himself, but he'd always managed to steer the conversation in a different direction.

Clearly, she would have to take matters into her own hands.

Was he as wakeful as she this night, or was he sleeping, over there in the big house only a few yards away from where she was curled up in her own bed? Janna assumed he must sleep; he seemed to eat and drink like a normal human, and so she guessed his other biological processes probably weren't all that different. She could slip over there and....

You're crazy, she told herself. *Go back to sleep.*

But the thought had taken hold and wouldn't let her alone. Really, it was silly for him to keep hiding, all for no apparent reason she could determine. If it turned out he was hideous, well, she'd deal with that unpleasant reality when the time came. Wasn't it what was inside a person that really mattered?

Without stopping to think, she pushed herself out of bed. Since she already wore one of her old T-shirts as a sleep shirt, it was easy enough to slip on a pair of jeans and slide her feet into a pair of flats, then add a sweater to prepare herself for the short trek to the main house. She knew Sayid didn't lock the doors. What would be the point? For all she knew, the two of them were the only people in a hundred-mile radius.

She let herself out into the damp, chilly night. The scent of salt was strong on the air, carried by the perpetual sea breeze. She placed her hand on the door handle and slipped inside.

None of the lamps were on, of course, but all those uncovered windows let in plenty of moonlight. Although she'd never been upstairs, she knew that was where all the bedrooms in the main house were located.

Now she had to hope that none of the stairs creaked.

She inched her way up, step by step. No squeaks, no creaks, nothing to let Sayid know she was creeping her way to the room where he slept.

A pause in the upstairs hall as she stopped to take her bearings. Part of her brain was shouting at her to turn around and go back, but she told herself she'd come this far and it would be stupid to stop now.

The doorway opposite where Janna stood opened on a smallish room furnished with a desk and a small bookcase. Obviously not the master bedroom.

Following a hunch, she made her way down to the room at the end of the hall. The door stood open, and moonlight flooded in through a sliding door that opened on a private deck. The pale light clearly illuminated the room, which had a set of windows flanking a built-in bookcase, and a large bed with light-colored covers set up against one wall.

A man slept on that bed.

At least, he looked like a man. His face was in profile to her, but Janna could see the cleanly etched, elegant outlines of his nose and jaw, the close-cut beard, the heavy dark hair stark against a white pillowcase. Moonlight slipped over the well-defined muscles of his arms and chest.

He was…well, he was probably the best-looking man Janna had ever seen.

A startled sound slipped from her throat. Almost at once, Sayid sat up in bed, turning so his gaze met hers. Those eyes were dark, piercing even in the moonlit room.

"Janna!" he exclaimed, voice rough with sleep…and probably with anger. "What are you doing here?"

"I—" She swallowed a breath and forced herself to go on, even though she would have liked nothing more than to turn away from the fury in his eyes. "I wanted…no, I *needed* to see you."

"And now that your curiosity is satisfied?" he returned, a scowl twisting his dark brows.

He had been so mild, so kind and patient, up until this moment, that there was something especially off-putting about his anger now.

Especially since he was a djinn, and she still didn't know for sure all that he was capable of.

"I wanted to know why you were hiding from me," Janna said. "There didn't seem to be any reason for it. And now it seems especially pointless. You don't need to hide, not when you look like that."

She supposed she'd hoped that making such a statement might have mollified him, at least a little. Unfortunately, her words only seemed to anger him further.

"That is precisely what I was trying to avoid," he retorted, that same frown digging into the smooth brown skin of his brow. His fingers knotted in the duvet cover as he pulled in a breath. "But we can speak about this tomorrow. I think it's best if you go back to bed now."

Janna didn't think it was best at all. However, she could tell from the expression on Sayid's face that he was in no mood to further the discussion. And, to be fair, she was the one trespassing here.

"Fine," she said. "We can talk in the morning."

Without waiting for a reply, she turned and headed out to the hall, then back down the stairs. With each step, her own irritation increased. What was the big deal, anyway? He was acting as though she'd done him a terrible wrong, and all she'd done was gotten a good look at his face—a face that wouldn't have looked out of place on the poster for a Bollywood musical.

He really was gorgeous.

Luckily, she'd never been the type to allow herself to be distracted by a person's looks. What was in their heart and their mind was far more important.

Unfortunately, she couldn't begin to guess what might actually be going on in Sayid's head.

And just who the hell was he to tell her what she could and couldn't do?

A member of a race who's managed to wipe out most of humanity, her mind replied, but she brushed that aside. If he'd wanted to hurt her, he'd had plenty of time. No, it seemed much more likely that this was all about control and nothing else.

Well, he was about to find out real soon how Janna Sayers felt about being controlled.

She didn't have any luggage, but that didn't matter. One of the purses she'd "liberated" from a shop on Tiburon's main street was big enough that she could stuff an extra pair of jeans and a few tops into it, along with her laptop. Toiletries she wouldn't worry about, since the plan she was rapidly formulating in her head called for her to stop by her apartment and get anything else she needed before she headed out of town.

A faint thrill of worry went through her. Sayid had told her it was dangerous for her to be alone, that rogue djinn were out hunting any random survivors. Then again, that was a pretty convenient story if his main goal was to keep her here with him. What if there weren't any reavers? What if she'd be perfectly safe?

The more she thought about it, the more plausible such a scenario seemed to her. Keep her scared, keep her thinking that only he could protect her from the big, bad reavers. That was just the sort of story a gas-lighting jerk like him would want her to believe.

She slipped the purse over her shoulder and stepped outside. Once again, the cool night breeze caressed her cheek, but she ignored it, only pausing for a moment to make sure the main house remained quiet and dark, with no sign of its occupant stirring. It definitely looked to her as though he'd gone back to sleep.

Good. During their walks, she'd spied plenty of abandoned cars. What would happen to them eventually, she had no idea—probably, they'd rust where they sat—but she figured it wouldn't be too hard to find one that still had its key fob somewhere in it. All those cars had been idle for only a week, so she doubted she had to worry about any of their batteries being dead.

Two doors down from the home Sayid had taken for his own was a large, modern house, all plate glass and dark wood. Sitting in the driveway was a dusty Mercedes SUV.

Janna went up to it and peered inside, thankful for the bright moonlight. A little shudder went over her as she realized the black leather driver's seat had a pile of that ominous gray dust resting in the middle of it, but horror gave way almost immediately to relief as she saw that a black and silver key fob lay on top of the dust.

Gritting her teeth, she opened the door and reached for the fob. A few brushes with her hand, and the dust was dispersed to float on the night air.

"Sorry," she murmured to the universe, and to the former owner of the SUV in particular. It felt horribly disrespectful, but she really needed to get out of there.

The engine started up right away, and the electronic gauges on the dash told her the gas tank was nearly full. Good. She'd have to fill up along the way, but she should still be able to get pretty far before she had to stop for gas.

Because she'd realized that the only place she wanted to go was home. Yes, she knew she'd probably be greeted by a few more of those awful piles of dust, but she could gather it up and bury it in the yard, maybe under the big willow tree her mother had loved so much. And Turlock was such an out-of-the-way place, Janna had to think she'd be able to hide from the djinn reavers there.

If they even existed at all.

She eased the Mercedes out of the driveway and drove slowly down the street, headlights off. With the moon so bright, she really didn't need them, and she figured it was safer that way.

The entire trip to her apartment continued at that same snail's pace, since the roads were so littered with abandoned vehicles that she basically had to inch her way along, squeezing between trucks and SUVs and semis as she laboriously made her way across the Golden Gate Bridge and into her neighborhood on the border of Chinatown.

In fact, it got so bad there that the streets became impassable, at least in the big Mercedes SUV she was driving. With a pang of regret—it was definitely the nicest vehicle she'd ever driven—she got out and continued on foot, figuring she could just get another car after she was done fetching the few items she needed from her apartment.

By the time she reached the building, the sun was just beginning to ease itself up over the eastern horizon. Janna looked at it and shook her head. Crazy to think that a trip of some fifteen miles could take so many hours. She might have done better on foot.

Well, it didn't matter now. She climbed the stairs to her second-floor apartment, then got out her keys. Thank God Sayid had fetched her purse for her along with all those other items of clothing, since at least she didn't have to worry about getting in without a key.

The apartment smelled stale, and the collection of thrift store furniture looked even shabbier after spending a week in Sayid's quietly luxurious house in Tiburon. Janna did her best to ignore the contrast and went into the bathroom to get her toothbrush and toothpaste and a few other toiletries, then paused in the bedroom so she could pick up the framed photo on the nightstand of her and her parents at her graduation from UCSF. The Janna in that photo looked bright and confident, as if she knew she could take on anything the future had to throw at her.

Well, anything except a bunch of genocidal djinn and a devastating plague, she thought, then resolutely stuffed the photo into her bulging purse. A quick stop in the kitchen to grab a couple of Kind bars from the pantry—she figured those would keep her going on the trip to Turlock—and then it was time to leave. She didn't experience any kind of particular pang as she closed the door behind her; the apartment had basically been a place to crash, a temporary refuge. It had never felt like home.

Unlike Sayid's home by the bay.

It wasn't home, either, she told herself. *It just felt that way.*

Her inner voice didn't sound terribly convinced, however.

She set her jaw and continued down the steps, then emerged on the street. Parked just slightly down from her apartment building was a big Ford pickup so new, it still had the paper plates from the dealer.

Perfect. She could definitely use a truck where she was headed.

Praying she'd find the Ford's key fob in the cab, she began to hurry toward the vehicle. She'd only gone a couple of paces before a tall shape came sailing down from the sky, dark robes fluttering around him.

An unfamiliar djinn came to rest right in front of Janna, blocking her way. He shot her an unpleasant smile, then said, "Going somewhere, human?"

Sayid blinked awake and pushed himself up on his elbows. Although he'd had a difficult time composing himself after that confrontation with Janna, he'd managed to fall asleep again after a while, albeit a sleep that was uneasy, plagued by nightmares. And as soon as he focused on his bedroom and the bright sunlight beaming in through the windows, he knew immediately that something was terribly wrong.

Janna was gone. A djinn could sense his Chosen, and so he should have been able to detect the warm glow of her life force in the guest house just across the patio. But that bright beacon was gone.

Cursing under his breath, he snapped his fingers and summoned his garments to him. Once dressed, he went out onto the balcony—not to enjoy the crisp, beautiful morning around him, but to send those same senses questing forth, trying to determine where she had gone. If she'd somehow managed to leave the city altogether, he would have a more difficult time finding her, but....

No, there she was, like a bright spark in all those canyons of steel and brick. She had gone back to her apartment.

He would ask her why later. For now, he cared only about getting to her as quickly as he could, before the reavers found her.

A blink brought him to the crowded street of mixed apartment buildings and shops and restaurants where she'd once lived. And yes, there she was...but she was not alone.

Sayid didn't recognize the djinn who confronted her, a gloating smile on his dark features. Not that it mattered. What mattered was that the reaver had no right to take her life.

"Stop!" he thundered, and the strange djinn turned toward him, even as the fear on Janna's features began to transform into shock... and relief. "This woman is my Chosen!"

The other djinn didn't look terribly impressed. "If she is your Chosen, then what is she doing wandering the streets of this city alone?"

"That is none of your concern," Sayid returned. "What matters is that you will certainly bring down the wrath of the elders if you harm the merest hair on her head. Go, and find your sport elsewhere."

The strange djinn crossed his arms. "It is not 'sport,'" he sneered. "It is a necessity to cleanse this world of its human plague."

"Call it what you want," Sayid said. "But you have no business here."

And he sent the faintest tremor through the ground beneath their feet, a warning that he would not stand idly by and allow any harm to come to the woman he loved. This was a calculated risk, for there was no guarantee that the other djinn might not summon his own elemental power—whatever it may be—in retaliation.

But apparently he thought better of it, as he gave a negligent shrug and said, "Perhaps not. But you should put a leash on your little pet, lest she get herself into more trouble."

She bristled, but the djinn disappeared after delivering that remark, leaving Sayid and Janna alone on the street.

His gaze met hers. She appeared still defiant, but also somehow chastened, as if she knew she had made a mistake.

"You are all right?" he asked, trying to keep his tone neutral.

"Yes," she replied. "He showed up only a minute before you did." A pause, and then she asked, "How did you know where to find me?"

"I always know where you are," he said simply. "That is part of the bond that ties us together."

"I see," she said. Her clear blue eyes met his, and she added, "I think we need to talk."

The djinn method of traveling was definitely faster than driving. Sayid held out his arms to her, and she went to him, not sure what to do about being so close.

As soon as his arms tightened around her, though, a delicious thrill went through her body. Oddly, it felt right to be held like this, even though that second or two of swirling darkness as they traveled from Chinatown to his home in Tiburon was disconcerting, to say the least.

But he let go of her quickly, shimmering burgundy silk robes fluttering as he went to open the door to the deck. "We can talk out here."

Yes, it did seem like a good idea to sit out in the sun and let the fresh ocean breeze wash away the dregs of fear from her encounter with the reaver djinn. Janna nodded and went outside, taking a seat at the patio table there. Sayid followed, and as soon as he sat down, two large cups of cappuccino appeared on the tabletop.

Much, much better.

She wrapped her hands around the mug and lifted it to take a sip. After she'd swallowed a mouthful of cappuccino, she said, "I'm sorry."

"No, I am the one who should apologize," he replied. Dark eyes met hers, fringed with some of the most amazing lashes she'd ever seen. Once again, one of those little thrills went through her. Had he hidden himself because he'd known what kind of an effect he'd have on her?

"I don't know—"

"I do," he cut in, but gently. "I had thought only to ease you into this life, to allow you to get to know me for who I am. I did not realize that not being able to see me would cause you so much turmoil."

Janna wished she could protest that statement, but since it was true enough, about all she could do was give a helpless lift of her shoulders. "And I should have said something earlier, rather than let myself stew over it. It was stupid to run off like that. If I'd known how dangerous it could be—"

"I told you about the reavers," he said simply, with no accusation in his tone.

"I know you did. I just didn't know whether I believed you, not when you'd purposely hidden yourself from me. It made me think there were a whole lot of things you weren't being truthful about."

His mouth tightened, but he only reached over and laid his hand on top of hers. It was a very human-looking hand, browned and strong, with a heavy gold ring set with a smooth wine-colored garnet on his middle finger.

"I'm sorry," he said. "Can you forgive me?"

Janna gazed at him, taking in every detail, from the finely drawn brows to the way his dark hair waved back from his forehead to the close-cut beard that couldn't obscure the chiseled lines of his jaw. It should have been a stranger's face, but she knew that voice, knew its warmth—a warmth echoed in the eyes that now watched her closely.

"I forgive you," she replied. "As long as you forgive me."

His fingers closed on hers as he stood. She rose as well, and in the next moment, he was pulling her close, his mouth warm and welcome and tasting of delicious cappuccino froth. Heat flushed through her, telling her that her body didn't care if he was a djinn—she only knew he aroused her in a way no man ever had.

When he spoke, his voice was husky with desire. "There is nothing to forgive, beloved," he said. "Only promise that you will never leave me again."

Janna hesitated…but only for a second. Deep in her soul, she knew this was where she was meant to be, who she was meant to be with. She still had so much to learn about this strange new world she found herself in, but she also knew she couldn't ask for a better companion in that world than the man who held her now. The wish of her heart—that she might one day find someone who would love her for who she was, all her stubbornness and grit and drive—had been answered. She never could have imagined standing here in this bright sunlight place, never could have imagined the world she now found herself in. But she wouldn't have to face that world alone. This man, this djinn had chosen her above all others. His love would help her to heal.

"I promise, Sayid," she whispered, hoping he could hear the sincerity in her voice. "I want to be with you…always."

He bent and kissed her again, and she pressed herself against him, let herself finally be lost in his embrace.

Her mind now knew what her soul had already accepted.

She had come home.

THE END

AUTHOR'S NOTE

"Unseen" is set in the world of my Djinn Wars series and can serve as a prequel of sorts, as it takes place at about the same time as the first book in that series. The inspiration is the myth of Cupid and Psyche, although I stripped the story to its bare bones—no vengeful goddess mother-in-law here—and instead focused on the relationship between the two protagonists and a love that developed despite...or possibly because of...the way the hero has hidden himself from the heroine.

ABOUT THE AUTHOR

USA Today bestseller Christine Pope is the author of the Witches of Cleopatra Hill, Djinn Wars, Project Demon Hunters, and Hedge-witch for Hire series, along with many other books (eighty and counting!). A California transplant, she now makes her home in New Mexico with her husband and the world's fluffiest dog. Find out more about her books at christinepope.com.

FIRST SNOW

ALEXIA PURDY

There's powerful magic in a name, like a wish.
Especially when there is no other magic to be found.

SEVEN JET BLACK RAVENS LANDED ON THE ICY BRANCHES, disturbing the quiet of this wondrous other world with their flapping wings. Snow crystals lined my eyelashes as I peered into the tree line. The tapping of snowflakes against the ground was the only sound in the vastness of the forest. My cheeks stung from my tears freezing in the cold air. Puffs of steam spilled from my mouth as I spun in the middle of the clearing, my heart frantically beating in my head.

I closed my eyes and inhaled a sharp, freezing breath. The weight of the world held me down, but there was nowhere to go. It was my own fault. I could have been back at the camp lodge sipping hot chocolate and warming by the fireplace. Instead, I was lost in the middle of the endless wilderness without a clue about how to get back. If only I hadn't come, but it was the only place left to look.

I needed to find my brothers. My heart called to them through the frost.

As the snow fell harder, it covered my footprints faster than I could backtrack. Before long, there was nothing to mark where I had come from, and I pondered staying put to await rescue. Sitting still was far worse than moving around to stay warm, and I had no patience to wait for death. Plus, no one was looking for me. I was the one searching.

I shivered. My fingers ached from the cold, stiff and numb inside my gloves. *I'm lost*, I thought. *I'll die out here.*

"You're far from home, human," a voice said from behind, startling me.

I jerked around and came face to face with an unusual stranger. He was a man, but he wasn't just any normal man. There was no way he could have ever been human. My blood ran cold as I stared into pearly-white eyes, gleaming with a swirl of colors as he blinked, intensely focused on me. His stark, white hair was long, tied back away from his face, with a single, thick lock of black hair. Several strands lifted in the wind.

"Who are you?" I demanded, my eyes widening in horror. I'd never seen anyone who looked like him. No one had ever *felt* the same way either. I couldn't explain it, but something swirled around us, moving the snowflakes up into the air and dropping them back down outside the constraints of its power. Whatever it was, it reached out from him, like invisible fingers, caressing my skin and examining every inch of me, even winding their way into my head and sifting through my thoughts. It was an intimate violation without a single touch.

I froze, too petrified to move. I wasn't even sure I was breathing anymore. Time stood still as he stared at me. Was I imagining him, a vivid hallucination due to hypothermia setting in? Was he a devil? I couldn't tell. His skin was as porcelain white as the snow surrounding us, with just a hint of pink to his lips. His breath made no steam in the frigid air as he breathed, which made me wonder if he even had a heartbeat beneath his pale exterior.

His dark outfit was made of black material, maybe leather, but I'd never seen clothes like his on anyone. It clung to his body as though painted on, tightened by leather straps and ties. A pair of gloves matched his outfit perfectly. I heard a whinny and snort behind him and found a horse as dark as a moonless night eyeing me with unnatural red eyes. Its breath steamed as though he breathed fire, smoky and black with soot. It shook its head, rippling its shimmering hide, which looked like it was made of iridescent dragon scales.

The man is death himself riding on his hell horse to claim my soul, I told myself. This was the end of me for certain.

"I am Corb, the ruler of the Winter Realm and the Great Divide."

"What do you mean?" I stammered, shaking with fear. My voice trembled as my lungs filled with cold air, and I shivered madly. "I-I need to go home. Do you know how I can find a way back to the campgrounds?"

He cocked his head to the side as he watched me shiver. How was he not cold? The fur-lined cape he wore looked warm, but it blew in the wind as the storm grew stronger. He didn't seem to care or feel any of the chill. I would have given anything for something more to wrap around me or a crackling fire to warm my soul. I encircled my arms around my body and tucked in my chin.

So cold.

"You're not made for this weather. Death awaits you," he said.

"You're not kidding," I muttered, feeling my throat seize. Cold penetrated my eyes until my tears were no longer warming them but froze on my lashes in crystals. I closed them, afraid they'd freeze into icy globes. The snow fell harder now, almost making the strange man nearly disappear into it. My body stopped shivering as a warmth as sweet as heated syrup replaced the cold.

This is it, I thought. *I'm freezing to death with some strange apparition watching me die.*

The man, Corb, was suddenly in front of me as my legs gave out, unable to hold my weight any longer. He swept his fur cape around me, wrapping me in its warmth. How could a person who looked like death personified have any warmth to spare in his body? My thoughts hung in suspense as my mind shut down, and I barely noticed him carrying me to the demon horse and somehow jumping onto it while holding me to his chest. The rhythm of the horse trotting away into the fierce storm lulled me to sleep.

I blinked, the brightness of light stinging my eyes, and I reached up to shade them. Where was I? I looked around and attempted to sit up. Ice cracked and popped around me as I straightened, finding myself in a massive room made completely of ice.

"What is this?" I asked myself, mystified. Everything—chairs, tables, and decorations—was intricately carved of ice. I shook my head as I squeezed the edge of the blanket covering me. It was Corb's cloak, but it was warm and moved like water over me. I couldn't see how it was possible.

I flung it off. My clothes, jacket, and boots were still on me. Wiggling my toes, I wondered if they'd frozen solid. Surprisingly, they moved easily and didn't hurt. Neither did my fingers, which felt fine. I flexed them then crossed my arms, expecting to freeze, but felt no cold at all. Was I dead? Lifting my hands, I looked at my palms and arms. They were a pale color, almost bluish-white. I glanced around the room for a mirror and found one hanging on a wall near me, above a table carved from the ice. I hurried to it and studied my reflection, sucking in a sharp breath at what I found.

I didn't recognize myself. My hair was long and brown, but ice streaked the strands, making it look like it had been turned to glass. My eyes were rimmed with tiny crystals flashing in the light. I touched the icy blue skin on my face, appalled at what I'd found. I looked dead except for the fact that my lips were a dusty pink.

"I'm dreaming," I concluded. "Wake up. Wake up." I patted my cheeks harder, hoping to break the dream. Or nightmare. Whatever it was, I didn't want to be in it anymore.

"You're awake. Good. Please join me for dinner."

I spun around in shock, backing away until I nearly tripped on a bench seat. This entire place felt unreal. But it also felt very real. As real as the man standing in front of me.

He held out a dress made of ice crystals so dense that they shone an eerie deep blue color. They chimed softly as they tapped against each other, and I froze, stunned by its beauty.

"You want me to wear that?" I asked.

"Yes."

I took the dress from him and held it out at arm's length, still awestruck at the gown. "How was it made?"

"It's made of ice. My power siphons from the cold. It bends to my will."

I was still mesmerized by the dress but glanced up. He was studying me with hard, sharp eyes.

"Um, where can I change?" I asked, afraid that denying this creature such a simple request would set him off.

"No need," Corb said and snapped his fingers. The sound cracked through the room like thunder, and I sucked in a breath. I looked down, feeling a different weight on my body, and found the dress clinging to my skin as though it'd always been made just for me. My feet were bare. I took a tentative step, feeling nothing of the cold, frigid ice beneath me.

"How did you do that?" I asked.

"Magic, of course. Now let's have dinner, shall we? You must be famished." Corb smiled, offering me his hand.

I swallowed my apprehension and glanced around. There was nowhere to go except to dinner. Maybe then I could ask Corb to take me home. Reluctantly, I took his hand.

He led me to a table I could have sworn hadn't been there before. It was long and covered with a feast that could feed hundreds. He let go and pulled out a chair, motioning for me to sit. I did so and watched him take a seat at the head of the table.

I needed to find my brothers, or all would be for nothing. It was the only thing I wished for. Maybe Corb could help me find them. If he could make a dress and palace from ice, he might be able to conjure a miracle. If this place was preternatural, what sort of fate awaited me here?

Then, a horrid thought crossed my mind. Did he have my

brothers? What if they were trapped here? Wherever they'd gone, it had been deep into the forest I'd entered earlier. If this was where they'd ended up, trapped, I would find out soon enough.

I looked around the room again. The walls were also sculpted of ice, designed with intricate swirls and patterns I couldn't discern. The lack of cold on the pads of my feet confused me and didn't make sense to my brain. I kept my feet tucked up onto the brace of the chair even though it too was made of ice. The dress touched the tops of my feet with crystal beads tapping against each other, chiming softly. For a few moments, it was the only sound in the desolate ice palace.

A crack and pop boomed above me, and my arms went flying to cover my head. I expected to be crushed by a massive chunk of ice, but nothing happened. My breath turned ragged as I squeezed my eyes shut, my stomach knotting up. When nothing else happened, I gathered the strength to open my eyes and look around.

There were no cracks, nor were there any signs of collapse in the roof above me. I let out the breath I had been holding, my heart still fluttering in fear. The smell of food made my stomach roll until it realized I hadn't eaten a meal for a good long while. How long had it been? How long had I slept, near death from the icy weather outside? I couldn't know, but maybe it'd been too long.

"You may eat what you like." Corb waved his hand toward the massive feast, seemingly untempted by the mounds of food.

I gazed at the empty plate before me and wondered if the tales of the fae were true. He had to be one of them. A faery. I'd heard of those who lingered in the forest and preyed on humans and stole children from their cradles. Could he be one of those? I couldn't imagine him being friendly even though he had saved my life. Or imprisoned me. I still wasn't sure. But I'd heard a legend that if you ate food offered to you from a fae creature, you would belong to them for all eternity.

My eyes hovered over the delectable spread, my mouth watering at the sights and smells. I struggled to hold my hands back. I couldn't lose my freedom to this ice king.

"Are you not hungry?" Corb asked, leaning forward and narrowing his mother-of-pearl eyes.

"Yes, but…." I hesitated. How did I do this and not insult him? Insulting a fae could be a lethal gamble. "It's just… I heard stories."

"Stories?" he asked abruptly. "Indulge me."

"Um, yes. I heard legends about eating food offered from the fae. You are fae, are you not?" I asked, keeping my eyes focused on his collar. I dared not insult him by meeting him eye to eye.

He leaned back in his chair and began to laugh. It was frightening to hear, for it didn't suit his hardened exterior. He radiated magic, which felt ethereal, unnatural. This all felt like a dream. I was stuck in this odd reality without any recourse. How did one escape a dream prison?

"You may eat without worry. I do not offer such trickery here. The lower fae may use such petty charms to ensnare the weak-minded, but I am not an ordinary faery." His eyes flashed and turned a shade of blue so light, the color nearly disappeared aside from the stark black pupil in the center of each eye. His color even changed. His skin warmed, and his lips grew even pinker. Was he trying to look human? What for? To comfort me?

"You can change the way you look?" I asked, more to just say something out loud than to ask a question, but I was quite frankly stunned. He nodded. "And what guarantee do I have that you won't trick me and use the food to enslave me?"

He chuckled, looking amused at my concerns. "If it will put you at ease, I will swear it."

"Okay, yes, please do." I nodded, waiting for him to complete the promise. Faerie tales weren't that far off, from what I could see. The fae couldn't lie. You could make a faery powerless by having them swear to do you no harm. It had to be done right, or the promise would be nothing but empty words.

"Very well. I swear upon the Land of Faerie that I will not enchant, enslave, or otherwise trick you into staying with me forever by eating food and drinking drink from my table. Happy?"

"Yes."

It took all my strength to not swipe half the table onto my plate. Instead, I carefully picked out food from each hot, savory dish and began to eat, forcing myself to chew slowly. I didn't want to seem desperate or in need, or worse… choke to death. I could never show weakness to a faery. They would do whatever they wanted with it and relish the torment they could lay on a person. Or so I'd heard.

Corb watched me intensely as I ate. If I hadn't been so hungry, I would have lost my appetite to his unblinking eyes. After washing down my first plate with a cup of sweet honey wine, I began plucking more pieces of food off the platters. My stomach roared, unhappy with its still meager meal, slow to be satisfied. I had to eat more and more. There was no end to my ravenous hunger.

"What is a girl like you doing out in the winter forest alone, in the middle of the dead season?" Corb asked, tilting his head as he studied me. His eyes seemed to pierce my head, and I dropped a drumstick of chicken to grasp at my temples with both hands, a sharp pain striking my brain.

"Ah!" I gasped, squeezing my eyes shut. As quickly as it had come, the pain receded, a tide of agony with the edge of a threat.

"Forgive me. I've not had the company of a human girl for an exceptionally long time."

"You invite humans here? Is that often?" I pulled my hands from my head with a sigh of relief and a twinge of annoyance. "What happened to them?"

He shrugged. "They are in far grander places."

"You wouldn't happen to have come across seven young men, all with hair the color of raven feathers and dark brown eyes, would you? They actually look just like me, but male."

If my brothers were around, I'd get it out of this faery man if it was the last thing I did. If he wanted to skirt around things, I would have to become adept at playing his game.

Corb narrowed his gaze, amusement swimming in his eyes. He may have looked more human now, but his heart was all ice-cold faery.

"There may have been such people here at one time." He waved into the air nonchalantly, leaning back in his chair and crossing one leg over the other knee.

"May have been? I need a definitive answer." I glared at him, making sure he knew I meant business.

"They are important to you?" I didn't respond. He leaned forward again, an eyebrow cocked. "Of course. Your siblings. Brothers." He folded his hands together, appearing bored with the issue at hand.

"Where are they?" I demanded.

"Where are who?"

"My brothers," I nearly yelled. Already, my appetite was gone, the plate of food before me forgotten.

"Who are your brothers?" he asked. Corb's eyes turned back to their pearly look, white without pupils. The magic in the air sharpened as his face settled into a stoic mask, cold and unmoving.

"Their names are J—J…J—J…." I screwed up my face in annoyance. "I know their names. I do. They're… they're…."

"What is your name?" Corb lifted an eyebrow, a smirk rising in the corners of his mouth.

"I—I'm," I stammered. I hadn't been expecting that question, and for the life of me, my name eluded me. "My name… my name is…."

"You have no name?"

"I have a name," I snapped. "So do my brothers. I know them. They're in here." I pointed to my head. "Just on the tip of my tongue, but I can't… I can't remember."

"Ah," Corb said. "The first snow of the Winter Realm can do that. It robs memories in exchange for life. Names are powerful, and the winter is ravenous for power. But don't fret. There's powerful magic in a name, like a wish. Especially when there is no magic to be found."

"What?" I asked, confounded. "What are you talking about?"

He waved his hand, and the room became flooded with people. Some were dancing to music I had not heard playing before. People bustled all around in fancy suits or ball gowns almost as beautiful as my dress. I felt odd being the only one seated at the table with Corb. The others continued as though we didn't exist, except if one walked by Corb, then they would bow, smile, and giggle while admiring him. Servants glided around the table, clearing empty plates and refilling goblets as though it was all they desired to do. I had wondered who had prepared such a feast and had refilled my drink over and over again as though the cup had refilled itself.

"What's this?" I asked, swinging my head around the decadent room, taking in the sway of the crowd and the murmurs of others speaking. "Who are they?"

"They are part of my court. Faeries, humans, any creatures who desire to belong somewhere they can enjoy their lives."

"They were here the whole time?" I asked. He nodded. "Why couldn't I see them?"

"Because you do not have the sight. You're a human. I took the liberty of enlightening you and opening your eyes to my world."

"Is that what you were doing when my head hurt?"

"Yes."

"I didn't ask you to show me this."

"Oh? Are you not intrigued?" His face hardened again as he snapped a finger, and everyone faded away as though they had been nothing but apparitions. I sucked in a breath. I didn't want to anger him. I was already in dangerous territory asking him all these ques-tions. The most important question was yet to be answered though.

"Yes, but I just didn't expect it." I fidgeted from nervousness as he continued to look at me. "Can you not stare? It's rude."

Corb smiled, a wicked gleam in his eye. "I don't mean to make you uncomfortable. I am just interested in knowing why you would follow your brothers out into the snowy wilderness without support. Without food, water, shelter. Unprepared for the harsh, frigid winter."

"I wasn't going to search for them today due to the inclement weather. I was just walking around the campgrounds where I'd parked my camper and planned to ride out the storm there until morning when it would hopefully clear. I was out of water and waiting for the water truck to deliver to the main tank at the grounds. The pipes froze from the cold, and there was no water but from a truck. It was the last place anyone saw my brothers. Their RV was found there, but the harsh weather kept a search at bay."

"Why did you go into the forest, then?" he asked.

"I—I don't know. I had to search for them immediately. The longer I waited, the less of a chance there was to find them alive. I had a feeling they'd taken a trail into the woods and felt like they had led me to it, whispering in my mind and showing me the way. We were always awfully close, all eight of us. Everyone always called us of one mind, eight souls. I followed the trail for a bit, but then I lost it under the snowfall and couldn't find my way back."

"I see." Corb scratched his chin, finally letting go of my visage as he thought over my words. The crowd reappeared as though he'd dropped the curtain they stood behind. I searched through them for my brothers. Would I even know them if I saw them, transformed into ice people? My heart sank. They were not among the party. Would I ever find them again? I had to follow the trail they'd set for me. So far, it had led me to this place, but why?

"Where can I find my brothers?" I asked again, avoiding a look at the faery king. I was too afraid to see a mischievous gleam in his eyes. If he wanted to play with my feelings, he very well could. Maybe he already had.

"I'm afraid they are not here. But they are close."

I held my breath. "Where?"

"There's a place near here. A ring made of statues, beyond the edge of the forest. The frost witch cursed the land. Some say she sleeps until a soul has the misfortune of wandering into her territory, and none have ever escaped her clutches."

I slumped in my chair. "This witch, what does she do with the people she traps?"

Corb looked away, watching the crowd as they danced. I began to wonder if they ever stopped dancing. No one ever left the dance floor, and the ones who weren't dancing remained on the sidelines, never joining.

"She collects them. Adds them to the ring of statues or curses them to fill her deadlands with creatures where no natural animals could live. They belong to her forever. I don't know what she demands of them, but no one has ever returned from there."

Corb snapped his eyes back to me, the iridescent coloring of his eyes hypnotizing. "Your brothers... I believe she has them there."

"How do I get there?" I rose from my chair, ready to leave once more for the storm outside. "I'll need my own clothes back."

He held out a dark blue ice crystal attached to a chain made of clear ice. I didn't know how he'd gotten it, or if he'd conjured it out of thin air, but it was enchanted. I could feel the waves of magic pouring off of it. I feared taking it would curse me.

"This is for you. It'll make you impervious to the cold. Once you leave my realm, you will have one day until the spell wears off. If you get to the witch's domain and are able to find your brothers and release them from her hold, you will be able to protect them as well until you return to your campground, or the final hour of the day has passed. Whichever comes first."

"And if I refuse?" I trembled beneath his stare. I knew it couldn't be so simple.

"Then your brothers will die—or worse. It's your choice, really."

"I see." I groaned internally, but it was a risk I was willing to take. "And there's no trick?" I asked. I was waiting for the other shoe to drop. He hadn't shown me any malice or trickery, but I just couldn't be too safe. There was always a price for a favor from a faery. I remembered that from the stories as well.

"No. It's just a token, from me to you. To help you and your brothers."

I took the charm and held it up. It sparkled despite its opacity. "Why would you help me? I'm merely a human. What do you ask in return?"

Corb smiled to himself, his eyes drifting to the crowd as though he were remembering something. "Let's just say I'm quite fond of humans who defy the odds. I have no need to add to my court or keep you from your mission. You remind me of a good friend of mine who would be adamant to help you."

"A human?"

"Yes. Though she was part human and part faery. Her humanity had a way of enchanting everyone far more than her faery blood."

"Oh." I pressed the crystal to my chest, tears of gratefulness blooming in my eyes. "Thank you."

He rose from his chair and waved his hand once more. The dancers cleared the floor, hurrying to the sides to watch him return to the dais. There, he sat on his throne and looked at me once more.

"How do I get to the witch's ring?" I called out, hoping he wasn't yet done with me.

"My first lieutenant, Aeathil will take you to get your things. Then he will escort you to the borders of my realm and point the way. After that, you are on your own."

He snapped his fingers. Everyone, including him, disappeared. All except for his lieutenant who stood in armor made of black metal decorated with ice crystals. He was taller than I was and loomed over me with cold white eyes and even whiter skin. His hair, long like Corb's, was a dark brown color, frosted with ice.

Alone with him in the throne room, I shuddered, not from cold but from the sudden silence. This soldier's cold company felt far more suffocating than the boisterous crowd. The table was gone along with all signs of my dinner. I sighed and turned toward Aeathil, who had begun walking down a long icy hall to a room where my clothes sat neatly folded, cleaned, and pressed. Even my jacket was fluffed and renewed. I gripped the crystal in my palm, glad I had an ally in this search.

"You may dress. I will return when you are ready." Aeathil's deep voice sent a shudder down my spine, like he was made of ice as well. All I could do was nod before he turned and left. Alone at last, I felt no comfort in the silence.

Aeathil arrived a half-hour later as I finished putting on my parka.

"Are you ready, milady?" he asked, waiting at attention at the doorway.

"Yes," I answered. "I'm ready."

I tugged the necklace over my head and tucked it into the top of my coat. I felt its cold facets against my skin, but it warmed with my body's heat. Its frigid magic didn't make me cold, but I could feel its potency demanding attention to the fact that I only had one full day to find my brothers and get back to my world. I wouldn't want to wear it for too much longer anyway; the pull to stay in Corb's ice castle intensified with each moment I wore it. I wondered what would happen to me if I kept wearing it. Letting such worries slip from my mind for now, I followed Aeathil out into the cold of the forest.

When Corb had said his lieutenant would take me to the border of his realm, he meant it. Aeathil stopped right at the edge and moved no further. He lifted his hand to point the way.

"Straight ahead is the ring. I go no further."

"Wait, that's it? This is as far as you'll go?" I asked.

He turned to stare at me with his dead, uncaring eyes. I gasped as I watched his body melt away into the snow at my feet. Even his armor sunk away as though he were but a specter made of ice magic. I shuddered, feeling more alone than ever.

Peering around me, I could see why this was the border of Corb's realm. This was where the forest ended. It was a sparse, barren land full of stone and packed earth with dead tundra and whatever frost-defying vegetation grew here. Their scrawny stalks reached out toward the meager sunlight as though crying out for more.

It was still daytime, but the constant cloud covering made it impossible to know what hour. My breath steamed in the air, and I felt as though I should be shivering to my death like I'd been in the forest. But I was warm, as if it were summer, and no frigid cold could touch me.

Corb's magic is potent, I thought.

I stepped across the border, feeling a shift in the air. Corb's magic was gone, and in its place was a colder and far more treacherous presence. I swallowed down my fear and kept going the direction Aeathil had pointed out. I just needed to find the ring of statues and make sure I outsmarted the witch. I had no plan, nor did I have any inkling of what she'd ask me. I only had faith that everything would be all right.

I travelled for a few miles and felt my body grow wearier with every step. Breathing hard from the effort of treading through the waist deep snow, I wondered if I'd ever find the witch's circle. I came upon a dead tree, its branches reaching out like fingers snagging the cold air. Leaning on its crumbling trunk, I paused to catch my breath as my lungs burned. There was nothing but the same scenery every place I looked, all whited out. Cursing under my breath, I coughed from the exertion.

You'll die out here as sure as all things die in the frost. You are mine.

I gasped, jerking my head around to see where the whisper had come from. I heard only the howling wind, making ghastly intonations that made my heart skip a beat.

It was only the wind. Only the wind. I breathed in deeply, feeling slightly better from the quick rest, and resumed my trek through the snow. Suddenly, I stepped not on snow but solid ice. Sliding a bit, I moved to keep my balance and looked down at the mirror of ice reflecting my face back at me.

I was standing on a lake or river. I wasn't sure which, but it was frozen solid. I wondered how long it had remained that way, or if it ever thawed. I took a tentative step forward, slowly so as to not slip. It became easier as the snow began to fall and spread across the ice like a carpet. I walked on and on and wondered just how wide this body of water could be. It felt like I'd walked onto the ocean. It seemed never-ending until I came upon some mounds of broken ice. The mounds stuck out from the surface of the ice like stalagmites, but I couldn't see how they'd been formed. I pressed on until I decided to examine one of the broken pillars closely. I could see that it wasn't just a jagged piece of ice, but it'd been carved into with tools. Maybe even magic. I rounded the pillar and gasped as I peered at a smaller mound next to it with a face carved into it, blank eyes staring back at me.

"Oh, my god!" I screamed, falling onto my rear end and crawling backward as I realized the pillars were not just mounds but disintegrating statues of people. Not just people, but also faeries with wings, trolls with gigantic bodies and pointy teeth, and other creatures I couldn't identify. I could see that many of them were probably humans as well.

I scrambled to my feet, sliding about once more on the smooth surface of the lake. I turned in a circle, not seeing which direction I'd been walking, but it didn't matter. Up ahead was a clearing. The statues were in rows, spreading out from it like rays shooting out from the center of a star. I swallowed down a hard lump in my throat as I took step after tentative step toward the clearing, knowing deep in my core that this was it.

It was the witch's ring of statues.

Approaching the ring, I knew the moment I stepped into it there would be no turning back. I looked around, not seeing anything at all but the white of winter. The snow fell harder, and the wind blew louder, wailing in my ears. I took a breath in and stepped into the ring. The moment I was inside of it, the noise silenced, and the snow no longer pummeled into me.

"Hello?" I called out. This had to be the place. Where was she? Where were my brothers?

At that thought, I saw the ravens from the forest settling down atop some of the ice statues. Their beady eyes stared at me as they cawed loudly, speaking to each other in their own language. They were enormous and almost the size of some of the statues. How had I not noticed how large they were before? They'd been so far up in the trees, it'd been too hard to tell.

"You've come to see me. How lovely."

I jerked around and came face to face with a beautiful woman with long, grey hair and matching eyes. She smiled, not a wrinkle on her luminous skin or her pouty pink mouth. She looked radiant, as though time would not betray her age, but I knew better. I could sense how old she was through Corb's pendant. It flared to life beneath my coat and whispered to me that this was not a woman but a creature older than most things on earth and as inhuman as a being could be. Ancient magic encircled me and would have swallowed me up but for the crystal.

"You have my brothers. Let them go," I demanded. Reasoning with this creature was not going work, but what would?

Her expressionless face looked almost as still as the statues around us, their empty eyes watching our every move. Their mouths were all open in silent screams.

"I cannot let them go. They belong to me." Her face never moved; instead, her voice came from all over. I felt an icy cold finger run itself down my cheek and flinched. She was playing with me, trying to terrify me. Was that what she'd done to these people? Scared them into submission?

"They do not belong to you or anyone. They are my brothers!"

She smiled, breaking the mask she'd been wearing. I watched her eyes wrinkle at the edges, as though using magic slowly wore away her glamour.

"Do you really want them back?" she asked, her sinister grin digging into my chest.

"Yes. Of course I do."

"What would you do to save them?"

I was taken aback. "Anything," I whispered. "What do you want?"

She moved toward me, her long thin hand looking far older than her youthful face.

"You wish for me to return them to you?"

"Yes." I could barely speak the closer she got to me. Her haggard hand reached me, and the crystal slipped up and out of my coat, hanging off the chain around my neck and floating in the air. It was gleaming with light, bright azure swirling around the crystal.

"What would you give for them?"

"I have nothing to give you," I whimpered, feeling my knees weaken as her ancient power pressed me beneath its weight.

"Your crystal is beautiful." She touched it, but I heard a faint crack, and she jerked her hand back. She stared in horror at her blackened finger. Frostbite traveled toward her palm. She squeezed her finger, trying to make it stop. My mouth hung open as I dropped to my knees.

"How dare you trick me?"

I shook my head, trembling from the effort to stay awake. "I didn't. I swear."

"Whose magic is this?" She held her wrist now, the darkness on her flesh slowly staining her skin more and more.

"Corb gave me the crystal. He said it would keep me from freezing."

"You dare bring him into this circle?" She reached into her pocket and brought out a curved dagger and promptly sliced it into her wrist until the blackening hand fell onto the ice below. It slid away from her and toward me, stopping a few inches away. I gagged as the smell of burnt flesh filled my nostrils.

"I didn't," I gasped, her magic receding just a little as she repaired her arm, creating a new hand from ice she funneled from the frozen water below. When she was done, her ice hand shined like liquid, moving and flexing with ease. I instinctively knew it wouldn't ever return to normal.

"You won't need that anymore." She held her good hand out and flicked it to the side. The chain snapped, and the crystal necklace disappeared into the storm surrounding the circle.

"No!" I screamed, feeling the frigid air immediately. I would die without the crystal. We would all die. There was no way to save my brothers without it. Tears filled my eyes as I shivered, my lips trembling.

"You will be a fine addition to my collection." She smirked, looking older as the minutes ticked by. I wondered if she used enough magic, would she continue to age and crumble to ashes? I hoped so.

"Give me my brothers!" I yelled, shivering so hard, I could feel my teeth cutting into my tongue from chattering. "Give them back!"

The witch narrowed her eyes at me and laughed. "They are mine, just as you are now mine as well."

I shook my head, closing my eyes as my tears froze on my cheeks. I wished for a warm fire to sit at and remembered such a fire while my brothers and I sat around telling funny stories of the past, drinking hot cocoa with large marshmallows melting in the hot mugs. I saw each of their faces, knowing them by heart. We were of one mind and eight souls. We were powerful together and weak when apart.

I flicked my eyes open and glared at the abomination in front of me, slowly crumbling beneath her mask of youth and time.

"They are not yours. Neither am I. I am Jonna, and my brothers Jonathan, Joseph, Jonas, Joel, Jack, Jacob, and Johan, will never be yours—ever!" I screamed out our names with the last of my breath.

There's powerful magic in a name, like a wish. Especially when there is no other magic to be found.

Corb's words rang in my head as I dropped to the ground, staring off into the frozen world around me, buried in ice and snow. The only thing I registered was screaming coming from either the witch or the ravens circling above. Either way, I knew it was over.

I couldn't move anymore, nor did I want to. It was only the warmth in my hand that woke me from the grip of death, and I moved my cold eyes toward the hand curled in front of me. In my fingers lay the crystal Corb had given me, glistening in the now rising sun. Somehow, it returned to me. There was no doubt Corb made it that way.

I felt arms grab ahold of me, and familiar voices echoed in my head, but I couldn't move. My bones slowly warmed; the crystal was working to help me. I could see flashes of images—the icy lake cracking into large slabs of ice, the pillars of statues melting down into people, fae and other creatures, all looking around bewildered at their new freedom. Then, as quickly as they had awoken, they bounded out of sight, running to where there was still life in the earth. I wasn't so easily recovered, knowing full well it might be too late to save me, even with the crystal.

I blinked now and then, feeling the warmth of the sun caressing my skin as we walked. My brother's voices murmured, reassuring me and speaking words of comfort. I knew I was safe and that we were all out of the frost witch's control. Her power had dissipated when I'd ripped my brothers from her grasp all at once, severing her hold on the ring of magic funneling its power from the frozen creatures.

I awoke later in a warm bed in my brothers' tricked-out RV. It had eight beds in it, one always for me as though they knew that one day, I would need it. I sat up, feeling woozy and disorientated. I heard voices from the front of the RV and knew my brothers were all up, chatting and playing cards, waiting it out until the icy roads were plowed. I slipped on a robe and walked precariously to the front, moving the partition to find my seven brothers. They turned to stare at me.

"Jonna! You're awake! Are you all right?" Jonathan asked. He was the oldest of us and always the one to take control.

I nodded, slipping into the booth as my brothers moved to make room. "I'm fine. Thirsty and hungry." I paused, looking at all of them with happy tears in my eyes. "How did we get back?"

"We don't know really," Johan said. "We just kept walking, and suddenly a path appeared in the snow, and we followed it straight back to camp. We didn't even feel cold. It was like we were standing in some warm bubble."

"Yeah, totally weird too!" Jacob said.

"How did you guys end up in that witch's hands?" I asked as they served me tea and a plate with a sandwich that Jack had quietly made as we all spoke. He grinned at me and winked. He wasn't much of a talker but was the chef of the bunch. Even his sandwiches were gourmet.

"We were going on our annual ice fishing trip and decided to find a new spot. I guess we ended up taking a wrong turn because we couldn't find our way back. Then it began to snow, like tons and tons just dumped from the sky. Then we were at her circle. I don't remember much, but I remember the feeling of floating in the air and flying."

"Ravens. She turned you into ravens," I said, understanding so much now. "You guys showed me the way. I saw you guys, seven ravens in the trees waiting for me. You called to me, and I had to follow."

The seven of them were silent as they rolled my words around in their heads. I could hear their minds making sense of it all. I knew immediately why the witch had taken them.

"That witch. She used us for power. She was old, and her magic was dying. She needed others to keep the power flowing for her youth and magic. If she could get the eight of us, who are connected and stronger together, she would have had power for a long time. That's probably why she turned you into birds instead of ice statues, to lure me to her."

"Jonna, we're so sorry. We didn't know we were leading you to her." Joel scooped up my hand between both of his. "We'd never do anything to hurt you."

I smiled. "I know. Just like I would never let anyone hurt any of you. That's why I let it lure me in. I somehow knew it would lead me to you guys. Luckily, I got some friendly help along the way."

My brothers smiled, hugged me, and began chatting about how when the roads cleared, they would head south where it was warm and hit up the beaches. I couldn't agree more.

It was then that I felt something cool on my collarbone. I reached up and felt the crystal Corb had given me still hanging from my neck. I wondered how long I'd been wearing it. It hummed beneath my fingers, still very much infused with magic.

I whispered a thank you to the ice king who had helped me find my family. He hadn't even known my name. I hoped that I'd be able to tell him my name in person one day. Deep inside, I knew that I would.

END

AUTHOR'S NOTE

I chose the story of The Seven Ravens to retell because it resonated so much with my love for my family. I have brothers I'm close to and miss every day. You could say I would do anything for them, just as Jonna risked her life for her brothers. They may not live near me, nor do I see them often enough, but I think of them every day of my life.

I wanted to convey that the ties that bind family can never be broken and stretch through distance and time, no matter what. Some are not fortunate enough to have this, but all those who have such family ties, whether by blood or choice, will surely understand.

Magic is all around us, including the magic in names and in family.

ABOUT THE AUTHOR

Alexia is a *USA Today* Bestselling author who currently lives in Las Vegas and loves spending every free moment writing or hanging out with her four rambunctious kids. Writing is the ultimate getaway for her since she's always lost in her head. She is best known for her award-winning Reign of Blood series, and A Dark Faerie Tale Series. Find out more at www.alexiapurdybooks.com.

THE DREAMER'S CURSE

RACHEL MORGAN

CHAPTER 1

ALL CRESS WANTED FOR HER BIRTHDAY WAS TO DISCOVER SHE'D been cursed at birth and would die the day she turned sixteen.

Wait. No. She definitely had not included *death* on her wish list. "I'm...sorry?" she said, frowning across the dinner table at her parents. "Did you just say I'm going to *die* tomorrow?"

Mom looked at Dad as she took a deep breath, but no words left her tongue. The only sound in the tastefully decorated penthouse dining room was the jazz music playing softly in the background. "Well, uh ..." Mom's hand fluttered near her throat. Her gold bangles clinked against one another as they slid down her arm.

"You may not be aware of this, Cress," Dad said, unable to meet Cress's eyes, "but we struggled to, uh ..." He scratched the tip of one pointed ear. His phone, sitting beside his plate of untouched dinner, beeped. He made no move to reach for it.

"Fall pregnant," Mom supplied. "We saw many doctors. We tried all the potions and concoctions Grammy came up with. We scoured the wish catalog, hoping to find something that would help. We even sent in a request to the Mages' Guild, but apparently not even a third-tier wish can fix infertility."

"So we summoned the Godmother," Dad said gravely.

"The Godmother," Cress repeated, incredulous. She couldn't

imagine her parents—highly regarded members of fae society—in the same *sentence* as the Godmother, let alone the same room.

The Godmother was fae too, but that wasn't nearly enough to make up for her illicit activities. According to the stories, she'd been a member of the Mages' Guild once, more talented at wish magic than anyone before or since. She had escaped the Guild, taking the knowledge of wish magic with her instead of surrendering it, as law dictated for anyone who wished to cut ties with the Guild.

The manufacture and trade of wishes was tightly regulated. No one operating outside the Mages' Guild and its registered network of sellers was allowed to deal in wishes. But the Godmother did. And unlike other black-market dealers, her wishes were flawless. The only catch? Her prices were steep, and they were not the kind that money —or even Essence, the fae's magic—could pay.

"Yes," Mom said. "The Godmother. We told her we wished for a child. She said this was a wish she could grant."

"But ... the price?" Cress asked.

"She would not say. We had to agree to the bargain first. She would then return to us on the day of your birth and inform us of the price she'd decided upon."

"Well." Cress tucked a lock of peacock-blue hair behind one ear before folding her arms. Like her parents, she was dark-skinned, dark-eyed, and dark-haired. It was boring, in her opinion. She wanted more color in her life, and the easiest feature to change with a charm was her hair. "I have to say, Mom. That sounds like the worst possible deal you could ever have agreed to."

"I don't expect you to understand now, Cressida, but you will one day when you—" Mom cut herself off, sucking in a shuddery breath. It seemed she'd momentarily forgotten that there would be no 'one day' for Cress.

"A life for a life," Dad murmured. "You were barely hours old when the Godmother appeared and told us the price: Your mother and I had to choose which of the two of us would die."

"What?" Suddenly, Cress was standing. "That's awful, even for the Godmother! What's the point in granting a life if you're only going to take another one away?"

"Great magic requires a great price," Dad answered. "That's what the Godmother said. I would never choose your mother's death, so of course I offered my own life. But your mom refused to let me, saying that she would die instead. I argued, reminding her that you would need a mother more than a father, and she argued right back, saying that you would always need both of us. We couldn't come to an agreement, and that was the worst mistake we could have made."

"The Godmother chose for us," Mom whispered. "And she chose you instead of either of us."

"Like the lunatic that she is," Cress growled, trying to smother her fear with anger. "Of course, grant a life and then take it away." She swept her arm through the air. "That makes total sense."

She shoved her chair back and stalked toward the impressive glass doors that led to the balcony. With her arms wrapped tightly around her chest—as if that might calm the racing of her heart—she watched the vibrant sunset colors light up the sky above Vale City. Was this the last she would ever see of the sun? Would she truly be dead by the time it rose tomorrow?

"So I'm simply going to…die?" she asked quietly, still facing the city.

"Well, the Godmother didn't mention any specifics. She only said that you would die the day you turn sixteen."

Cress inhaled deeply. Her mind raced through all the things she would never do, never see, never be. There was the Winter Dance in three weeks, and all the friends she would never hang out with again, including the new girl Emma she hadn't told her parents about, because Emma was human, and Cress's parents wouldn't approve of that. She would never get to master all the potions and charms she wanted to learn about, or one day take over Grammy's apothecary, or—

Cress turned to face her parents. "Does Grammy know?"

"Yes," Dad said.

Cress felt a stab of betrayal. Grammy was *her person*. The only one who truly understood her endless fascination with potions and her tendency to say exactly what was on her mind and her somewhat unorthodox opinion of the other High Races. Grammy knew about the friendship Cress had already formed with Emma, and she didn't care that Emma was human. She wouldn't have cared if Emma was shifter or even vampire. Like Cress, Grammy knew a person's worth extended beyond his or her race.

Cress thought she and Grammy shared everything. Apparently she'd been wrong.

"For most of your life," Dad said, "Grammy has been working to find some potion or charm that will release you from this curse. But nothing has worked so far."

"How do you know? If I'm not yet sixteen, then perhaps something she's done has—"

"You still have the mark of the curse," Mom said gently. She rose from her chair and moved to Cress's side. "It's here, on your right wrist. A freckle shaped like a diamond. It appeared when the Godmother cursed you and has never gone away."

Cress swallowed, staring at the freckle with growing dread. "Where is Grammy?" she asked, trying to keep the shudder from her voice. "Why isn't she here? I can't die without saying goodbye to her."

"She's going to meet us at the Mages' Guild. We're going there this evening, after dinner. Or now, I suppose, since I doubt any of us can stomach a single mouthful right now."

"The Mages' Guild?" Cress pictured the grand institution located at the end of a winding avenue of oak trees just outside Vale City. Surrounded by solid walls and grounds almost as extensive as Belmont Palace—home to the country's fae royal family—it wasn't the most...*accessible* of places. "I don't think they allow people to just walk in there, Mom. Not even in the middle of the day, let alone after hours."

"I don't care. Someone there *has* to help us. We'll pay anything. We may not be the wealthiest family in the city—not like those living in the Arabesque Hills—but we are most certainly high society and they *will* help us."

Cress would have rolled her eyes if the situation wasn't so serious. In her opinion, Mom placed far too much value on the concept of *high society*.

"Apparently there is no wish, no potion, no Essence—no magic of any sort—that can save you from this curse," Mom continued. "But that doesn't mean magic can't bring you back to life. When you die, the Mages' Guild is the best place we can possibly be. They are the most skilled, the most powerful—"

"Not as powerful as the Godmother," Cress pointed out. "Why not summon her again and ask to change the terms of the deal?"

"Do you think we haven't tried that?" Dad asked. He was standing now too, striding toward Cress. He took her hand, his grip almost painful it was so tight. "I would do anything—*anything*—to save my little girl. Both your mother and I have tried many times to summon the Godmother again. But either she hasn't received our summons, or she chooses to ignore us."

"The last thing she said to us was that she does not deal a second time with those who refuse to pay the price of a wish," Mom said. "It would seem she was telling the truth." She exhaled heavily and looked at Cress. "We have to fix this ourselves. Go and get ready. We're leaving in twenty minutes."

CRESS SHUT HER BEDROOM DOOR AND LAUNCHED HERSELF onto her four-poster bed. She pulled her laptop closer and opened it. Her parents might believe her only hope lay with the Mages' Guild, but she refused to leave her future in the hands of a bunch of entitled fae who would probably get her arrested before they'd help her. Her future belonged to *her*, and she needed to take charge of it.

Her fingers paused over the laptop keys. She bit her lip. What she was about to do was stupid. A huge risk. But apparently this was her last night alive, so what did she have to lose?

It took only a single search for Cress to find what she was looking for: the Godmother's symbol. Though she'd seen it before, she needed a reminder. Cress clicked on the first video result, then watched as someone—either human or shifter, based on his non-pointed ears—painted the symbol onto a stop sign with a can of spray paint. She paused the video and peered closer. She watched it a second time. Then a third.

Then she climbed off her bed and hurried to the vanity. Her fingers searched through the items scattered across the top until they landed on a tube of lipstick the same shade of blue as her hair. That would work. She pulled the lid off and positioned the tip against the vanity mirror. After a final glance over her shoulder at the frozen image on the laptop screen, Cress drew the symbol onto the glass surface.

She drew her hand back and stared at it, slowly releasing the breath she hadn't been aware she was holding. The summoning required no words. Cress simply had to wait and hope the Godmother had—

A throat cleared somewhere behind her. Cress spun around. There, leaning elegantly against her bedroom window, was a woman. Cress blinked, taking in the Godmother with one sweep of her gaze. From her short, perfectly styled white hair down to the points of her impossibly high heels, she was the last thing Cress had expected.

"Well, what is it?" the Godmother asked. She shifted her purse from one flawless alabaster hand to the other and checked her watch. "I'm due at an art auction in precisely eight and a half minutes. You're lucky I decided to deal with you myself instead of sending someone in my place."

"I—oh." Cress swallowed past the dryness in her throat and lifted her chin. "My parents made a wish before I was born that affects me. They refused to pay the price, and you decided I should die when I turn sixteen. That's tomorrow."

The Godmother made a get-to-the-point motion with her hand. "You're not telling me anything I don't already know, Cressida."

Cress blinked at the Godmother's use of her name. "Um, right. Well, I don't want to die. I'd like to…negotiate with you."

"I don't negotiate."

"But I'm not the one who made the wish and then couldn't pay the price. Why should I be the one to die?"

"Life isn't fair, Cress."

"It doesn't have to be *fair*. You can make me pay some other price, even though I didn't bring any of this about. Just make it something that isn't *death*. Please," she added belatedly.

The Godmother checked her watch again and sighed. "Fine. You can exchange one curse for another. Instead of death you can have …" Her gaze moved to the vase of white roses sitting on Cress's windowsill. She slid one from the vase and lifted it to her nose. "An eternal slumber. Which," she added, returning the rose to the vase, "can be ended with true love's first kiss. That's always a fun one." She smiled. "See? I'm not completely evil."

Cress stared, her heart sinking. "Are you kidding? That's *definitely* evil. You know I've planned to never fall in love."

"I know nothing of the sort," the Godmother replied.

"You seem to know everything else," Cress said. "And even if I *was* fine with the idea of being tied to some guy for the rest of my life, how am I supposed to find him while I'm *asleep*?"

The Godmother shrugged, somehow managing to make the movement seem refined. "That isn't my concern. You've got …" She consulted her watch. "Roughly seven hours to come up with a plan."

Cress's eyes darted to the small clock beside her bed. "Midnight is less than five hours away."

"You were born just after two in the morning. You're not sixteen until the same time tomorrow. Now, do you accept the new terms?"

"I…uh …" Cress shut her eyes, her scrambled thoughts tumbling over one another.

"Five, four, three—"

"Yes," Cress blurted out. An eternal sleep with the remote possibility of waking up was better than death, right? Or was it? Now that Cress thought about it, eternity was very…well, eternal.

"Wonderful. Sweet dreams, Cressida."

"Wait—"

The Godmother snapped her fingers and vanished.

CHAPTER 3

"There must be something here," Cress murmured, her fingers hovering inches from the dozens of bottles, boxes, and pouches lining the shelves of Apollo's Apothecary. "Something, something ..."

She and Grammy were searching for a potion or charm that might help Cress, either before or after she fell into an eternal slumber. Dad was sitting at the computer behind the shop's counter, scrolling through the wish catalog to see if he could find anything useful. Mom was hovering nearby, wringing her hands and being generally unhelpful.

"Nothing this side," Grammy said. "I'll check the next aisle." She fluttered past Cress in her purple and gold kaftan dress.

"I still can't believe you summoned her," Mom whimpered from behind Cress. "You should have told us what you were planning. We could have—"

"What? Stood in the room with me while I summoned her? She probably would have ignored me then. You told me she's ignored you every other time you tried to summon her."

"We could have tried to negotiate something better than a cursed eternal sleep!"

"She doesn't negotiate," Cress said, her eyes continuing to slide across the many labels on the shelf in front of her. She hadn't mentioned the part about 'true love's first kiss' ending the cursed sleep. There was no point. Love wasn't something she was cut out for. She'd seen the way Mom couldn't do anything without first conferring with Dad, and she'd never wanted to be bound to someone in that way. She had always wanted to be like Grammy, strong and independent.

If Cress could change her beliefs in order to escape a curse that was possibly worse than death, she would. But she figured it was too late now to alter something so fundamental about herself.

"We don't even know what we're looking for here," Mom said. "We're wasting time. We should be at the Mages' Guild, explaining what's happened. Someone there will help us."

"More likely they'll get us arrested," Cress muttered under her breath as she stepped around the row of shelves and into the next aisle where Grammy had just removed something from a shelf.

"These are all charms designed to keep one awake," Grammy said, holding her hand out to reveal three different bottles, "popular among students at exam time. But I doubt any are powerful enough to counter an enchanted sleep brought on by the Godmother's magic. And even if they are, the effects won't last longer than a day at most."

"Well, we'll try them anyway," Mom said, swooping past Cress and grabbing the bottles from Grammy's hand.

"Thanks, Grammy," Cress said as she walked past, aiming for the door with the Staff Only sign that led to the workshop and store rooms. There were more supplies back there—and Cress needed to get away from her mother's anxiety.

She hurried into the workshop, ignoring the benches laden with open flasks, scattered powders, and crushed herbs, and trying not to breathe in too much of the green smoke that drifted near the ceiling. How Grammy didn't get herself blown up in here on a daily basis was a mystery to Cress.

She moved to the only shelf that held Grammy's completed products. Her eyes scanned the bottles, taking in each label in under a second before sliding to the next. The weight on her shoulders grew heavier. Her hope began to fade. There was nothing here that could—

Dream Traveler. Cress's eyes caught on the tiny label. In the next instant, she snatched the glass bottle from the shelf and raced back out to the store. "Grammy, what's this?"

Grammy's kaftan rippled around her as she turned. She eyed the bottle in Cress's hand with a frown. "Did you get that from my workshop?"

"Yes."

Grammy glanced over her shoulder. Mom was with Dad now. They were bent together over the computer, their heads almost touching. "That's an experimental potion," she said, turning to Cress again. "It hasn't been through the Guild approval process yet. I decided not to submit it because…well, I don't think they're going to like it."

Meaning it probably violated at least one law. Not that that bothered Cress. "What exactly does it do?"

Grammy pressed her lips together before answering. "It will give you the ability to travel into other people's dreams and communicate with them."

Yes, that sounded like something the Mages' Guild would refuse to approve. It also sounded like something that would be useful to a person stuck inside an eternal sleep. "Does it work?"

Grammy paused. Cress figured she was probably about to point out that it was illegal, but instead she simply said, "It does."

"Do you think I should—"

"Cress, we need to go." Mom appeared at Cress's side. "We've wasted enough time already. Potions can't help you now, and we can't possibly look through the entire wish catalog before you turn sixteen." She steered Cress away from Grammy and toward the apothecary's front door. "We'll be better off at the Mages' Guild. Someone there will know what to do about an eternal sleep."

Instead of arguing, Cress slipped the tiny bottle of *Dream Traveler* into her back pocket. She would take it when Mom wasn't looking. She would also take the stay-awake potions and charms, just in case they were strong enough to combat the Godmother's magic for a few hours and keep her awake long enough for someone at the Guild to help her.

Unfortunately, just as Cress had feared, no one at the Mages' Guild seemed interested in the plight of a single fae girl whose parents had been foolish enough to make a deal with the Godmother. In fact, the man on the other side of the tall metal gates threatened to call the police at the mere mention of the Godmother's name.

After various threats, a few embarrassing attempts at bribery, and some name-dropping of several celebrity fae—old friends of Grammy's—they finally made it through the gates, up the long driveway, and into a reception area. But hours later, they hadn't made it any further than that, and Cress's parents were still arguing with a tired-looking woman who appeared to be wearing a nightgown beneath her partially buttoned-up dress.

As the hands of the giant clock behind the reception desk passed two a.m., an irresistible tiredness stole its way through Cress's body. Mom and Dad didn't seem to notice. Dad jabbed a finger at the air as he shouted something. Mom carried on sniffling.

Cress tried to stand, tried to call out. But she was so…darn… tired. Her limbs were liquid. Her eyelids were lead. She slid down in her chair, Grammy holding her hand as the curse of eternal sleep tugged her into darkness.

CHAPTER 4

An Unknown Amount of Time Later

Traveling through dreams was like wandering through a house where every door led to a new life: A girl standing naked on a stage in front of a hall full of school children; a woman wrapping a scarf of lettuce leaves around her neck in a shopping mall fitting room; an overgrown forest of prehistoric creatures seen through binoculars; a human-turned-wolf shifter trying to outrun the rising moon and his first change.

Most dreams were boring, albeit a bit odd. Some dreams were disturbing. Even if Cress couldn't see through the shadows to exactly what caused her heart to seize, she could hear slithering, or a scream, or the grunts of a struggle. She could feel icy breath on her neck or sense invisible shackles around her ankles. Those were the dreams she dove away from, willing herself to flee into someone else's head as quickly as possible.

To a certain extent, she could control whose dreamscape she entered. She could think of someone—Grammy or Mom or one of her friends—and open a door into that person's dreams. Mostly, though, she wandered through worlds that belonged to people she didn't know, seeing indistinct faces and hearing snatches of conversation.

In the beginning, she'd explained her story to anyone who would listen. She'd asked each dreamer if they knew of a way to save her from an eternal enchanted sleep. Most seemed to believe her story. But of course, that was the way it was with dreams. You believed them when you were in them. But there were others—those who were shifter, vampire or human—who tried to fight her off, screaming about how they wanted nothing to do with her cruel, selfish kind.

No matter what kind of response Cress received, no one ever seemed to remember her after they woke up. If she found her way back into the dreams of someone she'd already met, she had to explain everything all over again. It was the same with Grammy and Mom and Dad. They knew as soon as they saw her in a dream that she had traveled there, but they couldn't remember any previous dream conversations they'd had with her.

After a while, she'd stopped asking if anyone could help her.

When Cress wasn't traveling through someone else's dreams, she was stuck inside her own. Stocking shelves at the apothecary, rushing to finish a homework assignment on her laptop, trying out for the cheerleading squad at school—*that* had never happened in real life —or that one specific recurring nightmare involving the Godmother, a dragon, and a tower of thorns.

How many dreams had she traveled through now? How many people's heads had she lived inside? How long had she been asleep? The trouble with dreams was that time was a meaningless concept. It disappeared like water through Cress's fingers when she tried to hold onto it. Sometimes it seemed she'd been asleep for only minutes. At other times it felt like years.

Perhaps there really was no way out of this dream world.

Perhaps she should never have wished to change her curse.

CHAPTER 5

CRESS WAS IN THE NIGHTMARE AGAIN. THE ONE WITH THE Godmother, a dragon, and a tower of thorns. The tower was actually the skyscraper Cress lived in, wrapped in ropy, thorny vines. The dream always began with her about halfway up the outside of the building, clinging to the vines as she tried to find the next handhold. With magical telescopic dream-vision, she could see the Godmother standing at the very top, laughing down at her.

Cress never made it to the top, but some urgent force always prompted her to try. Maybe this time would be different. Maybe this time she would finally make it into her bedroom. She would find herself asleep on the bed, and she would shake herself awake. This nightmare—this never-ending dream world—would be over.

A whoosh warned Cress that the dragon was close. Giant wings beat the wind at her back. Heat burned her ankles. She yelped and hoisted herself a little higher, gasping as thorns bit into her palm. The dragon swooped past again. Hot breath curled against Cress's neck. She shuddered and pulled her body closer to the vines. Peering through the leaves, her eyes found the reflective surface of a window —and saw the dragon right behind her.

Her heart almost stopped. Her dream-vision zoomed in on the

dragon's eyes. Solid rings of orange flame surrounded narrow, vertical pupils. They were eyes that *burned.*

Don't. Stop. Moving, Cress instructed herself, forcing her gaze away from the dragon's. Though she was almost paralyzed by terror, she managed to pull her body upward. She had to keep going. That was the only way the nightmare would end. She would reach her window, raise her fist to bang against the glass, and the Godmother would stretch down and grab her hand. Then she would tug Cress free from her thorny perch and let go.

Cress would fall, fall, fall…

… and land in a new dream.

That was the way it always ended.

A roar startled her. She froze. There wasn't supposed to be a *roar* in this dream. The dragon never made a sound. Clinging tightly to the vines, Cress swiveled to look behind her.

Two dragons. *Two.* Both sweeping low over the glimmering structures of Vale City before soaring back up toward Cress. One was the orange-gold dragon that always chased her. The other was black and green.

Cress turned back to the vines, looked up, and saw that somehow, she was closer to the top than she'd ever been before. This was definitely a different nightmare. That must surely mean it would have a different ending.

She pulled herself a little higher. Then higher still.

"Hey!" a voice yelled from above her. She knew before looking that it wasn't the Godmother. Where the mysterious fae woman had been, there was now a young man brandishing a computer keyboard like a sword. "Come and get me!" he yelled at the dragons.

Cress looked behind her. There was only one dragon now. Gone was the orange-gold one she knew and feared. And the other one… Cress realized with a jolt that it wasn't a real dragon after all. It was the *shape* of a dragon, made up of rows upon rows of bright green computer code.

The code-dragon flew at the young man. With a cry, he swiped his keyboard at it, sending tiny green numbers and letters scattering through the air. He swung the keyboard back and forth, again and again, until the code-dragon was gone and numbers and letters rained down toward the streets below.

A hand gripped Cress's. She looked up again. She was now at the very top of the building, though she couldn't remember climbing any further. The young man pulled her all the way up. She took a moment to catch her balance before noticing all of a sudden that the Godmother was standing behind him.

"Finally," the Godmother said with a twisted grin. Then, in a blink, she was gone.

"Thank you," Cress breathed, focusing on her rescuer. As was the way with all her dreams, she couldn't fully see his face. Whenever she tried to look directly at him, it was as if her gaze slid off to the side. Or perhaps she *was* looking directly at him, but somehow immediately forgetting what he looked like. "Is this your dream?" she asked.

"Oh. I'm not sure. I thought it was your dream." He scratched his head. "Though the computer-coded dragon would suggest otherwise."

Perhaps it was the dream world that was making it difficult for Cress to place his accent, but he sounded...posh. "Did you buy a dream traveler potion, by any chance? From Apollo's Apothecary, perhaps?"

"I think I made one. I mean I *did* make one. I just wasn't sure if it would work. I experiment with all sorts of charms and concoctions," he explained. "Drives my parents crazy. They think I'm going to accidentally give myself a third arm or turn myself into a frog or something."

"And is that—" Cress's gaze moved toward his right hand "—a computer keyboard?"

"Oh. Uh...yes." He attempted to hide the keyboard behind his back, but it was larger than a real-life keyboard and stuck out a little on either side. "I, uh, also like to code. Seems my nerdy pastime followed me into my dream. Or your dream. Or...whoever's dream this is. You have to admit, though—it made quick work of that dragon." He raised the keyboard above his head and let out a nervous chuckle. "Nerds rule."

Cress couldn't help it. A loud laugh burst from her lips. In all the dreams she'd experienced, no one else had ever felt as *real* as this guy. "What's your name?"

"Bren." He thrust the keyboard toward her. "Oh, sorry." He lowered the keyboard and extended his empty hand.

"Cress," she told him, taking his hand and giving it a firm shake. "It's very nice to meet you."

CHAPTER 6

"Where do you live?" Cress asked Bren. "I'm in Vale City in Astranerica." As she spoke, the remnants of her nightmare melted away. The twisted thorny vines rose around her to form trees. A cool breeze drifted over her arms, and the sound of water tumbling over pebbles reached her ears. A bench sat behind Bren, and not too far beyond that, a familiar bridge curved over a stream. Cress recognized the tranquil scene as part of the Vale City Botanical Gardens.

"Oh, yes, Vale City," Bren repeated with a smile. At least, Cress figured he was smiling. She could hear it in his voice, even if she couldn't see it on his face. "I'm not too far from you. A few hours' drive, I think. You can probably tell I'm not originally from your part of the world, but my dad moved for work recently. Hmm." He paused for about half a second before continuing. "What are the chances of me ending up inside the dream of someone I'm close enough to meet up with in real life? If you think about it, we should be able to travel through the dreams of anyone anywhere in the world. Is this merely a coincidence? Although, now that I think about it, there's something that feels familiar about your dream. As if...I've been here before." He turned and looked around. "Not *here*, specifically. Maybe the previous scene? I don't know. It just *feels* familiar."

Cress bit her lip to keep from laughing again. "You talk a lot, Bren."

He faced her again. "Right, I know. I'm sorry."

"Oh, don't apologize. I like it. Other dreamers don't generally talk much. You know, people who are just having a normal sleep and a normal dream, not magically traveling into dreams the way you and I are doing. Sometimes they don't even talk in full sentences. It can be difficult to have a conversation that makes sense."

"How very frustrating."

"Yes. Especially since…well, I've been here a very long time." Cress hesitated. It had been so long since she'd shared her story with anyone. She'd decided years ago—had it been years? Or was it only months or weeks?—that there was no point. But Bren was the first person who might actually remember what she told him.

She took a breath and began her tale.

"Oh, it's you again," a surprised voice said from behind Cress. Surprised but pleased, she noted as she turned to face Bren. She'd just stepped into a beach dreamscape where a laptop sat on the sand, frothy white water washing over it before receding.

"Hi," Cress said, smiling as she faced him. He was tall and…tall. That was pretty much all she could tell in a dream world where physical details were impossible to pin down. Bren was…warmth, curiosity, unexpected bursts of laughter, the scent of freshly brewed coffee.

"You know," he said, "I still haven't taken that potion again. Seems the effects are…well, slightly longer-lasting than I expected."

Cress raised an eyebrow. "Not wild about traveling through dreams forever?"

"After you sold the idea so well?" Bren laughed. "Slightly less wild than I was while crafting the dream traveling concoction in the first place. Although, if you're always here, it certainly won't be that bad. Oh dear, is that my laptop?" He craned his head to see past her.

"I've been worrying about it all day. A friendly classmate of mine managed to fit it into a toilet bowl at school. Quite impressive, actually. The size of the toilet bowl, I mean. Anyway, I haven't attempted to switch the poor drenched thing on yet. Figured I'd subject it to one of my mother's hair dryer charms first."

"Friendly classmate? Sounds like a bit of an *arse* to me," Cress said, mimicking Bren's accent.

He chuckled. "Yes, well, unfortunately these things happen when you're a—" He cut himself off.

"Nerd?" Cress finished.

Bren took a deep breath. "Uh, yes. A nerd in a school full of jocks. Let's call it that."

Okay, so 'nerd' wasn't what he'd been planning to say. Cress was about to ask what he really meant, but Bren took two steps toward the laptop and disappeared.

Cress kicked the water as it rippled over her feet and then vanished in the same way Bren had. Dreams were so annoyingly short sometimes.

"Mom," Cress called. "Mom. Mom!"

Her mother looked up. She was sitting on Cress's bed, one of Cress's journals in her hand. Everything about her was out of focus except for her large, tear-filled eyes. This was Cress's dream, not Mom's dream, which meant Cress wasn't communicating with her real mother. Thank goodness.

"I'm so sorry, Mom. The part where I said I never want to be like you…I just meant…it seems like you love Dad *too* much. Like you're half a person when you're not with him. And I want to be *whole*. Individual. I don't want love to steal part of my identity."

"Love doesn't do that, Cress," Mom said. "Not if it's the right kind of love. I thought I told you this already, but perhaps you don't remember. I was broken. Love put me back together."

Cress shook her head. "I think that's a line you got from a cheesy love song. Actually, since this is my dream, I think that's a line my *subconscious* got from a cheesy love song."

"Or maybe you're remembering something I told you long ago," Mom said.

"Either way, I still don't want love stealing anything from me."

"I think you have it backwards, honey. Love doesn't *take*, it *gives*."

"Cress?"

Cress whipped around and saw Bren. How much had he heard? It didn't matter. He wouldn't remember any of it when he woke up.

She spun away and fled the dream.

"It's a cloak made of daylight," Bren explained. He stood up from the library table they were sitting at and shook the wrinkles from the silvery piece of fabric. Then he drew it around his shoulders and raised the hood over his head. Instantly, he became almost too bright to look at. Cress had to shield her eyes.

"Is it real?" she asked.

"Unfortunately not. I keep daydreaming about it, which is probably how it ended up appearing in this dream. If only I could take it back with me when I wake up."

"Why? Are you afraid of the dark?"

"Um…not the *dark*, exactly. More the—"

"Hey, put that away!" Bren's boss called from behind the library's front desk. "You'll blind the books!"

"Aren't you supposed to be telling us we're being too *noisy*," Bren pointed out, "not too *bright*? And what about the fact that I'm drinking coffee in the library?" He pointed across the table at the takeaway coffee cup with the words *A MAGICAL BREW* printed on the side.

And then he vanished before he could properly explain the reason for the daylight cloak.

"Did you remember?" Cress asked Bren the moment she stepped into his dream. She'd been waiting ages for him to fall asleep, stepping into one boring dream after the next, always thinking of Bren and never finding him until—

There he was in the middle of a fairground, a Ferris wheel turning behind him. The air was filled with carnival music, laughter, and the burnt-sugar scent of cotton candy.

"Cress, good evening." Bren's grin was invisible, but Cress could hear it in his voice. "And, uh, remember what exactly?"

Cress sighed and turned her gaze toward the moonless night sky. "You forgot again. For like the four hundred and seventy-fifth time."

"Surely not," Bren said. "I don't think I've known you a whole year yet."

"Really? It feels like multiple years."

"True. It does. In a good way, that is. Anyway, what is it I'm supposed to remember?"

"Vale City and Apollo's Apothecary," Cress said. "You're supposed to find my grandmother there. She never made any more dream traveling potion after the one she gave me because it was an old experimental one she was never planning to get approval for, and she couldn't find her notes on exactly how she'd made it. You're supposed to find her and tell her how you made yours so she can travel into my dreams and I can have real conversations with her. She's probably the only one who can come up with something that'll get me out of this enchanted sleep."

Bren sighed. "I'm sorry. That's a lot to remember. Perhaps it's just me and my silly, cluttered mind, but the details of my dreams fade as soon as I wake up."

Cress smiled, feeling something melt inside her. "You don't have a silly, cluttered mind. Your mind is brilliant. I think most people have trouble remembering dream worlds once they've left them."

"I suppose. Anyway, whether you can have proper dream conversations with your grandmother or not, I'm sure she's hard at work on trying to figure out how to wake you up."

Cress nodded. "You're right. I'm sure she is."

Bren looked over his shoulder at the slowly turning Ferris wheel. "I was at the Belgravia Fair this evening."

"That must have been fun," Cress said, unable to hide the wistful tone in her voice. She'd been to the fair with her friends last year. They'd ridden the bumper cars, and she'd laughed so hard her stomach ached by the end of the evening.

"Yes and no," Bren admitted. "I rode the Ferris wheel with a friend, and the view from the top was splendid."

Friend? Cress wanted to ask, an unexpected flash of jealousy warming her insides.

"But I couldn't help thinking that it would have been more fun if I'd been there with you."

"Oh." The heat of jealousy morphed into the heat of...something else.

"I figured if I could get myself to dream about it then we could go together." Bren held his hand out toward Cress. "What do you think? Want to ride the Ferris wheel with me?"

Cress reached for his hand. "There's nothing I'd like more."

"Brewing coffee in there?" Bren asked, pointing to the cauldron that stood between them.

"It's a potion that will make us all the same," Cress explained. They sat together on the grass outside the library Bren worked at. This was Cress's dream, not Bren's, but she'd seen the grand library entrance with its stone pillars and impressive archway so many times now that it had become a regular feature of her own dreams, even when Bren wasn't around. "Which means," she added, "that like most others things we create in our dreams, it will never exist in real life."

"Why would we all want to be the same?" Bren asked. "Life would be so boring."

"I mean the same…High Race," Cress said carefully, staring at the cauldron of purple liquid. "So there would be no difference between fae, shifter, vampire and human. No reason for people to hate one another."

Bren was quiet. Then he said, "That would be nice." Several more moments passed before he added, "It would also be nice if we didn't *enslave* one of our four High Races."

Cress's gaze shot up. She wished she could see Bren's expression. "I agree one thousand percent. The slave charm should never have been created." She lifted a glass rod and stirred the contents of the cauldron.

"What would be even nicer still," Bren said eventually, "is if we could *keep* the differences between High Races but remove the hate."

Cress nodded. "You're right. This should be a potion that removes hate from the world." She became quiet again, slowly stirring her make-believe potion and leaving space for Bren to ask the one question that would be natural for someone to ask right now: *Which High Race do you belong to?*

The two of them had spoken about everything under the sun, but they'd never spoken about this. Not being able to *see* Bren properly meant Cress couldn't tell just by looking. She wondered what his reason was for not asking her. Or had the question simply never crossed his mind because he assumed they were the same? It seemed likely he was also fae, given his ability to work with charms and potions. But she knew shifters and vampires brewed certain concoctions as well. It wasn't nearly as easy for them to send their magic into such things, but it was possible.

Cress's own reasons for never asking were simple: First, it didn't matter to her whether or not they were the same. Second, she was worried it *would* matter to him.

"Try adding unicorn tears," Bren suggested, stepping past Cress's not-so-subtle invitation to discuss the topic of High Race.

"Good idea," Cress said, relief filling her chest. Perhaps whatever differences existed between the two of them mattered as little to him as they did to her.

A tiny glass bottle of Lawson's Unicorn Tears appeared on the grass beside Cress. Dreams were convenient that way. She added the tears to the cauldron and continued stirring, watching as tiny gold sparkles appeared. "What do you think? Should I add anything else?"

"Of the two of us, my dear Cress, you're the potion master. I don't think my opinion matters much."

Cress's brain almost got stuck on the 'my dear Cress' part, but then she focused on the rest of Bren's words. With cheeks still warm from the compliment, she said, "Of course your opinion matters. It doesn't mean mine *isn't* important, it just means I value yours too."

"Is that a line you got from a cheesy love song?"

Cress dropped the glass rod and looked up. It was her mother who sat across from her now, not Bren. But after another blink, Mom was gone too.

"I NEED TO TELL YOU SOMETHING," BREN SAID. HE SAT DOWN beside Cress on the bench inside the glass greenhouse above Apollo's Apothecary. This wasn't Cress's dream, but since she'd shown Bren the greenhouse and told him it was one of her favorite places, it had begun to appear more often in his dreamscapes. "I don't want to wake up before I've finished explaining," he added, "so I'm just going to get on with it, okay?"

"Okaaay." Cress's heart beat a little more rapidly. Something brushed her finger. She looked down. Bren's hand was so close to hers on the bench that their fingers were touching. Something fluttered low down in the region of Cress's belly.

She looked up, and for the first time, she could actually *see* Bren's eyes. The rest of his face remained blurry, but his eyes…Cress felt her chest tighten and her heart leap. His eyes were beautiful. A warm brown that was almost gold. Without realizing it, she was leaning closer.

But Bren's eyes…the pupils….

Cress froze. The pupils were changing shape. Growing narrower. Narrower and narrower, until they were impossibly thin and vertical. Orange flames burned around the pupils, threatening to engulf them. Burning orange eyes that she *recognized*.

"I'm…a shifter."

Cress pushed herself up and backed away. "It was you," she gasped. "You're the dragon. Holy stars, you're a *dragon!* The one in my nightmares, always chasing me up the side of the—"

"No, Cress." Bren stood quickly. "I mean yes, but it wasn't like that. Do you remember I told you something seemed familiar when I first met you? It took me a while, but those old dreams have slowly been coming back to me."

"You were part of my nightmare," Cress whispered. She didn't care that Bren was a shifter. She didn't even care that he was a *dragon* shifter, which was all but unheard of. The only thing she cared about was that he was *that specific dragon* who'd chased her through so many nightmares.

"No, wait, just listen. I…I bought a wish, you see. It was silly. I know one can't wish for love, but…but who would ever naturally fall in love with a dragon shifter? Even among shifter-kind we're looked upon with revulsion or—or something bordering on reverence, which doesn't help in the romance department."

Cress shook her head. "What does this have to do with being in my nightmare?"

"Right, sorry. Rambling again." Bren tugged at his hair. "So, I— I bought a wish, and I added an extra charm to it, and then I wished for love. And then…I started having those dreams. I was in a forest of thorns, running after someone. Someone I cared deeply for and was desperate not to lose. And every time, right at the end, I realized the reason that person was running from me was because I was in dragon form. But I could never change back before the dream ended. I could never—"

His words came to an abrupt end as his body suddenly went ramrod straight. Then his right shoulder dipped down, as if an invisible weight had dropped onto it. "No, no, no," he muttered as his left shoulder shoved itself forward and his fingers curled into claw shapes. "Not now. Wake up, wake up!" He fell to the floor, and Cress clapped a hand over her mouth as Bren's body arched. He cried out…and then vanished.

CHAPTER 8

CRESS PACED THROUGH DREAM AFTER BORING DREAM, SEEING nothing and communicating with no one. Her mind was in turmoil. How could Bren—the gentle, funny, nerdy Bren she had come to know so well—be the dragon who had chased her through nightmare after nightmare as she'd tried repeatedly to get to her window and wake herself up? That dragon was so fierce, so terrifying, while Bren was so…Bren.

Cress sat on the edge of a pier and stared out at the rippling water with a frown. That dragon *had* been terrifying, hadn't it? So much time had passed since she'd been forced to live through the nightmare that she was starting to forget. In fact, now that she thought about it…had the nightmare happened again since she'd met Bren? Perhaps it hadn't.

And perhaps the dragon *hadn't* been so terrifying. Other than appearing to chase her up the side of the building, it had never actually given her a reason to be afraid. She had felt the heat of the flames from its mouth, but it had never once burned her, bitten her, or even scratched her. Perhaps her mind had simply manufactured fear where there had never been a need for it.

She wasn't afraid of Bren, and she didn't want to start being afraid of him now. The idea seemed laughable. How could she be afraid of someone she l—

Cress's thoughts slammed to a halt at the startling realization. Her heart pounded, and something hot and heady rushed through her veins. She sat frozen for several breathless moments, then scooted forward. She slid off the edge of the pier and into the water, then dropped straight down, into the next dream.

Bren, she thought immediately, looking around. In the way that one somehow *knows* things in a dream, she knew that this was his. But she could barely see a thing here. It was dark, damp, earthy. Water dripped nearby. She turned slowly, feeling wet ground crunch beneath her shoes.

Flickering white light caught her attention. She hurried toward it, struggling to figure out what she was seeing. Finally, her brain managed to make sense of the writhing shape ahead of her. Understanding snapped into place.

It was a dragon—wrestling with the moon.

Bren tumbled and spun and struggled with the glowing white orb. It seemed he was trying to tear it apart with his claws. Cress rushed forward, desperate to help. But if dragon claws were no use against this miniature dream-moon, then what could her tiny fae hands do?

She looked down and realized she was holding a glass rod. The type of glass rod she might use to stir the contents of a beaker or flask. Odd, but she'd seen stranger things in her dream travels. And if a computer keyboard could fight off a dragon, then by the same illogical dream-logic, a glass rod could fight off a moon.

Cress ran forward with a cry, raising the glass rod like a dagger. "Bren!" she shouted. "Get back!"

It was probably surprise more than the fact that he was obeying her, but the great orange-gold dragon paused, swung around, and pinned Cress with his gaze. She skidded to a halt. Her heart lodged in her throat. What had she been thinking? Those fiery eyes *were* terrifying.

No. She forced herself to look closer. Bren's eyes were burning with *fear*, not ferocity. The white orb, lying at his feet, blazed brighter. Bren roared in pain and tossed his head. He scraped at his sides, leaving deep gashes in his glimmering hide.

Cress launched forward and brought the glass rod straight down into the miniature moon. A burst of white light blinded her, and Bren's roar rang in her ears. Then darkness and silence descended upon them.

Cress waited for a new dream to begin. But instead, the faint glow of sunrise illuminated Bren, no longer in dragon form, lying at Cress's feet. A gleaming puddle of silver—was that what remained of the moon?—covered the ground beside him.

Bren stirred and looked up. "Cress?" He pushed himself up, glancing toward the silvery puddle and shivering. "I was in so much pain." He stood. Cress noticed his hands shaking. "You saved me. Thank you."

"Thank you for saving me first," Cress answered, thinking back to the nightmare Bren had rescued her from. The nightmare she hadn't returned to since the day she'd met him.

She stepped closer, reached for his face with both hands, and kissed him.

CHAPTER 9

Cress dragged her heavy eyelids open and blinked through her blurry vision. What day was it? Did she have to get up for school now? Hopefully it was a weekend and she could sleep in for a—

Her eyelids flew open. Everything came rushing back to her, stealing her breath in an instant like a box of books dropped onto her chest. She sucked in a gasp as she sat up.

The curse. The Godmother. Eternal slumber.

How long had she been asleep?

She scrambled off the bed, her mind whirling as her eyes darted wildly about. Everything in the room appeared exactly as she remembered it: The untidy collection of objects on her vanity, the white roses in a vase on her windowsill, the laptop on the corner of her bed. She touched her head, then looked down at her hands, her clothes, her feet. She was wearing the same jeans, the same sneakers. Her fingernails weren't grotesquely long, and her hair wasn't down to her knees. Everything was the same.

The only thing that had disappeared was the diamond-shaped freckle on her wrist. The mark of the Godmother's curse.

If nothing else had changed, was it possible Cress had been asleep for only a few days? She raced out of her bedroom, calling for her parents as she aimed for the kitchen. There was a digital calendar stuck to the refrigerator. The date changed automatically every day, along with—

Cress came to an abrupt stop in the kitchen doorway as her eyes landed on the date. She swallowed. Five years. *Five years.* The Godmother's curse must have frozen everything inside her bedroom, keeping it in exactly the same condition. But now she was awake, which must mean …

Love. She'd found love.

Bren! Holy stars, she was forgetting everything already! What did he look like? Where did he live? How would she find him? Her pulse drummed wildly as she tried in vain to grab hold of the unraveling threads of her dream world. "Think!" she hissed, squeezing her eyes shut and pressing her fists to her face.

A library. Bren worked at a library. Cress couldn't remember the name, but she knew it wasn't too far away—several hours, perhaps?—and she could see the entrance in her mind.

Back in her bedroom, she opened the laptop and searched for libraries nearby. Her eyes scanned the images that came up. "Not that one…not that one …" she muttered, her fingers scrolling and her eyes darting from picture to picture.

"Yes!" she shrieked, finally spotting a familiar archway with pillars on either side. She leaned closer and squinted at the details below the image. Then she tugged open the left-hand drawer of her vanity, grabbed a transportation charm, and ran for the door.

Cress's sneakers squeaked on the polished floor as she entered the grand old library and looked around. Her breath caught at the sight of the elaborately carved wooden shelves, the artwork painted onto the domed ceiling, and the intoxicating scent of old books. She'd seen glimpses of this place inside Bren's dreams, but it was even more beautiful in person.

She was just wondering how many aisles she would have to

search before finding her true love when her eyes landed on the main desk and a tall, somewhat gangly white guy standing behind it. He was facing away from her, giving her an excellent view of the cauldron-shaped coffee cup on the back of his T-shirt. *A MAGICAL BREW*, read the words beneath the cup.

Cress knew without a doubt that it was Bren.

He turned toward her, and after years of traveling through dreams together, she finally saw his face. Warm eyes, glasses that gave him a scholarly, intelligent air, and a mouth that…well, hopefully Cress was the only one who could see this, but his mouth definitely wanted to be kissed.

He looked up, met her eyes, and smiled. It was the most perfectly glorious thing Cress had ever seen. With her heart thumping wildly and happily, she strode forward and stopped in front of the desk. Bren's smile faltered ever so slightly. "Do I know you?" he asked.

"You're Bren," she said.

"Yes." He paused, his eyes traveling her face. "Wait …" The frown deepened. "Cress?"

She reached across the desk, grabbed a fistful of his T-shirt, and kissed him. The library, which had been quiet to begin with, became suddenly, noticeably silent. Then someone giggled. Someone else let out a *hmph* of disapproval. Someone else started clapping.

Cress didn't care. Neither, apparently did Bren. His fingers slid into her hair, pulling her as close as the desk between them would allow. A shiver raced from Cress's brilliantly blue hair all the way down to the tips of her toes. Her heart danced in her chest. She would happily have stayed in this moment for the rest of time, but the desk was getting in the way, and there was the annoying fact that she needed to breathe.

She removed her lips from Bren's and sucked in a breath. "Thank you for waking me."

"Um, wow," he breathed. "No problem." He leaned back, adjusted his glasses, then laughed. "Thank you for being real.

Everyone keeps doubting my sanity every time I try to tell them about the girl of my dreams."

Cress grinned. "Well, if you said it like *that*, I don't entirely blame them." Suddenly, she noticed something she'd missed before: the tips of Bren's ears were pointed. "Oh, you're not just a shifter," she said in surprise. "You're fae, too."

"Uh, yes. That's another story I haven't told you yet."

Cress reached for Bren's hand. "I'm looking forward to hearing every story you haven't told me yet."

"So it...it doesn't bother you?" He lowered his voice. "The dragon thing."

"Not at all." She gave him a half-grin. "I think it's sexy."

Bren's face turned adorably red. "You can't say things like that in a *library*."

"Why not?" Cress leaned closer and whispered, "I think books are sexy too."

Bren looked like he'd just won the jackpot. "I'd fall in love with you right now if I didn't love you already."

Cress beamed. Then she climbed onto the desk and kissed him again.

FIN

AUTHOR'S NOTE

Thank you for reading *The Dreamer's Curse!* A fairytale-inspired story involving wishes was the perfect opportunity to return to my City of Wishes world. I'd been planning a Sleeping Beauty retelling for one of the characters, so when that particular fairytale became available for this anthology (just after I'd decided I was done with the stress of 2020 and would sadly have to pass up this perfect opportunity), I figured it was meant to be after all!

If you enjoyed Cress's story and want to dive deeper into a world where fae, shifters, vampires, and magic are real (and the Godmother rules the illegal wish trade like some Devil-Wears-Prada mafia queen) I hope you'll check out the rest of my City of Wishes series.

ABOUT THE AUTHOR

Rachel Morgan is the author of the bestselling Creepy Hollow series, the Ridley Kayne Chronicles, and the City of Wishes series. Her first love is fantasy, but she's also dipped her toes into the sweet contemporary romance genre under the name Rochelle Morgan.

You can follow Rachel on most major social media platforms, or find out more about her and her books at rachel-morgan.com.

LADY OF THE LAKE

JULIA CRANE

Rising out of the mist, the Lady of the Lake soaked in the lush beauty surrounding her. Laughter filled the air as young mortals passed. A flicker of anger surged to the surface, causing the water to ripple around her. They didn't know how blessed they were. Being human was a gift. However, most of them that were lucky enough to wear the earthly garment of flesh took it for granted.

By the gods, how she would love to experience the thrill of being a mortal just for a day. So often throughout the eons of time she dreamt of such an experience. Even with all her power, she could not turn spirit into bone.

There was only one person who might be able to make such a feat happen—Merlin. But she also knew he would never do such a thing. Not for her. While there was mutual respect between the two, he was wary of her. Merlin didn't trust her, and she wasn't quite sure why. As far as she knew, she'd never done anything to warrant the feeling. Yet, it was apparent anytime they interacted.

Mentally, she sent out the clarion call to the wizard before dipping back into the lake. Once again, her body particles merged with the water. Her enchanted human form was no more as she became one with the lake. As she envisioned the cavern, her energy moved through the current, swiftly bringing her to the entrance.

Calling on her magick, she formed a body before stepping out of the water and onto the cave floor. She felt nothing beneath her feet. She could pretend that the ground was cool and the soles of her feet stung stepping on a pebble. However, that was not the case. The body was an illusion and nothing more.

Within moments, Merlin's form flashed before her. She studied him. He looked the same, handsome as ever. His black hair hung loosely above his shoulders. The plain robe that made others appear dreary somehow made him look more assertive with his confident stance, broad shoulders, and sparkling eyes. Her gaze lingered a while longer before she spoke. "Hello, old friend."

"What do you want, Viviane?" His tone was one of annoyance. Which did not sit well with her, yet she held her tongue. She needed him if she were to get her one genuine desire. Somehow, she would get her way.

She stepped forward, reducing the distance between them. Lowering her voice, she asked, "Why do I displease you so?"

Merlin sighed. "You do not displease me. I am busy, and you call me like a lost sheep only around to do your bidding. Believe it or not, I have important matters at hand."

"You could say no."

His expression clouded. "We both know that is not true. Don't insult me."

She didn't bother to engage in that debate. For Merlin was correct, she being of Earth and Water and he of Fire and Air, Earth always triumphed. Sophia, the Goddess of the Earth, was the most powerful being of all. Viviane received her power directly from the planet, whereas Merlin came from the stars.

"I would like you to grant me a wish."

Merlin laughed. "My dear, you have more magick than I. Grant your own wish."

"This I cannot do," she protested. "I assure you, I have tried over the centuries to no avail."

Curious, Merlin leaned forward on his staff, peering deep into her eyes. She knew he was searching for the truth in her energy field.

"What would you have me do?"

"Make us both mortal, just for a day. We could truly make love and experience all the sensations of being a mortal instead of imagining how it would be. I know you've wondered what my touch would feel like." She grabbed his robe and yanked him toward her.

He pulled back, appalled. "That was not at all what I expected. Dear gods, why in the world would you want to be a mortal? You are the most exquisite creature on the planet. What good would it do for you to have a clunky human form?"

She was not surprised by his reaction. "I'm curious, and I know you must be as well. You've traveled this land nearly as long as I. In the world but not of the world. A mirage. Don't you want to be real, even if just briefly?"

"I can't say that I do. I want to leave and never return. However, like you, I am stuck here on Earth. It is our fate, and it must be accepted."

"What good is all this power? It's wasted on those that don't appreciate it. All this time, and we've not improved anything. The humans continue to attempt in vain to destroy the planet with their selfish ways. Our powers haven't even dampened the darkness that hangs over this world. If anything, it's worse."

"I could make you mortal," Merlin's voice dropped, "but you could never return to your enchantress form. You would be like me, and walk the Earth, only you would die and be reborn again and again, like a normal human. Trust me, you do not want that suffering."

Viviane let that sink in. It surprised her to feel such a thrill at the idea. "Do you mean that? Is this true?"

Merlin's eyes widened. "Do not tell me you would even consider such a thing. You know how vital your element is to the Earth's existence. Water makes up nearly the whole surface. Not to mention most of the human form."

With a wave of her hand, "There are others like me."

Shaking his head, , "There is no other like you, and you know it."

The excitement was building within. Yet, Viviane knew she should listen to Merlin's reasoning. After all, he was one of the wisest beings to ever enter this sphere. With a tilt of her head, she asked, "What makes me so special?"

Tapping his staff on the ground, he said, "Your heritage. Don't act dim-witted, it doesn't suit you."

She frowned. "We all come from the same lineage."

"But not all are so closely birthed from the source as you are."

"Merlin, just help me. I want this experience. Why can't we just do it for a day? An hour even? You're making this much more difficult than it should be. I can't believe it would have to be permanent. With magick, there is always a way to circumvent energy."

"You have no idea what you are asking."

"As you said, my magick is potent. If you do not grant me this wish, I will unleash that power on you."

Merlin's eyes narrowed on her. "Do not threaten me. A battle between the two of us would not serve the divine will. It would only end in destruction, making the radiant one very unhappy."

"Do you think I care?"

"You should."

Moving closer, she placed her hand on his chest. True, she could not feel the touch any more than could he, but they could imagine it. "Merlin, you cannot tell me you have not thought of what it would be like to feel the touch of another? Perhaps you've even imagined my own hands caressing your skin?" Her fingertips traced down his chest with an enchanting smile.

His chest rose up and down. "Viviane, you're playing with fire. You must stop this foolishness."

Dropping her hand, she met his gaze. "I could command you to grant my wish."

Merlin laughed and took a step back, putting distance between them. "That you could, and the fact that you haven't shows me you are aware it would be a terrible idea."

"You don't know me as well as you think, Merlin."

"No one knows you." His form began to flicker before he faded out, leaving her alone.

Viviane's body dissolved into a trickle of water, sliding off the cavern floor back into the lake. Was Merlin right? Did she care even if he was? Not necessarily. The idea had been brewing in her mind over the last century. The thought of tasting food, feeling the vibration of laughter in her chest, enjoying the sensual touch of a lover? Why had she denied these earthly pleasures? It was not fair!

There must be a way to convince Merlin to grant her desire. Perhaps she could weave an enchantment to lure him. Doubtful, but possible. After all, she had eternity to work it out. Until then, she would work on getting to know him better to find his weaknesses. They all had them. Humans and deities alike.

She waited two days before calling on him.

"Merlin, I request your presence." She sent the message through the airwaves.

Before long, he was standing outside of the lake, his body a rigid line of annoyance. "What is it now?"

"I've given your refusal a lot of thought, and for now, I will agree with you. I've decided to put off the fantasy at least until I can figure out how to do such a thing without your assistance."

"Hmph, is that why called me? I have important matters I'm dealing with."

"No, don't go, not yet. Merlin, I'm so lonely. Please can't you keep me company for a little while? You have no idea what it's like for me. At least you have Arthur and the knights. Perhaps if I had a companion, it would get this idea out of my head. I am so close, Merlin, to releasing my energy from this lake and taking on a human form, knowing that I would be trapped in the cycle of birth and rebirth."

"Viviane, do not even jest of such a thing. You could not survive being a human. There would be no access to your power. You would be a mortal in the true sense. There is no middle ground with this. It is a universal law. There have been others that have taken this path, and it has not gone well."

"What do you mean there have been others? Why haven't I heard of this?"

"Of course there have been others. Do you think you are the only one that would have such a longing?"

"What happened to them?"

"As far as I know, none of them have been able to get off the wheel of life. They are stuck."

"Is it possible for humans to get out of the cycle?"

"It is indeed, but it is no easy feat. Very few have crossed that threshold."

Viviane was fascinated by this information. The water around her rippled as her energy increased with excitement. "Merlin, you could teach me! You could teach me how to get off the wheel of life, and then I would only have to do one cycle, and I could return to the lake."

He lowered his tall form to sitting and crossed his legs so he could be closer. "That would be impossible. There is a veil placed over humans. No memory remains of any one-time gifts they may have once had. It is truly a blank slate."

"What if you made it your goal? What if from the moment I became human, you took me on as a student. You know my strengths, and you could lead me back to my power. It would be quite the feat. The higher realms would take notice. After all, you are known as one of the greatest master teachers to have ever graced the Earth. I know you need a challenge as much as I need change."

"It's a bad idea, Viviane, and we have no idea how it would turn out."

Merlin's curiosity was ignited. She could sense him going over possibilities in his mind. There was not much more the wizard loved than a puzzle to solve. A mind as great as his needed to be in constant motion.

"I will think it over, but I must get back to the castle. Give me time."

"Thank you, Merlin. I know you do not care for me, but truly you are my only friend."

Without responding, he disappeared, and she eased herself back into the water.

Merlin wandered the halls of the castle, lost in thought. Viviane was such a temptress. Not only had she dangled her power and beauty before him, but now a challenge that would be very hard to resist. He'd known she was appealing to his pride, and yet he still found the complexity very alluring. What if he could teach her how to regain her powers while in human form? Sure, there had been others who had fully awakened in their lifetime, but that was after several hundred failures. If they could do it in one …

Despite the nagging feeling in his spirit, he knew he was going to move forward with it. After all, it was her choice, not his. He was only performing a simple spell. If the powers that be didn't want him to do such a feat, they shouldn't have given him free rein of his powers while leaving him on his mission to keep the energy of the Earth's ley lines moving smoothly across the sphere. Which he was able to do by simply being himself. His energy acted as a generator, a fail-safe. Of course, he found other ways to make himself useful to the divine goddess, Sophia. However, Viviane was correct. He was in need of a challenge. Like her, he'd long grown tired of the role they were serving.

"Meet me in the cavern." Merlin sent the telepathic message.

When he stepped outside of the castle, a strong wind hit his face, and dark clouds covered the skies. It should have been a warning, yet he ignored it. Storms were quite common in their world.

He pulled his hood over his head and made the short journey to the lake. He could use his powers to settle the storm, but it was often necessary for the sphere to release pent-up energy due to the humans' emotions. Humans were either very quick to temper or the opposite…stuff down emotions until they blew up. Weather patterns were a way Earth could release this negative energy.

As he entered the cavern, Viviane's energy crackled with excitement. He found he had to gaze slightly above her shoulder, so he didn't stare too long at her beauty. She was unmatched in all the realms as far as he had seen. He wondered how her human form would appear. Surely she wouldn't be able to retain such other-worldly beauty.

"You're going to do it?" She reached out and clenched the cloth on his arm.

He glanced down at her fingers, curled on the fabric. He could not feel her touch or the clothes on his skin, but the mind knew there should be a sensation. For the first time, he too longed to feel the touch of another. Not just any other, hers.

"Viviane, you must be sure this is what you wish to do. There is a huge potential that you will not be able to come back to your power. You may lose it forever."

For an instant, he thought she might change her mind. A flicker of doubt marred her features but was quickly replaced with resolve. "I believe in you, Merlin. I trust that you will not lead me astray and will be able to bring me back to my natural state. If not this lifetime, perhaps the next. What do we have to do to make this happen?"

"You are very stubborn."

"You would be too if you were stuck inside of a body of water."

"It can't be that bad. You can merge with most of the sphere itself. There are other water elementals you could befriend."

"Stop talking nonsense. You know it's not that simple."

One thing he knew was he wouldn't be able to talk her out of it, and he also wasn't sure he wanted to. His curiosity was piqued. He would have to deal with the wrath of Sophia, but she needed him so she would get over it.

"Exactly how would it happen? How can I become a mortal?"

"As you know, we're not truly here. We are a conglomerate of energy that has kept awareness of our soul. Which is why we can form and reform at will. So, if we're not actually here, then where are we? That is a question I've pondered many a moonrise. I've searched all the records I could get my hands on for more under-standing. It finally occurred to me that our essence had to be somewhere on Earth. Those like us, born of the gods and goddesses. Where would Sophia keep such a precious energy source? Closest to her, of course. At first, I thought perhaps they were stored in the ley lines surrounding the sphere, but that was not the case. After much pondering, I knew it must be within the Earth itself, inner Earth, the core…where Sophia's heart beats."

"Okay, that does make sense, but how in Hades do you think you can gain access?"

"With magick, of course." Merlin smiled.

"I'm still not understanding. What do you mean by essence is stored? Are you saying we have another dormant form?"

"Not exactly in the way you are thinking, but you are close. What is the only thing that could hold such power? It would have to be of Sophia herself."

Viviane gasped. "Crystals."

"Exactly."

"Is there a storehouse of crystal essences? For all the divine beings on the Earth?"

"There are, and I have seen them."

"How can you tell which one is mine?"

"We all have our energy pattern that transmits in wavelengths. It is easy to know yours."

"If it's easy for you, then certainly Sophia will know right away it's gone."

"Of course, but you didn't expect her not to find out, did you? If so, you're not as smart as I thought."

"She will be angry."

"Wrathful is what she will be. But she'll adjust. As you said, others can take your place. Not quite as powerful as you, but it will not disrupt the sphere's cycle. At least it shouldn't." Merlin paused. Had he gone over all the possibilities? Likely not; there was always something that could go wrong.

"What will you do with the crystal?"

"Destroy it."

Viviane gasped. "There's no other way?"

"No, that is the only way. This is why I have told you this is not a game. There is a possibility you will never return to your current stature."

"How soon can we do it?"

May the gods and goddesses help him. "Now, if you wish."

"Now?" She absently bit the inside of her mouth. "Yes, now, let's do it. I'm ready as I'll ever be."

Merlin reached for her hand and wondered what it would feel like for her when she experienced the sensation of touch. He'd always found it interesting that even though they couldn't feel, they still went through the motions. Even at court, Merlin enjoyed grasping onto Arthur's shoulder when they talked. Or if Guinevere greeted him with a hug, he received a certain satisfaction just in knowing the sentiment was there. Would it be drastically different for Viviane? Would it be worth all she was willing to sacrifice?

He was unsure, but he was curious.

Viviane tried desperately to conceal her nervousness from the wizard. If he knew she was having doubts, he would call it off instantly. She knew him well enough to be sure of that much. What would it mean to have her very spirit destroyed? She would be starting over. Very much a sliver of the crystal he would have to destroy to bring her to the lower state to live on the Earth plane as a human. It all made sense, but it was no less terrifying than it was thrilling. Becoming mortal would be the most daring thing she'd ever done. And for what, to feel the touch of a human man? Had she truly lost her mind? She wished they had more time, but Merlin was testing her when he said now. If she said later, he would sense the weakness within her, and she would lose her chance. So long she had desired this outcome, and now it was presented to her, she couldn't back out.

Taking a deep breath, she forged forward.

It was interesting that he took her hand. He had not done that before; the wizard always came off as so aloof and above them all. He would be the first being she would be able to feel. At least she hoped she could feel him. "Merlin, do you think I will be able to feel your skin even though you cannot?"

The wizard stopped in his tracks, dropping her hand. "Yes, of course you can. If not, others would have mentioned it. Arthur is quite touchy; he likes to show his affection to the ones he cares about."

"Oh, thank goodness. I didn't want to have to wait too long. And if I'm honest, you've always been very appealing to me. Something about how you see me for who I am and yet are seemingly unaffected by my magick. I wonder how you will feel when I have no power. Perhaps you will find me a bore."

"It is possible." Merlin continued forward.

She found she didn't like that idea at all.

They were now deep into inner Earth. The hum of energy radiated around them. Indeed, Sophia could sense their presence by now. Yet, she hadn't chosen to engage them.

"Do you know where you're going?" Viviane hissed.

"Quiet, we're very close. I need to concentrate."

As they rounded a corner, a light shimmered from the ground off to the left. Merlin veered in that direction. Following the silvery glow on the rock flooring, they came to a stop before a rock wall. Merlin placed his hand on the surface and recited an ancient spell. Golden sigils danced in the air, and the wall wavered before them as they stepped through it.

Viviane gasped at the sight. Surrounding them was a room full of crystals from very tiny to quite large. They glimmered, energy pulsating off them. Merlin didn't have to tell her which one was hers, the power called to her. And it was breathtakingly beautiful with so many facets. It was clear and yet all colors at the same time. Radiance danced from within to without. Reaching out, she pulled it from the slot. Could she allow Merlin to destroy something so stunning? All she was and ever had been was stored inside of this object.

"Merlin, when you say you will destroy it, what exactly do you mean?"

"I will not shatter it as you believe. That would be disastrous. I will simply dissolve the structure of the stone. Breaking down the molecules and dispersing them. The energy will still be alive. It will just not be condensed into one object. This means to fully awaken and remember who you are once you're mortal, you will have to recall the energy and bring it back into your soul. It will be extremely challenging"

This explanation was much simpler to digest. If the energy pattern was not destroyed, Viviane knew she would find a way back to it. Much like it was effortless for her to find her stone amongst so many. "Merlin, do you promise you will take me on as a pupil?"

"I promise. This will be my greatest life's work, and I will follow it to completion even if it takes you a thousand life cycles."

Nodding her head, she handed the crystal to Merlin. She felt an ache within her being but pushed it aside. "I am ready."

"We cannot do it here. Your body wouldn't be able to withstand the energy of inner Earth. I have a cabin where I go when I need solitude. We will go there, and I will perform the ritual of release."

"Thank you, Merlin. I know you are risking much by granting me this wish."

"We shall see. Let us hurry before Sophia decides to intervene."

Viviane knew Sophia well, and she knew the goddess always allowed free will and would not intervene. She was aware that Sophia would be very angry and consider her foolish, but that was something she would deal with at a later date.

Once they were back on the surface of the Earth, they only had to think of the cabin, and they were there. Viviane hadn't known about his place of solitude and was surprised at how charming it was. The outside was covered in vines and had a thatched roof. Beautiful flowers covered the mossy ground. It struck her that this would be her last memory of being the Lady of the Lake. She would miss the water.

Merlin prepped the altar to prepare for the releasing ritual. For the millionth time, he wondered if he was out of his mind playing around with such things. And yet, he knew he would not back out at this point. Soon Viviane would no longer be the enchanting creature she was, but a mere human. Quite a shame, but the choice was hers.

The spell, like most, was quite simple. Long ago, Merlin had given up the theatrics of drawn-out spell casting. It was unnecessary. He held the crystal in his hands, felt the waves of energy emanating from it as they mingled with his own. He entered into communion with the encoding of the crystal and commanded the molecules to disperse and only return at the command of the soul's owner. The crystal remained in his hand, but the light was no more. He had believed the crystal itself would disappear, but that was not the case.

A loud thud caused Merlin to glance over his shoulder, and there on the ground was a heap of naked flesh and long, curly hair. He placed the crystal in a vault he conjured on the spot.

Hurriedly, he dropped to the ground and turned over the unresponsive body. She appeared the same; her beauty had somehow remained in the human form. After checking for a pulse, Merlin lifted her, brought her into the bedroom, and covered her with blankets. He did not know how long it would take her to revive; it could be minutes or days.

Sophia's voice startled him. "Merlin! What have you done?"

He turned and saw the supreme goddess standing in front of the fireplace.

His shoulder lifted and fell. "I was curious, and you know it's hard to say no to her."

"You have no idea of the consequences this will have on the very fabric of the sphere itself. As you know, Viviane is not a normal elemental. She is my daughter! Her energy is vital in sustaining the very delicate balance on Earth."

"I understand, but you have other daughters who can take her place until this experiment's completion. Imagine how much information we can receive with having one of your own go through the cycles. We could find a way to shorten the human wheel of life, so mortals don't have to suffer so long. Give me time. If it all goes to Hades, you can step in and fix it."

Sophia sighed. "She will break your heart, Merlin. Over and over again."

He glanced toward the bedroom. "Of that, I have no doubt." And it was unsettling, but he was the one that agreed to put this craziness into play. He would have to deal with the consequences.

"Who will take her place?"

"Nimue, and like Viviane, she will not be happy about it."

Tough. "She will adjust."

"This will not be easy for Viviane. My heart breaks when I glance through the seasons of time to see what this little project of yours will do to her. But in the end, she will be stronger for it. Perhaps even strong enough to take my place so I can move on. You're not the only one exhausted with this Earth experiment, but we to have see it through to completion. I must go. I cannot help you with this, Merlin. We have to let it play out as it will now that it has been set into motion. One thing I can assure you, you're delusional to believe you could complete such a feat in one lifecycle." With that, she was gone.

Merlin put another log on the fire since Viviane would be cold when she woke up. He created a robe for her to wear, laid it on the end of the bed, and then formed several simple dresses for her as well. They hung neatly in the closet. With a mere thought, the room expanded, morphing into a room fit for a lady. He placed flowers on the chest, and the bedsheets became softer, more comfortable than his own.

Three days passed before she stirred.

Stretching, Viviane rolled over on the bed, felt the soft, fur blanket on her skin. She went to toss the blanket off and then stopped. Confusion settled over her. Her eyes popped open. Pulling the blanket up, she covered her nakedness. Her body jerked when she looked to the right and saw a tall man standing in the doorway. "Who are you? And where the hell am I?"

"I am Merlin, and I am your teacher." His voice was low and calm. "Get dressed and come out. I've made soup for you."

Shock rippled through her. "I don't think so." She stood up, wrapped the blanket around her body, and walking backward, putting more distance between them. Her eyes were wild.

"Please calm down. I know this is alarming. I mean you no harm. There was a terrible accident," the man said softly. "You were riding an untrained horse, and a snake startled it, causing it to throw you off. You slammed your head quite hard. Memory loss is common in these situations. But don't worry, your memories should return with time." He paused. "For now, it's best to continue where we left off with your studies and see if it sparks anything for you."

She rubbed the middle of her forehead. There was a strange pressure in her head. Why couldn't she remember anything? Her stomach rumbled loudly, and she noticed the fragrant smell of food.

"I know you're upset. But please just come sit down and eat. I'll answer any questions you have. You'll feel better with some food in your stomach. You've been out for nearly three days."

Viviane's eyes narrowed suspiciously for a long moment. "Three days?" How could that be?

Merlin's gaze was fixed on her face, reading her expression. It made her uncomfortable. What if he wasn't telling the truth?

"Let's go into the kitchen. We can talk while you eat. I don't want you passing out."

Despite herself, the soup smelled incredible. Waking up in a strange bed was terrifying.

Yet, she found she needed to eat and think before making any drastic decisions. For all she knew the man was telling the truth.

Sinking into the chair, she reached forward and grabbed a piece of bread. "I'm sorry, but I don't know why I am here or even who I am. You have to understand that this is beyond disturbing." She stared at him across the table. "How long have I been your pupil? And what exactly do you teach?"

He studied her face before saying, "You've been with me a very long time. I teach magick, I am a wizard of the highest order."

She smiled faintly. "Magick? Like witchcraft? I'm into that?" Viviane dipped her bread into the soup and sighed when she tasted it. "This is good. Are we lovers?" The words tumbled out of her mouth before she had decided to say them.

Silence.

Merlin's lips tightened, "No, I do not have romantic relations with my students. Ever."

"There are others?" For some reason, that set her mind at ease a little. Perhaps they could help her remember who she is.

"Well, not at the moment, but there will be in the future."

"That's very convenient." Her words hung in the air. The calmness she had previously felt vanished just as quickly.

Merlin nodded. "I understand your distrust. It would be unusual if you weren't upset. I assure you I mean you no harm."

"What were we working on before the incident?" She continued to eat, savoring the soup. She was hungry. When their eyes met, she could feel the intensity of them. He was intelligent and maybe felt a warmth toward her, even if it was strictly as a teacher. Every ounce of her felt like bolting. And yet, for some reason, she thought she should at least stay long enough to find out if he was telling the truth. Plus, where else would she go? She didn't even know where they were. Suddenly, she realized she didn't even remember her name.

Abruptly she pushed her chair back, stood up, and paced the room. Merlin remained seated, watching her. Her heart thudded in her chest. She wanted to scream or throw something. How could she not even recall her name?

"Viviane. Your name is Viviane."

Her mouth hung agape. "How could you possibly know what I

was thinking?" Viviane wrapped her arms across her chest, and her eyes darted side to side. Fear rose in the pit of her stomach.

Just as quickly, sudden calm energy washed over her, soothing her frayed nerves. Her eyes snapped in Merlin's direction. "What did you do to me?"

"A simple calming spell. You were clearly about to get out of control. As I said, I am a wizard; telepathy is easy for me. You were upset and broadcasting your thoughts very loudly. The calming wave is effortless, something you were quite adept at…controlling others' emotions. You will be again." He paused. "We just need to practice. Even if you can't recall your past, I can still teach you everything you once knew. It will just take time, like any novice. Please, Viviane, you must trust me."

"You're asking me to trust a stranger. You must understand how absurd that is?" She paused, looking up at him. "Viviane is my name?"

"It is. Why don't you go into your bedroom, and look through some of your items? Perhaps that will put your mind at ease."

Taking a deep breath, she nodded. Perhaps that would help. She turned on her heel and strode into the bedroom. This time she took it all in—the flowers, the clothes in the closet, the pretty rug on the floor, a mirror with a chair. It was a nice room. There was a box on top of the shelf. She reached up and grabbed it. Inside were letters, drawings, and pressed flowers. Closing her eyes, she ran her hand over the objects, begging them to return any memory to her. But she received nothing. Placing the box back, she went over to the sitting area; there were several jewelry pieces, all beautiful. She had exquisite taste.

"Look under your pillow."

Viviane tossed the pillow aside and saw what appeared to be a journal. She opened it, surprised to see ancient symbols. Turning the page, she realized it was a book of spells, along with apothecary ingredients. He'd been telling the truth. She was into witchcraft.

After several moments, Merlin came closer. "You asked what we had been working on before the accident. We've been focusing on the element of water. It's something you are very gifted in."

Her brow furrowed. "I am? In what way? I don't recall any of this even though I want to."

"When you are ready, we'll take a walk to the lake and see if it stirs any memories. We used to spend a lot of time there."

She tried to absorb all the information she'd received in such a short amount of time. Her mind couldn't seem to move quick enough to process. She should at least go to the water and see if the wizard was correct. And if she had to, she would clobber him with a rock or something and make a run for it. "All right, but I'd like another bowl of soup first."

His lips quirked into a half smile. "Of course, as much as you'd like, you must be starving. Would you like some tea?"

She nodded. Tea sounded good to her right now. Perhaps she loved tea before she lost consciousness and memories. She felt foolish for doubting him. But any sane person would have felt the same she would imagine.

She watched as the man crossed into the kitchen area. It was interesting she remembered what a kitchen was but not yesterday. Hopefully, as he said, the memories would return quickly. She studied him. He was quite attractive, and his movements were sure. A wizard of the highest order, and he claimed they were not lovers.

After he cleaned up the dishes, they made their way down to the lake. The mossy ground felt incredible beneath her feet. When she saw the lake, her heart quickened. Without thought, she dropped her robe and stepped into the lake. The sensation was indescribable. Even though the water was frigid, as was the air, it was invigorating. When she immersed herself in the water, she laughed. "Come in, Merlin."

He hesitated for a moment before dropping his robe. His body was lean but muscular. If he found the water cold, he didn't show it. "It's wonderful. What are you sensing?"

"Sensing?" Viviane asked warily. "I don't know. Water? Coldness, wetness."

"Do you feel the energy?"

"I don't even know what that means."

"Water is an element, and it has an energetic signature you can tune into. It should feel very natural to you." He swam closer. "Close your eyes. The human body is made up mostly of water, as is the planet itself. Ask to feel the energy of water and tell me what it feels like."

She closed her eyes, feeling slightly foolish. "I do feel a slight flowing sensation, but it's not very strong. How would I have answered this question before the accident?"

"You would have said you felt one with the water."

"I don't feel that now. Do you think I've lost what I learned?"

"Do not fret, what was unlearned can be relearned. We will work with all the elements."

"How advanced was I?" she asked

"Top marks, my prized pupil, and you will get back there. Of this I have no doubt."

"Merlin?" She closed the distance between them, placing her hand on his bare shoulder. His body felt warm even in the coldness. Their bodies were so close she felt her chest touch his. Her eyes widened as desire coursed through her. She wondered if she was sexually drawn to this man before the accident and, if so, how she was able to resist seducing him. There was no denying—by the reaction of his own body—that the attraction was mutual. However, she would not cross any lines, at least not until she could assess the situation better. "Thank you for making sure I survived the accident and taking care of me."

He pulled back. "It is my duty. One I take very seriously. You've done well today, but you should rest. Let's get back to the cabin, and tomorrow we will start your training. As if it were day one, and you were an untrained sorceress."

She swam after him, pulling herself out of the water. She noticed Merlin would not glance her way until her robe was back on. "How did you become my instructor?"

"Your family sent you to me when you were quite young."

"My family?" Her voice turned urgent. "Can I go see them? Maybe that will jar something in my mind."

"I'm sorry, but they are no longer here," he said quietly. "That's how you came to me. A plague killed your family."

Her hand touched her chest. She was feeling bewildered, frustrated, and a little scared. It seemed as if no one but this man knew anything about her. The confidence she had felt being near Merlin had quickly dispersed. Her emotions were all over the place. "That's terrible. How old was I?"

"Seven, and had already shown great signs of your gifts. They are yours and will be returned to you no matter how long it takes. Your mother was a dear friend of mine, and I promised to bring you into your full potential. She, too, was a great sorceress. Your parents were very fond of you."

Her eyes narrowed. "How old are you? You do not appear to be much older than I."

"I am much, much older, but I am a wizard, so I only age as much as or as little as I would like."

Viviane allowed the information to rattle around her head. In a flash, she became determined to reclaim her lost knowledge. For her family name, she would do whatever it took to remember who she was and what her abilities were.

"Merlin, you must teach me," she eyed him steadily, "everything you know."

His head dipped slightly. "It would be my pleasure. No matter how long it takes."

"Hopefully, not too long." She frowned.

"Indeed. We will take it one day at a time."

They walked back to the cabin in silence. Viviane knew she would spend the rest of her life learning. Her heart ached for a family she couldn't recall. So many emotions coursed through her body. So many unknowns.

"Merlin, what was I like? Before the accident."

He stopped walking. "Stubborn, powerful, and impulsive."

Not a very appealing description. "Was I a bad person?"

Taking her by the elbow, they continued walking. "Bad is so subjective."

Finding herself smiling, she gave him a nudge with her elbow.

"Viviane, you've been given a chance so few receive. Losing your memory allows you to have a clean slate, to start anew."

She had not thought of it in such a way. Perhaps the wizard was right. Plus, it didn't sound like she had anyone she was close to, so maybe she could take this as a chance to see life with fresh eyes, embrace every moment as if it were her last because one never knew when it might come to an abrupt end.

END

Ever since I was a child, I've had a fascination with Knights and King Arthur's world. There's so much mystery and magic. The Lady of the Lake is such a pivotal part of the story, but we don't know very much about her, so it's always interesting to use the imagination to see what story reveals itself.

Thanks for reading,

Julia Crane

www.Juliacrane.com

THE WISHING THORN

JAMIE FERGUSON

I hadn't planned to make a wish.

I could have made my wish of the hawthorn tree at the top of the little hill, and tied colored ribbons or even strips of cloth on its branches. The hawthorn is the traditional wishing tree, after all, and was the obvious choice.

But hawthorns like to solve problems by cleansing your heart of negativity and creating or strengthening love and romance in your life. Not only was romance the complete opposite of what I wanted, I couldn't figure out if that kind of wish could possibly be granted by that kind of tree.

And so I did not ask the hawthorn.

I could have made my wish of the old willow that hung far out over the little lake, for a willow will grant wishes as well, but only if you ask in the right way, by telling the tree one of your secrets. But I didn't have any secrets I wanted to share—although I *did* have secrets. Willows deal with healing, protection, and peace, all things that my wish would have given *me*…but which I could only receive if they were taken away from someone else.

And so I did not ask the willow.

Instead, I chose the blackthorn, the tree of warfare, the tree of ill omens and the keeper of dark secrets…

If I hadn't noticed the message light up his phone that day in the middle of May, I might never have found out at all that Tyler was seeing someone else.

He'd left his phone in the middle of the kitchen counter while he went to take a shower. The text came through right as I went to grab a paper towel to wipe up the olive oil I'd spilled while making quesadillas for dinner. The words appeared on top of his lock screen image: a photo of the two of us at the opera last fall, Tyler in a tuxedo and me in a fancy, sequined dress, our arms around each other and big smiles on our faces.

See you at the hotel next week…don't be late! I have a surprise for you… Hugs, Janice.

My blood felt as though it had turned to ice, and the only thing I could hear was the thump-thump-thumping of my heartbeat ringing in my ears.

I took a deep breath, then smiled and shook my head. It was just a wrong number.

After he got out of the shower, I asked him about the message anyway.

"Someone must have texted me by accident," he said with a laugh. "I don't know anyone named Janice. Don't worry, Leah, no one can hold a candle to you. I'm going to marry you, and you'll be stuck with me for the rest of your life."

He snapped his towel at my backside, then wrapped his arms around my shoulders and kissed me.

Fortunately I hadn't turned the oven on yet, as dinner was a bit delayed by what ensued.

But later that evening, I noticed he wasn't leaving his phone lying around the house like he normally did. Every time he got up, whether to get a drink, or brush his teeth, he picked it up and took it with him.

Later that night I grabbed his phone while he was sleeping. I carried it into the bathroom, unlocked it, and pulled up his calendar, my fingers trembling.

A two-hour block was on his calendar earlier that day, with the name of a ritzy hotel in the foothills about forty-five minutes away. On a Monday. A workday. When he was supposed to be *at work*.

And the event was called Tyler & Janice.

He'd said he didn't even know anyone by that name.

He'd lied.

I bit my lip, then opened his text messages. Sure enough, the person he claimed he didn't know had sent him multiple messages, and he'd replied to them. All of their conversations were about meeting at different hotels and restaurants, and Janice had sent a few photos of the two of them with picturesque backgrounds.

Multi-colored heart emojis were sprinkled throughout her messages to him.

I tiptoed back into the bedroom and put the phone on his nightstand. I crawled back into bed and scooted to the very edge of the mattress, as far away from him as I could possibly get. My head spun and I felt like I couldn't catch my breath, even though I could hear myself breathing. I didn't know what to do. Should I wake him up and tell him I'd spied on him? Should I show up at their next rendezvous—and surprise him and the trollop he'd apparently been seeing for who knew how long?

The only thing I was sure of was that my life would never be the same again. Tyler and I had been together for over three years. *Three years.* We'd talked about kids, the dream house we wanted to build, the places we wanted to travel to over time…everything we wanted to do while we spent the rest of our lives together. We were happy.

But apparently only one of us was happy…or at least I had been until I found out about…this.

Finally I shook him awake, and asked—okay, confronted—him about it. "Janice is my cousin," he said, and let out a big sigh. "We're planning a big family event. It's supposed to be a surprise, and I promised her I wouldn't tell anyone else."

"I've never heard of Janice before," I snapped. "I've met all your cousins."

He swallowed. "She's my second cousin. Or my first cousin twice removed, or something like that. You've never met her."

"Obviously not."

"I'm telling you the truth, Leah. I promise. I love you and I want to spend the rest of my life with you. Only you."

He looked so sad and forlorn that I wanted to believe him. I wanted to forgive him. I wanted to tell him I loved him.

But I didn't.

Instead I got out of bed and got dressed.

Tyler tried to stop me, to tell me things weren't what they appeared to be, that he loved me.

I ignored his words, grabbed my car keys, and left.

Now, not only was he cheating on me, I no longer had a place of my own to go back to.

I drove to an old dirt road on the north side of town, pulled off on the side of the road, and cried for my lost love, my lost dreams. My lost life.

After a while I checked my phone. He'd sent several messages, all saying variants of: *This isn't what it looks like. Please believe me. I'll explain later. I love you.*

I stared at his ridiculous messages for a few minutes, then I typed out a response. My fingers shook, but I finally got the words out.

I hate you. I never want to see you again.

I blocked his number and cried some more.

Around one in the morning I ran out of tears. But as my sadness diminished, my anger grew...as did my resolve as I realized I knew what I wanted to do.

Moonlight turned everything to shades of gray as I trudged across a wide, open area in the city park, my sneakered feet making tiny scuffing sounds on the grass. A tall hawthorn tree stood near the little creek that marked the northern edge of the park, and a weeping willow grew on the bank, its long, elegant branches hanging down, some of them touching the surface of the water. During the day the park was full of kids, joggers, and happy dogs, but tonight I was the only one there to admire the picturesque scene.

I headed toward the western edge where a clump of blackthorns clustered at the edge of the woods. The spring air was that in-between temperature that was not quite comfortable, yet not quite chilly. I zipped up my hoodie while my eyes darted around, scanning for potential danger. This park was considered relatively safe, and in theory the police patrolled here every night, but I had my pepper spray ready in one hand just in case.

As I got closer to the row of blackthorns, I realized there were five of them, or maybe seven—it was hard to tell for sure since they were all bunched up together. The tallest was about ten feet tall, and maybe a little wider than that. In the day they looked unobtrusive, more like big, scraggly shrubs than trees. But tonight they seemed darker, their leaves casting eerie, flickering shadows that moved when the wind rustled the branches.

My grandmother had told me tales of the magic of trees, which she'd learned from her own grandmother, who'd grown up in Ireland in the early 1800s. The stories weren't true, of course. Worst case, I'd end up going back to my car to find a spot to park until morning. Then I'd find an empty little apartment to rent and live there with my empty, broken heart. Eventually I would heal enough that I'd be able to tamp down my feelings of anger and betrayal and spend time with my friends and family again. But tonight, I'd allowed my emotions to take control.

Because...why not?

I was always calm, thoughtful, open-minded. I never lost my temper, wasn't quick to judge. But I'd never had anything like this happen to me before, and I was furious. Anger was a new, heady sensation. So why not try to see if Gram's tales were real, and could help me to get back at the man who'd turned my entire life upside-down?

I balled my hands up in fists, stared at the blackthorns, and hoped with all my might that the old stories were real.

I jammed the pepper spray into my pocket, hurried over to the little thicket, and walked around the trees. Their leaves looked silvery in the light of the half-full moon. Clusters of tiny blossoms dotted the trees with bits of white, and rather sinister-looking thorns over an inch long studded their dense, black branches.

Gram's tales had never explained *how* to make wishes of trees. They usually started with the tale of the person's plight, then jumped forward in time to where the person and the tree were having a conversation, so I didn't know how to start. Was I supposed to bow? Was there a specific phrase I was supposed to use? Should I sit? Stand? Sing a song? Tie ribbons on the branches? Was I supposed to talk to all of them, or just one?

I glanced over my shoulder to make sure I wouldn't be surprised by anyone else lurking in the park—or by the police clearing out punk kids, drug dealers, and crazy people.

I wasn't unaware that I might fall in the last category.

I pressed my lips together and looked up at the moon, then I glanced back at my car.

It looked small and far away, even though it was only a short walk from where I stood. I could leave, but where would I go? I couldn't go home. Tyler would be there. Or at least I assumed he would be, unless he'd gone to Janice's house after I'd left. How many times had he hooked up with her? Or with other women—maybe she wasn't the first.

I had thought I was going to spend the rest of my life with him. How could he do this to me?

I sank to my knees on the cool grass about ten feet away from the blackthorn thicket, screwed my eyes shut, wrapped my arms around myself, and muffled my gasping sobs with the sleeve of my hoodie.

After a few minutes I raised my head, the hurt and anger inside of me hardening into determination. I might be crazy to be out here in the middle of the night to try to talk to a tree, but what-the-fuck-ever. If it didn't work, it didn't work.

But if it did...

...Tyler would pay.

I grinned, wiped my nose on my sleeve, and straightened my shoulders. The breeze fluttered the leaves of the little trees in front of me. I took a deep breath, made an attempt at a bow, and sat down on the cool grass in front of the tallest blackthorn.

"Hello," I said, looking up at the tree. I cleared my throat. "I'm... My name is Leah. I...I am here to make a wish."

Nothing happened.

I ran a hand through my hair. There was probably some special saying I was supposed to know, but didn't. Or maybe I was supposed to make an offering.

Or maybe I was crazy.

I screwed my eyes shut, clasped my hands together, and thought about the stories Gram had told me. I remembered her voice and the way her face lit up when she talked about magic, as if she really believed in it. I concentrated on my desire to make my wish, how important it was to me, how much I believed in the magic of the trees—or at least how much I wanted to believe. I focused as hard as I could on the tree in front of me, willing it to hear me, to grant my wish. A gust of wind ruffled my hair, making it tickle the side of my face, but I ignored the sensation and put everything I could into my will, my determination, my need.

A small, scratchy sound, like twigs rubbing together, jolted me out of my reverie.

I opened my eyes and blinked. The only light was from the not-quite-full moon, but it seemed super bright after having my eyes closed for who knew how long. My back had grown stiff and one of my feet had fallen asleep. I stretched out my legs, wriggling the toes on the foot that had fallen asleep, and looked up at the tree. Apparently it wasn't magic after all.

The scratchy sound came again, but this time I could see something moving in the tangle of branches and leaves next to the base of the tree.

Whatever it was, it was making some of the smaller branches move back and forth.

I sighed. This whole thing was stupid. As soon as my foot stopped tingling, I'd head back to my car. I'd have to –

I froze, prickles running down my spine, as I realized the branches were actually moving *toward me.*

At first it just looked like a bundle of twigs, but as it grew closer I realized it was a thin, wizened, human-like creature maybe a foot and a half tall. Its skin looked as if it were made from bark. Tiny spikes, like miniature versions of the thorns on the tree in front of me, jutted out from its head. Its ears were long and pointed, and its arms and legs were narrow and looked more like branches than limbs. Black, beady eyes were framed with eyebrows that looked almost like they were made of very small leaves.

It was one of the Lunantisidhe, the moon fairies who guarded the blackthorn.

Gram's stories had been real after all.

I held my breath as the creature approached. It stopped just outside of my reach.

"You have a wish to make," it said, its voice deep and raspy.

"Yes," I said. I swallowed. "My name is Leah. I, um, I would like to ask, um…I'm not sure how to do this."

The fairy's brow narrowed. More of the Lunantisidhe were approaching, some from the tree I sat in front of, and some from the other blackthorns.

"I mean…I'm sorry, I apologize for whatever I'm doing, or not doing. But…I do have a wish. Should I ask you?"

The Lunantisidhe all burst out in raucous laughter, the sound like thousands of pieces of wood being scraped and smacked together. Then, as if on cue, they stopped. They stared at me, their beady little eyes fixed on my face. I swallowed. There were over twenty of them, some as tall as the first, some half as high, and all of them looking up at me. A few more skittled in from the sides, their movements sharp and jerky.

A trickle of sweat ran down the side of my face. I had no idea what to do next. I didn't remember a lot about the Lunantisidhe from Gram's tales, but I did remember they were never very friendly. They definitely didn't look at all friendly in person. At least I hadn't accidentally shown up on Beltane or Samhain, since the folklore said they cursed anyone who disturbed blackthorn trees on those days. Maybe I should just go sleep in my car and find an apartment to rent in the morning. Maybe—

I gritted my teeth. Remembering I was now homeless—there was no way I was going to spend another night with Tyler—pushed my nervousness aside.

"Please, let me know what I need to do."

The Lunantisidhe began whispering to each other, their beady little eyes fixed on me. One started giggling, covering its mouth with its tiny, twiggy hands.

The breeze rustled the leaves of the trees, and the fairies grew silent. They moved to one side or the other, shuffling sideways on their gnarled, thin legs, and splitting into two groups separated by several feet. They were making a pathway for me to the tallest of the blackthorns.

I took a deep breath, wriggled my toes on my now-awake foot, and scrambled to my feet. Then my breath caught at what I saw.

The shape of a woman in the tree.

It was as if she were a shadow, for I could see the branches of the tree through her, *inside* of her. I could even see leaves moving gently in the light breeze.

She walked toward me, and as she approached, she coalesced and became more solid. Her pale skin looked almost translucent in the light of the moon, and her dark hair cascaded below her waist in thick waves. She wore a gown made of what I first thought to be white lace but realized was made up of blackthorn flowers.

She stopped before me, her emerald-green eyes fixed on mine.

I bit my lip. "Hi. I, uh, my name is Leah. I came to ask for a wish. I'm sorry but I don't know the protocol."

"You may ask however you'd like." Her voice was warm, rich, melodious. She smiled. "The rules are about how wishes are fulfilled. Not about how they are requested."

"Okay. Um. I... I wish to punish my...my boyfriend. He...I found out..." I took a deep breath, my anger rekindling itself. "My wish is to make him regret what he did to me, to hurt him like he hurt me. I don't know exactly what I'm asking for, just that my wish is for whatever hurts him the most."

Her smile faded, and her face grew somber. "I will ask once, and only once. Are you, Leah, sure that this wish is what you truly want?"

Was I sure?

I thought of him meeting his "cousin" at the hotel earlier in the day, and what that must have entailed.

I set my shoulders and nodded. "Yes. I'm sure."

The woman raised one hand toward me, spread out her fingers, and turned her hand in the air as she made a fist, as if she were grabbing hold of something invisible.

She nodded at me. "Your wish has been granted."

I blinked. Was that all there was to it?

She turned and walked back toward the tallest blackthorn. I realized with a start that the Lunantisidhe were gone, although I hadn't heard them leave. I swallowed and watched as the woman walked back into the tree, becoming translucent as she moved toward the trunk, the branches once again visible inside of her. She dissipated, almost like smoke.

For a split-second I could see tiny lights twinkling in the space where she'd been. And then they, too, were gone.

I blinked.

The moonlight was gone, the sky now the pink and purple of dawn. Had I imagined the fairies, the woman, everything? Maybe it was a dream.

I turned around to go back to my car, but it was no longer there.

Someone had stolen it, and I hadn't heard a thing.

I fumbled in my pockets for my phone, but it wasn't there either. I looked around on the grass, then retraced my steps, but my phone was nowhere to be found. I must have left it in my car. So much for getting a ride...not that I had anywhere to go.

There was a gas station about half a mile away. I could walk there and call the police to report my car had been stolen. And then after that...

After that, maybe I'd check in on Tyler, and see how my wish was working out for *him*.

Early morning fog had sprung up. I jammed my hands into the pockets of my hoodie as I walked down the street, the scents of concrete and exhaust tickling my nose. It felt as if I'd been walking for an hour or so. I could have sworn the gas station was closer to the park than this. At least I wasn't sleepy. I felt oddly alert.

I still couldn't believe that Gram's stories from Ireland were real. Nor could I believe I'd been so angry that I'd decided to ask a tree to grant a wish.

Where was that stupid gas station? At least the fog was finally dissipating. I needed to –

I skidded to a stop as I realized I was outside my parents' house.

Not only was there no way I'd walked the ten or so miles to my parents' house, but their front door was ajar, and Tyler's truck was parked on the other side of the street.

What the hell was he doing there?

I stormed up to the front door and went inside.

The muted hum of conversation grew louder as I walked through the foyer, up the stairs, and into the great room my parents had added on to the house a few years before.

There were at least twenty people there, gathered in little groups: my parents, my brothers, my friends from book club, several of my cousins...and Tyler, his arm around that woman Janice's shoulders.

"You asshole!" I was so angry I could feel myself shaking. "Tyler, how dare you bring that bitch here?"

He didn't even have the decency to meet my eyes, much less respond.

I stood in front of him, my hands on my hips. "Get out."

My cheeks were burning—everyone else in the room must be staring at me, wondering what was going on. I set my jaw. Let them wonder.

"Now, Tyler. Go away. And take your…your new girlfriend with you."

He continued to ignore me. My mom walked over, a tissue in one hand.

"Thank you so much for reading that poem, Tyler," she said. She dabbed at her eyes with the tissue. "It was absolutely perfect. Leah would have…"

She sniffled, waved her hand in the air, and then burst into tears.

I took a step toward her. "I'm right here, Mom. What's going on?"

Janice stepped in front of me, took my mom by the arm, and led her over to the sofa. The back of my neck prickled.

My eyes darted around the room. Bouquets, vases, and baskets of flowers were piled on the table, the hutch, and scattered about the floor. Everyone wore suits and dark dresses, as if this were a formal event. Boxes of tissues were scattered around the room.

I hurried after Tyler, who now stood alone next to a window. He stared out at the foothills to the east.

"Tyler?" I asked, my voice sounding tinny and hollow. "Can you hear me?"

"Leah," he said, his voice low. "I miss you."

"Oh, thank god!" I said, my anger swept away, at least temporarily. "I know this is going to sound weird, but I was starting to think I was invisible. I –"

He bit his lip. "I hope you liked the poem. I was going to read it to you when I proposed."

My entire body felt as if it had turned to ice.

"I wanted to surprise you," he whispered. His jaw clenched, and a tear trickled down his cheek. "I should have just told you about my cousin being a wedding planner. I should have…"

He screwed his eyes shut, took a deep breath, then opened them, blew his nose, and walked over to one of the tables. I realized with a start that there were pictures of me scattered amongst all the flowers.

I swallowed.

His mouth a thin line, he ran his fingers over the edge of a framed photo of us from last Thanksgiving. We had our arms around each other and happy smiles on our faces.

I'd made a wish to punish an innocent man.

My steps slow and hesitant, I walked over to the big, flower-laden dining table, and read the open cards.

Our condolences about the loss of your daughter, Leah…

We're thinking of you…

Sympathies…

Our thoughts are with you…

We miss Leah so much…

I stepped to the side as a couple of my girlfriends approached the table.

"I still can't believe it," one of them said. "We just went out for happy hour last Friday. I can't believe she's gone."

"Me either."

"Did you see the photos of the accident in the paper? Her car was completely unrecognizable. It didn't even look like a car anymore…"

I couldn't listen anymore. I pressed my hands to my ears and watched my friends walk away.

My knees felt wobbly as I remembered my words to the fairy woman:

"My wish is for whatever hurts him the most."

I ran outside, then skidded to a stop as I realized I had no car. The park was at least ten miles away, maybe more.

I took a deep breath, balled my hands up into fists, and began to run.

The late afternoon sun warmed my shoulders as I walked across the wide, open area of the city park again, heading toward the thicket of blackthorns at the edge of the woods. They looked innocuous, a cluster of short, scraggly trees covered with tiny white flowers. I set my jaw as I neared them.

I sat down in front of the tallest of the blackthorns, screwed my eyes shut, clasped my hands together, and concentrated on the tree, thinking about the woman with the emerald eyes and the twig-like moon fairies. I focused with every fiber of my being, willing the fairies to hear me.

After what felt like hours I opened my eyes. No one was there. My shoulders were stiff and sore from sitting for so long, and it had gotten chilly. I glanced up at the darkened sky, and realized the sun had set. I bit my lip and stared at the tree.

"Please, please come back," I said.

A cool breeze rustled the leaves of the tree, but no fairies appeared.

"Please." I took a deep breath. "I don't know what to do.".

"*Please!*"

The leaves of the tree moved again, but this time there was no wind. I squinted, and saw the faint shadow of the fairy woman in the tree.

I scrambled to my feet as she moved toward me.

As before, she walked through the tree as if the leaves and the thorny branches were ethereal. Her long, dark hair had been plaited into hundreds of braids with the small, white blackthorn flowers woven through them. Her green gown was made from leaves that looked exactly like those on the trees in front of me. She stopped several feet away from me, her emerald eyes bright in the fading light of the evening.

"Good evening, Leah." she said.

The sound of her voice hung in the air after her word finished, like the hum of a ringing bell.

"I'm really sorry, but I made a mistake," I said, the words spilling out. "I need to undo my wish."

"Once granted, a wish may not be undone," she said.

"But I *have* to undo this. I was wrong. I misunderstood what was going on."

The fairy woman stared at me, her pale face as still as if it had been carved out of stone.

I sank to my knees and began to sob. I curled into a little ball and cried and cried.

"I am sorry," I said. "I made a wish. I should not have made it… but I did. You granted it. You said there are rules about how wishes are fulfilled, and I did not ask what they were. I acted out of anger, and I hurt not only the man I love, but my family and friends as well. And now…now I'm dead."

"You are not dead, mortal woman," she said.

I blinked.

She glanced up at the moon. I realized with a start that it was full, as if several days had passed.

"You belong to Faerie now. You may walk among your people, but they cannot see, or hear, or even touch you."

I belonged to Faerie? What did that even mean?

"But…that's not fair! I didn't ask for that!" I felt as though I'd been punched in the stomach.

Her eyes narrowed as she looked at me. It felt as if I were being appraised, as if she were looking into my very soul.

"Leah, why did you come to the blackthorn to make your wish?"

My voice was small. "I wanted to hurt Tyler, and the blackthorn was the only tree that I thought would grant my wish."

The breeze rustled the leaves of the tree behind her, and the thousands of leaves that made up her dress fluttered.

"You may call me Áine," she said after a moment. "The blackthorn is tied to darkness, but also to light, to protection and home even in the midst of devastation. Unlike other trees, the blackthorn pulls in *both* energies. There is great power involved in keeping the balance between the two. And the balance must be kept."

"Did my wish mess up the balance?"

"No," she said. "But if I undid your bargain, that would."

I took a deep breath. "But I—I didn't make a bargain. I just made a wish."

"The rules are clear. Your ignorance of them, and your failure to ask about them, is your burden."

I opened my mouth to reply, then snapped it shut as what she said sunk in. She was right. I, and I alone, was to blame for the foolishness of my actions. I'd made my wish without even thinking there might be a cost. Nor had I thought about the ramifications—not just for Tyler, but for everyone else I knew and loved.

I pressed my hands to my mouth and sank to my knees in the cool, damp grass. I screwed my eyes shut, and my entire body shook.

Finally, I raised my head and met her gaze.

The fairy woman appraised me for a moment. "I see. Your wish may not be undone, and the bargain will stand. But, if you can find a way to change your fate, I will not insist upon it being fulfilled immediately."

Áine glanced up at the top of the blackthorn nearest her and nodded, almost as if she and the tree were in agreement about something, and then she met my gaze. "When you are ready, come back to this thicket and walk through the trees and into Faerie. I wish you luck, Leah."

She turned and walked back into the trees, her shape fading, becoming translucent.

I could hear voices raised in song coming from where she had gone, the sound so beautiful and compelling that I stood up and took a step forward, and then another.

No!

I clamped my hands over my ears and screwed my eyes shut.

When I opened my eyes, Áine was gone, and the tree that stood in front of me was just a tree.

I looked up at the top of the blackthorn tree, the tips of its branches swaying in the light of the full moon.

I had a price to pay…someday.

But now I had to try to find someone—or something—willing to help me undo—no, not undo, *change*—what I'd done.

To help me heal what I'd broken.

I set my shoulders and began to walk toward the other side of the park, toward the hawthorn tree.

END

AUTHOR'S NOTE

My story was inspired by the folklore of the blackthorn, the tree known as the "wishing thorn." This is one of the trees thought to straddle the boundaries between our world and that of Faerie. The Lunantisidhe, thin, wizened fairies with pointed ears and teeth, inhabit these trees and are bound to protect them. These fairies do not like people *at all,* and will curse anyone who disturbs their trees at Samhain or Beltaine.

The blackthorn is associated with warfare, death, power, and malevolence—but also with hope and protection. I found the complexity of the legends intriguing—rather than being a source of good or of evil, the blackthorn is both at once.

ABOUT THE AUTHOR

Jamie focuses on getting into the minds and hearts of her characters, whether she's writing about a saloon girl in the Old West, a man who discovers the barista he's in love with is a naiad, or a ghost who haunts the house she was killed in—even though that house no longer exists. She lives in Colorado and spends her free time in a futile quest to wear out her two border collies, since she hasn't given in and gotten them their own herd of sheep. Yet. You can find Jamie at jamieferguson.com.

WOVEN FROM PURE STARLIGHT

JENNA ELIZABETH JOHNSON

"Caitlin!"

My name, when spat from Sorcha's foul mouth, sent shivers of dread up my spine. I dropped the shears I'd been using to harvest the garden herbs, and turned to catch sight of the bane of my existence moving down the cobblestone path like a flock of ravens descending upon a battlefield. Sorcha was Cheadmorr, a willing servant to the Morrigan and one of the goddess's most loyal underlings. She had also murdered my mother.

Before she could get too close, I said, "Sorcha. What did you need?"

Sorcha stopped fifteen feet away, her lip curling in derision. No, she wasn't like a flock of ravens, but a golden eagle. Precise, cold, cruel, and beautiful. Sorcha's eyes dropped to the braid trailing down my torso. Instinct had me twitching my head, shifting the braid out of view.

"The Solstice nears," she purred, her arms crossing over her chest.

Behind her, a half dozen of her favorite generals stood in full regalia, their eyes studying me too closely. And the smirks they wore had nothing to do with what happened on the Solstice. I'd noticed their regard drifting towards me five summers ago, just before I turned fifteen. That was one of the reasons I had voluntarily moved into the old grain tower far away from the manor compound.

"I know," I said, finally replying to her comment. "A fortnight from tomorrow."

Sorcha sneered at me. I knew the precise date of the winter Solstice, knew it and counted down the days more obsessively than the days until my birthday. For it was on the Solstice that Sorcha cut my hair, almost to the scalp, to wrap up and send off to the Morrigan as some sacrificial gift. Upon her death, my mother had begged the spirits of Eile to protect me from suffering the same fate. What resulted could be considered more of a curse than a blessing. All the rich magic the Morrigan coveted manifested in my hair instead of where it should, a place right beside my heart. As a result, I became akin to a sheep, its only value the wool it had to offer. But, in my case, it was hair.

I sighed and reached for my shears. "Do you mind? I wish to explore the edge of the Weald before sundown, and there is still plenty of gathering I must do here first."

Sorcha nodded, her dark eyes narrowing. "Very well. So long as you remember what you owe me. I don't want you to succumb to temptation and allow the evil creatures lurking in that forest to drag you away."

The Weald was dripping with magic, some good, some evil, but far too powerful and unpredictable for any normal Faelorehn man, woman or child to resist. I had never felt that twinge of unease during the few hours I'd spend just inside the forest's edge. Instead, it would bring me peace and calm my tumultuous thoughts.

As Sorcha's dark form retreated around the corner, more of the servants springing out of her way as she went, I knelt down and got back to work. It was late in the year, and the sun wouldn't last much longer. Still, I was determined to collect as many specimens from the Weald's edge as I could. Winter's first frost and snowfall would soon arrive, and then, I'd have to wait once again for spring, and my current supplies wouldn't last until then.

The great beech trees of the Weald's eastern edge towered over me, like silent guardians offering me quiet passage. Some still held their gold and russet leaves, others were mostly bare. Hawthorn, blackthorn, and holly grew in tangled rows between the trees. The holly's glossy leaves and bright berries were a vibrant splash of color against the dull browns and greys of early winter. I drew in a deep breath of crisp air, then twirled around, my braid whipping around me as I laughed. I loved the autumn and winter, despite the cold.

I stopped along my path, breathing in great gusts of frosty air, and picked up my braid, carefully studying the tasseled end. My hair was a very unusual color, somewhere between golden blond, pale red, and that softest of mauves witnessed only when the sun dipped low on the horizon. I was told, after my mother was murdered and her geis fell upon me, that it had once been more yellow in color, and that the rose gold hue was a result of my glamour being trapped within the strands. I always believed it because I had never seen any other Faelorehn man or woman with hair my color, and I had seen many come and go at Sorcha's whim. The fact that most of those strangers stared unapologetically at my hair when they visited was further proof of that fact.

"It's a shame you can't utilize any of that glamour," I muttered to myself. If I could, perhaps I might find a way to escape my forced servitude.

Before I could reflect on my sorry state of existence much longer, a twitch of movement grabbed my attention. I snapped my head around, thinking a singular cloud had passed before the lowering sun, but when my eyes caught the source of my distraction I gasped, nearly dropping my basket. Some fifty yards away, weaving through a young stand of birch, paced a large stag so dark brown he was nearly black. Tall, regal, with a pair of elegant, bone-white antlers, the buck didn't seem to notice me. I stood absolutely still, holding my breath, not wanting to spook him. As if sensing my sudden existence, the deer's head turned, his soft ears swiveling forward. Dark eyes locked with mine, and my heart picked up its pace.

"C-Cernunnos?" I breathed in disbelief. For who else could this be but the god of the Wild himself in animal form?

The stag shook out his head, those antlers threatening to tangle with the hawthorn branches weaving through the birch trees. A feeling of mirth struck me then, as if the buck was laughing at me. I frowned, wondering if this was the magic of the Weald weaving its spell.

To my relief, or perhaps disappointment, the buck did not transform, but kept moving forward at that leisurely pace. As he slipped into the shadows of the deeper wood, I called out, as loudly as I dared, "Well, if you aren't Cernunnos, but a regular deer, and you can understand me, be careful along the edge of this part of the Weald. Sorcha's generals and soldiers would love to take you down if they saw you."

I spent the next half hour searching for herbs. By the time the encroaching twilight forced me to give up my chore, I hadn't collected as many as I'd hoped. I tried not to let it disappoint me. So long as the hard frost held off a few days more, I should be able to gather enough for both the winter pantry stores as well as the medicinal ones. I had an interest in both healing and cooking, but it was merely a hobby. I'd never get the opportunity to practice either. At least, so long as Sorcha lived and held favor with the Morrigan. My dreams were futile, but they kept my mind busy and took me away from the manor. And perhaps, one day, I would discover some berry or mushroom that would free me of Sorcha's grasp forever.

Before leaving the edge of the forest, I tucked away my two botany books – both rescued from my mother's library before Sorcha ordered everything destroyed. As I broke away from the edge of the forest to cross over the rolling fields skirting the manor, I stopped for a moment to gaze upward. The Solstice Rose was already glittering high in the darkening sky, a pale red-gold point of light. I closed my eyes and thought of all those things I'd wished for over the years, sending my deepest desires up into the unknown. Mother had always said wishing upon the Solstice Rose held its own sort of magic, and that more likely than not, some of those wishes would come true. I had been sending up my most precious hopes and dreams my entire life, and not one of them had yet come true. Along with the desire to find a friend, a family, to know freedom, I also asked that star to keep watch over the stag I'd seen earlier. Perhaps that wish, at least, was small enough to be granted.

A group of arguing ravens just outside my window drew me from sleep the following morning. I sat up in bed, dragging my quilt up with me as my teeth chattered. I threw the dim coals in my tiny fireplace a nasty look. It would have been nice to get dressed in a warm room instead of one just above the edge of freezing. Despite the cold, it was my one day off from chores at the manor, and I didn't want to waste one minute of it. I was dressed and ready to go with my satchel and botany books in a quarter of an hour. A cool misty morning greeted me, but I just pulled my cloak tighter and secured the door to my tower behind me before stepping out onto the footpath leading to the Weald.

I was only halfway across the field when I noticed him, the stag from the day before. He skirted the edge of the forest, making his way up a familiar rise in the land. I stood absolutely still, but as soon as he disappeared over the rise, I bolted, running as swiftly and quietly as I could. Once I broke the tree line, I climbed the low hill, picking my way around shrubs and saplings, as well as a collection of large boulders. I tried not to make a sound because I did not want the buck to hear me. Why he still lingered in this place, the edge of the woods where he would be most vulnerable to hunters, was a quandary. His rare color and extraordinary antlers would make him a coveted target. The fact he had lived as long as he had proved he was no careless yearling. Yet, here he was. Drawing in a slow breath through my nose, I came to the top of the game trail.

An outcropping of dolerite monoliths that had once been an

established stone circle ringed the small rise like an ancient, weathered crown. I crossed over the outer diameter of the taller stones, some only a few inches above my head, and the gentle hum of ancient magic thrummed through my veins. Sorcha and her generals ignored this particular setting as a potential well of power, thinking it ruined because so many of the stones had toppled over the years, but I knew better. At least, my trapped glamour did.

Using the standing stones to cover my presence, I moved quickly across the circle to the other side. When I dared, I peeked around the edge of one of the taller stones down to the wide, shallow pond I knew lay several yards below. Trees ringed the edge of the pool, and several feet of saturated earth teeming with reeds and cattails extended from the water's edge. I scanned the entire area, my brows furrowing when I failed to find my quarry. Odd. Where else could he have gone?

I lifted the hem of my skirt, ready to step forward when a flash of movement and the press of a strong arm jerked me off my feet. I let out a gasp that was half surprise, half pain as the arm tightened around my waist, another pressing hard across my chest. I drew in a breath to scream, but metal flashed and the cold bite of steel at my throat had me reconsidering.

A skein of sleek, dark hair brushed my cheek and spilled over the front of my shoulder.

"Who are you?" a harsh, masculine voice whispered against my ear. His breath sent shivers of apprehension across my skin.

Apparently, I didn't answer fast enough, for the steel's cold bite pricked and I hissed at the sudden sting. A warm trickle down my neck convinced me to go utterly still.

"C-Caitlin."

"And why are you following me, Caitlin?"

He spoke barely above a whisper, but I was able to pick up a slight accent to his speech. An almost lilting cadence that didn't quite match the harsh brogue of those living on my mother's land. It almost distracted me from registering his question.

"I, I'm sorry?"

"What is your business on the edge of the Weald?"

That knife stayed pressed against my throat, but it no longer threatened to cut me.

"I am a servant of the Cheadmorr, Sorcha, who lives in the manor house just east of here. I am interested in cooking and brewing medicines. I scour the edge of these woods only in search of edible plants and herbs. I swear to you."

His grip didn't change, and as the seconds ticked by, I became more aware of the heat seeping through the back of my bodice. Slowly, his hold loosened until he shoved me away from him. I nearly tripped, catching myself against a nearby standing stone. I whipped around, not wanting to expose my back to this threat, only to gape in utter astonishment. A tall man stood no more than twenty feet away. His hair was dark and fell straight just past his shoulders. And he was completely naked, from his masculine face all the way to the soles of his feet.

Blushing furiously, I dropped my gaze. Oh, spirits of Eile. What I had managed to avoid with Sorcha's generals and soldiers all these years was about to be visited upon me now, in a place I held sacred. Fear sent tears prickling at the corners of my eyes. Sorcha had taken everything from me: my mother, my home, my freedom, and once a year, she cut off all my hair. The ancient, crumbling stone circle was all I had left. The place my mother and I used to visit on Solstice night, where she would tell me ancient tales as we watched the stars wheel above us in the dark sky.

"Please," I managed, dropping to my knees. "Please, I meant no harm. I didn't know you were here. I was only trying to catch a glimpse of a beautiful stag who has been lingering in this part of the forest for the past few days."

One tear sprang free and dropped to splatter against the stone below me. Out of the corner of my eye, I registered movement.

"No!" I cried out, scurrying back and trying to put as much distance between myself and the naked stranger as I could.

He had taken a step forward, but paused, holding out a hand.

The other rested against the side of his thigh, the knife's blade now pointing downward.

"I have no design to molest you," he said, his voice pitched louder now. If it wasn't for the threat he represented, I would have been calmed by that voice.

I glanced up at him, careful to keep my eyes fixed above his waist. He was well-built and possessed the body of a man who didn't remain idle. His was the form of a warrior or soldier. Or someone who spent his days running through the deep forest with the woodland animals at his side. I blinked away that strange thought as my eyes continued to take in every detail I could, in case he had a physical weakness I might exploit. I only noticed more muscle and several knotwork tattoos finely painted over sun-bronzed skin. Yet, even the parts that would normally be covered in clothing suggested that the copper undertones were not the result of exposure to sun. I had only ever been around Faelorehn men and women with skin as pale as my own. This man's exotic beauty was mesmerizing, and distracting.

"Is it my lack of clothing that bothers you?"

That question snapped me right out of my fog of confusion. I shot my gaze up to his. Like the other striking parts of him, his eyes slanted slightly at their corners and their pale gray color shone like silver beneath his dark brows. He reached for me again, and I cringed backwards. As intriguing as his physical form appeared, I had no idea who he was or what he wanted.

He dropped his outreached hand and ducked his head. He took a deep breath and let it out, then stepped toward the edge of the stone circle.

"Excuse me for a moment. Please. Do not leave."

He disappeared down the hill, and I simply sat there, still dazed by the sudden turn of events. That inner voice that had kept me relatively safe from Sorcha and her minions screamed at me to get up and run, but even as I tried, my legs gave out beneath me. In what seemed like mere moments, the stranger returned, this time wearing a pair of deerskin pants. The knife was also nowhere to be seen. I let out a squeak of despair, but he stopped abruptly, leaving plenty of space between us. He crossed his arms and tilted his head to the side, studying me. This time, I felt like the one who was naked as he took me in from head to toe. Those silver eyes traveled back upward and stopped just above my eyes, where my head rested against the stone. I knew what had caught his attention before he named it.

"Your hair," he began.

"Yes," I snapped, my ire returning with a vengeance. I never liked to speak about my hair for many reasons and liked even less when strangers commented on it. "It is unusual. But surely no more unusual than a naked man attacking an innocent woman out collecting herbs."

It might have been a flinch I noticed, or a failed attempt at a grunt. Either way, my snappish comment made a mark, if only a small one.

The man sighed again, the action lifting his shoulders. "I don't suppose I can make amends, can I?"

He smiled, and I almost returned the gesture. And nearly forgot why I was keeping my distance from him.

"My name is Riordan, and I am here on behalf of Cernunnos. I am one of his forest scouts and I was tasked with the mission of checking this portion of the Weald's edge," he opened his arms wide, then continued, "for weaknesses or breaches. The god of the Wild is confident that the original spell holds strong, but he does not wish to take any chances. The Morrigan is always trying to find ways into the sacred realm of the Weald, and it would be foolish of the Tuatha De to underestimate her determination."

I could only blink at him. Was he being serious? And if so, why would he share with me, a perfect stranger, something that, in my opinion, ought to be kept secret.

"How do I know you aren't lying to me?" I pressed. "Wouldn't a man poking around the edge of the Weald draw unwanted attention to himself?"

I knew how paranoid Sorcha was. True, there probably wasn't a spy of the Morrigan posted every few miles along the Weald's edge.

However, enough wild tales had been born of strange and powerful magic and beings living in the Weald that common Faelorehn folk living in small villages might see this Riordan as a danger and take action.

He merely lifted one brow, cocked his head to the side, and smiled. That smile was dangerous, I decided. "You do have a point, but I know how to be discreet and stay out of sight. This isn't my first scouting mission."

I would have argued with him, but he did manage to sneak up on me from out of nowhere. Still, I wasn't about to trust him. I made to stand up, and he took a step forward, reaching out a hand. Before he could speak, I shook my head. "No. I'm quite capable of getting to my feet on my own."

He didn't push the issue. Once standing, I reached up to rub at my neck, only to hiss at the sharp sting that simple action caused. I pulled my hand away to find crusted blood smeared across my fingertips.

"I'm sorry," Riordan said, a genuine hint of remorse in his voice. "I had no idea if you intended ill will towards me."

I laughed a little and almost told him he had absolutely nothing to fear from the likes of me, but thought better of it.

"May I see your wound?"

I stilled and snapped my eyes to his face. "Why? It can't be all that bad."

"Still, I was the cause for it."

This time, my eyes narrowed. "And what will looking at it do?"

His mouth curved into that familiar grin I liked too much. "My mother is Fahndi and gifted with powerful healing glamour. She passed a good deal of that glamour on to me."

I merely blinked at him. I'd heard of the Fahndi before. A race of immortals very similar to the Faelorehn who lived deep within the heart of the Weald. They were said to be Cernunnos' chosen race of fae, but that was all I knew of them. Perhaps, one of my mother's books would have told me more, if Sorcha hadn't burned them.

"How do I know you aren't trying to move in close to overpower me again?"

He crossed his arms and regarded me. "Do you think I'd ask permission if that was my intent?"

I considered the logic behind that. He had a point.

"Here. Take my knife."

He flipped the hilt in his hand and caught the tip of the blade, then slung it forward. Before I could leap out of the way, the point sank into a patch of moss a foot away from me.

I glanced up at him.

"If I try anything nefarious, you can stab me," he vowed, holding both palms outward.

Despite my apprehension, and better judgment, I was curious. I reached down and picked up the blade, holding it the way some of Sorcha's less vile soldiers had taught me. Apparently, that surprised Riordan because that dark brow shot up again.

"Fine. But only because I don't entirely believe you."

He let out a breath and stepped towards me carefully. "If I heal the cut in your neck, will you begin to believe me?"

I wrinkled my nose. All my life, I'd been wary of strangers, and male strangers especially. But I'd never once had a true friend either. The servants working under Sorcha weren't exactly friends because despite how close I grew to them, I was always considered more valuable. We were objects to be owned, livestock to be used. We weren't allowed to show or even possess the other emotional bonds free Faelorehn men and women shared. And in that moment, I realized I was incredibly angry about that fact. I deserved to rule my own life. I deserved freedom. I couldn't control either of those things thanks to my mother's geis, but I could control what I did next. Even if Riordan wasn't as trustworthy as he appeared to be, I wanted to give him a chance.

"Very well," I said, my chin tilting upward. "Show me what you can do."

He ducked his head once, then began moving forward again, his right hand outstretched. "I'll need to touch you in order for my glamour to work."

I swallowed back the last vestiges of apprehension and jerked my head down once. When his fingertips finally brushed my skin, I nearly jumped. They were warm and slightly rough, but it was the tingling sensation they left in their wake that had me catching my breath. It wasn't unpleasant, but strange. He traced his index finger in a short line down the side of my neck, the odd touch leaving a slight itchiness behind.

The process was over quickly, and as he stepped back, taking his hand with him, I noticed a golden glow fading away from his first two fingers.

"There," he said. "Good as new."

I reached up and rubbed my neck. No stinging, and when I studied my fingers, no blood. I blinked up at him, unsure of what to say.

"I'd like to strike a bargain with you," Riordan said without preamble.

My eyes narrowed. Bargains with the fae were never good, but since I was Faelorehn myself, perhaps I had little to worry about.

"Oh? What sort of bargain?"

"I know a great deal about plants and herbs and their various properties," he said, slipping the knife back into a hidden sheath along his belt. "You mentioned that was your reason for exploring the edge of the Weald."

I crossed my arms. "Go on."

"I am good at keeping out of sight, but most places I scout have only the occasional hunter or village farmer. This area is practically crawling with Faelorehn men and women trained by the Morrigan's best. They might be a bit better at noticing my presence."

I waited for him to finish.

"I imagine since you live at the manor, you must be familiar with some of the soldiers' activities. More specifically, when they run perimeter checks and if they venture into the forest."

I did know their routine quite well, because I tried to avoid frequenting the woods and fields when they were making their rounds.

"I might," I offered. "What is your bargain?"

"I will teach you all I know about the plants and herbs in this area and how to use them, if you will educate me on the schedule of your mistress's army."

My heart kicked up its pace, my eyes going wide. What he offered was a priceless gift.

Riordan must have misread my reaction because he lifted a hand and added, "My mother and I possess the power to heal, but we are also great scholars of the medicinal uses of the natural world around us. She always taught me I should never rely entirely on the use of my glamour because there would be times in my life where it might fail me. I assure you, I'm well educated."

I didn't even have to think about it.

"Done," I said. "But, I want you to prove it first. Teach me about one of the plants or herbs nearby, and I'll tell you all I know about the movements of Sorcha's soldiers."

Riordan offered that charming smile and proceeded to inform me about not one, but half a dozen plants. Some I already knew about, like how marsh mint made a wonderful tea that soothed the stomach, but could also repel biting insects when ground into a paste and applied to the skin. Riordan added that the oil, when heated, soothed the symptoms of a cold. By the time he finished his lesson, I was thoroughly convinced.

"Sorcha's generals never venture beyond the walls of the manor house, unless the Morrigan calls them to her realm or they are going on a hunt. The last hunt was two weeks ago, so they shouldn't plan another one until after the Solstice."

The mention of winter's shortest night also reminded me of the tithe I owed Sorcha. Shaking off the unpleasantness of that thought, I continued on. "Parties of four scour the forest just after sunrise, just after the midday meal, and just after the sun sets. They fear the forest, so they are not thorough in their task, and they do not step within the boundary of the trees."

He arched a brow. "You do not fear the woods?"

I actually thought about that question for a moment. Eventually, I shrugged. "Nothing within these trees could be worse than what I currently live with."

As soon as the words left my mouth, I wished for a net to scoop them back up.

Riordan's gaze became more intense then. "What do you mean by that?"

I waved a hand, feigning nonchalance. "Nothing, nothing. Just the whims of a girlish daydream that never came to fruition."

Riordan didn't press the issue, but somehow I knew he wouldn't forget it, either. I bid him goodnight after that, for twilight had deepened and despite my lack of fear of the Weald, I wasn't foolish enough to linger after dark. By the time I reached the oak door of my stone tower, I could barely see the silhouette of my hand. A strange prickling sensation creeping up my neck had me whipping around, my heart thudding against my chest. I peered up to the rise where the tree line started a half mile away. It was too dark to make out anything but more shadows and outlines, but I could have sworn the dark shape of a buck stood between the trees, its figure statue still.

The next several days passed swiftly. In the mornings, I'd do the chores required of me, then after the late afternoon meal, I'd venture into the edge of the Weald to collect my herbs. Most days, Riordan met me between the second and third perimeter shift, taking full advantage of the short daylight hours. I always made sure to bring my botany books, a fresh quill, and small pot of ink with me, furiously scratching away in the margins of the tomes to soak up every drop of knowledge he so freely gave.

Before meeting Riordan, I thought I knew so much about the various uses of herbs and plants. He proved to me I had only scratched the surface. Shade nettle, a nasty weed that left small welts on the skin if touched, was a wonderful remedy for chronic headaches if the leaves were simmered for half an hour. Faewort, a plant that grew along the edge of creeks and ponds, had a tuber that when added to stews and soups, proved to be highly nutritious and plentiful when winter killed everything else. But my favorite had to be a leafy vine he called spirit's balm. The leaves, when dried, made a delicious tea that soothed a troubled mind and helped one fall asleep. The plant also contained a substance that could fight fever and, according to Riordan's Fahndi mother, often brought people back from the brink of death. Once steeped, the leaves could be used to create a highly effective poultice.

As the days slipped by, I found myself looking forward to our meetings. While we collected our specimens, I peppered Riordan with as many questions as I could think of. Mostly, they pertained to the plants we studied, but I also yearned to know more about him. For once, I could have a true conversation with another being without worrying what Sorcha might do to him for daring to show kindness or interest in her source of extra glamour. He told me about his childhood, about growing up in the heart of the Weald with his siblings and his mother, father, and cousin. He recited the story of how his parents met, and I hung on to every word.

"My mother was cast out of her clan, and my father shot her."

"What?" I said, dropping the small knife I'd been using to cut the stems of a young willow tree.

Riordan nodded, a knowing grin on his face. "The Fahndi can transform into deer. She was in her doe form when my father found her. After the arrow struck, he followed her only to discover a young Fahndi woman instead. Feeling guilty, he carried her home and nursed her back to health. They fell in love as she recovered."

I couldn't help but smile brightly at that. "I think you're making that up," I insisted. "It sounds like a fae tale to me."

Riordan held his hand over his heart and proclaimed it was the truth. "They can tell you themselves, if you ever come to visit."

The smile disappeared from my face. Visit? Had we become good enough friends for him to offer such an invitation? My excitement died the moment I remembered I didn't have the freedom to do such simple things as visit friends. I could sneak away in the night, but I wouldn't make it very far. I was a valuable commodity to Sorcha. Despite her attempts to belittle and humiliate me, I knew my value to her. Without my wealth of glamour-rich hair, she would have nothing to stay in good favor with the Morrigan. I could never leave, but Riordan eventually would.

"Are you well today, Caitlin?"

Riordan's voice pulled me away from my thoughts. We had been uprooting a purple and white fungus to dry and grind into a flavorful powder. I forced a smile and shook my head. "I'm fine. Just tired."

"Would you like to rest a while?"

"No, we only have a half hour before the next perimeter check heads this way. I'll be fine."

So, we fell into companionable silence as we finished our task.

Later that evening, I was so distracted by the inevitable loss of my friend, that I didn't realize it was the eve of the Solstice until the next morning when Sorcha's soldiers woke me from a deep sleep. As soon as I pulled open the door, they grabbed me by the arms and half marched, half dragged me across the field. I protested, asking if I could at least dress myself first, but it was in my nightgown that I was flung before my enemy upon the cold cobblestones in the courtyard of what had once been my mother's beautiful estate. Around us, soldiers and Sorcha's generals held torches, their flames flickering as the breeze-tossed fog licked at them. All was silent, including the myriad of servants who had paused in their morning activities to watch the annual ritual.

"You assured me you had not forgotten," Sorcha sneered. "Yet, my soldiers had to fetch you here. Perhaps, I should cut back on your privileges, or give you more work to do."

I gritted my teeth against the freezing cold to keep them from chattering. My hair hung down over my shoulder in its usual long, woven plait.

Sorcha clicked her tongue, her hand darting out to grab the tip of my braid. She yanked hard, forcing me into a kneeling position. Tears stung the corners of my eyes, and I gasped.

"Your mother gave me a gift when she set her foolish geis upon you," the Morrigan's Cheadmorr mocked. "I wish I had a dozen more like you, but I'll take what I can get."

She drew her knife, slicing it swiftly past the nape of my neck, barely missing my skin. Another tug, and then, I was suddenly sprawled against the stones again, a few short strands of hair tickling my ears. I didn't have to look up to know what I would find. Sorcha held my shorn braid high for all to see. Her generals and soldiers shouted and cheered, some laughing and jeering. I curled my fingers into fists, trying so hard to stop the encroaching shame and rage. Fresh tears sprang free, and without even glancing up, I shot to my feet and ran from the courtyard, followed by more cruel laughter. I made my way through the herb garden and headed for the outer wall. Before I escaped into the open pasture, one of the other servants pushed a cloak into my hands.

"You'll freeze out there, dear girl," she said.

I took it blindly and wiped at my eyes, but didn't stop. Every year, I told myself I wouldn't let it get to me, but every year, I failed. I needed to go somewhere safe. Someplace that didn't remind me of my pathetic existence. Without looking back, I headed for the ruined stone circle where once upon a time, I had a mother who loved me and taught me how to dream.

The broken stone circle stood in a halo of golden light, a gift from the sun as it broke the horizon and slipped between the wisps of mist. The dazzling beauty of it only made my tears come faster, and by the time I reached the top of the hill, I was practically crawling. I came to the center of the ring and curled into a ball, perfectly content to wallow in my own self-pity. One would think after more than a decade of suffering under Sorcha's cruelty, I would have been hardened against it. It would have been easier that way.

Before I could reflect much longer upon it, a shadow passed over me. I inhaled sharply and sat up, ready to face whoever Sorcha had sent after me.

"Caitlin?" a familiar voice asked.

Relief and no small amount of embarrassment washed through me.

"Riordan," I managed, wiping at my face with my sleeve. "I'm okay. Please. I want to be left alone."

Either he didn't hear me, or he didn't believe my words.

"Your hair." His voice held disbelief, but hardened with his next words. "Who did this to you?"

I turned my head away from him and wrapped my arms around myself. "It's nothing, really."

He moved before I could react, before I could think, kneeling down before me and taking my face in his hands. It was a strangely intimate action, and for a few blissful seconds, I forgot about my anger and sorrow. His fingers slid into my hair, and only then did I realize just how short it was. Reaching up, I grasped his wrists, but he didn't budge. When I met his eyes, I lost all control of my willpower to hold onto my dignity, and in the next breath everything came flooding out.

"Sorcha did this. She's been cutting my hair every year since I was five. I am not a servant at the manor. It was my mother's, but she was murdered by the Morrigan for her glamour. Before she died, she placed a geis upon me, that all the glamour I would ever be capable of possessing would gather in my hair. She did it so they wouldn't kill me, too, but because of that, I have never been free. I wish my mother had never cursed me! I wish Sorcha and the Morrigan had killed me then and just taken my glamour, for I am stuck here. I tried running away, several times, but they always found me. They always caught up, and I was punished each time."

Riordan pulled me close, and I clung to him, my face pressed into his shoulder.

"Don't say that," he said, his voice rough. "If you had died then, I never would have met you."

He ran one hand down the back of my skull, the short strands of hair springing back up as his fingers passed. Of their own volition, my arms reached up, and I hugged him back. I hadn't been hugged since I was a little girl, and I was like a person starved. I clung tight, afraid to let go, and he continued to stroke my short hair, his fingers leaving a tingling sensation in their wake.

"It's only hair," I managed to say between sobs, "but my mother always brushed it and braided it for me. It is the one connection I still have to her."

Riordan's arms tightened around me, a source of comfort and strength as I fell apart. None of those living at the manor had ever showed this much compassion towards me, and it only made that ache of loneliness grow tighter.

"Well, well, well, what have we here?"

The sound of Sorcha's cruel voice sent ice water through my veins. I tore free of Riordan's embrace and spun around. Sorcha stood at the base of the rise, two dozen or so soldiers forming an arc behind her.

"I thought you were spending more time in the woods than usual these past few weeks. And now I can see why."

She arched a golden brow, her eyes slowly regarding Riordan behind me. That look was more than curiosity. A foul hunger lingered there, too, and I felt myself shifting to block as much of him as I could. How dare she look at him that way?

"Not only is he handsome, but it appears as if he possesses healing glamour as well. Your hair is nearly as long as it was before I trimmed it for you just now."

The tone of her voice, or perhaps some inner intuition, had fear grasping at my heart.

"No," I whispered, my hands snapping up to grasp at my shorn hair. Only, the rose gold strands I gathered between my fingers were as long as they had been the night before.

"Soldiers, seize them both and bring them back to the old silo tower."

"No!" I shouted, shoving at Riordan. I turned to face him, my eyes wild. "Run! You must run or she will imprison you, too!"

Riordan's face was unreadable, his gray eyes shifting to a dark, dangerous color.

"I'll not leave you," he snarled softly.

"You don't understand! She'll lock you up forever if she doesn't kill you outright and take your glamour! She is Cheadmorr! One of the Morrigan's greatest devotees!"

Riordan reached down and took my hand, his grip strong. I tried shoving him again, but it was no use. He wasn't budging, and Sorcha's soldiers had already surrounded us, their swords and bows at the ready as a few of them tied our hands together. We were marched back to my tower and shoved inside. A spear point guided us upstairs where four soldiers and Sorcha crowded in with us. Sorcha ordered two soldiers to hold me and cut my hair short once again, the other two keeping Riordan back at sword point.

"Take the bed and the blankets," Sorcha snapped to her soldiers once they handed her the bundle of my shorn hair. "We can't have them using the sheets to climb through the window."

"No!" I cried. "We'll freeze."

She glared at me and Riordan, her gaze cold and unyielding.

"You have cloaks and a fine pile of wood, and surely your lover can warm you well enough. You will survive just fine. You will receive food and more wood only if the two of you can somehow produce a length of hair by morning. And the same from now onward. Provisions for survival in exchange for a foot of hair each day. I think that sounds fair."

Riordan glared at Sorcha, his dark eyes sparking fire. His fists tightened at his sides, but I leaned ever so slightly towards him. His tension eased at my small warning.

"Do not even attempt escape. The door will be locked, and a pair of guards will stand watch at all hours. The sooner you accept your fate, the better. We shall see how you two fare in the coming weeks. If you behave yourselves, and I feel I can trust you, I may allow you to come outside every now and then. But that means cooperation."

With that, she ordered our bonds cut and made her exit, her soldiers covering her back as they left. The moment the trap door slammed shut, I fell to my knees.

"I'm so sorry, Riordan," I said, my anguish making it hard for me to breathe. "I should never have befriended you. I should have not made that bargain with you. Now, you may never see your family again."

Riordan took me by the shoulders, then lifted my chin so that he could look me in the eye. His were dark with emotion when he said, "Why did you never tell me how terribly you were treated here?"

I shrugged, once again attempting to wipe away my tears. "I don't know. I didn't want you to worry or to feel sorry for me."

He hugged me close again. "We'll find a way out of this, Caitlin. We'll comply for now, but we will find a way to break free, and both you and I will escape this horrible prison for good. We'll escape deep into the Weald, I promise. The Morrigan, and those who belong to her, cannot enter where we will go. The ancient, powerful glamour won't allow it."

Freedom. He promised freedom so easily as if it were even a possibility. He did not know the power or determination Sorcha possessed. We would never be free.

I clenched my teeth, fighting back against the despair as Riordan rocked me gently, his hand brushing over my short strands of hair. That tingling sensation crackled against my scalp once more, and I knew he was keeping true to Sorcha's demands, growing my hair out for her to take in the morning. In an attempt to fight my misery, I let my mind wander. How much of Riordan's glamour did it take to grow my hair, and would my hair grow even longer if he just kept feeding it magic? Like a sudden spring cloudburst, an idea flared to life.

"Riordan," I exclaimed, pushing him away just enough so I could see his face, "how long do you think you could make my hair grow before dawn, if you spent all night feeding it with your glamour?"

He blinked at me, then said, "Maybe five feet an hour, until my glamour begins to run low, then perhaps a couple of feet or even just a few inches after that."

"Do you think you could grow my hair to a length of sixty feet by the morning?" I pressed.

Riordan's eyes sharpened, their color flashing more silver than gray. He gave me a small grin and leaned forward to press his lips to my forehead.

"Brilliant!" he said. "I don't know for certain, because I never tried, but I'll do my best."

I grabbed his hand and leaned up to give him a quick kiss. But Riordan scooped me up, deepening the kiss and leaving us both breathless.

"I'll start now," he said, lacing his fingers through the hair at my temple. "And if the spirits of Eile are on our side, we will have more than what we need before morning."

We were up the entire night, Riordan pushing his glamour into my hair, making it grow to ten feet, then fifteen, then twenty. I kept busy by gathering the ends and folding the strands into neat piles to keep it from getting knotted. It would all have to be braided in the end, but that shouldn't take too much time.

"Done," Riordan said a few hours after midnight. He drew in steady breaths of air, his frame shaking a little.

"Are you well?" I asked, brushing his hair from his forehead.

He nodded, reaching out to gently lace his fingers with mine. "I'll be fine. But, we'll need a way to cut it."

"I keep a pair of old scissors hidden in the wall. Sorcha didn't think to check for them."

I got up and located the scissors, then began cutting away my hair.

"Now, it is my turn to work," I told Riordan. "You rest."

He didn't argue. He threw a few more meager branches onto the dying fire and collapsed against the wall nearby, his eyes already drifting shut in sleep. And so I began. I tore off a bit of my cloak to secure the strands of hair on one end, then began to braid as swiftly as possible. Even when the work became tedious and threatened to drag me into sleep, I shook it off and quickened my pace. I reached the end of the long make-shift rope just as the deep blue sky outside my window began to shift.

"Riordan," I whispered.

Riordan jerked awake, his hand reaching for the knife that used to hang from his belt. When he realized it was me calling his name, his lips parted in a smile and his eyes warmed.

"The rope is done," I hissed eagerly. "Now, we get to see if it's long enough."

He nodded, and together, we tied off the end of the rope of hair on one of the broken iron bars that once covered the window. Riordan gathered the braided hair into his arms and pushed it over the ledge. The tip just brushed the ground some sixty feet below. I nearly fainted from relief.

"I'll go first," Riordan said, "and take care of the guards."

I nodded, then kissed him one more time before he began the climb down the side of the tower. He reached the bottom rather quickly, then his dark figure disappeared around the curve of the wall. I waited several moments, my heart pounding in my throat, and nearly jumped when the latch securing the trap door scraped open. The door swung wide, and Riordan's dark head pushed through the opening.

"Let's go," he said.

I grabbed my satchel, already packed with the meager food I had in the tower and my precious botany books, and bolted for the door. We made our way as fast as possible down the stairs and stepped around the guards, now slumped against the stone wall. Riordan grabbed my hand, and we set out across the field. The day was growing lighter by the minute, and it wouldn't be long before Sorcha arrived with more soldiers, demanding her foot of hair. She could have the sixty feet hanging from the window. That would be the last time she ever took anything from me.

We reached the edge of the Weald and paused to catch our breath, but the sudden clanging of bells and blasting of horns froze my heart. I gave Riordan a look of sheer terror.

"We've barely ventured into the Weald! They will surely know which way I went and hunt us!"

The not-so-distant baying of hounds only drove my point home. We may have escaped the tower, but the dogs would track us down, and no doubt Sorcha and her generals were mounting their horses as we spoke.

Riordan grabbed my hand once more and pulled me deeper into the woods.

"We will escape," he insisted, "I have just enough glamour left, but I need you to trust me and not to question anything."

He let go of my hand and immediately started stripping away his clothes. I gaped at him, "Riordan, what are you doing!? They'll be here in a matter of minutes!"

In answer, he tossed his coat to me, followed by his shirt and boots.

"Trust me!" he hissed, shrugging out of his trousers. "Put everything in your satchel and prepare to hold on tight."

My jaw dropped, but I did as he bade, shoving the clothing into my now bursting satchel. The baying grew closer, and now I could make out the shouts of men and women crackling over the rumble of horses' hooves. I peered over my shoulder only to spy Sorcha and her ilk thundering across the fields.

"Riordan!" I shouted, tearing around to face him again. Only, instead of a naked Faelorehn man standing before me, I found the large, dark stag from a few weeks ago.

The great animal snorted and pawed at the earth with one hoof, and from this close I could see the color of his eyes: smoky gray.

"R-Riordan?" I whispered.

The buck tossed his antlered head, then lowered himself to his knees. Riordan was the stag. So that was what he meant when he accused me of following him… There was no time to stand around wondering about it. I took the strap of my satchel and looped it around one antler, then climbed onto his back. He stood quickly, and I grabbed at the thick fur encircling his neck.

"Sorry," I whispered, hoping I hadn't pulled too hard.

He snorted once, his only warning before springing forward with great speed. I hooked one arm through my satchel and then dug my fingers in deep, using my legs to keep steady on his back. The wind whipped against my face, cold and crisp and clean. The baying of the hounds and shouts of Sorcha and her generals faded as we fled deeper into the forest.

I pressed my face into Riordan's strong, furred neck and breathed deeply. He smelled like his Faelorehn form – a comforting blend of wind, tall trees, and old, strong magic. I smiled, and the tears that broke free this time were ones of joy. The Solstice Rose had finally granted me my wishes. I was free, I had a friend, and soon, I'd be part of a family once again.

END

AUTHOR'S NOTE

Woven From Pure Starlight began as an idea several years ago while I was thinking of putting together a collection of retold fairytale pieces for my Otherworld series. When the *Once Upon A Wish* anthology was announced, I decided now was my chance to work on that particular story. My Rapunzel is named Caitlin, and in the strands of her hair resides her powerful glamour. Because of this, she is held captive by a servant of the Morrigan and once a year, her hair is harvested like a sheep's wool.

For the most part, my version takes on a life of its own and veers from the traditional tale of *Rapunzel*, but at the end of the story, the famous long locks of hair are still utilized to climb a tower. Furthermore, those who have read the books in the Otherworld series will get to meet a character who is closely connected to a previously featured couple. Whether you've read the other books in the Otherworld series or not, I hope you enjoy *Woven from Pure Starlight*.

ABOUT THE AUTHOR

Jenna Elizabeth Johnson is a bestselling, multi award-winning author of contemporary and epic fantasy. She has written multiple books in the Otherworld, the Draghans of Firiehn, and the Legend of Oescienne series. For more information, visit the author's website at www.jennaelizabethjohnson.com.

LAST WISH

C. GOCKEL

At the end of the last ice age, there was no death for the People of North America. Spirits walked among them, and giant game animals sustained them. But as the ice caps melted, and the animals that fed the people of the plains began to disappear, something worse than death came to the world ...

YOU DO NOT KNOW MY NAME

You do not know my name.

You only know me as the wife of Coyote. Coyote the shapeshifter who, with the Great Spirit, helped bring the world forth from the sea, and helped create man. Coyote who gave man fire by stealing it from the spirits. Coyote who cursed all people to die by following me to the land of the dead, bargaining a reprieve from death for all, but then capriciously failing to abide by the terms. You think that it is his fault you will one-day face death.

But that is a myth.

Let me tell you how it really happened.

Would you deny my last wish?

IN THE BEGINNING

In the beginning bridges of silver and emerald crossed oceans. Giant mammoths roamed the world. Saber-tooth tigers stalked the mountains, dire wolves and giant lions roamed the plains, and giant, short-nosed bears haunted the forests. They were brothers and sisters of humans, and there was no death for any of us.

That was the world into which I was born.

I was one of dozens upon dozens of brothers and sisters. You probably do not believe me, but there was no death, and no age beyond grown. We all had more siblings than we had fingers and toes.

I was a happy child and a happy grown woman. It was easy to be happy. Death did not stalk us, nor did disease or hunger. The world was full of plenty for any people that would but shoot an arrow. Although the great mammoths had skin too thick to pierce, there were giant bison who weighed twice as much as the creatures you now call large. And there were slow-moving, giant sloths and enormous armadillos that could feed entire families for months. If one did not wish for meat, all one had to do was put a basket in a stream to catch fish, wade through the verdant plains, or wander through the towering forests to find edible things.

We were all beautiful, the way all young are beautiful, the way people who are happy, without care can be. So there was nothing special about me to catch Coyote's eye, but somehow I did. It was on a summer day when I was gathering reeds for the baskets I loved to weave.

I was with my not-grown siblings by a stream. They were using some of my previous creations to gather strawberries. It was the hottest day I could remember, but the stream was glacier melt, and was wonderfully cold and exceptionally clear. We were cooling ourselves and resting, sitting upon the bank, dipping our feet, our laughter bubbling with the water gurgling over rocks. One moment I was staring at the current turning gray stones to rainbow hues; the next my siblings were screeching in surprise. I looked up and saw Coyote on the opposite bank.

He stood in his four-footed form. Silhouetted against the sky, he was only a shadow, except for his eyes, shining orange, a little bit of the fire he'd stolen for us burning bright within him. My siblings went quiet without me admonishing them to hush. We all knew a spirit when we saw one. Although he couldn't kill us, he could cause us a great deal of trouble: kidnapping us, or twisting the pathway home through the spirit world so it would take us years to find our way back to our kin.

Thinking about those unspoken dangers made me fearful, but Coyote looming there, silent as a stone, frightening my little brothers and sisters made me angry. My anger made me reckless. Picking up a basket of berries, holding them over the water, I said, "Would you like some?" I did not offer them meekly. I did not stand in respect, did not bow my head, and I met his fiery gaze.

Coyote opened his mouth revealing glistening white teeth and he laughed the high-pitched, yipping song of a laugh that all coyotes have. And then his shadowy body twisted like smoke and sank into the water. A glittering fish with orange eyes appeared there, flashed in the sun, and darted towards my feet. I made myself not flinch, even when the fish leaped from the stream in a great splash that rained down upon us. The fish's nearly serpentine body lengthened and broadened. Gills retreated, fins stretched into limbs, his back became upright, and scales fanned into hair. Back to the sun, he still was a shadow except for his glowing orange eyes. He took the basket from me. "Thank you, I would like some." Grinning, teeth flashing, he popped a handful into his mouth.

I was too shocked to react. My little brothers and sisters whispered, "Sister is so brave," and backed away. I wasn't brave at all, in fact, I was becoming more and more alarmed, but I was determined not to show my fear.

He was completely naked—which wasn't shocking, who swam in clothes?—but he was too close. I did not know him, and he was a spirit, an immensely powerful spirit, an obviously very male spirit. Coyote's appetite for all things was legendary, and as he gulped down another handful of berries it occurred to me that if his appetite for food was not exaggerated, his appetite for other things might not be, either.

I did not rise, and I did not look at his naked body, not wanting to show fear or give invitation. Meeting that fiery gaze again, I asked, "Are you cold? We have a spare blanket."

"I am never cold. And no one near me is ever cold either." One flaming eye winked at me. And I did go hot, and not just with anger. Although I could only see him in outline, that outline was strong and beautiful, and his voice made me think of lying beside banked fires on long nights, soft furs above and beneath, naked limbs twined between.

But he was toying with me. Whatever brief heat he might offer, nights after would be made colder by the memory of warmth. I found my anger again. Pointedly looking down at his naked body, I said, "Parts of you say they are *very* cold."

There was no sound except the gurgling stream. My blood went cold, as I realized my mistake. Such barbs brought out the worst in the worst of men.

Coyote huffed, and his breath ruffled my hair, hot as wind over summer sands.

My hand went to the knife at my belt, and I silently prayed to the spirits for protection from their enemy. Was Coyote still an enemy of the spirits? It had been a long time since Coyote had stolen fire from them. I was doomed if they'd made peace ...

Thunder clapped in front of me. My fingers tightened on my knife ... and then I realized Coyote was laughing. He'd thrown back his head, had one hand on his belly, and I thought I saw tears sparkling in the shadow that was his face. The thunder became a rumble, that faded to a chuckle, and he sat upon the boulder beside me, but not too close this time. I could see him in the sunlight then. His shadow had been beautiful, but in sunlight he was breathtaking. His face and his body were the models after which all men were formed, and I could see now, all other men were crude copies. His skin was gold, his hair alternated between jet black and sun burnished red, and even in bright light, his eyes still glowed. His smile was like the horizon just before dawn, when you waited breathlessly for the sun to explode into the sky.

The glowing eyes fell to my waist and the knife, and that sun-rising smile vanished. "I frightened you. I did not mean to. Forgive me."

Swallowing, I glanced at my hand. My fingers were clenched so tight my knuckles were the color of ivory, and I could not release the weapon. There was no point in lying. It was the time to be humble, the time to accept his apology. I opened my mouth and did not recognize the words that came out. "If you didn't wish to be frightening, you should not have come in shadow, slithered like smoke, and erupted from the water like a water spout!"

Whispers arose from my brothers and sisters.

Coyote's head jerked back as though I'd slapped him, and he sneered at me. "A mean tongue you have, woman."

The whispers behind me became a roar, and then the eldest of my little brothers ran forward and flung an arm around me. "Big Sister is not mean! She is the nicest of all my sisters and all my aunts, and if you didn't want to scare her, you should not have been scary!"

Coyote blinked at my little brothers and sisters. "I was scary?"

Wide-eyed, and mute, they nodded at him.

Crossing one arm over his middle, he put his other hand to his chin, and fluttered his fingers, very much like a woman. Considering the horizon, he mused. "That was not my intention at all."

One of my little sisters snickered.

Little Brother cocked his head. "What was your intention?"

Dropping his arms, Coyote turned to me, naked body much too close, even if the distance was not improper. He stared at me with those glowing eyes, his expression very serious. A bird called, the wind whistled, but those sounds weren't as loud as the silence of my siblings and me holding our breath.

"I wanted to impress her so she might be my wife," Coyote said, lips quirking.

My cheeks caught fire at the jest. I have mentioned his appetites were legendary, as was his wandering. Coyote did not marry. He roamed from camp-to-camp, taking partners as he pleased. Now that I saw him, I knew how he could.

He narrowed his eyes and addressed Little Brother. "But how do I know she is kind, as you say?"

Little Brother, up until that point my protector, betrayed me. "Oh, she is the kindest. Let me show you the shoes she made me!" He dashed from the bank into the bushes.

My littlest sister and brother said, "Look at the necklaces of flowers she made."

"She made us mittens," said the twins, in unison.

"She fetched water for Mother this morning because she is about to have a baby! Mother is going to have a baby, not Big Sister."

"She helped my dog when he broke his leg."

"See the baskets? She made them."

"She makes the most beautiful baskets and clothes."

"She's here gathering reeds for baskets."

"And to see we don't play with the baby bears again."

"Or fall in the rapids."

"It makes Mother Bear mad."

"If we play with the babies. Mother Bear doesn't mind if we get wet."

"See, here are the shoes!" declared Little Brother, dashing from the bush.

"May I?" Coyote extended his hands.

Little Brother dutifully handed them over.

Examining them, Coyote said, "These are well made."

I saw every flaw in the shoes—and there were many—just as I saw all the flaws in my baskets, beadwork, clothing, and finger-woven sashes and belts, too. But people often told me I was clever with my fingers, so I was used to being praised, and unmoved by his flattery.

"Pity they are too small for my feet," Coyote said, slipping them on his hands. "But look, they almost work as mittens." He made his hands dance through the air, mimicking the hand gestures of a winter dance we all knew—notably taking the woman's part. All of my little brothers and sisters giggled. I bit my lip to keep from smiling.

Handing them back to Little Brother he said, "You praise your sister very much, but I cannot believe she is without flaws."

I smiled triumphantly, seeing my escape. "I am a horrible cook." I had a tendency to become overly engrossed in my weaving and sewing, and to forget the maize mash bubbling in the skin or the meat roasting over the fire.

Little Brother glared at me meaningfully, as though in repri-mand. My other siblings covered their mouths.

"It is true," said my Littlest Sister, and Biggest Little Brother hissed, "Shhh ... don't you want her to find a husband?"

But I smiled. If Coyote knew, he would at least try to tempt me between the furs honestly, without the farce of prospective matrimony.

Coyote answered my smile with a wicked smile of his own. "Lucky for you I am good at everything that has to do with heat, and am a wonderful cook."

My smile melted. His did too, and his face was as somber as the sky before a thunderstorm. I couldn't tell when he was more handsome, serious or smiling. I wasn't sure when he looked more dangerous either.

"You're brave, talented, but humble and honest," he said. "I am sure I want you as my wife."

The air between us rippled like it does over sunbaked stones. His golden skin became tawny fur punctuated with a black ruff. Arms became forelegs, and long legs coiled and shortened. A tail appeared and thumped. He looked at me with glowing eyes that hadn't changed when he'd reverted to his coyote form. Tipping back his head, he laughed, and then rising, trotted away.

It was only then that I realized how hard my heart was pounding.

"Will we see him again?" asked Little Brother.

"No." I swallowed. "He was just playing." It surprised me how much it made me sad to say it. I shrugged. "You know how coyotes are."

HOW COYOTES ARE

I WAS SITTING BEFORE THE FIRE WITH MY FAMILY, JUST BEFORE
the sun slipped behind the mountains. It was getting dark, but not
so dark I needed to pause weaving the basket on my knees. From the
side, the design appeared to be repeating triangles, but if you looked
into the basket from above you would see a flower. A happy thing to
see just before you had to go through the trouble to refill it. We were
at our summer camp, and the strong smell of the fresh tule mats that
covered our tents was as thick in the air as the smoke from our fire.

Laughing, my father smacked his hands on his thighs. "How I
would have liked to have seen Coyote wearing shoes as mittens." His
latest wife, not my mother, pantomimed the winter dance, and my
father, my grown sister and her husband, my grown brother and his
wife, my grandfather, they all laughed. Everyone who was there
laughed, and there were so many of us! More than sixty, it was a
huge number for a summer hunting trip. But the land was richer
then. We knew the seeds we'd dropped in the streambed would all
sprout and flourish, and we'd only need to slay a few of the enormous game to fill our winter stores. We even needed so many
people! If we slew one of the giant bison, we'd need many hands to
smoke the meat before it went bad, and a giant armadillo was even

more of a challenge. Though, that summer we'd only caught smaller game up to that point.

I joined in the laughter, perhaps a little wistfully. Coyote had been very handsome. I knew I'd never meet a man quite that beautiful ever again, but I'd just gotten to the point where the encounter seemed like a dream. It was good that it was dream-like. Love with spirits was fraught. My aunt loved Dire Wolf spirit once long ago; he was a great black wolf with eyes like the sky. In his human form he kept those sky-blue eyes, his skin was darker than you can imagine, and his midnight black hair never bleached with the sun. I did believe he loved her, too. I never saw or heard of him seeking out any other woman. Dire wolves mate for life. They were together for many years and had more than a dozen children. All my Dire cousins had an uncanny sense of smell, but none slipped from dire wolf to human and back again. Though the dire spirit loved my aunt, he loved his own kind, too, and eventually, he retreated to the spirit world. "The world is changing," Uncle Dire told her before that final journey, "I have to go back to the spirit world. I have to teach my kind how to return home."

I caught my aunt's eye across the fire. She gave me a timid smile. She hadn't remarried or taken a lover since he left. "I wish," Dire Aunt, had told me once, "that he could have taught me to go to the spirit world as well. After him, I cannot marry another. My spirit is now part dire wolf." That was why she was still Dire Aunt, though Dire Uncle was gone.

My sister grinned at me. "You scared him off with your cooking skills! Typical Sister!" And there was more laughter. I smiled, not upset. I preferred weaving baskets and making clothes to cooking, and was good enough at it that my family let it occupy my time, trading food for the work of my fingers. I bent my head, prepared to resume—and a coyote's laughing song came rippling through our camp. Human laughter stopped. A pattering sound rose like rain at the beginning of a storm. I held out my hands to catch a drop, but the sky was clear. We looked at each other in confusion, and then the pattering became the pounding of a drum. My father yelled,

"Buffalo coming this way!" As soon as he said the words we all knew it was the truth. I threw my basket aside. In my family, it wasn't uncommon for a woman to pick up a spear if she needed to, and women without children often participated in hunts—though not me, my skill as a weaver was better than my skill with a weapon. In any case, I had no spear, and there were children sleeping, oblivious to the danger. I grabbed two children sleeping close beside me. Men and some sisters and cousins got out their spears and bows, forming a wall between us and the approaching thunder. I looked around, not sure where to run, the sound of hooves was everywhere, and the earth was reverberating, as though it was the surface of the giant drum making the thunderous noise. The next moment a bull buffalo roared into our camp and reared. I remember its eyes, wide and surprised as ours. Arrows and spears flew, hitting the beast head-on—but one spear came from the side, long and fletched with black feathers. It embedded itself between the beast's ribs, directly into its heart. The beast groaned and fell sideways. In an instant it was dead.

Everyone stood and stared, dumbfounded. My heart beat loud in my ears, and my arms shook. A baby cried, though the children in my arms didn't have the sense to wake.

"It's not every day," said Coyote, striding from the shadows into the firelight, "that dinner comes to you."

He was not naked now, but his clothing was unusual. He wore buckskin leggings with what I now know was a breechcloth. People in my family more commonly wore pants beneath dresses or tunics. Coyote's leggings were beaded with seashells, rare so far inland. More seashells adorned his neck. He was bare-chested beneath a cloak entirely made of jet-black raven feathers that seemed to have nothing holding it together. Coyote gestured out into the darkening night. "I have brought the whole herd." And we heard them then, milling and moaning, not far away.

His eyes burned bright as he stared straight at me. "And since you *can't* cook, I will cook for you."

No one dared argue with a spirit.

Except me. I set the children down gently and glared at him. "I did not say I will marry you."

My father hummed a low warning, but Coyote only smiled like a child smiles before you present them with a gift. "That is only because you haven't tasted my cooking."

There were a few chuckles from my family, and my brother said, "Finding a man who cooks might be the only way you *ever* marry, Sister."

That wasn't true. I had been asked for a few times at the yearly gatherings. I once almost said yes, but he wanted to travel south, to where it was never cold, where every stone was gold. At the time, my sisters had just had babies, and my mother, too, and I couldn't leave them when they needed me most. Even if we didn't die, we could be hungry, and hunger is pain. I might not have been able to cook for them, but I gathered food and tule, brought water, and helped clothe their babies. I hadn't taken a lover since. There was no shame in a baby without marriage among my family; it happened when groups of People gathered. But my father's wife is not my mother, and I know what it is like to always wonder where a parent has gone and why they went.

"It won't work," I said.

Coyote's smile only faded a little bit. "Why not? Do you have another man?" He looked off into the night. "Perhaps if you do, you should not say, because then I might murder him." I did not know what murder was—but I guessed he meant to hurt, because we could feel and cause pain, even then—but then he said, "That means nothing to you because you are my people and I would never let you die." His words were confusing. He would not hurt this imaginary lover?

Approaching me, smile gone, he brushed my cheek. His fingers were warm; the light touch had a strange heaviness to it, and heat spread from his fingertips to my entire body.

I wanted to lean into him. I did not. "You are only playing with me. Your ways are well known. You wander. You have lovers in every camp. I don't want to be abandoned. I do not want a child to be abandoned. I will not play your game." No matter how much I wanted to. He must have felt me trembling; it wasn't fear.

"You are right, I have played. But I don't want to play anymore." His eyes drifted over the children sleeping beside the fire and in their parents' arms and grew soft. "I want to be part of your family. Traveling between your winter and summer camps will be enough wandering for me." His eyes burned blue, like the hottest part of the fire. "Ask your Dire Aunt, she will tell you, Coyotes may play, but in the end, we mate for life." He grinned a smile as bright as sunshine. "Before I ask or you decide, let me cook for you."

He turned toward the giant bison already being skinned, but then paused, and brought out a satchel from beneath his raven feather cloak. "I almost forgot, these are yours."

He held the satchel out to me.

Father whispered close by, his words filled with warning for me, or Coyote, or both of us. "Take it, Daughter. There is no obligation in accepting a gift, but not accepting it would be rude."

Coyote canted his head. "That is all true."

For my family's sake, I took it. It was very heavy.

Coyote immediately walked over to the downed beast, and I couldn't help peeking inside the bag. It was filled with beads the color of the sky, seashells, and cotton thread that even in the firelight I could tell was brilliant crimson and bright white. I couldn't help imagining all the beading and stitching I could do with these rare things.

Dire Aunt had come up behind Father and I so quietly I had not heard her, probably because Coyote was loudly telling the tale of how he brought us *all* the giant bison, to many exclamations of surprise and laughter. Dire Aunt whispered quietly, "My husband did say that coyotes do mate for life. It was their sole redeeming quality in his opinion."

I should have thought about the word "murder" that I didn't understand, and had, at first, understood as a threat. I should have thought of how Coyote's gifts always seemed to come with a price. Fire was dangerous as well as useful. The giant bison he had brought down might have injured someone, and the recovery would have been painful and long.

What I thought of instead was how his eyes had softened looking at my brothers and sisters, and how he was talking and laughing so easily with my family. Those things were even weightier than the treasure in my hands.

I did not think at all of how Coyote had given us life, or what the price might be for that.

THE PRICE

I DID NOT MARRY COYOTE THAT SUMMER, BUT HE STAYED WITH us. With his gift of the giant bison herd, roaming an easy half-hour walk from our camp, our winter meat stores were soon filled. But we stayed in the summer camp anyway, waiting for the seeds we'd tossed before we'd headed south last year to ripen. Coyote had a raven form, sharp-eyed as any bird, and he used it to search for rarer delicacies: mushrooms uncommon on the plains, more strawberries, and later blueberries. We worked very little that summer, and it was a good thing. The heat was uncommon. It wasn't truly hot—not like the heat that would come later—but it was hotter than I'd ever remembered. Buckskin pants and dresses became too heavy. In the heat of the day, men began copying Coyote's breechcloth that had first looked so strange, wearing them without leggings. Women began wearing grass skirts and aprons. I wove the grass clothing with the cotton thread. They were bright and cheerful things that fell apart quickly. I was constantly reclaiming the thread.

As summer turned to autumn, and the familiar bitter cold began to fall upon the land, I couldn't resist Coyote's warmth. He hadn't paid any attention to any other person in my family, nor had he paid attention to anyone in the friendly families that visited ours frequently, drawn by the giant bison. He did make the meeting of our families merrier, always with a new story to tell of one of his outlandish adventures. He also had not lied about his cooking. People are happier and more inclined to love when their bellies are full and they don't have to work very hard. Laughter doesn't hurt either. It was because of him that by fall I had lost a record number of brothers, sisters, aunts, and uncles to marriage, and gained some new ones besides, as our groups mingled, mixed, and broke apart.

And watching these new couples form, exchanging my grass and cotton skirts for buckskin dresses, how could I resist Coyote? We were married in the tradition of my family. I was not prepared for how happy it would make me. I was not prepared for how long that happiness would last. Winter turned to spring, which turned to summer, and fall, and winter again. Countless seasons sped by and the happiness continued, like some strange, beautiful dream. He had not lied about always being warm—and nor had myths exaggerated his appetites. Perhaps it was that leftover fire he stole?

Sometimes I might go to sleep with clothes on, but by morning they would be gone, and I would invariably wake with my naked body tangled with his, an arm and a leg, sometimes my whole body free of the skins, because even in the depths of winter, he was too hot.

There was only one thing that saddened me. We had no children, and although I was fulfilled by all my sisters and brothers, nieces and nephews, I worried that Coyote would leave me for it. Many men would blame the woman. But not Coyote.

He found me one time, tears on my cheeks, hiding between the furs on a winter afternoon. I'd gone to bed early, when most of the family was still out by the fire, laughing, telling tales. He followed me into the tent soon after, bringing firelight with him in his eyes; it turned our cold, dark shelter warm and orange. "What is wrong Little Badger?" he asked. Sometimes he called me that. We were very different, Coyote and I. He was, and is, quick-witted and swift-footed. I was slower. Coyotes fill their bellies with inspiration. Badgers fill their bellies with faithful labor. Despite their differences, badgers and coyotes are often friends, finding life easier when

Badger's industry is combined with Coyote's swiftness. Coyote also said that I was like Badger in that I was utterly unafraid of him and would never put up with his nonsense. If only I was a Badger spirit! I might have understood him then, and saved countless suffering later. But if I was Badger, I wouldn't have been one of the People, and would not have cared to spare them. Perhaps there is reason in all things, or perhaps there is only luck.

When he asked me what was wrong, I told him, "I have given you no children." I did not say that I was afraid that he would leave me for it. No one likes to be accused of what they have not yet done. Also, my answer was truthful. I was sure that I had failed him, that something was wrong with me.

At my words, he dropped down beside me and pulled me into the furs. "Ah," he said. "It is my fault. I made this world, and that means I cannot be completely of it. I am part spirit, part flesh, and that is why it is taking so long. Forgive me. I should have known. I should have told you."

It wound up me comforting him. I would have been in my rights to leave, but I assured him that he had made me the happiest of wives, and I would never leave him for lack of children. I had my siblings and cousins, and if I ever needed a baby to hold, I could always borrow one. Comforting turned into trying to make a baby again.

Outside the tent, I heard one of my brothers grunt. "They're at it early tonight."

Someone else commented, "Maybe they'll be quieter later and it will be easier to sleep."

I think I remember Coyote and I both laughing at that. We were not quiet at our normal time at all.

I was the happiest of wives, and I think that if the world had stayed the same, I would still be. But the world did not stay the same. Not every summer was hotter than the last, but we went from summers in pants and dresses to summers in breechcloths and skirts more and more. The glacier melt turned what had once been streams to rivers. Instead of dire wolves, we saw more and more of a different type of wolf, longer in the nose, thinner in the body, shorter. A similar thing happened to the short-nosed bears. The saber-toothed cats and the giant lions vanished, leaving only the slender, subtle cougars and the feisty bobcats. The mammoth and the giant bison ranges shrunk. The giant sloths and armadillos became rarer and rarer.

I did not notice at first. Coyote's presence sheltered my family from the change. He had a Coyote's nose, and a raven's eyes and vantage point, and we always could find game, no matter how rare. But after a while, I couldn't help but notice that the giant bison herds were smaller, though we never took more than what we needed. The other large beasts were more sluggish as well, easier to kill.

Once, we found a dying mammoth.

It was a day when we'd all exchanged buckskin pants, tunics, and dresses for breechcloths and grass skirts. No one had left their hair unbraided, and I'd pulled my braid into a bun, desperate to keep it off my neck. We hadn't worn our warmer clothing in nearly the cycle of the moon.

We came upon the mammoth, on its side, panting furiously, in a dry riverbed. The most frightening thing about the creature was that there didn't appear to be anything wrong with it. If anything, it looked overly well-fed, and yet it lay on the ground looking at us with piteous, knowing eyes.

We did not hunt mammoths. Mammoth hide was too tough for spears or arrows. I had heard stories of People driving them over cliffs, but I think that was more likely luck, that the creatures killed had slipped and fallen and People had found them and then embellished the tale. If such a thing happened, it did not happen more than once. Mammoths were like People and taught their young. They would have taught their calves not to go near the fields by the cliffs if those stories had ever been true. And how many fields do you know conveniently by cliffs? Mammoths were like People in other ways, too. If you tried to hunt them in a group, they would defend themselves in a group, keeping their weak and vulnerable safely behind the strong. Wave fire at a mammoth and they'd trample the fire and you at the same time. Wave spears and they would break the spears and then break you. It could take years to mend from a mammoth attack. There was no sense in attempting it.

But here was a great bull, lying before us. Not starving. Not near a cliff. Chillingly, alone. Like People, Mammoths aided their wounded.

We could see many tracks around it. My father pointed at them and said, "They were moving slowly, see—their feet were dragging, especially the large ones."

"It's overheated," Coyote said, standing just out of its striking distance. "Their fur keeps the heat out as well as the cold, but once the heat gets in, they cannot release it. All their fat stores and their size do not help. It's happening to all the large animals." He smiled and slapped his naked thigh. "Luckily we can remove our buckskins. You are cleverly designed."

The Mammoth spirit must have entered the beast just then because it spoke. "I told my herd to keep going. Please. You may have my body. Send me to the spirits."

Coyote put a hand to his chin and fluttered his fingers in a way that was calculated for a laugh. "How to do that when your hide is so—"

My father walked up to the creature's head. The trunk moved, and I ran forward to try and hold it off.

Coyote shouted, "No!"

But when I caught the trunk, the mammoth did not struggle. It's enormous, dangerous trunk gave me only the lightest of touches, almost a caress, and it huffed. "Little Sister, do not worry. I will let your father finish."

My father speared the creature in the eye, plunging the weapon deep into the mammoth's brain. And then he pulled back, bowed his head, and gave thanks to the mammoth spirit. The trunk slid from me.

"For once you are cleverer than me," Coyote said to my father with a grin.

Expression grim, my father laid his hand on the great creature's head. He did not say anything to Coyote, and I think that silence speaks a thousand stories. I think that as much as Father was grateful for Coyote's presence, he could see then what I could not. Coyote's care was narrow. Coyote loved me, so he loved my family. Outside of the circle of kin, he could be blithely unconcerned. If he hadn't spent those seconds being silly when he asked us how to kill the mammoth, he might have put it out of its misery faster than my father had done.

It was good that my father did not challenge Coyote, and that he kept his misgivings to himself. We needed Coyote's help, we would soon see how much.

It was the winter after my father killed the mammoth. You don't hear tales of that feat, because my father never allowed it. "It wasn't bravery. It was mercy," he said. So it never became an epic adventure of my father chasing the mammoth over a cliff, or cornering it with fire, or just getting a lucky spear shot. Maybe that was a mistake on my father's part. Perhaps if more tales of mercy were told, there would be more of it.

The mammoth was the only large game we took that season. We salted and smoked the meat. Salting wasn't common so far from the sea, but Coyote would change into his raven form, fly to the seashore, and bring back salt for us, or for him—he couldn't stand bland food. We ate a lot of mammoth that summer. Still, we had too much meat to carry back to the winter camp. It would have been wasteful to leave it all behind, and surely would have angered the mammoth spirit, so we did our best. Everyone helped carry the dried meat. We tied saplings to our dogs, allowing the ends to trail behind, and loaded them up to help carry the bounty. My baskets were filled. Great satchels were filled. Small satchels were filled. If you could walk, you carried as much as you could. Normally we would have stopped on the journey to hunt, sparing the summer's takings for the long winter, but we ate mammoth on our return trek, just happy to get rid of it. We still had too much, and we had to walk slow. My husband was not patient, and he grumbled the entire trip, mostly about the Mammoth Spirit punishing him with the weighty burden. According to Coyote, it was all because Mammoth was jealous. Coyote had designed a more adaptable creature than Mammoth himself had, and our burden and "boring menu" was mammoth's revenge. You might think we were annoyed, but we couldn't be. Coyote was so outrageous when he complained. He'd put a hand over his own chest, and declare, "Don't I look like someone you should consult when designing the creatures of the Earth?" He'd then make a point of stumbling on a pebble, crossing his eyes, and making his legs bow, nearly tipping over his baskets. He was the only thing to laugh at, and he took our mind off our blisters.

He behaved the entire journey like a fool, but a kind fool. He had a basket on his back, and one in the front, like all of us, but when the children got tired, he'd take his walking stick, sling it over his shoulders with one basket on the end, and say to the smallest child, "Ah, my load is unbalanced! I need one for the other side," and urge the child to put their own basket on the opposite end of the pole. Then he'd declare the original basket was too light, and ask for another basket to "balance the load." This would go on until he had three baskets on either side and one on his head along with the one on his back. By the end of the day, he'd have the largest load.

So we didn't mind him complaining so much. Nor did we mind, on the day we reached the campsite, that he put down his load and declared, "I can't eat mammoth another night! Let's go hunting!" He batted his eyelashes at me and grinned. Sometimes I would go with him. He liked me to go with him, because "the others are too quiet."

Thinking back on it, I believe that the others were just a little afraid of him. He often made himself the butt of jokes, but he had fire in his eyes, and sometimes it jumped from his fingers. Sometimes, even when he was a man, his teeth were long and sharp, like his other form.

That day I was having none of it, I had blisters on my blisters, and the winter tent needed to be prepared.

He rolled his eyes when I said so. "Fine Little Badger, prepare your den." But there was no real bite in the barb. A few of the other hunters went off with him. Not my father that day though.

He muttered as they left. "We still have more than enough mammoth meat. It's rude to not accept a gift."

I didn't know the word "murder" then, but I think to my father, his mercy to the mammoth had felt like murder—the mammoth had spoken to him, and gently caressed his daughter as though she were a sister. He couldn't think of wasting the mammoth's meat.

He didn't know that would never be a possibility.

When Coyote and the others left, we went about preparing the winter tents. We constructed them in much the same way we constructed summer camp, angling tall, thin, saplings together in a circle. However, in the summer we'd covered them in tule mats, now we covered them in hide. With the mammoth's gift, we had plenty of it. The tule mats we used inside the dwellings, covering the earth that would soon be frozen solid, leaving a space for a fire pit in the center. Once we finished, we began moving stores into the lodges. I was bent over a basket taller than my thighs, doing just that when my cousin screamed. There was a thud. Before I'd thought of it, I had a knife out. It was a long, slender thing, with a long blade of flint, and a bone handle. Coyote had given it to me. The flint had been tempered by fire, and it was sharper and more dangerous than the one I had when we first met.

A step out of the tent, I paused. I didn't know what I was looking at. It looked like the back of a man, but he wasn't wearing clothing appropriate for the cold weather, and he was so thin, his hair was so matted, and skin was so dirty, I wasn't sure. But whatever he was, he was holding a spear at my cousin. I almost charged, but then a twig cracked and another. I saw more of the creatures in the trees.

"Give me the meat!" the man-thing with a spear demanded of my cousin.

My father crept out of his own tent with a spear, and he nodded at me. Together, we crept closer. I saw others of my family emerging from their tents. A child cried. The man-things in the trees were quiet.

My cousin said, "Of course we will give it to you, Cousin. Why are you threatening me with a spear?"

At her words, the man-thing dropped his weapon and put his hands to his eyes. He began to weep. "I am sorry. No one else will share! We had no large game this summer, none! We came to the winter grounds and found the forest almost picked bare. We are so hungry we began eating our skins."

This time, when he spoke, I recognized him as one of my family, a distant cousin. I looked out at all the forest and realized I was seeing my own kin, shrunken by hunger. They had lines in their faces, lines of care, and pain. They didn't look *very* old, but to someone who had never seen age, they appeared ancient.

My father said, "You'd better eat broth at first, or you'll be sick."

Some of them listened to him. Some of them didn't. The ones that hadn't listened were busy being violently ill when Coyote and the hunting party returned with a black-tailed deer, and herbs, tubers, and other edibles beside. Seeing the retching People, he sneered. "What is this?"

My cousin explained before I could. She left out the part where she'd been threatened with a spear. My family knew my husband better than I did.

"How long are they staying?" Coyote asked, nose wrinkling in disgust.

We gaped at him. With their pathetic state, the answer was obvious. "They will stay with us at least until spring."

"There isn't enough food or enough tents," Coyote replied, scanning our relatives through narrowed eyes. He was right. The mammoth was too much, but with the addition of our relatives, it wouldn't last. We didn't have enough tents to sleep comfortably, or enough hides to cover more tents, or enough saplings to make more frames. Nor did we have enough tule mats for the floors, and our relatives were in no shape to help mitigate these matters.

"We'll manage," said my father.

My husband huffed, and his breath hung in front of his face like an angry cloud.

"They have told us there is no game," I said, "But you've found a deer and more."

"I had to turn into a raven," he said.

"You'll find enough for all of us," I said confidently.

The scowl crawling between his brows retreated. "I suppose you're right." He sighed. "And it's only for a season."

We were both wrong.

That long winter Coyote and I shared our tent with three other childless couples. It was more a sacrifice for them than for us. We didn't have the same concept of privacy in those times. But my husband's appetites had not slackened with marriage, and he was a bit of a show-off ... every single night and some of the days. The men complained that he was showing them up, the women verified it—I hadn't appreciated until then how unsatisfied some women were. Men and women both complained about not getting any sleep.

Thankfully, winter turned to spring. The family split apart as normal. Farming and herding were thousands of years away, and not as many People could successfully stay on a single plot of land for long. We'd all been hungry those last weeks in the winter camp, even with Coyote.

My family found another mammoth that had died on the way to the summer hunting ground. We knew it had died the previous summer, it was just bones upon a plain just coming into spring. The tusks were gone. Other People had found it.

Coyote in his raven form found a giant bison herd, further from our usual winter camp than we'd ever gone before. The herd was smaller than we were used to but still more than we needed. Our summer camp was in the shadow of a glacier and filled with the normal cornucopia of the summer prairie and more, strange, delicious things. Plants that Coyote said came from the East that were making their way west as the glaciers pulled away. There was more than enough—until our relatives from winter appeared again, leading other more distant related People—my distant cousins' distant cousins. They were not as hungry as they'd been when we'd first encountered them in winter, but they were not as well fed as us. Coyote had led us straight to the herds and summer bounty that suddenly wasn't so bountiful. Our cousins had tried to find a herd of their own, but had given up, and followed our trail. Their cousins had joined them.

It wasn't an emergency that summer. Or the next. But gradually the number of People multiplied, but the giant bison did not. The years grew warmer and warmer, the glaciers further and further away. Dead and dying mammoths were more common, and when those were found there was more than plenty, but only for a while; there were more People to share the plenty with.

Though the winters became shorter, they also became hungrier, and the spring march to the summer hunting ground became harder, as there was less food to fuel our steps.

And one summer it finally happened. We traveled further North than we'd ever gone before, not just my family, but many families of the People ... and the giant bison were gone. We were hungry and tired from our journey. There were too many of us, it had been a dry winter, and the normal largess of the land—tubers, berries, and young leaves that usually supported us on our journey—had been sparse. When we reached the shadow of the glaciers, and the plains were empty, my husband vowed he would find food for all of us. He kissed me as though it would be the last time—for he always did that before he left—took to his raven form, and to flight.

He was gone for hours. Hours turned to days. First came hunger, and then came blame. Coyote was to blame for not returning, everyone's cousin was to blame for hunting too much, or both. People began speaking of the land that belonged to everyone as only belonging to one immediate family. Then came fights. Days turned to weeks, and then no one had the strength to fight. Weeks turned to cycles of the moon.

We had endured short-term hunger before. Usually, it was not enough food, not an absence of food. This was absence. Holy men fasted regularly for extended periods, but holy men sat during their fasting while others around them worked and saw that they had water.

We didn't stay put, maybe we should have. I think we spent more energy searching for new land than we derived subsistence from it. The dry winter had become a dry spring, and then summer. Rivers and streams were full of glacial melt, but cutting through the land they didn't nourish anything beyond their banks. By middle summer we were too exhausted to move. We camped as close as we could to water because we could barely lift ourselves to drink. It wasn't my stomach that pained me so much; it was everything else. Skin cracked and peeled. We threw up bile. Every muscle and every organ ached. Though we hardly ate, our bodies attempted to defecate, and it was long and excruciatingly painful. Worse than childbirth, my sisters cried. The suffering was terrible, but the worst was watching our children suffer. They reached each stage of agony earlier than we did, and there was nothing we could do but watch. None died of course, but I was relieved when the children fell into sleep, and were no longer in pain. That was painful only to we adults, because their muscles withered away and their cracked skin clung to their small bones. It was the first time I'd seen human skeletons—and they still had souls attached to them.

Of course, we prayed to the spirits from the moment Coyote left and had never stopped. And at last our prayers were answered, not by my husband, but by other spirits. Mammoth, Giant Bison, Lion, Saber Tooth, Short-Nosed Bear, and at the head of them stood Dire Wolf Uncle, blue eyes burning in the dark skin of his human form. Dire Aunt was the first to leave her body. She ran to her husband, but he held up his hands, and warned her, "Once you enter the spirit world, there will be no coming back."

"I don't care!" She exclaimed, clasping his hands. "The world hasn't been whole since you left."

My father and my not-mother went to Mammoth, and he gently gathered them to him with his trunk. One by one, the children's spirits rose from their bodies whole and well. Their parents cried out and followed.

I was one of the few that remained behind. Although others doubted that Coyote would return, I knew he would be back. I might have stayed in this world, but when my not-mother called out to my Littlest Brother and Littlest Sister, they said they would remain with me and wait for Uncle Coyote. I looked at their skeletal remains with cracked skin and lips, eyes bulging even beneath their lids, limbs twisted and frail, and ribs like claws across their tiny chests, and my pain doubled. What was worse was the agony of knowing what was on the inside, the pain that we had experienced in every organ had to have left scars. I didn't think they could ever recover and knew I couldn't stay. My spirit rose from my body and I held out my hands to them. "Come, Uncle Coyote will find us in the spirit world."

My tiny siblings took my hands, and we stepped over into the spirit world and all our pain was gone.

THE BARGAIN

How do I explain the spirit world? There is no hunger, cold, heat, or hurt. All the maladies of the body vanish, but all the desires as well. It is not a place, but every place. It is also not a time, but every time. Because there was no time, I'm not sure how long it took for Coyote to find us; but he did find us, at a time that was comfortable and familiar—a spirit-version of winter camp, with a bonfire tall as the trees, my family around me, and the spirits of all the animals. The Great Spirit was there in a place of honor. His being changed constantly, evolving and churning, like a whirlpool: now a man, now a woman, now a lion, now a monster, never frightening, but not one you would ever confront.

Of course, my husband did confront him. One moment Coyote wasn't there, the next moment a giant raven was at the fire's edge. The raven became a coyote, and then the coyote became the man that was my husband. His eyes met mine, and they burned brighter than the firelight. There is no cold in the spirit world, but I felt cold in that moment, remembering my husband's warmth. Jumping from my place, I ran to him, but he held up his hands, as Dire Uncle had. I was close enough then to realize I could not feel his heat.

Looking sorrowful, he put his hands behind his back and clasped them, as though to restrain himself. He turned back to the Great Spirit. "You must give me back my wife and my People!"

The Great Spirit's voice boomed, "I *must* not do anything. You left them to starve. I have shown mercy."

"I did not leave them to starve," Coyote roared. "I left them to create a new bison, one smaller and stronger, that will survive the glacial retreat."

Thunder rumbled in the spirit world. "You did not create the new bison, you stole it!"

Coyote waved a hand. "It is the same."

There was a warning crackle of lightning and another roll of thunder.

Coyote rolled his eyes. "The same in outcome." He held up a hand to me. "You cannot keep her or them. I helped create them; they are as much mine as yours. I have a say in their fate!"

The air crackled again, though not so loud. Wind whistled, and then the Great Spirit replied, "Very well, you may have your wife back, and keep her and her kind in the world on these conditions: first she must stay here and feast on the food of the spirit world for three days and three nights; second, you must lead her back to the world for three days and three nights—"

Coyote's hand rose toward me, as though to touch my shoulder reassuringly, I could see the word, "Done," on his lips. Before he could say it, the Great Spirit added, "During all that time you must not touch her."

My shoulders fell, and my husband's jaw sagged. I don't think either of us thought he could abide by those conditions.

My sister whispered, "He'll never manage that." I think I have mentioned several times, that our bed was never, ever, cold.

One of my brothers said, "Well, here is not so bad, after all," already resigned.

Coyote snapped his hands back behind his back, and he glared at the Great Spirit. In the spirit world, I think I understood why his passion had never abated. Here there was no passion, no hunger, but no satiety either. Coyote came from this world, he created our world for the flesh, and after an eternity of spiritual pleasures, his sensual pleasures could not be quenched.

"It will be done," Coyote said, and smiled at me, the timidest, most uncertain smile I had ever seen from anyone.

I wanted to touch him, to reassure him, but clasped my own hands behind my back.

The feasting commenced. The food in the spirit world is not for your body, it is for your soul. We devoured what had been and might have been, what was and could be, and what would and might be. The feast included all the knowledge of all the creatures of the world and beyond, before, present, and after. That is how I know your language now, and how I speak to you.

For three days and nights in the spirit world we "ate," and Coyote did not touch me with more than his eyes. Every time he looked at me, I remembered the warmth, and as much as the sustenance of the spirit world tempted me—I saw how I could weave the light of stars!—his eyes tempted me back into my own flesh. When the feast was done, Coyote and I set out, the People to follow after our journey was complete.

The first day, walking along the border between the land of living and spirits, I heard of how my husband stole the new bison by coordinating with other animals of the living world, at great personal risk and sacrifice. It made my steps quicker and made me lock my hands more tightly behind my back. I smiled at him though, and he smiled back. Even if his fiery eyes didn't cast warmth, his smile was still like sunshine spilling over the horizon at dawn.

We traveled another day, and I saw the People who hadn't journeyed to the spirit world, enjoying the bounty of Coyote's smaller bison. I had thought that my family's end was the end of the People, but I saw that there were more of us, spilling through the North and the South, East, and the West. Where the new bison were, there was happiness, but in places beyond the bison's range, the hunger that had set upon my family was still being felt. People had fished too much, hunted too much, and cleared too much land. And the People's numbers kept growing, they couldn't stop.

That was when my feast in the spirit world began to sit heavy in my stomach. I could see what my return would do. I'd spare my own family from the pain of starvation ... for a while. But the other People by the coasts, along the rivers, in the mountains, and great forests of the East and the South, would be doomed to never-ending pain as their sources of food dwindled. They wouldn't be able to die. Maybe they'd move into the plains, drawn by the buffalo. Maybe they'd be too hungry, and maybe the fall leaves would fall on them, burying them deeper and deeper each year, in a state near comatose, too weak to seek food, and unable to journey to the land of the spirits. They'd be trapped forever in a world that would be only pain.

And that would be my family's fate, too. One day the smaller buffalo would be gone, slain not by the changing climate, but by us. Coyote would have to steal again from the spirits. Maybe next time he would be gone even longer. In such a circumstance wouldn't I wish for death again?

That fear grew stronger that night, as we drew closer to our last camp. Beneath the moonlight, the tents were in shreds. Our bodies were barely more than skeletons, covered by dust where they weren't covered by flies.

Coyote turned to me, clasping his hands behind him more tightly. I saw the strain in his shoulders.

"Don't worry, you will be whole again. You will! You will see!" His tone was all eagerness and hope.

My lover was leading me back to an inescapable trap, not because he was malicious, but because he missed me, he missed my family. He loved us, our world, and we were his People.

But he wasn't the one who would feel the pain.

In the East, the sun was a blush on the horizon. When it rose, I'd be back inside my broken body, breathing in dust. I might not ever recover completely, whether I did or didn't, I was doomed to repeat the cycle again, and maybe next time the spirits wouldn't be able to answer.

I made a decision for myself, and for my People. For you.

I didn't have much time.

"In my body, I will be sick for a while, my love." I held out my arms. "Please, love me now just a little."

He stared at me, but then looked over his shoulders at the not quite risen sun. It was the first time he had ever resisted me.

"My love, I need you now," I implored, stepping toward him. It was too much for him. He was like a spark, leaping toward me, perhaps in his ardor missing that the sun was not quite up. Or maybe the blaze in his own eyes deceived him. For just an instant his lips were on mine, our bodies were pressed together and I felt his flesh and his heat, and I had flesh and heat too. Just for an instant.

And then the journey we had traveled was spinning past me in reverse, and my husband's cry of anguish was ringing in my ears. I still hear it.

THE LAST WISH

HE COMES TO VISIT ME IN THE SPIRIT WORLD SOMETIMES. IT isn't the same without the fire of his touch, though I still enjoy his wit. He can still make me laugh. He doesn't stay. He belongs to the other world as much as this one.

He isn't precisely welcome here. Those who came after those first of us who passed over are often surprised to arrive here. They fell from a tree, or a cliff, or were struck by lightning. They felt no pain and they are angry to be stolen from the world and their loved ones. They blame Coyote for death.

And he isn't precisely welcome in the world of the living, your world, either. The living are haunted by the loss of loved ones, and by fear of the unknown.

Coyote blames himself for death. Because he should have taken care of our physical forms so I wouldn't have been frightened to re-enter mine. Because he should have come to us earlier. Because he can't blame me.

Someday humankind will escape death again. You'll find new unexplored frontiers. You won't have to worry about exhausting the earth, and you or your descendants will be free again to live forever. But for People in my time, endless life was endless suffering not just of us, but for all creatures.

I miss my husband, his fiery nature, and the fire between us. As much as I enjoy weaving with starlight, I miss the world. And I regret that my husband unfairly gets labeled as the bringer of death.

But do I regret the choice I made, my wish for death for my People?

Never. I only wish you'd know my name, so I might get the blame.

Fin

AUTHOR'S NOTE

Coyote was worshipped, revered, or reviled by many of the First Nation peoples (sometimes all three by the same nation.) He was depicted as a bumbling trickster, an unrepentant lothario, the creator and savior of man, the bringer of the sun and fire, and the destroyer of an endless winter.

Coyote's trip to the spirit world to retrieve his wife and loved ones is told by the Nez Percé, Zuni nation, and possibly others. I've adapted it most noticeably by making the story from his wife's point of view. I could find no reference to her name in any versions of the story I've read. Also, in the original versions, it was normally five days and nights that he had to restrain from touching her. In all the tales, he fails.

Setting the story at the end of the last ice age is purely my addition. In researching the ice age I learned that the First Nation People most likely did not just arrive by the land bridge in the Bering Strait, but also came by boat along what is known as "The Kelp Highway," a sea route that followed the landmasses of the Pacific Rim and a string of islands just south of the Bering Strait Land Bridge.

The giant bison in the story are *Bison antiquus.* It seemed unlikely North America's first people would describe an existing species as "ancient." Since the modern, smaller, *Bison bison* did not exist at the time, it's also unlikely they would have prefaced it with "giant," but I wanted to make some distinction for readers.

There is a lot of disagreement as to the nature of the woolly mammoth and *Bison antiquus* extinction. It has been popular in the past to blame the woolly mammoth extinction in particular almost exclusively on humans. However, elephants have survived to modern times in both Asia and Africa. Without the aid of modern weaponry, they are very difficult to kill. I chose to make the mammoth and the "giant bison" extinction purely a matter of climate change. Overheating as a mode of death for the mammoth and Bison antiquus in the story is purely speculation on my part, but I would love to see it explored with computer models. Particularly in the case of mammoths, I think it would be an issue. Modern elephants use their ears for cooling purposes. Mammoth ears were proportionally smaller. Also, as modern elephants flap their ears, they are fanning their sides, letting heat escape from their flanks. Even if mammoths had larger ears, with their furry hides they wouldn't lose heat as effectively in this manner. Finally, that modern bison survives to this day, lends credence to the idea that the mode of death wasn't the rapacious appetites of First Nation hunters.

ABOUT THE AUTHOR

If you enjoyed this story, you may enjoy my depiction of the Norse trickster Loki in *I Bring the Fire.* The first book is available free. I am currently working on a new series inspired by fairy tales and folklore; sign-up for my newsletter for updates or follow me on Facebook.

HEART OF THE FOREST

ANTHEA SHARP

CHAPTER 1

Prince Kentry of Raine leaned low over his mount's lathered neck, his heartbeat echoing the thud of his horse's hooves, until he was a single pulse of purpose.

Ride. Hunt. He must capture the impossible creature fleeing before him—the fable he'd only half-believed, until the force of his need propelled him into the treacherous reaches of the forest.

Ahead, his quarry flickered through the trees in full, leaping flight. Flashes of sunlight limned the wide crown of its antlers, struck silver from its hide.

The White Hart.

One handed, Kent reached for the net slung across the pommel of his saddle. So close…

The creature veered off with a sudden burst of speed as the dark lacing of cedar branches opened to a clearing. Kent spurred his horse after it. The sharp scent of crushed ferns hung in the air as the pale shape of the stag vaulted back into the Darkwood's embrace.

Undaunted, he followed.

"Kentry! Prince!"

"Wait!"

The shouts of his companions faded as he reentered the cool shadows beneath the trees. The White Hart fled along a game trail barely wide enough for Kent's mount to follow. Bushes raked at his sides and he was forced to duck to avoid low-hanging boughs. The wet, musty smell of upturned loam hung in the air.

Faster. Faster.

Surely he was closing the distance. Behind him, the mournful cry of a hunting horn sounded, as faint as a mother's call to her wayward child.

A red-breasted bird fluttered, startled, past his head. Shafts of sun speared through the evergreens, striking down like solid columns through the dark branches. Pale yellow flowers nodded on graceful stems, blurring past so quickly he scarcely glimpsed them. The path swerved around a bush laden with translucent red berries tucked among coin-shaped leaves.

Other than the rasp of his breathing, the silence pressed down. His horse's hoof beats were muffled by the carpet of cedar needles strewn over emerald moss. The birds had all stopped singing. No more shouts sounded behind him.

It was only him, his gelding, and the glowing White Hart leading him into the depths of the forest.

When he'd announced his intention to ride into the Darkwood in search of the fabled beast, his family had thought him mad. The dinner conversation had halted while his older brothers exchanged skeptical looks across the long, candle-bedecked dining hall of the palace.

"Certainly not," his mother had said.

His father, the king, had cleared his throat and asked Kent to present himself in the royal parlor after supper.

The parlor, at least, was cozier than the formal throne room. The late evening light scattered shadows over the ornate Parnesian carpets, and the room smelled pleasantly of leather and his mother's rose perfume. Despite this, Kent stood uncomfortably, stance wide, hands clasped behind his back as he faced his parents.

"Don't go," his mother begged him. "I know your heart is sore, but once your brother is married, surely it will mend."

Kent shook his head, sending a lock of overlong dark hair into his eyes. He swiped it out of his face impatiently. "I will always love Maired, and seeing her as the future queen will only twist the blade in my heart. Every single day."

"But is this mad quest necessary?" His father rocked forward onto the balls of his feet. "I know you're young and hot-headed, much like myself at your age"—he gave a rueful chuckle, and the queen smiled at him—"but there are other ways you might cool your emotions. You've often expressed a desire to see more of the world. We could appoint you as our ambassador to the Fiorland court. Or to a post in Caliss, if that doesn't suit."

"I want neither of those things," Kent said, hating the roughness of his voice. He *had* wanted them, before love had submerged him in a ferocious storm—but now it was too late. "The stories say that, once captured, the White Hart will grant your heart's desire."

His mother's delicately arched brows rose. "And what of your brother's desire? He cares deeply for Maired, too. What kind of man would steal away the future king's bride and cast such melancholy over the throne of Raine?"

Kent made a slashing motion with his hand. "Both of you are in excellent health. Ian won't take the throne for years. He'll have plenty of time to find another wife."

Still, he couldn't help the curdling suspicion that they were right. Although he'd tried to tell himself that Maired had agreed to marry his brother only because he was to be king, Kent couldn't deny that she and Ian shared a deep affection.

Not as deep as Kent's own hot and piercing love, of course. It had shattered him when Maired had, ever-so-gently, told him that Ian had proposed—and that she'd accepted.

"Surely the White Hart, being a creature of Raine, wouldn't do anything to endanger the kingdom," Kent said.

"Hm." The king regarded him steadily. "Do recall, the Darkwood is older than the kingdom, and full of strangeness. There's a reason no one dwells close to the forest's edges."

"Well, perhaps we should!" Kent retorted. "It's time to stop being so afraid of a collection of trees."

"That 'collection of trees,' as you term it, spreads across half the country." His father's tone dipped with disappointment. "It's teeming with bear and wolves, not to mention other creatures—if the tales can be believed. And might I point out that if you're going after the White Hart, you can't dismiss the darker things rumored to lurk in the forest."

Kent shifted impatiently. Surely his need was great enough that he would prevail. After all, if the burning in his brain scarcely allowed him to sleep, it would certainly guide him to the creature that could grant his greatest wish.

"In any case," he said, "I'm going into the Darkwood. The huntsmaster has agreed to let me bring two of his best trackers and their hounds."

"But you must have other companions!" The queen clasped her hands in agitation. "What if you become lost in the forest?"

Kent heaved a sigh. He'd anticipated his mother's concern, however, and was prepared for this objection.

"Lord Carkin and Cousin Sean will accompany me." He couldn't leave his oldest friend behind, and Sean had a talent for inviting himself along, whether he was wanted or not.

A touch of relief smoothed his mother's expression. "At least your cousin can be depended upon."

"Then it's settled," Kent said. "I'll ride out in the morning."

He hadn't been able to bear the thought of seeing Maired again. Since the announcement of her engagement, even the briefest encounter with her in the palace corridors had set a torch to his lungs.

And so, before the summer sun had dispelled the misty dawn air, Kent and his companions rode out. It was a long day's journey from Meriton to the edge of the Darkwood, and though he'd wanted to begin the hunt that evening, Cousin Sean had persuaded him to make camp and wait until daybreak.

For the next three days they'd searched fruitlessly for signs of their quarry, until one of the hounds had finally caught a scent.

Baying joyously, it had led them deeper into the forest. At last Kent had glimpsed the silvery stag that was his prize.

Now, the White Hart bounded before him, leaping gracefully down a fern-carpeted slope. Kent followed, blessing his surefooted mount, aptly named Nimble. He set one hand to the net he carried. Although his bow was slung across his back, his goal was to snare the stag, not kill it.

The White Hart burst into a meadow, Kent at its heels. He grabbed the net and bent lower over his horse's neck. Closer. Closer. He could hear the beast snorting for breath, see the white of its eye and smell its sweet, wild odor.

In the corner of Kent's vision, he glimpsed a tall stone, sparkling eerily—but he had no time to pause. He readied the net, lifting it overhead...

The White Hart glowed beneath the encroaching darkness of the trees, the sunlight gone between one breath and the next. Kent's mount faltered. His throw missed, the net capturing nothing but a bush covered in glowing purple flowers.

The pale form of the stag slipped between the enormous tree trunks and was gone.

Heart pounding, Kent drew Nimble to a stop. He leaned down and gathered up his net, inhaling the richness of loam and cedar, and then took stock of his surroundings.

Between one heartbeat and the next, the Darkwood had transformed, growing fierce and magical. Strange blooms glowed with their own radiance beneath the fronded branches of the evergreens that now towered high above him, blocking all the light.

He squinted up, dismayed to see a huge golden moon floating in a dark sky brushed with unrecognizable stars. And was that another moon, trailing behind its brighter sister?

Where, by all the seas, was he?

Movement again, between the trees. For an instant the shape of the silver deer was outlined against the green-black shadows. Casting aside his confusion, Kent urged his mount forward. This time, he vowed, the White Hart would not escape.

Fanyaleth Lasgalen woke with a start from her moss-cradled sleep. The tall cedars of the forest waved above her in an invisible breeze and she stared up at them from the green depths of her ferny bower. Something had echoed through her dreams—a strange, mournful call, a shimmer of magic…

Sitting, she lifted her palm and called a blue sphere of foxfire, then sent it to hover overhead. She'd been wandering the Erynvorn for three days, and was wary of encountering the strange creatures said to roam the depths of the forest. But her light revealed nothing dangerous—no insidious spawn of the Void that could only be vanquished by the power of a warrior-mage. No red-eyed dire wolves skulking in the underbrush, no scaled drakes or poison-fanged basilisks lurking, ready to pounce.

Not that Fanya was sure the latter creatures existed, beyond the tales told to Dark Elf children to warn them to approach the Erynvorn with caution. If at all.

She'd had no choice, however. The prophecy spoken at her birth had commanded her to enter the dark bastion of the forest on the doublemoon after her seventeenth birthday. Since ignoring the Oracles was a sure path to madness and ruin, here she was, sleeping in the bracken, picking twigs from her long silver hair, and spending her days foraging for berries and mushrooms.

That shiver went through the air again, and Fanya rose, half crouching beneath the huge moss-covered log that had given her shelter. She dismissed her foxfire and took up her bow, which she'd laid close to hand. Quickly, she drew a sharp-tipped arrow from her quiver.

Something was coming toward her through the trees. Silver flashed, and she glimpsed a regal set of antlers. Then the creature was upon her, its graceful form soaring over her hiding place with a mighty leap.

As the White Hart sailed past, it sent her a look from one dark, liquid eye, as though it were trying to warn her. She caught her breath at its majesty, the luminous magic it trailed.

Then it was gone, and whatever was crashing through the underbrush after it burst through the trees. A figure on horseback, sword at his side, net in his hand. She hesitated a moment—but no one with pure intent would hunt the White Hart.

Fanya raised her bow, aiming for the rider's shoulder. She wanted to wound, not kill.

Her arrow flew—just as his net descended over her, fouling her bow and pulling her arms against her sides with its weight. A cry of pain made her smile grimly, even as she twisted within the net. She might be snared, but her arrow had met its mark.

"Cruel beast," the rider said, his words oddly accented. "How dare you wound me?"

He brought his mount to stop in front of her and slid down one-handed, clutching the arrow shaft protruding from the meat of his upper arm. Not quite what Fanya had intended, but close enough.

"How dare *you* hunt the White Hart?" she replied hotly. "It is a sacred creature."

"But I've caught you, despite that." The hunter grinned, though his smile turned to a grimace of pain as he leaned forward. "Now you owe me my heart's desire."

Belatedly, Fanya realized she was facing a mortal man. His oddly short hair should have alerted her, his strange human eyes and round-tipped ears—just as in the tales her people told. It had been a long time since a human had been spotted in the Erynvorn, however. Clearly, the White Hart had brought him.

"Let me go," she said, forcing one elbow through the net. Given time, she'd be able to free herself, but it would be much easier if he'd simply remove it.

"Not until you grant my wish." Despite his bold words, he ended with a small grunt of pain.

She narrowed her eyes. "Free me, and I'll pull my arrow from your arm and dress the wound."

He glanced down at the protruding shaft, then back at her. "Although that's a pressing need, it's not my heart's desire."

"I'd think not bleeding to death on the forest floor would be anyone's wish."

"The injury's not that bad." He sent her a smile, his jaw clenched in obvious pain.

"Are all humans so foolishly stubborn? I nearly pierced your arm straight through." She impatiently shrugged at the net covering her. "Release me, and I'll help you."

"You won't run?"

She glanced at his mount, which stood patiently behind him. "You'd catch me again easily enough."

It wasn't *quite* true—he was a stranger to the forest, and she could possibly find a hole to hide in, or scale one of the huge hemlocks and disappear among the feathery treetops. But beyond the fact that she wouldn't relish being chased through the Erynvorn, she had injured him, and could not leave him to wander.

Not to mention that the smell of his blood could call other, darker things out of the depths of the forest to menace them both.

"I'd only catch you if didn't transform again," he said tersely.

Fanya blinked at him, belatedly realizing he thought *she* was the White Hart. Despite being the wrong gender. Still, it seemed to her advantage to say nothing and let him believe she was, indeed, that powerful, enchanted creature.

"Free me, and I will not flee from you," she said. "I promise—and my kind do not break our word."

He nodded, once, then stepped forward, fingers still clenched around the arrow buried in his arm. At least he was wise enough not to wrench at it. The barbed head would tear through his flesh if he tried to pull it out, making the wound far worse.

"Crouch down," he said as he awkwardly tried to pull the net off of her, one-handed.

Her shoulders tensed and she forced herself to breathe deeply of the rich loam as she went to her knees. Should this human try to attack her again, she had the knife at her belt—and her magic, although she'd never been taught the dangerous combat runes her people traditionally used in battle.

An oversight she would most certainly remedy as soon as she returned to the Moonflower Court.

The human had peeled away half the net when a long, wavering howl shivered through the forest. Fanya struggled out of the rest of the strands, fear spiking her blood while the human's horse danced backward a few steps, eyes rolling in fright.

"What was that?" he asked, plucking at the net still wrapped about her bow.

"Direwolf. Hold still." She stepped forward, nostrils flaring at the strange, spicy scent of him. But this was no time for distraction, no matter how strange it was to stand so close to a human.

With quick, efficient movements, she tore a larger hole in the arm of his shirt around the protruding arrow. Taking hold of the shaft in both hands, she snapped it, removing the fletched end. He winced at the movement. Then, before he could protest, she drove the arrow point through the rest of his arm and out the other side. He made a strangled sound of agony, but, impressively, didn't cry out, even though the pain doubled him over for a moment.

She tucked her broken, bloody arrow back into her quiver, then placed her hands on either side of his arm and murmured a quick rune of healing to staunch the blood. Wide-eyed, he turned to look at her. Their gazes caught, and she blinked at his nearness.

"You *are* magic," he whispered.

Then the wolf howled once more, and Fanya jerked away.

"It's only a minor rune," she said. "But it will help until we reach a true healer."

She turned and plucked her bow free of the net, which he quickly folded away.

"And where will we find one of those?" He turned and scanned the forest.

"Not here—and we should go." Though a part of her might wish to, she couldn't abandon him in the Erynvorn. Even though he was no longer bleeding, he was still wounded. And though she wasn't pleased at the fact that prophecy had thrust a human into her life, there was no arguing with fate.

He turned to his horse, lifted his hands to the saddle, then let out a grunt of pain.

"You're not healed," she said. "Only slightly mended. You must favor your arm."

He gave her a tight nod and, face pale, mounted. As soon as he was settled, she set her hand on the horse's side, accustoming the animal to her touch.

"I will ride with you," she said. Then, before he could protest, she murmured a quick feather-light rune and leapt up behind him.

His mount whuffled softly, but didn't object to her presence on its back.

"Oh." The human turned to look at her over his shoulder. "I thought you might…"

"I told you I would not transform," she said—which was not a *complete* falsehood. She couldn't turn herself into a white deer, even if she wanted to. None of her people could change their forms, no matter what this mortal man seemed to think.

His eyebrows drew together in question, but before he could voice any objection, she prodded the horse into motion. Quickly, he swiveled to face forward and guide his mount around the mossy hollow beneath the log where she'd taken shelter.

"That way." She pointed to the left, trying to ignore the heat of him seated before her, the musky, not-unpleasant mortal scent drifting from his shorn hair.

"How far are we going?"

It was a good question. She frowned, thinking. Certainly not all the way to Moonflower, which was a journey of nearly two double-moons. No, they'd have to make for one of the outer courts. Nightshade was the closest, if she wasn't mistaken.

"Some distance," she finally answered. "We'll have to sleep in the forest tonight."

She would set wards, of course.

And, somehow, once he was healed, they must determine how to send him back to the mortal realm. But that was a powerful magic indeed, and one she had no hope of performing on her own.

CHAPTER 3

Following the maiden's directions, Kent guided his horse between the massive evergreens and around great tangles of briars studded with dark purple berries. The wound in his arm pulsed unpleasantly, but not as painfully as it ought to, given the nature of the injury. He supposed he ought to be grateful that the deer-maiden had tended to it, even though she'd been the one to wound him in the first place.

He hadn't anticipated that she'd be armed, or quite so combative in nature. Some of the tales he'd discovered in the palace library had mentioned that the White Hart, once captured, might turn into a silver-haired maiden. He'd been prepared for that possibility, although the stories differed on whether or not she was a princess or simply an enchanted creature.

None of them had mentioned that she carried a bow fitted with wickedly pointed arrows and possessed a tongue nearly as sharp.

"Do you have a name?" he asked.

Despite her assurances, he couldn't decide if she were truthful in nature. If only he could see her face when she answered, so he might study her pale, mist-blue eyes for the flicker of a lie. Her delicate features were mostly human, though her cheekbones were sharper, and he'd noticed the pointed tips of her ears peeking out from the pale fall of her hair.

"Of course I have a name." She sounded offended by his question, though she didn't offer him an answer.

Kent shook his head. He'd never imagined a deer to be quite so cross in nature. Though he supposed any creature would be irritated by being chased down and captured.

"I am Prince Kentry Larnach of the Kingdom of Raine," he said, belatedly realizing how pompous his title sounded, spoken into the hushed depths of the forest. There was no need for such ceremony here. "But Kent will do."

The maiden at his back was quiet for a moment, as if weighing her words.

"You may call me Fanya," she finally said.

"Are you a princess?"

She let out a soft snort of amusement, her breath briefly warming the back of his neck. "Do such things matter greatly to mortals?"

"It matters who governs a kingdom, who the ruling family is." He frowned, though she couldn't see it.

"Then are you destined to rule some mortal realm?"

"No," he said shortly, wishing he hadn't started the conversation.

Better to have a silent deer-maiden at his back than these sharp-edged questions prodding at his old pain.

At least the wolves were no longer howling in the distance.

"Is that your heart's desire, then?" she asked. "To rule a kingdom?"

"Not necessarily. It isn't what drove me to seek you out, if that's what you mean."

Another quiet sound of disbelief at his back. "Then what did?"

He shot an annoyed glance over his shoulder, catching a glimpse of her shimmering hair and one pointed ear.

"Aren't you supposed to know such things?" he demanded. "You're a creature of magic and fable, after all."

She didn't reply immediately, and Kent concentrated on guiding his mount around a fallen tree, its roots a twisted snarl above a moss-filled depression.

"Even the most magical being cannot read a heart that does not know its own way," she said at last.

"I know what I want." He kept his voice low and controlled, though he wanted to shout the words. Wanted to yell his frustration into the forest until the very trees shook with the depth of his longing.

"Hm," the maiden said.

The doubt in that single syllable almost made him leap from his horse and confront her, force her to immediately grant his wish. Of *course* he knew what he wanted! For Maired to love him back, as fiercely as he loved her.

But he was wounded, as his aching arm reminded him. And even though the howls of the wolves had faded, his demands could wait until they made camp.

"You didn't answer my question," he said, trying to turn the tables.

"Did I not?" Her voice was lightly amused. "You have so many, it's difficult to keep track."

He clenched his jaw, beating back annoyance. This wasn't how he'd envisioned the triumphant end of his hunt—wounded, and burdened with a strange maiden who refused to grant his wish and instead seemed to take a great deal of satisfaction in needling him.

And yet, he was familiar enough with hiding his own pain behind a veneer of mockery that he recognized that Fanya was doing the same. Why else would she jab him with her questions if not to deflect his own queries in return?

"So," he said, drawing his own conclusions, "you *are* a princess, after all."

He felt her go still behind him.

"Can an enchanted deer even *be* a princess?" she asked, though the amusement in her voice sounded forced. "It seems unlikely. Wouldn't my circlet tangle in my antlers? Which item, might I point out, I'm not wearing."

"Just because you don't currently have a crown atop your head doesn't mean you're not entitled to wear one. My question stands."

She blew out an annoyed breath, and a small, grim smile crossed his face. Pursuing the truth from her was almost as enjoyable as running his silver-coated quarry to ground, and a welcome distraction from the sharp throbbing in his arm. He suspected he would win this battle of words, too.

"We have no kingdoms, here," she said.

A slippery answer, but he was learning to hear what she left unsaid.

"Then what *do* you have?"

She shifted behind him and went silent for several moment. He was opening his mouth to ask her again, when she replied, "We have courts."

His brows lifted. Courts, but not kingdoms? It seemed a small distinction. "And what court do you hail from, Lady Fanya?"

"Moonflower."

She hadn't challenged his use of *lady*—which he guessed meant she was used to the title. And that he was wearing her down.

"Is that where we're going, to finish tending my injury?"

"No. That court is too far. We're headed to Nightshade."

"That sounds…ominous."

As if underscoring his words, a bird flashed from the under-brush. The blue of its startled wings matched the memory of the daylit skies of Raine.

"Nightshade might be one of the outer courts, but it's not entirely unpolished," Fanya said. "There's no cause for alarm."

"Perhaps." He would make his own determination once they reached the court. "Will we make camp soon? Your two moons are very pretty, but I'd rather travel by daylight."

"Daylight?"

He made an impatient gesture, then winced as it jarred his wounded arm. "When does the sun rise, here in your land?"

"If you mean a great glowing sphere of fire burning across the sky, we do not have a sun."

"No sun?" For the first time a wisp of fear wreathed around his heart. How far had the White Hart led him from the mortal world? And would she send him back, once his wish was granted?

Surely she must.

Yet other tales tickled his memory, of humans trapped for decades—centuries even—in a mystical land where time moved differently, if it existed at all. Enthralled by fey creatures, like the one who rode at his back. Ensorcelled until they forgot what it was to be mortal.

No. Such a fate was not for him. He would return to Raine, where Maired would be waiting with open arms, her eyes alight with a smile meant only for him.

And then what? a treacherous part of him whispered. Would he truly remain at the palace in Meriton, after stealing away his brother's fiancée? That could only result in bitter unhappiness, for all involved.

Well then, he and Maired would travel, as he'd always dreamed—visiting Fiorland in the summer, and Parnese in the winter. When they were ready, they'd find a pleasant place to settle down and raise a family.

Far from their own families…

Enough. Kent reined his thoughts back to his current predicament—injured and trapped in a shadowy realm with nothing but an irritable maiden for company. Whatever the future held, he still had a rough road to travel before he reached that happy ending.

"Is this as bright as it gets?" He waved his good arm at the dark forest, the dimly glowing flowers scattered beneath feathery ferns.

"It is." The hint of a smile lurked in her voice. "This is the doublemoon—when both the palemoon and the bright ascend together into the sky. On the morrow, we'll be left with only one."

"I fervently hope it's the brighter one."

"Alas." Now she was outright laughing at him. "The brightmoon will not show itself until the palemoon has soared the sky thrice."

"So you spend your days stumbling about in the dark?" He certainly didn't welcome the idea.

"Of course not. My kind can summon light at will. And I believe our eyes have a greater ability to adjust to shades of brightness than your poor mortal vision."

They rode in silence for a time as Kent pondered her words. Around them, the Darkwood was unchanging: a carpet of velvety moss interspersed with fallen evergreen needles, the black columns of the trees rising in every direction, the occasional shaft of moonlight drifting down through an opening in the interlaced branches.

He could barely make out the shapes of fallen logs or the contours of the bushes ahead—and this was the brightest this realm became?

"Can you enchant my eyes, so that I might see better in the dim light?" he finally asked. He wouldn't admit how poor his vision was, for fear she'd take advantage and flee.

"Is that your heart's desire?" she asked, a teasing note in her voice.

"I'll pretend you didn't ask me that."

A soft chuckle, and then he felt her lean forward, her breath against his neck once more.

"It is possible, I suppose," she said. "Let me think upon it."

He nodded. Such a small enchantment should be within her powers—though he'd make absolutely sure she knew it was *not* the wish he claimed in return for her capture. If he'd learned anything from his fable-reading, it was that magical creatures could twist the terms of any bargain, and that mortals had best take care.

CHAPTER 4

As they rode, Fanya pondered the human's request. She knew the rune to call light, of course—*calya*—and several others that created a small glamour, such as adding extra sparkle to gems or a sheen to her court gowns. Perhaps a combination of the two would work.

"I will attempt to enchant your vision," she told Prince Kentry the next time they halted for a rest.

"Just to be clear," he said, moving stiffly to perch on a nearby fallen log, "this is *not* my heart's desire."

"Understood." She nodded gravely, pretending she actually had the power to perform such a life-changing magic as reading his heart and making that wish come true.

She started by quickly refreshing the healing rune on his arm, frowning at the reddened flesh surrounding the arrow hole. It was not mending at all, and she worried that he might develop wound-fever. She added a murmured rune of pain-ease over the injury, and he drew in a deep, relieved breath. Clearly, he'd been concealing the extent of his discomfort.

Once she was finished with his arm, she came to stand before him. He watched her calmly.

"Close your eyes," she said.

He did, and she rested her fingertips gently over his eyebrows, trying to ignore how her pulse jumped. Truly, this wasn't a difficult thing she was about to attempt. Why her breath should be trembling, she could not say.

"*Calyagalad*," she said, drawing upon her wellspring and directing the power through her hands.

Blue light flared across her fingers, throwing his face into sharp relief, then fading. Slowly, she pulled her hands away.

"Open your eyes."

He did, blinking. A hint of astonishment crossed his face as he turned his head, looking at the trees, the flowers, and then her.

"Astounding." His gaze held hers. "Thank you, Fanya. I no longer feel as if I'm stumbling about in a dark room."

"Good. If, once we reach Nightshade, the light becomes too bright, tell me. I should be able to remove the enchantment." At least, she hoped so.

He nodded, and they mounted and recommenced their journey through the Erynvorn.

The palemoon had fled from the sky, and the brightmoon was dipping low when they finally reached a small clearing where they could make camp. As soon as Prince Kentry halted his horse, Fanya slipped lightly off and laid her hand against its warm back in gratitude for bearing her.

The prince dismounted more slowly, wincing in pain from the movement. A sluggish flow of blood had begun trickling from the arrow-hole in his arm, and she frowned in sympathy. Once she'd foraged for their dinner, she'd once again tend to the injury as best she could. It was her fault he was wounded, after all.

Though it was also his fault, for capturing her in the first place...

"This is where we'll spend the night?" He turned in a slow circle, then glanced up at the star-specked sky.

"Yes." She indicated the tumble of boulders on one side of the clearing. "We'll sleep beneath the shelter of the rocks. Now, rest. I'll fetch water."

"Here." He unslung an empty water skin from his belt and handed it to her.

Soft-footed, Fanya made her way to the stream that lay deeper in the Erynvorn. She filled his container, and her own, with the clear sweet water. On the way back, she gathered a pouchful of tart red berries and the long, moist shelf of a tree-growing mushroom.

Those, plus the supplies she carried in her pack, should feed them well enough. She didn't know if Kentry would have anything to contribute. He seemed rather ill-provisioned for a trip into the forest. Mortals were strange creatures.

Though not without their small charms.

He'd borne up stoically, though she knew his arm pained him with every movement. Despite that, he'd met her pointed words with jabs of own, which she couldn't help but admire. In the Moonflower Court, she was often chided for her sharp tongue.

Though, if she were a warrior instead of the youngest daughter of the Moonflower Lord and Lady, such bluntness would be appreciated, not frowned upon.

The fact that this mortal prince didn't feel any need to mince words with her made her like him all the better. Even if he thought she was an enchanted deer. He was clever, too. The suggestion she enchant his vision had been a good one, and she was pleased she'd been able to create a rune to suit.

When she returned to the clearing, she found that Kentry had made the rudiments of their camp, despite his injury.

"You were supposed to rest," she reminded him, glancing at the unsaddled horse that now browsed the clearing, the armfuls of long grasses he'd cut and laid at the foot of the stones to cushion their sleep.

"I did." He lifted his uninjured shoulder in a shrug. "For a short time, anyway."

She deposited the food she'd gathered on a flat stone and went to fetch the cheese and last bit of bread from her pack. The prince rummaged in his satchel and brought out dried fruit and a small piece of salted meat.

"I'm sorry I don't have more," he said. "I didn't expect…this." He looked at her, then the cedars towering above them.

"Do you have any bedding?" she asked, though she feared the answer was clear enough.

"Just my cloak. It won't get too cold, will it?"

"No—perhaps a bit cooler than it is now, once the brightmoon sets." She was reluctant to add her fear that he'd become feverish. Even with magical healing, wounds sometimes went bad.

But tomorrow they would reach Nightshade, and the healer there was certainly skilled enough to tend this stray human.

Then what?

Her mind shied from the question. Her current task was to bring Kentry safely out of the Erynvorn. Whatever happened after that was in the Oracle's hands.

"Come, sit by me and let me tend to that," she said, nodding to his arm.

He dabbed at the ooze of blood on his upper arm, then looked at his fingers, smeared faintly with red. "It doesn't hurt."

"Whether or not it does, it's never a good idea to bleed in the middle of the Erynvorn." She patted the grass covered ground beside her.

"The Erynvorn." He glanced at the trees surrounding their small clearing. "In my land, we call this forest the Darkwood."

"It is the same meaning," she said.

"I like your language better." He sent her a quick grin, then held out his arm. "Do your magic."

She poured a little water over the wound, wiping the liquid gently away with a torn-off strip of her undertunic and taking care not to touch the injury itself. Then she held her hand just above his arm and closed her eyes, reaching within herself for her wellspring of power.

As she'd not been healer-trained, she only knew those two runes; one to ease pain and the other to staunch blood and knit together small wounds. The hole in Kentry's arm could not be called small, of course, but her meager efforts would have to suffice until they reached the Nightshade Court.

She spoke both runes, infusing them with as much power as she could, conscious of his intent gaze as she worked. When she finished, she glanced into his face, glad to see that the lines of pain creasing his forehead had eased once more.

"Thank you," he said.

"Since I caused your injury, it's only fair that I tend it. But soon enough you'll be healed entirely, and free to return to your own land."

"With my wish granted," he reminded her.

Since she had no idea how to do such a thing, she made no reply. Instead, she turned to the flat stone and busied herself with portioning out their food.

They took their meal, though the prince was clearly distrustful of the mushroom, and only ate sparingly of the berries.

"I'm not trying to poison you," she said. "Eat. Your body needs fuel."

Slowly, he picked up a slice of mushroom and sniffed it. "It's unfamiliar."

"This whole realm is unfamiliar to you," she pointed out, a bit tartly. "That doesn't mean you must starve to death."

He shook his head, then took a bite of the mushroom and chewed it slowly. "I hope you have better food at your courts."

"I didn't think it wise to light a cooking fire. But I assure you, my people don't subsist on raw foods gleaned from the forest."

His eyebrows twitched, but he finished the piece of mushroom. She noticed he didn't reach for any more.

The last golden radiance faded as the brightmoon slipped away behind the trees, chasing the absent palemoon. A bird chirped sleepily from a nearby thicket, and the glowing blossoms of the *quille* furled themselves into shadow. Fanya tidied up the remains of their meal, then took her spidersilk blanket from her pack.

Normally she bound the two edges together with a simple rune, creating an envelope to sleep within—but it was large enough to spread over two, if they settled next to one another. She didn't welcome the thought of lying beside Kentry all night, but he was her responsibility, and she would let no harm come to him.

Speaking of which, she needed to set the wards about their camp, before the darkness brought anything unpleasant their way.

"If you need a moment," she said to the prince, "best take it now. I will be warding the clearing, and once the protections are in place, you cannot cross them."

"Why not?" He gave her a keen glance, curiosity glinting in his dark brown eyes. "Will the enchantment hurt me?"

"No. It will simply dispel, leaving us vulnerable."

"Can I watch you cast them?"

"I suppose there's no harm in it—but I doubt you'll be able to see anything."

He nodded, then rose to tend to his needs. In his absence, Fanya spread her silken blanket over the mounded grass he'd gathered for their simple bed. She did not like it, but there was no other option.

When the prince returned, he rinsed his hands and splashed water on his face, leaving a small amount in his waterskin. He glanced at the bed, then back to her.

"Where will I sleep?"

She shot him a look. "Do you think I mean to take all the comfort for myself and leave you on the hard ground?"

Color reddened his face and he glanced away. "I didn't want to presume. But if you're inviting me to share your bed—"

"I am not. We will simply sleep next to one another, for warmth." And so that, if he took a turn for the worse in the dark hours, she would sense it and be able to tend him.

"Ah." He nodded sagely. "For warmth."

Now it was her turn to blush.

"You're wounded," she said. "And even if you were not, I do not find you appealing in that manner."

Which, she had to privately admit, was an untruth. Though his features were not as sharp as those of her people, she found his full mouth and the soft planes of his cheeks appealing. The warmth in his eyes reminded her of the taste of dark honey, and for a fleeting moment she wondered how his hair would look, grown long and braided in the fashion of the warriors of Elfhame.

He raised a clenched fist to his heart. "You wound me! I am considered one of the most handsome men in Raine."

"I *have* wounded you, yes." She gave his injured arm a significant glance. "And as for what passes as comeliness among humans, I cannot say."

"You would be thought quite beautiful." There was no mockery in his voice. "By mortal standards, at least."

She ducked her head, letting her hair cover her blush with a silvery veil. By the moons, this human had a surprising ability to discomfit her.

Well, he would be gone soon enough, and then she wouldn't have to worry about how uncomfortable he made her. Strangely, she did not welcome the thought.

KENT LAY BESIDE FANYA, STARING UP AT THE UNFAMILIAR STARS spangling the deep violet-black of the sky. He was tired, his body heavy with exhaustion, but his clamoring thoughts would not still enough for him to find sleep.

His moonlit-haired companion slept—or at least he thought she did. After their meal, she'd walked a circle about their campsite, humming beneath her breath and pausing at what he guessed had been each of the four directions. Although he'd watched her closely, he could detect no signs of magic, but he trusted her word that she'd set protective enchantments around them.

The magic she'd performed on his eyes, however, was much more tangible. The soft radiance of her realm bathed his vision, and though it wasn't like moving about in the sunlit world, he'd adjusted readily enough.

Her healing magic wasn't as effective, unfortunately, although when she'd murmured the strange, liquid syllables over the injury one last time before they took their rest, he'd sighed with relief. The waves of pain receded like the tide pulling away from the shore. The discomfort would be back, he knew, but hopefully not soon.

He didn't tell her that he felt hot and restless. Even if the wound was beginning to fester, there was nothing Fanya could do to aid him. Tomorrow they would reach the court she'd told him of. Nightshade.

It did not sound appealing. He imagined a dark and eerie place, filled with purple shadows and strange, pale beings who would not be pleased to see a human in their midst.

But they would heal him, and then Fanya would grant his heart's desire.

Although…he had to admit that the burning devotion for Maired he carried like a coal in his chest had cooled, ever since he'd chased the White Hart into this strange realm. But surely, once he returned to Raine, the force of his yearning would again pierce him with every breath he drew.

And, even better, Maired would love him back as passionately as he loved her. He pulled the knowledge over him, as comforting as the wood-smoke smell of his cloak laid atop them. Finally, he slept.

Fanya woke suddenly, her senses humming. Something had triggered her wards of protection.

Slowly, she reached for the bow set on the ground beside her. Once her fingers were wrapped about the grip, she sat in one smooth motion, pulling an arrow from her quiver and nocking it to the string.

Bow drawn, she scanned the shadows beneath the trees. Nothing stirred. Her pulse beat through her, hollow and insistent.

Then, suddenly, a rush of air over her head. She sprang to her feet, calling out the rune for foxfire. The blue light illuminated the underside of batlike wings, the sinuous neck and baleful eye of a drake as it passed overhead.

"Prince," she said softly, nudging his sleeping her form with her foot. "Awaken."

In credit to his obvious warrior training, it took only a single heartbeat for him to roll from beneath his cloak and draw the sword he'd kept sheathed on his side of their makeshift bed.

"What is it?" His voice was heavy with sleep, and he blinked, squinting at the clearing. "Are we under attack?"

"Imminently—from above. My wards will deflect one strike, but after that, we'll be unprotected."

"Not entirely." He shot her a tight look. "Good thing you didn't shoot my sword arm. What's after us?"

"A drake. Luckily a small one, by the look—"

Her words were cut off by an angry shriek as the creature plunged down, wickedly sharp claws extended. The horse, tethered nearby, let out a shrill whinny of fear, and Fanya spared a sliver of hope that the drake would leave it alone.

She tilted her bow up, aiming for one of the drake's yellow eyes, and let her arrow fly. It struck the creature near the mouth, which seemed to enrage it. Her wards of protection flared blue, and then were gone.

"Take cover beside the rock." Kentry gestured. "You shoot at the beast while I keep it distracted."

"Beware the claws," she said, stepping back. "They're poisonous."

"Wonderful. Here it comes."

He moved away from their sleeping area, giving himself room to maneuver, and Fanya set another arrow to her bow.

"Strike the underbelly," she called. "It's not as heavily scaled there."

At least, not according to the few accounts of how to fight drakes she'd found in the Moonflower scrolls while researching creatures of the Erynvorn. The best hope for a fatal blow, however, was an eye shot. The stories she'd read had not mentioned how difficult that would be. The drake's head was set at the end of a long, scaly neck, which whipped about constantly.

The creature descended and Kentry ducked, swiping at its belly. His sword flashed blue in the light of her foxfire. The blade grated across the drake's scales, doing no noticeable damage, and the prince was barely able to avoid a vicious rake of the creature's claws. Fanya kept her arrow trained on its head, but it moved too quickly for her to be sure of hitting her mark.

With effort, she kept her breathing controlled, her hands steady. There wouldn't be many chances to make her shot, and when one came, she must be prepared. No matter that her blood raced with fear, that the looming jaws of death gaped wide above their heads.

As the drake made another pass, Kentry stabbed up at its belly with the tip of his sword. The creature screeched as the blade penetrated. Thick, dark blood dripped from the injury and fell, sizzling, upon the ground. The prince wrenched his blade free and dodged away as the drake darted its head down with a vicious snap of teeth.

So far, Kentry had managed to stay away from the creature's attacks, but Fanya saw how clumsy his movements were growing. A sheen of sweat covered his face, and his blade wavered as he held it at the ready.

With another screech, the drake backwinged into the air, keeping its baleful yellow gaze on Kentry. It was poised for another diving attack—but that momentary pause in the air was all Fanya needed. She sighted along her arrow, then let it fly.

It struck the creature directly in the eye. Shrieking, the drake turned toward the rock where she sheltered, and dove directly at her.

"Fanya!" the prince cried, horror in his voice.

She dropped into a roll, desperately trying to avoid the drake's poisonous claws. A touch along her back, feather-light. He jerkin parted, her skin stung. The creature let out a bellow and made an ungainly landing, then lurched around to face her once more.

Shouting, Kentry threw himself forward and plunged his sword into the drake's other eye.

It froze, swayed, and then, with a gurgle, collapsed upon the trampled grasses.

They stared at the fallen drake a moment, and Fanya felt a trembling wave sweep from her legs up through her whole body. Grimacing, Kentry wrenched his sword out of the creature's eye, then wiped the blade clean and sheathed it. He plucked the arrow from its other eye, and brought it to Fanya.

"Did it touch you?" he asked.

Still kneeling, she reached to take the arrow, then winced at the flare of fire between her shoulders.

"I…think it did." Slowly, she turned so that he might view her back.

A hiss as he sucked air through his teeth. Gently, he folded her jerkin away from her skin. "It scratched you—lightly, but enough to draw blood. Is the poison…" He faltered, voice catching. "Does it act quickly, or do you have time?"

"Don't worry—I won't drop dead at your feet." At least, she didn't think so. "But we must head for Nightshade immediately."

"I don't think I'd fancy sleeping next to a dead drake, in any case," he said, then laid his cool fingers upon her back. "Do you have something I could clean and bandage this with?"

"I'll tear strips from the blanket." She went to their makeshift bed and sank down upon the piled grasses.

With the help of the small dagger she kept belted at her waist, she set about ruining her silk blanket. While she was at it, she tore several extra pieces to use as new dressings for his arm.

"Won't you need that?" he asked, watching as she shredded the cloth.

She glanced up at him, noting the pallor of his face, the shadows beneath his eyes.

"Either we'll take our next rest in beds at the Nightshade Court, or we'll have no need of blankets ever again."

He gave her a grim nod. "At least the creature didn't attack my horse. As soon as you're tended to, I'll saddle up and we'll go. Can you bring your light a bit closer?"

Through he tried to be gentle as he dabbed at her back with a water-dampened piece of silk, she winced whenever he touched the scratch.

"I presume you can cast your healing magic upon yourself," he said. "Will it help slow the poison's effect?"

"I don't know. But I'll try."

She murmured the runes, dismayed to find her wellspring sluggish and partially depleted. It seemed that the drake's inimical touch affected the source of her power, as well as her flesh and blood—though the stories had made no mention of that effect.

"Let me tend to you, as well," she said, neglecting to add that her powers were fading.

She would do what she could for both of them, then pray to the brightmoon that they reached Nightshade alive.

CHAPTER 6

KENT BLINKED, HIS VISION BLURRY. SOMETHING LAY AHEAD, but he didn't know whether it was a fever mirage brought on by the relentless hours of their journey, or the Nightshade Court at last. Certainly the pale, gracefully-arched palace shining faintly under the sickle of the small moon didn't match his dire imaginings.

Perhaps it was an illusion after all.

After they'd left the clearing where they'd defeated the drake, he and Fanya had spent an eternity riding through the huge, dark forest. They'd taken turns supporting one another through the long hours, coaxing each other to drink, one holding the other upright when either of them veered into unconsciousness—which happened more often the longer they traveled.

They'd tried placing Fanya in front of him as they rode—but any time his clothing brushed against the thin, angry line across her back, she winced. So she rode behind him, her arms about his waist, her head resting against his shoulders as they both fought to remain awake.

Eventually, the palemoon had risen, sending a soft lavender light through the trees. Some endless time after that, they'd passed from riding between the huge columns of the evergreens to smaller stands of white-barked saplings that shivered with every breeze. Following

Fanya's murmured instructions, he'd guided Nimble through silvery swaths of meadow grass and past a quiet lake rimmed with phosphorescence.

And now, he hardly dared hope, they'd finally arrived at their destination.

"Fanya." He reached behind him and gently touched her leg. "Is that the Nightshade Court?"

She murmured and stirred, and he felt her lift her head from his shoulder.

"Yes." Her breath whispered past his ear. "Make for the main gates."

A smooth dirt road curved to intersect their course, leading to the wide, pillared opening framing the palace. As they passed through, Kent noted filigreed gates, folded back like wings against the graceful outer walls.

A stretch of garden, planted with beds of pale flowers and trailing vines, lay between the gates and the long building ahead. Slender turrets rose at either end of the palace, and lights glimmered from multiple arched openings that must be windows.

Lights danced about him and Fanya, too, as they rode forward; small balls of radiance that looped over their heads and then darted back toward the palace.

"Glimglows," Fanya said. "They will alert the Nightshade Lord and Lady of our arrival."

He might have been apprehensive at the thought of meeting the monarchs, but sheer exhaustion, coupled with the pounding fever in his head, blunted all else.

Perhaps he drifted into unconsciousness, for it seemed that between one eyeblink and the next they arrived at the front door of the palace. Three wide, flat steps mounted to an arched doorway surrounded by carved vines and leaves. Instead of torches, the doorway was flanked by crystal bowls holding the strange blue lights he'd seen Fanya conjure.

A moment later, they were surrounded by four stern elvish warriors. Despite their long, intricately braided hair, and the fact that two of them were women, they had the air of hardened fighters. Kent drew his horse to a halt, careful to keep his hand well away from his sword.

"Who are you?" the lead warrior demanded, staring intently at Kent. "And what have you done to Lady Fanyaleth?"

"Peace, Pilinor," Fanya said. "He saved my life."

"But he is a mortal." The warrior gave her a distrustful look.

"Even so," she said.

"What call have you to bring such a one—"

"The lady is wounded and in need of healing," Kent broke in, little caring for the formalities. "We both are. Such discussions can wait until later."

The warrior's brows rose, but the brusqueness of Kent's words didn't seem to anger him.

"Then we shall escort you to the healer. Naica, Hatal, assist Lady Fanyaleth. Ileth and I will keep watch on this one." He turned his pointed gaze back to Kent.

Gently, the assigned warriors helped Fanya dismount. Kent followed, though he received only suspicious looks instead of careful assistance as he slid from his horse.

"Will you tend to Nimble?" he asked, patting his horse's withers. "He's carried us faithfully." He kept himself from asking if they even knew what such things as horses were. After all, Fanya had seemed comfortable with his mount.

"A servant will take your horse to the stables," the warrior, Pilinor, said. "Now, come."

He led the way up the steps, Kent and his watchful guard behind, and then Fanya with her escort. As they passed through the arched doorway into a long corridor, the air turned pleasantly warm. More of the blue lights glowed at intervals, their soft radiance reflected by the polished marble walls and floor.

For a court named Nightshade, the surroundings were far more airy and graceful than Kent had imagined. Although, on closer inspection, the carvings of foliage about the doors did, indeed, depict that poisonous plant.

Pilinor turned left down a smaller hallway, then right at another, which soon opened into an atrium. A quiet fountain plashed in the center of the room, and a half-dozen beds were arranged along the far wall.

A silver-haired elf woman sat before a table, but quickly rose as they entered. Unlike Fanya and the warriors, she wore a gown, made of rich blue cloth. Her gaze fell upon Kent for a moment, then went to Fanya.

"Lady Fanyaleth," she exclaimed in concern, hurrying to meet them. "Your wellspring is dangerously low. And what poison is that I sense within you?"

"Drake," Fanya said, weaving slightly on her feet.

"Help her to sit," the healer said, gesturing to the nearest bed.

"My companion is wounded, as well," Fanya said, nodding at Kent.

"It can wait," he said, his own dismay ticking up at the healer's worried expression. "See to the lady."

Fanya's escorts assisted her to the bed. Kent followed, trailed by his own watchful guard, while Pilinor took up a post near the fountain, one hand resting on his sword.

"Can you heal her, Mistress Silweth?" the warrior asked.

"I believe so."

"And what of the mortal?"

The healer glanced at Kent. "A simple enough injury." She waved at the next bed over. "There is no need to hover, human. Rest, while I tend to Lady Fanyaleth. I sense a great weariness within you."

Reluctantly, Kent moved to the bed and slowly sat. The coverlet was woven of a soft gray material and the mattress gave slightly beneath his weight. With a narrow-eyed look, the warrior guarding him moved to stand at the end of the bed.

Kent didn't care. He harbored no ill-will toward the inhabitants of Nightshade. All his concern was for Fanya, whose pale skin seemed even paler, the silver luster of her hair faded as she gingerly lay down upon her side, facing the bed where he sat. She smiled faintly at him—more a grimace than anything—and Kent leaned forward, ignoring the throbbing pain in his arm. *Be strong*, he willed at her as their gazes met.

Her smile fell and she winced as the healer examined her back. From where he sat, Kent had a clear view of Mistress Silweth's expression, which didn't bode well.

"You *can* heal her, can't you?" he demanded.

"Hush," Pilinor said from his post by the fountain.

The healer didn't respond, but bent to her work. Her long fingers left glowing sigils in the air as she chanted. To Kent's relief, the pain in Fanya's eyes eased.

"You should rest," Fanya said to him.

"No." Despite the heavy exhaustion blurring his senses, he refused to close his eyes until he knew that, when he opened them again, she would still be there.

"At least lie down," she said.

"Sh. Don't worry about me."

She nodded, once, then drew in a halting breath as the healer touched her back again.

"It will take several turns for me to drive all the poison out," Mistress Silweth said. "But you will recover. That, I promise. When did you last eat?"

Fanya blinked. "I…not since last moonset."

Mistress Silweth frowned and sent one of Fanya's escort off immediately to bring food. Then she turned to Kent and peeled away the makeshift bandages around his arm. When she spoke the healing words, a great rush of ease went through him, and the bone-deep agony within him quieted.

"Thank you," he said.

"You are not fully mended," Mistress Silweth said. "You must take care with your arm for some time yet."

"Can I stay here?" He looked at Fanya, who was still watching him. Truly, he didn't know where else he might go. She was his only friend in this strange world.

"The Nightshade rulers will wish to speak with him," Pilinor said.

"Might it wait?" Fanya asked softly. "I would stand at his side."

The warrior looked displeased, but it seemed her request carried enough weight to silence his protests.

Time passed in a blur. Kent slept, ate, slept again, though most of his attention was focused on Fanya. The healer performed enchantments upon her twice more, and with each healing session she seemed improved.

In the quietest hours of the night, however, the drake's poison roused for a final attempt.

The room was dim, the fountain still, when Fanya's whimpers of pain woke Kent.

"Fanya?" He sat, blessing the enchantment upon his eyes that enabled him to see in the faint light.

She tossed upon her bed, her hair stuck damply to her face with perspiration. Quickly, he rose and dipped a pitcher of water from the fountain's basin, as the elves had done. He coaxed her to drink, then dampened a cloth and gently sponged her forehead.

When the worst of her fever passed, he made to rise, but she gripped his hand fiercely.

"Stay," she whispered.

"I will. Give me a moment."

He loosened her grasp and went to push his bed up beside hers. His arm twinged at the motion, but he paid it no heed. When he lay back down, she reached for him again, curling her hands about his. He bowed his head, their foreheads touching, and took a deep breath.

For the first time in months, Kent passed the rest of the night in a deep and dreamless slumber.

In the morning, the healer's brows rose, but she said nothing about the new proximity of their beds. She frowned when Kent told her of Fanya's fever in the night, but reassured him that the healing was well underway—for both of them.

The summons woke Fanya, and she blinked in momentary confusion, trying to orient herself. The soft splash of the fountain in the healer's enclave of the Nightshade Court, the soft radiance of foxfire—and the warmth of Kentry's hand in hers, their fingers entwined, his bed pushed beside hers.

"What is it?" She slid her hand from his grasp and sat.

He woke, too, and looked up at her, his brown eyes confused. The vulnerability in their depths made something within her twist with yearning.

"Yes?" She glanced at the doorway where the warrior, Pilinor, stood.

"An Oracle has come," he said. "They request an audience."

Of course. She looked at the mortal by her side. Her prophecy had sent her into the Erynvorn, where she'd found Prince Kentry. Now, his time in Elfhame was drawing to a close. She refused to acknowledge how her heart ached at the thought.

"Prince," she said softly, bending over him. "I have a confession to make." Now that the Oracle was at hand, there was no more use in pretending. "I am not actually the White Hart."

His brows drew together briefly, and then he smiled at her. "I know. Once we arrived at the court, I guessed as much."

Before she could say anything more, a figure stepped into the room, garbed head to toe in white. The veil covering their head made it impossible to tell their gender, and their low, mellifluous voice gave no further clues.

"Lady Fanyaleth of the Moonflower Court," the Oracle said, halting a few paces from her bedside, "I am here to complete the circle of your prophecy."

Fanya nodded, and swung her legs over the edge of the bed. She'd prefer to meet her fate standing. To her surprise, Kentry also rose and came to stand at her side.

"I'm ready," she said.

For whatever reason, the Oracles had sent her into the forest so that she might find this mortal prince and bring him safely to Nightshade. Now that he was healed, they would return him to the mortal world so that he might fulfill whatever destiny awaited him.

And for herself?

She supposed she'd return, a dutiful daughter of Moonflower, and resign herself to an advantageous political marriage with one of the other courts. The thought pulled upon her heart, and she refused to consider it too closely.

"Are you?" The Oracle sounded lightly amused. "And what of you, Prince Kentry of Raine? Are you ready to achieve your heart's desire?"

Fanya was conscious of the prince's gaze upon her, but she didn't —couldn't—return it. Something inside her was cracking in two, and she dared not name the sorrow rending her.

"I believe I am," Kentry said.

The Oracle bowed their veiled head. "Am I to send you back to the mortal world, then?"

The prince cleared his throat. "Actually, I have a question."

Fanya sent him a startled glance, and he slanted her a quick smile in return.

"What is your question?" the Oracle asked.

"If you sent me back to the mortal world," he said, "would I ever be able to return here?"

"No. The gate can only be opened once more."

Kentry blew out his breath, then caught Fanya's hand. His fingers were warm against hers, his clasp firm.

"Fanya," he said, turning to her, "I thought I knew what my heart's desire was...until I met you."

"What did you wish?" she asked, an unaccountable tightness in her chest.

His lips twisted into a crooked smile. "I wished that a certain lady would love me. And yet, the longer I was away, the less I thought of her. My feelings for her were a grassfire—hot and bright, and, ultimately, short-lived."

"What, then, is your heart's desire?" the Oracle asked him.

"I..." Kentry held Fanya's gaze. "If my love for that lady was a fire, now burnt away, I believe that you have planted a seed in my heart. I would very much like to see the tall tree it will grow into, if given a chance. Would you be willing to take me to your court, lady? To see what we might achieve, together?"

The sorrow ripping through Fanya mended in a wave of hope. "You would stay here? What of your mortal life?"

He shook his head. "I might not know the entirety of my heart's desire—yet. But I believe I will find it here, in your world."

Fanya closed her eyes. Opened them, and glanced at the white-veiled Oracle.

"It is your choice," the Oracle said. "Your birthright sent you into the Erynvorn for a reason."

That reason stood before her, entreaty in his mortal eyes. A memory of all they had endured together flashed through her. Prince Kentry of Raine—the courageous, irritating, handsome mortal man who wished to remain in Elfhame. With her.

"If you will take such a leap," she said to him, "then I can do no less. Prince Kentry of Raine, will you stay with me, in this realm?"

His smile blazed and she thought she'd never tire of the look in his eyes—warmth, admiration, companionship, and the seed of a deep love, waiting to open.

"Lady Fanyaleth, I desire nothing more."

"You are certain?" the Oracle asked.

Kentry nodded. "My future is here, at the side of this moon-haired maiden. Whatever may come."

"Then so be it," the Oracle said. "May your lives be long and filled with joy." They bowed their veiled head and began a soft chant of blessing.

As the Oracle's favor drifted over them, Fanya gripped Kent's hand.

"Do you fear you'll regret this choice?" she asked softly, staring into his eyes.

He met her gaze steadily, his clasp firm. "Never. This is my heart's desire."

His heart's desire. And hers. Twined together by fate.

It was all the answer she needed.

The inspiration for this story comes from the many tales concerning the magical deer called the White Hart, or White Stag. From Arthurian Legend to Celtic myth, this mystical creature has roamed the forest, leading princes and knights astray and, if they're lucky, granting their heart's desire. I chose to set this tale in the world of the Darkwood, which contains the mystical gateway between the mortal world and the realm of the Dark Elves. Read more in the Darkwood Chronicles, starting with Elfhame!

ABOUT THE AUTHOR

Growing up, Anthea Sharp spent most of her summers raiding the library shelves and reading, especially fantasy. She now makes her home in sunny Southern California, where she enjoys fresh citrus, plays the fiddle, and writes up a storm. Contact her at antheasharp@hotmail.com or visit her website at www.antheasharp.com

Anthea also writes historical romance (yes, like Bridgerton!) under the pen name Anthea Lawson. Find out about her acclaimed Victorian romantic adventure novels at anthealawson.com.

PIN OAK'S WISH

KAY MCSPADDEN

Pɪɴɴʏ ʟᴏᴏᴋᴇᴅ ᴏᴠᴇʀ ʜᴇʀ ꜱʜᴏᴜʟᴅᴇʀ ᴀᴛ ᴛʜᴇ ᴅᴀʀᴋ ɢʀᴀʏ clouds scudding across the top of Bullhead Ridge. She paused for a moment to catch her breath and test the wind with her outstretched hand. Snow—not now, but in a few hours. Lots of it, too.

In the trees, the birds broadcast their alarm. Closing her eyes, Pinny listened to the chitter of squirrels and voles and a family of red foxes who lived in an uneasy alliance in this sheltered hollow. *Go home*, they said. *Blizzard on the way. Get along to your nest.*

A good idea. Pinny shifted her rucksack full of the chestnuts and feverfew roots she'd come to find. She'd planned to look for ginseng near Sugar Creek but the anxiety in the forest was palpable. Already the top of Spruce Pinnacle was draped in clouds. If she lost sight of Pisgah Mountain, she'd have a hard time navigating back to Grandmother Blue's cabin.

She hadn't gone far before she felt the first drops of rain. Sometimes in the lower elevations this happened—a quick shower before the blast of cold rolled in, encasing everything in a sheet of ice. Then the snow piled up in impassible drifts. No wonder the animals were urging her home. The Mountain Folk who lived here, as skilled in woodcraft as they were, could die caught out in such weather.

Even her Grandmother Blue, the best woodcrafter Pinny knew,

was wary about snow. For half a moment—the time it took for her heart to flutter from one beat to the next—Pinny let herself worry. But her grandmother, rumored to be a thousand years old, her black hair shiny with indigo highlights in the sun, was safe, sitting at the bedside of a neighboring Folk-woman who was enduring a difficult labor. Pinny reached out with her mind and felt the familiar bond between them, like a warm tendril.

Get home, Grandmother Blue told her. *Get home*, hooted the barred owl who lived in the largest pin oak on the creek bank.

But the crow who often quarreled with the owl flew overhead and scolded its disagreement. It circled once and then disappeared into a thicket of rhododendron.

"This better be important," Pinny said aloud. Crows were, she knew, the cleverest of birds, and the easiest to understand. This crow was clearly leading her forward.

As she pushed aside the thicket of bushes she saw why. Two men, both dressed in drab brown-green jackets and pants, were sprawled where they had landed after falling over a steep scarp. Sharp edges of the mountain, hidden by thick undergrowth, were a danger for anyone not born and bred here. More than once an unlucky hunter had wandered too far into the woods and needed rescuing after a hard tumble.

These men might be hunters, though their clothes were different from any Pinny had seen before. She looked around and saw a rifle and a canvas knapsack a few feet away on the ground. With a start, Pinny realized that one of the men was watching her. His face was grimy but she could see him opening his mouth to speak.

"Please," he whispered. Pinny dropped her rucksack and pushed her way past the last rhododendron branches. Kneeling beside the man, she shut her eyes.

A wave of fear and pain washed over her. She dove after it, like a swimmer, and caught up to it. He was feeling fear, yes, but curiosity, too. She saw herself briefly through his eyes and blushed, bemused that despite his broken ankle—the snap clean, the ligament untorn —he thought she was beautiful. Without opening her eyes she reached out and put her palm on his chest. At once his heart slowed and quieted, his pain receding.

"How did you—"

She opened her eyes and turned her attention to the other man. His injuries were more severe. A head wound, internal. She could sense a trickle of blood in his brain coursing freely like a creek over-flowing its banks. If only her Grandmother were here. She would know how to staunch the blood with a touch. It was her gift, the healing of every type of physical wound. In time Pinny expected to grow into her own healing ways, but for now she was limited to simple magic. Broken bones were one thing. Silent injuries to the brain were quite another.

She saw clumps of the first lazy snowflakes wafting around her. Soon the storm—and the snowfall—would start in earnest. The first man was watching her intently. Cupping his ankle with both hands, she pictured the ends of the broken ankle bones. She closed her eyes again and saw the jangling nerves and swollen tissues. *Quiet, now,* she intoned silently. Make the world whole again. She felt the man's pain ebb as the nerves settled down and the bones began stitching the jagged ends back together.

The man sighed audibly. Pinny picked up a broken tree branch from the ground and handed it to him.

"We can't stay here," she said. He nodded and turned to get up on his knees. Face drawn, breath ragged, he pushed himself upright with the help of the branch.

Pinny slid her arm under the shoulders of the other man and started to lift him. With an awkward sloping gait they half carried, half dragged the unconscious man the remainder of the way to her grandmother's wooden cabin. By the time Pinny stirred the ashes into flame and laid the unconscious man on a folded quilt by the stone fireplace, the snow was coming down so hard that the surrounding forest disappeared from view.

"If my grandmother were here, you wouldn't need this," Pinny said to the man with the broken ankle. He watched as she held up a roll of cotton sheeting cut into long strips, motioning to him to remove his boot. Like the oddly colored clothes he wore, the man's boots were unusual—brown leather with double buckles that fastened over his heel. Sitting on a rocker pulled close to the fire, he slid his boot from his foot and sat back, clearly exhausted. Pinny brushed her hand across the top of his foot and the grimace on his face smoothed out.

Pinny had seen few people who weren't Mountain Folk. Outsiders rarely ventured into the forest, and Mountain Folk almost never went into town. There was nothing there they needed. Self-sufficient and proud of it, they shied away from anyone who might misunderstand the particular magic only they seemed to have—healing, and future sight, and communion with the forest animals. Pinny had grown up hearing stories of Mountain Folk whose gifts had gotten them labeled as witches or demons and had suffered for it. If her grandmother were here, she would warn Pinny against what she was doing now.

Leaning forward, Pinny deftly slipped the man's sock off in a single motion. As he let out a cry, she slipped her hands around his ankle. He quieted at once.

"How do you—"

"I'm going to wrap your ankle," she said, cutting him off. "It might feel tight at first, but by tomorrow you should be able to put your weight on it."

Her words seemed to shock the man. "Tomorrow? I have to report back right away. I'm pretty sure Jack has a bad concussion. We'll need to—"

"You see that storm?" Pinny pointed to the small window. Nothing except whirling white was visible. "You aren't going anywhere until that lets up. And maybe not then."

"But—"

"His name is Jack?" Pinny knelt beside the unconscious man and brushed his hair out of his face.

"John, I think. But no one calls him that. I'm Carl, by the way. Well, Carlo, but no one calls me that either. What about you?"

Pinny lay her palm on Jack's forehead. Unlike the pain and fear that washed over her when she touched Carl the first time, she felt nothing but a vague sense of unease from Jack, like being lost in the dark, alone.

"You are safe," she said, leaning close to his ear. "Sleep and heal." She placed her hand on Jack's chest and imagined a peaceful place for him—the bank of the creek near the waterfall, with fish jumping to snap at mosquitos and toads eying each other warily. His breathing steadied and slowed.

Pinny stood up and strode to a shelf filled with cans of vegetables and fruits she and her grandmother had put up that summer. Beside the shelf was a counter, a sink, and an ancient oven black with soot.

"What are you doing?"

"Are you hungry? I can make something to eat."

"You didn't tell me your name."

Hesitating a moment, she considered what to share. Grandmother Blue had always cautioned her about Outsiders, so perhaps she should go by an alias. On the other hand, Grandmother Blue had also warned her not to lie—and indeed, the few times Pinny had ever tried to, her nose watered and she sneezed until it was swollen and distended.

The truth, then, just to be safe.

"My name? Pin Oak. You know, after the tree? But no one calls me that. You can call me Pinny."

"You're named after a tree? Interesting. I've never seen a pin oak."

"Of course you have," Pinny said, laughing. "The forest is full of them. This cabin is in a hollow surrounded by them."

Carl snorted. "I'll have to pay better attention."

"Turkey tracks."

"I beg your pardon?"

"Turkey tracks. Turkey feet. The pin oak leaves look like the tracks a turkey makes in the mud."

"I've never seen a turkey foot. Now I have to pay attention to two things."

She could tell he was joking because he smiled, but it was confusing, this kind of conversation with an Outsider. Confusing, but pleasant. She tried a joke of her own.

"Do all—people—from Outside have such interesting gaps in their knowledge?"

"Outside?"

"Marshall? Or Asheville? I've never been to either."

"Oh, we aren't from around here. Jack and I are stationed at Fort Bragg. We're on weekend maneuvers. Or we're supposed to be. Survival training in the mountains, now that things in Korea are heating up."

"You are Army men?"

"I know, right? It's not like I didn't know about Army life. Two brothers served in the war. I was too young to enlist then."

"And Jack? Was he in the war?" She looked down at the unconscious man and tried to imagine him on a battlefield. His features were even and smooth, his dark hair and eyelashes a sharp contrast to his pallor. He was, she thought, one of the most beautiful people she had ever seen.

Carl moved his foot and winced. "Naw. Funny thing is, we went to the same high school in Norfolk, but we didn't really know each other. I was class of '50 and he graduated a year later."

"And now you are both Army men."

"And now we are Army men. Lowly soldiers training to be medics. I can't believe it either."

Almost on cue, Jack moaned softly and Pinny came back and sat on the floor beside him. She let her fingertips brush across Jack's forehead and the moaning stopped. Carl lifted his right hand and pointed.

"How do you do that?"

Pinny turned and studied him. Unlike Jack, whose features were pleasant and fair, Carl's face was a whirl of scrunches and freckles, his reddish, bristly hair reminding Pinny of her grandmother's old sow. He seemed to have too many teeth for his mouth, and when he talked his eyes darted about as if he were nervous.

"It's nothing special," she said, stifling a sudden sneeze. Any other revelations would have to wait.

As the birds had warned, the snow didn't let up all day. Warm and dry in her Grandmother Blue's cabin, Pinny passed the time cooking and talking with Carl. He was different from what she had thought Outsiders were like—inquisitive about her and an eager listener. To her surprise she found herself describing her world to him in detail —where she found her medicinal herbs and what they were used for, the names of birds who stayed through the winter and which ones returned only when the redbud bushes unfurled their leaves in the spring, how she bartered with the other Mountain Folk for lambs' wool and cotton bolls to turn into her clothes. Carl made her laugh —teasing her and taking tentative steps from time to time to test his ankle.

"I really think it's getting better already," he marveled.

The sun had started to set when Jack woke up.

Pinny was busy stirring a pot of stew when she felt his consciousness in the room. With a start, she turned and saw his eyelashes flutter. Dropping the spoon into the pot, she rushed to the fireplace and knelt at Jack's side.

Carl stumbled over. "He's awake!"

"My head hurts," Jack whispered. Pinny drew her fingers across his forehead and the frown on his face disappeared.

"You took a bad fall," she said.

"Where am I?"

"Hey, buddy," Carl said before Pinny could reply. "You gave us a scare. As soon as the storm breaks, I'll get you out of here. Somebody's probably looking for us right now."

"You," Jack said, lifting his hand and touching his fingertips to Pinny's cheek, "were there. At the river with the fish and the frogs. I saw you."

"Can you sit up?" Pinny put her hand on his shoulder and he

struggled to rise. Unlike Carl's mind—curious and funny and bright —Jack's mind flickered with dark notes of worry and suspicion.

She and Carl helped him into a chair. He shivered visibly and Pinny tucked a quilt around his shoulders. Without being asked, Carl braved the weather long enough to collect more firewood from a pile by the front door.

As she prepared some broth, Pinny listened as the two men talked softly. They quickly agreed that between the storm and their own injuries, hiking out was impossible. A rescue, then, which would surely come when they failed to check in. Once that was settled, they turned their attention to asking Pinny about her life in the mountains. She could feel how exotic she sounded to them, though to her they were even more so. As the evening fell, Pinny began to get a picture of the world outside the mountains. Here she knew almost everyone. Mountain Folk were few and secretive with Outsiders, though if she concentrated, Pinny could sense where they were and what they were doing through the warm threads that tied them all together. Carl and Jack seemed to have none of those threads to anyone. Their stories were about life before the Army— the boredom of sitting through high school chemistry class, the joy of swimming in the sound, the difficulty of catching decent sized bluefish from the wharf, the football games they'd seen or played in. It was confusing and fascinating in equal measure, a glimpse of a world more chaotic and interesting than her own.

"Not to me," Carl said. "I think this place is far more wonderful. Quaint, you know. Peaceful. Tell Jack about the turkey foot trees. I'll bet he's never heard of those, either."

"Yes, tell me," Jack said softly, and Pinny felt an unwelcome flush on her neck when Jack's dark eyes met her own. "I want to know all about you."

She told them about the landslide that had killed her parents but spared her when she was too young to remember, how her Grandmother Blue found her right where she knew she would be in the fork of a tree, covered with sticky red mud, afterwards.

How she discovered her gift of healing when she freed a rabbit from an illegal sawtooth trap, its broken leg almost severed, held it until she could feel the shard ends of the bone reconnect, then set it down and watched it hop away into the underbrush.

How her Grandmother Blue taught her the language of animals so that as a child she was never lonely in the woods.

How some of the Mountain Folk had the gift of future sight, and some could summon crops from poor soil by appealing to the seeds to grow, and how even after they died, the ghosts of insects often whispered good advice into the ears of sleeping Mountain Children.

Jack laughed at that. "And what good advice have any crickets told you lately?"

Pinny's face heated up and she looked away, unsure if she was being teased.

By the end of the second day, Jack stopped dozing off so often and Carl was able to put down his improvised walking stick.

"It's amazing," he said, smiling at Pinny. "You're the best doctor I've ever known."

"My grandmother is the real healer," Pinny said. "I'm still learning."

"Then you should go to medical school or something. You know, work in a hospital. Or put up your own shingle."

"What?"

"Open your own practice. It's 1952, for Pete's sake."

"You mean leave the mountains?"

"Yeah, I guess that's a dumb idea," Carl said. He stepped gingerly to the window, brushed the frosted glass with his hand, and peered out at the snow.

By the third day the snow was so deep that it took all three of them to push the front door open. Carl shoveled a path from the door to the stack of firewood and Jack stood to the side and yelled unhelpful instructions, Pinny holding his elbow to keep him steady. Through his thick jacket she could feel his arm, almost fever warm, and sense how unfocused his thoughts still were. He flitted between worry about the snow and bafflement that he and Carl were here, un-rescued by the Army. His head hurt, even with willow bark infusions, and when Carl attempted to distract him with card games and tricks, he tired quickly. Both he and Carl slept curled awkwardly in rocking chairs pulled up close to the fireplace while she slept fitfully in the small room that did double duty as a pantry.

If only her Grandmother Blue would come home! Pinny reached out and found her Grandmother singing an old Folk tune to soothe the new, fretful baby and his anxious mother resting after a difficult delivery. She was miles away past Salton Gap and wouldn't be returning anytime soon. Pinny had a moment of panic. Jack was in no immediate danger but needed a better healer to make sure he would recover properly.

On the morning of the fourth day, she caught Carl watching her as she was setting a pot of soup on the stove. He lifted the pack of cards he'd been shuffling and gestured to the small round table where he sat, his cup of tea cooling. Jack snored gently in his chair. Pinny ran her fingers over his forehead and checked to make sure he was in the peaceful place by the river. Then with a sigh, she sat across from Carl, lacing her fingers together, waiting.

"What a time not to have future sight," she said. "If I knew when your Army friends were coming, I could stop worrying."

Carl's eyebrows rose. "Future sight. You mentioned that before. Like knowing what's gonna happen."

"Seeing it," Pinny corrected. "Being able to look when you need to."

"What's the difference?" Carl counted out several cards face down and flipped the last one face up. "Knowing, seeing. Either way, I don't want it. I would rather be surprised."

"But when you see the future, you can prepare," Pinny said. She picked up the card and examined it. "Which one is this? It looks special."

"It is. That's the Queen of Hearts." He paused dramatically and held up the card. "It means someone will fall in love." He put the card back on the table, smiled, and then flipped over the next card. "Well, look at that. Jack of hearts. You don't need future sight to see some people are made for each other. You know, they get thrown together by fate in an unexpected way. They have to fall in love. Don't you think so?"

He smiled again but Pinny felt his words were freighted with something serious. He tipped his head slightly at her as if he were waiting for an answer.

"What do you know about love?" The voice was Jack's. Pinny and Carl swiveled around to see him frowning at them. "Stop flirting, Carl. You'll steal my girl."

She knew Jack was joking—and Carl, too—with all this talk of flirting and stealing and love and fate. Blushing, she stood up abruptly and returned to the stove where the soup was starting to boil.

"She's not your girl," Carl said. Pinny could hear him shuffling the cards and tapping them on the table.

"Not yet," Jack said. He laughed and she let out a breath she didn't know she had been holding. Part of his game with Carl, that's all this was. She blushed again, this time in irritation.

"I'm no one's girl. I belong to myself." She kept her back turned, the soup pot apparently requiring all of her attention.

"I...I didn't mean anything by it," Jack stammered. "I just meant...well, I don't know what I meant."

She turned around and saw Jack and Carl exchanging glances.

"You'll have to forgive us," Carl said. "We're idiots."

His face was scrunched in an impossible expression. Pinny couldn't help herself; she laughed.

Jack gestured with his thumb in Carl's direction. "He's a natural idiot but I have a temporary head injury."

Pinny laughed again. How odd it was to joke and tease this way! The young men she knew who grew up on the mountain were so grave and silent in her presence.

"They're nervous," her grandmother had explained, "because

they know you must choose a husband soon. Why do you think they stop by the cabin so often? Did you think those flowers and herbs were gifts for me?"

Pinny had been taken aback by Grandmother Blue's words. "I thought they were here to ask a favor," she said. "To have you grant a wish or give a blessing."

"And so they were," her grandmother said with a smirk. "But I told them that was up to you."

By the time the snow stopped, the drifts were shoulder high. Pinny ventured outside, her woolen cloak pulled tight. The trees shimmered like a mirage against the backdrop of a bright blue sky. Birds flitted under the thickets, scratching the ground and complaining with hunger.

Overhead a crow warned that the creeks would overflow at the first warming spell.

Behind her Pinny could hear Jack taking cautious steps through the snow.

"It's beautiful," he said as he drew up beside her. "Almost as pretty as the boardwalk at Virginia Beach at night, all shiny and bright."

"I've never seen a boardwalk."

"Then I'll have to take you to the beach," Jack said, putting his hand on her arm, "when you come to see me."

He swayed slightly and for a moment Pinny thought he might be leaning forward to kiss her.

"The fire's getting low," Jack said, straightening. "I told Carl I'd help." He headed toward the woodpile.

Later Pinny would tell Grandmother Blue about how as she watched Jack walk he seemed to disappear, just as the snow magically vanished and the trees exploded with new leaves. Looking down she watched the grass spring beneath her shoes. The air was suddenly full of the songs of summer cicadas and gold-winged finches. Lovely scents of lavender and mountain laurel wafted in the warm breeze. In the distance the blue mountains rose like hazy sentries standing guard over this place where animals spoke and insects whispered sage advice.

She saw herself there in that summer scene with such clarity that she knew this was her first experience of future sight. She would walk out of her grandmother's cabin one morning and not only see but *be* in the vision. She looked around at the vision but didn't see Jack anywhere. That astonished—and saddened—her.

She told her grandmother that in the next moment she blinked and the world was again snowy, and there was Jack with his arms awkwardly hugging a load of split oak logs. Her grandmother crossed her arms and gave her a piercing look.

"And why are you telling me this?"

Taking a breath, Pinny spoke words she had rehearsed for months, ever since Jack and Carl left with the Army rescuers. "I want to ask a favor," she said, avoiding her grandmother's gaze. "I want to ask a wish. I want to go to the city."

"To find this man you told me of?"

There was no use lying to Grandmother Blue. Pinny nodded. "If I can. But also to see the city. To live there. To learn the medicine they know there. I've never even seen a boardwalk. I want to see what is beyond these mountains before—"

"Before you choose a husband. Is that what this is about?"

"Before I choose a life. And maybe, yes, a husband."

She heard her grandmother sigh. From the corner of her eye she saw her grandmother's blue-black hair shining in the sun.

"If I grant this wish," she said, "if you become real city Folk, you may not be able to return home."

Pinny was alarmed. "What do you mean?"

"You can't take your mountain gifts with you. The animals of the city will not speak to you. Your touch will have no healing there. And when you return—well, those gifts may not be yours again. Consider well whether you want me to grant this wish or not."

Her clothes were wrong. She could tell by the way the woman at the boarding house eyed her straw bonnet and sturdy brogans. Pinny pulled her sweater tighter around her thin cotton shift and put her shoulders back the way Grandmother Blue had told her the day she left the mountains on a bus to Fayetteville.

"Look adversity in the eye," her grandmother said, putting one bony finger under Pinny's chin. *"Don't flop over like some puppet that's lost its strings. The city will eat you up if you do."*

The landlady blinked. "You seem alright," she said. Nodding, she motioned to Pinny to bring her suitcase and follow her up a narrow flight of stairs. "Your room is the last one at the end of the hall," she said. "The bathroom's right there. No men visitors, curfew at 10. Keep quiet and clean and you'll get along with the rest of the girls."

The hall was poorly lit and the wooden floor creaked as she opened the door and walked into what was now her room. It was bare but not unpleasant, three narrow beds pushed against the walls. A small chest of drawers was the only other furniture in the room. Striped wallpaper pulled away in the corners and the oval rug on the floor was frayed. Pinny put her suitcase on the bed with the lumpiest-looking mattress, sat down beside it, and sighed. Already she questioned her wish. Instead of the pleasant twitter of birds in the trees, she heard the faint wail of a siren and the clatter of someone banging a pot or a pipe in the kitchen. Instead of lavender and wild rosemary, the odor of cabbage wafted in the halls. She opened her suitcase and removed the small drawstring pouch with all the money her grandmother had given her before she left. Now instead of walking through the meadows looking for herbs and wild mushrooms she needed to head out into the streets looking for a diner for an inexpensive meal. When her money was gone she'd need to find a way to get more. That was a new worry, almost overwhelming her.

It wasn't too late to walk back to the bus station and buy a ticket home.

"I'll have to take you to the beach when you come see me."

Idle chatter or a real promise from Jack? She wasn't going home until she found out.

First things first, then. Pinny closed the drawstring bag and returned it to the suitcase. The landlady might have a recommendation for a place to eat, or she could explore the nearby streets on her own and find out exactly what she'd gotten herself into.

As she was pulling the door to the room shut behind her, however, she heard the unmistakeable clatter of people walking up the wooden stairs at the end of the hall. Two young women about her age appeared, one dressed in a purple pencil skirt that fell just below her knee and the other in a white nurse's uniform. They wore their hair cut short with a part and a wave; Pinny reached up and touched her own shoulder-length hair pulled back with a ribbon, the way children wear it, she thought, embarrassed.

When the women reached the top of the stairs they saw Pinny.

"You must be the new renter," the woman in the nurse's uniform said. "I'm Cat, and this is Foxy."

"Cat and Foxy?"

"Well, Catherine and Frances, but no one calls us that. Who are you?"

"Pin Oak…uh, Pinny."

"Cute," Cat said as she brushed past Pinny and opened the door. "I see you made yourself at home already."

"I wasn't sure where—"

"You can have the bottom drawer," Foxy said. She sat heavily on the bed nearest to Pinny's and pulled off her high heels, letting them drop to the floor. "Where're you from? Mrs. Simpson wasn't sure. I'm from the beautiful city of Durham. That's a joke, by the way. It's just a college town wanting to be a big city. Full of stuck-up snobs and hicks hating each other, just like everywhere else. So where did you say you are from? You don't look like you're from around here."

"Give her a break!" Cat was also taking off her shoes—sensible flat ones, white like her uniform—and she dropped them on the floor. "Here, help me with this." She stood up and turned her back to Pinny. "You can tell a man designed this dress. Who else would think putting buttons up the back was a good idea?"

In a few minutes both Cat and Foxy had changed into floral-patterned dresses with full skirts puffed out with crinolines.

"What are you waiting for?" Foxy said. "Get on your party duds. We're going out!"

"I don't...I mean, this dress..."

"Don't tell me you don't have a decent dress." Foxy slipped her high heels back on and picked up a dainty-looking purse.

"Here," Cat said, grabbing Pinny's hand and pulling her to her feet. "Don't worry about your clothes. We're going dancing."

"I can't!" Pinny sounded panicked even to herself. Cat let go of her hand. Pinny saw her dart a glance at Foxy.

"Um, I was joshing you about the dress," Foxy stammered. "You look fine."

'It's not that. I...don't know how."

Foxy gave a loud snort. "Is that all? How're you gonna learn if you don't try it? Suit yourself, then. Stay here and do nothing all night."

She headed to the door, Cat close behind. Pinny closed her eyes and reached out for the thread that connected her to home. Casting about in her thoughts, she tried to conjure up an image of her grandmother, her cabin, the crows scolding from the treetops. To her dismay, the picture was blurry, as if she were looking through a clouded lens.

"Wait!" she shouted, not sure who she was calling to—her grandmother or the two young women walking out the door. Cat and Foxy stopped and looked back at her.

"I'm coming!"

They took her to a place called Hoot-n-Holler near the Army barracks at Fort Bragg, a building not much larger than Grand-mother Blue's cabin, smoke-filled and crowded with uniformed enlisted men and women dressed like Cat and Foxy. Foxy led the way to the bar, pushing through the couples trying to dance near the jukebox. She spoke to the bartender but the music was so loud that Pinny couldn't hear the conversation. In a moment the bartender set three sweaty glasses of beer on the counter.

Cat leaned close to Pinny's ear. "I don't know why Foxy likes this honky-tonk joint. All they have is warm beer and bad music."

Pinny took a sip and made a face. The honey brew Grandmother Blue made back home was sweet and almost silky, not like the astringent stuff in this glass.

"What'd I tell you?" Cat said. "I'll bet you're a bourbon girl."

"I wouldn't know," Pinny said. "I've never tried it. Some of the Folk back home are partial to 'shine but I don't care for it myself."

"Moonshine? Girl, where are you from? The backwoods?"

"Something like that."

Cat laughed, her teeth small and pearl-like. She lifted her glass and knocked the rim against Pinny's. "Drink up," she said. "We've got lots to do tonight."

"Lots to do" turned out to be catching rides with gypsy cabs from one bar to another, each one requiring a drink or two. Both Cat and Foxy found willing dance partners, mostly men in uniform who bought them drinks and offered them cigarettes. As the night went on Pinny felt hot and flushed, then woozy and sleepy and bored watching everyone else having a good time. The cigarette she tried turned her stomach—which was, she realized too late, very empty. She leaned back in the booth near the front door and focused on keeping the room from swirling.

"Pinny?" Carl's face swam into view. "Is that you?"

There he was, crooked teeth and freckles and eyebrows raised in amusement or astonishment. Pinny had never been so happy to see anyone before.

"What are you doing here!" she said. She sat up and patted the seat beside her. "Do you want to sit down?"

"Are you okay? You seem…not okay."

"I'm okay now!" She knew she sounded off but she was having

trouble controlling the volume of her voice. Too many beers and too much loud music, of course. She tried not to giggle. "How are you doing? I've been so worried about…you guys. So answer me—what are you doing here?"

"I'm just stopping by for a quick drink after my shift," Carl said. "What are *you* doing here?"

Pinny eyed the glass on her table. Not more than a swallow of beer remained and she debated whether to finish it or not. She looked up and saw Carl watching her. "Just got here today," she said, reaching for the glass. "I'm real City Folk now."

She described the boarding house and pointed out Cat and Foxy on the dance floor. "Tomorrow I'm going to get a job and then I'm going to buy a party dress and some fancy shoes and I'm going to see the sights. Why are you laughing? I can do it!"

"I know you can," Carl said. "What about your plans? You know, to be a healer in the mountains like your grandmother."

She ignored his question and held out her glass to him. "Can you go get me another drink? It's hot in here."

"I've got a better idea. Why don't you let me drive you home and you can tell me all about what you want to see in the city. I'm off duty for the next two days. I'll show you around."

Pinny took a breath and asked the question she'd been wanting to ask. "What about Jack? I mean, how is he?"

"Oh, he's fine. Fully recovered. He and Louise tied the knot right before he shipped out. I haven't heard from him since he got to Seoul."

"Louise?"

"Lou. I'm sure he mentioned her to you. High school sweethearts and all that. Some guys have all the luck."

Suddenly Pinny's eyes were strangely hot and dry. She tried to swallow and felt her tongue swell up in her mouth.

"Can you take me home now?" she whispered. Carl slid out of the booth and took her elbow. Across the dance floor Cat caught her eye and gave her an exaggerated wink and thumbs up.

Pinny was asleep as soon as her head touched the pillow. Her rest, however, was fitful, and she was dimly aware of flipping from side to side on the lumpy mattress.

Not quite what you expected, she heard her grandmother say. How's that wish working out for you?

There was her grandmother, blue-black hair falling loose around her shoulders. Her unlined face peered intently at Pinny, who in this dream—for surely that's what it was—stood barefoot on the grass in front of the mountain cabin. The sound of birds echoed around her. A cool breeze brushed her locks back from her fevered cheeks.

She remembered how it felt to really stand there, not in a dream but with the magic of the mountains coursing through her, her gift of healing in her touch just starting to emerge. She wondered if she could still feel her grandmother in her mind like a leash of blood uniting them.

It's what you asked for, her grandmother said. You wanted to be ordinary, an Outsider, a real City Woman.. And now you are.

A weight settled in Pinny's chest. She'd given up so much and gained so little for her loss. What she'd seen of town life was dreary and loud, and now she'd lost any hope of having Jack in her life. A sob forced its way up her throat.

A dark thought slithered into her thoughts. Perhaps she could ask her grandmother for a second wish! Her grandmother could part Jack from his new wife and make him fall in love with Pinny. They could have a life together after all!

As suddenly as the thought slid into her mind, she forced it back down. Magic love, enchanted love, compelled love, could never take the place of love gotten honestly.

In her dream, she stooped down and held out her palm. A cricket made a tentative hop onto her hand.

What should I do now? she asked it, but the cricket waggled its antennae at her and was silent.

When Pinny woke up the next morning, Cat and Foxy were

gone, presumably to work. Her tongue still felt too big for her mouth and her head throbbed. Worse, her stomach was queasy in a way she'd never felt before.

But she knew what she would do. Pressing her hands to the side of her head, she made her way to the bathroom at the end of the hall and took a long shower. By the time Carl came for her to show her around town, she was dressed and packed.

"I'm going home," she said. "This was all a silly fantasy."

"You just got here!" Carl's face showed genuine distress. "You haven't even given the city a chance!"

"You said you'd show me the sights first," Pinny said. "And maybe the boardwalk at the beach? Jack promised…I mean, Jack *said* he'd show me when I came. But now—"

She let her words drift off. Carl pressed his lips together and sighed.

"You really have a thing for Jack, don't you? I thought you might."

"No, I don't!" Pinny sneezed loudly and felt her nose wobble. She rubbed it with the back of her hand. "Besides, Jack's not here and you are. What do you say? Take me to the bus station so I can buy my ticket, then show me around?"

"You know we aren't near the beach, don't you? It would take hours to get there and back."

"I have nothing else on my calendar," Pinny said, "and I believe you are off duty. Of course, if you don't want to—"

Carl shook his head and laughed. "I'm yours," he said. "Let's get going."

"One moment," Pinny said, placing her suitcase on the floor and unlatching it. She picked up the drawstring bag and opened it.

"What's wrong," Carl asked. Pinny upended the bag and shook it. Nothing came out.

"It's empty," she said. "All my money was in there."

Cat or Foxy, while Pinny snored her way through a hangover. She pressed the heel of her hand to her forehead.

"So much for the trip to the beach," she said, a note of sadness in her voice. "I hate to ask this, but can you drive me home instead? I don't have any money for the bus."

"I told you, I don't report back for duty for two days. Let's go see the boardwalk, and then I'll take you home.

It was just as Grandmother Blue had warned. The animals weren't unfriendly, but they no longer spoke to her. A baby squirrel rescued after a fall from a tall pine, its forepaw bent in an unnatural angle, had to be soothed with a decoction of willow bark and wild parsley. She could feel the ends of the broken bones with her touch but that was all. No healing energy flowed between them, and she was forced to wrap the break and wait.

When she searched for the thread that tied her to her grandmother and the other Folk, she floundered. Nothing was there. The only spark she felt was when she pictured Carl walking her along the boardwalk at Myrtle Beach, the Ferris wheel and carousel gaudy with electric lights, food vendors wending their way through the crowds selling sodas and boiled peanuts and caramel apples and corndogs and ice pops and watermelon slices.

But all that paled to the sight of the ocean itself, slate gray and stretching to infinity, the rhythmic Siren voice of the crashing surf pulling her forward. The water was warm, sucking the sand from under her feet and almost knocking her off balance, causing her to squeal with alarm and delight. And Carl's hand on her back, keeping her from falling—she thought of that in the months after she returned to the mountains.

Best of all had been the long, long ride to the coast and back, and the even longer trip up into the mountains. They'd talked the entire way, Carl telling her about his medic training, and how he was considering applying for medical school in Wake Forest after his deployment to Korea was over. He would be close enough to visit— if she wanted him to. Pinny told him stories about people she knew, people for whom magic was as natural as breathing, and as necessary.

"Without our gifts," she said sadly, "we really aren't anything."

"I don't think you're nothing," Carl said. "And you seem magical to me."

Slowly she made peace with the change. She was useful even without her healing touch, a good nurse to the people who sought out her Grandmother's powers, and an even better potion maker. When she was lonely, she reread the letters Carl sent—not many, to be sure, but they made her feel as if he were standing beside her.

And then one day he was.

They were married in the orchard when the apple trees were in bloom. Grandmother Blue read some words from a book, and Pinny and Carl said some words they had written. Jack made a toast with a bottle of champagne. Their Folk neighbors made another one with a jug of moonshine.

After food and drink and a fiddler and some dancing until the sun went down, the guests left at last.

"Before you head off to your honeymoon," Grandmother Blue said, "I need to tell you both something."

They followed her into her cabin. Carl and Pinny sat down as Grandmother Blue settled in her rocker. How long ago it seemed since Pinny and Carl and Jack had hunkered down in a snowstorm, playing cards and talking nonsense about fate and love and wanting to know the future. What would she have done if she had known the end of the story all that time ago? What had Carl said? That he preferred the surprise? To her surprise now, Pinny realized she agreed.

"I want you to know," Grandmother Blue was saying, "that if I could undo the wish that took away your magic, I would, but no one can take away a wish granted in good faith. I know it pains you, Pinny, to be without your gifts."

"It's okay, Grandmother. I—"

"I'm not finished," Grandmother said. "I can't undo Pinny's wish, but I can offer *you* one, Carl." She looked at Carl so intensely that he squirmed. "I know you want to be a healer. Do you wish me to give you that gift? You could become one of the Mountain Folk. Your touch would ease the suffering of those in your care."

Pinny felt her heartbeat pounding in her throat. She watched Carl's face cloud up.

"Thank you," he said to Grandmother Blue. "But I'm going to be a healer after I finish medical school. Asking for a wish seems like cheating somehow." He leaned toward Pinny and took her hand. "And if Pinny isn't real Mountain Folk anymore, I don't want to be one, either. We'll stay real Outsiders, together."

Pinny knew her grandmother well enough to see that she was flustered.

"So be it," she said, nodding. "You may not have the magic of the mountains, but I can see that the two of you have created your own. I don't need any special sight to see that—or to see the blood link between you."

She shifted in her chair and held up her hands in benediction. "And maybe that's the best kind of magic after all. "

AUTHOR'S NOTE

This story was based on Carlo Collodi's The Adventures of Pinocchio, published in 1883. Later Disney would create a version that made Pinocchio less mischievous and more misled, and my version tries to combine elements from both. For example, what everyone knows about Pinocchio is that he is a wooden puppet who wants to become a real boy—and that he's given advice by a cricket (who in the original he kills!—and is haunted by the ghost of!), gets help from the Blue Fairy, is tricked by a rascally Cat and Fox, has misadventures with alcohol and tobacco, and watches his nose grow when he tells lies. (For the record, I think Stanley Kubrick's/Steven Spielberg's "AI" is a terrific sci-fi retelling—complete with allusions to the original Pinocchio story). In my tale Pinocchio is a naive young woman longing to be a part of the "real" world beyond her mountain home. Enjoy!

ABOUT THE AUTHOR

Kay McSpadden is a journalist and teacher whose published books include *Notes from a Classroom* and *A Child's Book of Virtues*. Her short stories have been published in *Kestrel*, *Orphans in the Black*,

We Are Not This, Once Upon a Ghost, Once Upon a Star, Once Upon a Quest, and *Heart's Kiss.*

WISH UPON A STRAW

DEVON MONK

Once there was a kingdom of great mountains, sprawling valleys, and rolling fields full of grain. It was a lovely place to live.

If it weren't for all the dragons.

It wasn't that the dragons were *bad*. They were just clever, secretive, and gold-hungry.

Unfortunately, everyone in the kingdom got by with trading and barter, so there was a woeful lack of gold to be found.

"All I see from every window is field upon field upon field of straw," King Kage thundered. He was new to his kingship, and determined to protect his land. "I can't be a king of straw."

"Perhaps if the straw were packaged in a pleasing way?" the king's attendant, Argentum, asked in his sterling voice.

The king narrowed his eyes and sniffed at the slender silver-haired man, trying to catch a scent of smoke. All he smelled was moonlight and spring dew.

"Are you sure you're not a dragon?" King Kage asked.

Dragons, it had turned out, had another favorite pastime besides hoarding gold—taking on the appearance of humans.

They were almost as good as it as the fairy folk.

Argentum had been a fixture at the castle when King Kage had replaced the last monarch, who had been eaten by a dragon.

King Kage had been that dragon.

The monarch had been delicious.

"*I* am not a dragon," Argentum replied, his long fingers spreading out in a graceful gesture.

King Kage *hrumphed.* "Well, I don't need straw. I need gold. Beautiful, buttery gold. Piles and mountains and oceans filled with so much gold, there is no room left for a spare breath."

"What would you do with that gold, Your Majesty?"

"Rule my kingdom in peace."

"Gold usually turns hearts to war," Argentum noted.

"Not dragon hearts. My rule shall be peaceful. With enough gold, there will be no need for war, nor for want. If I have gold, all my kingdom shall have it too."

"Hmm," Argentum said.

"You doubt?"

"I am curious." Argentum tipped his head and his thin, expressive mouth turned up into what appeared to be a smile. "You are not what I expected."

There was a glint in his eye and for the briefest moment, King Kage thought he saw a bit of a silver sparkle around the man. But just as quickly, it was gone, leaving nothing but the soft scent of moonlight and dew behind.

"Have we mined for it?" King Kage asked.

"Our mountains have no gold, Your Majesty."

"Have we panned for it?"

"Our rivers have no gold, Your Majesty."

"Have we fought for it?"

"There is peace on our borders, Your Majesty. No one wants to fight a kingdom infested with dragons."

That was true. There were dragons everywhere in the kingdom.

Kage strode to the window and locked his arms against the sill. He tipped his face to the sky and inhaled the sweet winds of autumn. It was a beautiful place, his kingdom. He intended to keep it that way.

"Go out into my lands," Kage ordered, "and find gold."

Argentum cleared his throat. "There is rumor of a farmer's daughter who spins straw."

"Again with straw?" Kage rumbled.

"It is said she spins straw into gold."

The king smiled and it was wickedly gleeful. "Well, then. Bring me the farmer's daughter," he commanded, "and throw her in the cellar."

The farmer's daughter had just finished cleaning the blood off the front step when the king's attendant arrived. Things had gotten a little out of hand. The farmer had put her life in danger by going around telling people she could spin gold.

Didn't he know the kingdom was full of dragons, and they were always listening?

Dragons wanted gold and weren't above eating people for it. The farmer should have remembered those two facts before blabbing about what she could or couldn't do with straw.

"The king requests your presence," the attendant informed her from atop a very fine horse.

"The king? The new king?" She clutched the door latch with both hands behind her back, hoping the attendant wouldn't want to enter the cottage.

"The old king is no more."

"Eaten by a dragon?" she asked.

"Eaten by a dragon," he agreed. "King Kage has requested I bring you...what is your name?"

The farmer's daughter hesitated. Names were powerful. Most fairy names were strong enough to bind spells and lock curses. Dragon names could do a bit of magic too. If she gave him her full name, would it be used against her?

"You aren't a fairy folk are you?" she asked.

The silver-haired man's eyebrows arched and his long fingers folded and refolded the reins in his hand. "Do I look like a fairy folk?"

She wasn't sure, since she'd never met one. All she knew was fairy folk, like dragons, could disguise themselves as human.

She sniffed, searching for dragon smoke, or the lemon-clover scent of fairy, but all she smelled was falling leaves and a hint of cool rain in the late summer air.

"Your name?" he repeated.

"Ruth," she said. "And yours?"

"Argentum."

"Why does the king want to see me, Argentum?"

"I can not say."

"Can I refuse his invitation?"

"Yes, but the king insisted I be very determined to bring you to him. Therefore, I will be *very* determined."

For a beat, the man was no longer mild-mannered. He suddenly appeared of the sort who might have seen a battlefield or two.

Ruth was optimistic by nature. Perhaps the king was taking time to get to know each of his subjects. She would enjoy that. She had been lonely lately.

"Very well, Argentum." She squared her shoulders. "Let us see the king."

It wasn't until she had stepped inside the great castle that she realized she had made a mistake.

The blow to the back of her head was hard enough to drop a dragon. The last thing she thought before she passed out, was that she had definitely smelled smoke.

She woke in a cellar. The floor was stone, the walls were stone, the ceiling was stone.

The door was also stone, except for a window at head height so small, only her hand could fit through it.

A spinning wheel sat near one wall, a pile of straw next to it.

She groaned. The king must have heard the farmer bragging.

"I hope you are comfortable," a low voice said through the door.

"I am not," Ruth replied. "Let me go. The king has requested to see me."

The door didn't open, the latch didn't twitch, but there were eyes at the little window now. Eyes that glittered green.

"I am the king," the voice said. "If you want to leave this cellar, you will spin gold from straw. I will return in the morning to collect the gold, or your life."

"Wait." Ruth rushed to the door just as a little wooden panel slid shut over the window.

"I can't spin gold! I have never been able to spin gold. I wish it were possible. I wish the straw could be spun into gold."

She also wished the king had heard her. But the floor was stone, the walls were stone and the ceiling was stone.

No one could hear her.

She was all alone.

Except for the pile of straw.

Except for the spinning wheel.

Except for the little crooked man standing next to her. "Hey, Babes."

"Ah!" she shrieked.

"Whoa, whoa." He held up long-fingered hands. "You wished, and I came. No need to yell about it."

Ruth took several deep breaths. One shouldn't commit more than one murder a day on principle.

"You smell like lemons," she said.

"I do."

"And clover."

"That too."

"You're a fairy."

His eyes, brown as pine cones went wide. "The tunic and pointy shoes didn't tip you off?"

"I don't judge a person by their clothing."

"The huge mouth?" He pointed to his mouth, which was a bit wide, she supposed.

"Mouths come in a lot of sizes."

"The glowing sparkles floating around me? That didn't make you think I might be magic?"

"Things," she said, annoyed, "are rarely what they appear to be."

"Fair."

He laced his large hands behind his back and rocked up on the balls of his feet. "So…you appear to be a prisoner."

"I think I am."

He pushed the spinning wheel so it slowly turned and gave the pile of straw a little kick. Dust puffed into the air, mixing with his golden magic and darkening his yellow hair.

"King Kage wants you to spin gold out of straw?"

Ruth worried at the ring on her finger. "Yes, but I can't spin straw into gold."

"I know," the little creature said. "That's why I'm here."

"To mock me?"

"To grant your wish."

"My wish?"

"You wished for the straw to be spun into gold. Here I am." He extended his arms and bowed.

"You can do that?" She wanted to believe the little creature, but she had been tricked before.

After all, there were dragons *everywhere*. And, apparently, fairy folk.

"Yes. For a price."

"But I don't have anything."

"You have that ring on your finger."

Ruth clutched it to her chest. It wasn't much as far as treasures went, but it matched the silver locket she wore. It was also all she had.

"Or maybe the king will just let you go once he finds out you can't spin gold from straw."

"Do you think he would?" Ruth asked hopefully.

"No," the little man said. "He's a dragon."

"Is that so?"

Interesting.

She glanced at the ring, at the door, and made up her mind. "I'll give you the ring."

The little creature snatched it out of her hand faster than a wink.

"Excellent! Leave it to me."

He bent and gathered straw, his foot already tapping the pedal. In no more than a second, straw was twisting and slipping through his fingers, the wheel spinning. A golden light filled the room.

Ruth didn't see any gold, though, just golden light.

"Will it take long?"

"All night," he said cheerfully. "Straw to gold is a tricky wish to fulfill. But a good wish. An impossible wish. Perfect for my needs."

"Needs?"

He waved a hand. "It's a fairy thing. Nothing to worry about."

Ruth sat in the corner and watched the little creature spin. "I don't know much about fairies. Perhaps you could tell me a tale to pass the time."

The little man tipped his head, his gaze assessing. "A tale?"

"A story." She drew her knees up and settled her skirts. Then she wrapped her arms around her legs and propped her chin on her knees. "Something about the fairy world. Is there much gold there?"

"Yes. But it isn't as valuable as magic."

"Is there a king?"

"Oh, yes." The little man's voice changed. Ruth knew anger when she heard it.

Interesting.

"Is he a terrible king?"

"The king in the land of fairy is a foul, cruel creature who delights in causing misery to all he rules."

"He sounds awful," Ruth murmured.

"He is. His rotted cruelty spread like a blight through those around him. Advisors became sycophants, their minds corroded by his lies and treachery. Every breath he exhales is a lie, every action, a horror. His rot even spread to the magic of the land, tarnishing and weakening it."

"Was there no one to stand up to him?" she asked.

The little man smiled ruefully. "Only one foolish, foolish knight. He was known as the golden knight."

The little man winked at her. She once again noted his hair was golden, and the magic surrounding him was too.

Interesting.

"Of course that wasn't his real name," he went on. "But he wore armor of the purest gold magic. He thought his magic would save him. Thought it would save those he loved. Thought it would save the land."

The flyer flew, the wheel spun, and despite wanting to know the end of the story, Ruth was becoming sleepy.

"What happened? To the golden knight?" she asked quietly.

"His family was imprisoned. Thrown into the deepest, darkest dungeon. Only one of his brothers escaped—a knight of pure silver.

"The golden knight was banished to the world of man. He was cursed to grant three great wishes before he could return."

"Did he do it?" Ruth asked around a yawn.

"What?"

"Did he grant three great wishes and return?"

"No," he said softly. "Not yet."

It was a strange answer. An *interesting* answer. But Ruth's eyes were closing.

The fairy began to hum and the tune blended with the whir and click of the wheel, becoming something more, a paintbrush of dreams, of slumber, of magic.

Ruth fell fast asleep and dreamed of evil kings and golden knights and magic made of straw.

When she woke she saw stone ceiling, stone walls, stone floor.

The little creature was gone, the spinning wheel still as if it had never turned. She wondered if it had all been a dream.

But next to the spinning wheel were three bright coins, stacked like little pats of butter.

"Gold!" she crowed, rushing over to it. "Did you spin it, you clever fairy, or did you have it on you the whole time?"

The gold smelled wonderfully of beeswax and honey and butter. She bit one just to be sure it wasn't a sweet.

The tang of soft metal filled her mouth.

It was gold. Solid gold. She loved it. She wanted to keep it.

At the sound of approaching footsteps, she quickly hid all three coins in her pocket before turning to face the door.

"Farmer's daughter?" said the deep voice on the other side of the door. "I've given you one full night. Have you spun straw into gold?"

Ruth's hand tightened around the coins in her pocket. The only weapon she had was the spinning wheel. But the flimsy wooden contraption wouldn't harm a dragon.

"Come in and see for yourself," she challenged.

With any luck, the door would open, and she could run through it before the king had a chance to catch her.

The king chuckled and the sound of it was alluring. "Come to the door," he coaxed, "and show me the gold."

Ruth followed his voice. She stopped in front of the door and held up two coins.

The King's eyes went wide. She shivered at the intensity of his gaze. "All of it," he rumbled.

Ruth hadn't gotten a look at the king other than his beautiful green eyes, but if his looks matched his voice, he was very handsome indeed.

She reluctantly pulled the last coin from her pocket and added it to the others.

"Good," the king said. "I am impressed. Now please stand back against the wall."

Ruth did so, her heart hammering. This would be her chance to escape.

The door swung open.

Ruth rushed. But before she'd made it halfway across the room, the king's men were there.

A sheaf of straw hit her in the chest. Several more pummeled her, hard enough to send her stumbling.

By the time she had regained her feet, the door slammed shut. The room was half-filled with sheaves of straw, the air thick with dust.

"Spin this straw into gold," the King said through the door, "and you will be rewarded."

The sound of retreating footsteps was replaced by the beating of Ruth's heart. No matter how handsome the king might be, she knew he was deadly serious about the gold.

She didn't blame him. He was a dragon, after all. And gold was deliciously pleasing.

She'd need another chance at the door. Tomorrow, when the king came, she would be ready.

But she'd also need a back-up plan.

She stacked the sheaves to make room in the tiny space, then planted her hands on her hips, and cleared her throat. "I wish someone would spin this straw into gold."

Silence.

She cleared her throat again. "I said, 'I wish some fairy creature would appear and spin all this straw into gold.'" Then she added, "Please."

But the little creature did not appear.

Ruth paced. Ruth wrung her hands. Ruth wished. But still no fairy rescuer appeared.

She even sat at the spinning wheel and fed straw into it. All that got her was crushed straw and a clogged wheel.

"I really do wish the straw was all gold," she said.

"Hey, Babes," a voice said from near her elbow.

Ruth yelped, her heart hammering. "You!"

The fairy creature gave her a wide bow. "At your service. You wished?"

"Hours ago."

"Yes, well. Time is tricky in this land. Straw to gold, is that the order of the day?"

She nodded. "You'll want something for it?"

"Yes."

"Is this enough?" She pulled off the thin silver necklace and held it out for him.

He darted forward and plucked it from her hand. "Perfectly." He tucked it into a pocket then strolled over to the mountain of straw.

He scratched his chin. "That's quite a lot of straw."

"The king said all of it must be spun. Can you?"

"Well, you did just wish for me to. It's an impossible wish, so, yes. Of course I can. I must."

He picked up several sheaves of straw as if they weighed nothing, dropped them next to the wheel, and got busy feeding straw into the flyer.

Ruth liked having him back again, enjoyed his company. "The story."

"Hmm?" he asked.

"Of the gold knight. The only one to stand up to the wicked king of fairy land. Does the knight have a name?"

The little creature pressed his hand against the flyer, stopping its rotation. "Why would you ask?"

Something about him had changed. He still wore pointy shoes. He still had a wide mouth and pine cone-brown eyes. The golden cloud of magic still surrounded him.

But his stance made him a spring ready to launch into action—

—or a knight ready to fight—

–with no fear of the consequences.

"Everyone has a name," she said carefully.

"Yes," he agreed. "But fairy names have power."

"Which is why they guard them so closely," Ruth said.

"Yes." He turned back to spinning. "I don't suppose you'd like to tell me your name?"

"It's Ruth."

"Is it?" he asked.

Maybe if she shared a part of her secret with him, he would share more of the golden knight's story. Everyone knew fairies were tricky. But then, so were dragons, and there certainly were a lot of those about.

"It is a part of my name," she admitted.

"And the rest of it?"

"I'll tell you if you agree to be my friend."

His foot paused on the pedal. "Your friend?"

She thought he could be trusted.

He was spinning gold for her.

He was saving her life.

He was keeping her company in this stone cellar. It had been a long time since she'd had a real friend.

"Yes. My friend."

His smile was a delightful thing. "All right, Ruth. I'm your friend. Care to tell me the rest of your name?"

"Less," she said.

"Less of your name?" he asked.

"No, that is the rest of it: Less. RuthLess."

He hooted a laugh. Straw continued to pour through his fingers, twisting into thin, glittering thread as he chuckled. The bobbin grew thick, the golden light grew brighter.

"RuthLess is a strange name for a farmer's daughter," he finally said.

"Yes, I suppose it is."

"Well, RuthLess, the golden knight's name is the key to his curse."

"So you won't tell me?"

"I *can't* tell you. Fairy rules."

"Oh."

"But you could guess."

Ruth smiled. That would be a pleasant way to pass the time.

She guessed name after name: common names, odd names, names she made up. She guessed names from other languages, names from old tales, names from the makers of goods imported from larger, older kingdoms.

With every name, the little man shook his head, or said, "No." "Nope." "I'm afraid not."

By the time she had exhausted her imagination, there was a tidy pile of gold coins stacked beside the spinning wheel.

"That's that then." The fairy dusted his hands. "All the straw is now gold. Your wish is fulfilled."

"But the knight," Ruth said. "He has to grant three wishes to be allowed back into his land. Is that right?"

"Yes."

"There's more to his curse than just granting three impossible wishes, isn't there?"

The little creature held her gaze. "Yes."

"Then I think there will be one more wish he can fulfill."

"The cost will be great," he warned. "All third wishes are. Too great perhaps, even for a friend."

Ruth blinked, and the little man was gone.

"What if I wish to leave this place?" she asked the empty air. "What if I wish for the knight to save his family? What if I wish for the evil fairy king to be defeated?"

But the empty air had nothing to say in return.

Ruth stayed awake and made another list of names. She also wondered what she could wish for that would be worthy of the price he would ask.

When she finally slept, she dreamed of the king's alluring voice, and the king's amazing eyes, and the king's amazing, dragon-y scent.

The king returned the next morning. Just as before, he demanded she show him the gold. She did so, and in return, the door swung open.

The king's men moved swiftly and packed and stacked bales of straw into the room so tightly, the spinning wheel barely had space to turn.

The lock slid shut with a click.

"Farmer's daughter?" the king asked. It was hard to hear him through all the straw.

"Yes?"

"If you spin this straw into gold, it will be the last time I ask you to do so. I will set you free."

"You'll set me free?"

"Yes and I will…give you some of the gold in payment." That last part sounded like it was difficult for him to say.

But this was wonderful. Gold! She would have delicious gold all to herself, and she would be free!

She thrilled over it for a moment, then remembered her plan. She squared her shoulders and took a breath.

"No thank you," she said.

"No?" the king sputtered. "No *thank* you? You wish to stay here, locked away in this straw-stuffed cellar for life?"

She didn't wish that. She didn't wish that at all.

What she wished were two things: a mountain of gold all her own—because who wouldn't want a mountain of gold—and for a way to help the little creature who must be the golden knight.

"I choose to stay in this straw-filled room forever."

"Spinning gold?"

"Doing nothing."

"But…*gold*," the king said as if it were everything.

It was a lot, but gold wasn't everything. Ruth wanted more. She wanted to help her friend and defeat evil. She enjoyed defeating evil.

"If I spin this straw into gold, you will give me gold, set me free, and agree to make me queen."

After a shocked moment, he said, "Queen? You would rule the land with me?"

"Yes."

"You would rule the people with me?"

"Yes."

"You would hoard—I mean, *own* the gold with me?"

"Absolutely."

"Will you make more gold if you were queen?"

"No."

"Well. Well then. Well."

Ruth waited. If the king said no, she could wish her way out of this cellar. But if the king said yes, she would wish for something that would help the little creature.

Something to defeat evil.

"Done," the king growled. Delicious shivers zigged down Ruth's spine. "Spin this straw into gold, and I will let you free and make you queen."

"And give me gold."

"And give you gold."

"Done," she said.

The king was quiet for a few seconds. "You are a very strange sort of farmer's daughter, Ruth."

"Yes," she said proudly, "I suppose I am. Now leave. I have gold to spin."

She waited until she heard his footsteps grow faint. Then she waited a few moments more. Finally, she made a third, a last—an undoubtedly costly—wish.

"I wish for the little creature to return and spin this straw into gold."

She held her breath. Moments ticked, a minute tocked, and then the little fairy was there, smooshed between a bale of hay and the spinning wheel.

"Hey, Babes," he said sadly. "Did you wish for me to spin all this straw into gold?"

"Yes. That is my wish. Spin this straw into gold. But I have nothing left to give you."

"This is the tricky bit. The costly bit," he warned.

RuthLess nodded, intrigued. She didn't think she'd have to give up her life. That was rather more of a demon deal than a fairy deal.

"I will spin all this," he tried to throw his arms wide, but his hands smacked into the bales, restricting his movement, "all of the straw into gold. But you must pay me with your firstborn child."

Ruth held very still. "My firstborn child?"

"Yes. I told you this wish would cost the most."

"But…if I'm hearing you correctly…you want a baby. As a gift."

"A royal baby. I heard you and the king. I heard the deal you made. If I spin this gold, you will give me a firstborn royal baby."

"I see. That seems quite an unusual thing to want."

"Does it? Fairies often steal babies. Replace them with changelings, that sort of thing."

"True." Ruth tapped her chin. "I think demanding a royal child for a third wish has something to do with a curse. A certain knight's curse. Could that be true?"

"Yes," he said so quietly, it might have just been the rubbing of straw on straw.

"Good! You shall have my firstborn."

"Just like that?"

"Just like that."

"Aren't you worried what will happen to your child? What I might do to it?"

Ruth laughed, and it was the first time she'd felt happy in a long while. "Not at all. You are my friend, aren't you?"

His wide mouth turned down, his long fingers wove together, the golden glow around him sparkled and sparkled. "Am I still?"

"You are," Ruth declared. "Now spin this straw and tell me the rest of the golden knight's story. He was exiled. Did he find a way to open the portal back to his world?"

The little man shook his golden curls, bemused, and set right to work. "He did. Although it was only because of a third great wish he granted to a very good friend."

"Isn't that fascinating?" Ruth said. "A third wish. A good friend."

"There was still one last thing he would need to open the portal to his world. A key."

"Such a complicated curse. What is the key?"

"His name."

"The knight's name?"

"Yes."

"He doesn't remember it?"

The little man laughed. "He remembers it. But it must be guessed by a creature of magic and must be spoken by the same."

"A creature of magic. Such as a fairy?"

He shook his head, his foot rocking the pedal, his fingers feeding twists of straw into the flyer. "Not a fairy. Some other magical creature. Like a phoenix, or a griffin."

"Or a dragon?"

He nodded.

"There are a *lot* of dragons in this kingdom," she said. "Do you suppose the golden knight knows about the dragons?"

"Oh, I think he must."

The wheel spun faster, straw catching sparks of yellow fire as it wound around the bobbin.

Ruth watched in silence, her thoughts spinning as quickly as the wheel, a new plan forming like threads of gold.

A year passed. The king had been delighted to find the cellar filled with gold. But he had been even more delighted to meet RuthLess.

In short, they fell madly in love at first sight.

It didn't hurt that they had more gold than any soul in the kingdom. Enough to distribute to all of their citizens, including the dragons, and still have a good and proper hoard.

It didn't hurt that they both enjoyed each other's company and ruling the kingdom together.

It didn't hurt that when RuthLess told King Kage–King WrecK-age–her biggest secret, he was thrilled with his luck.

After the baby was born, RuthLess waited in the throne room each day, watching her little daughter crawl on the floor. The fairy creature hadn't arrived to collect the child yet. She hoped he would soon.

"Hey, Babes."

RuthLess smiled. She had missed him.

"Hello," she said. "I see you are wearing beautiful golden armor."

"Like it?" He held his arms out and spun so she could see it from every angle.

"It suits you," she said.

"I see you are wearing a crown," he said.

"Like it?" She tipped it to a jaunty angle.

"It suits you," he replied. They both grinned at each other for a moment, then the baby made a noise and Ruth pointed at her.

"This is my daughter, Bel."

"Belle, is it?"

"No, Bel. TerriBel."

"You named your daughter TerriBel? That's a strange name for a princess."

"Perhaps," Ruth said. "But it's not strange for a dragon."

Just then Bel sneezed. The adorable squishy human baby popped into the shape of a little dragon, tough black scales flecked with red sparks. She yawned, revealing a terrifying collection of sharp teeth before popping back into the shape of a human baby.

"My stars," the fairy knight said, shocked. "That is…um…"

"I was thinking," Ruth said.

The baby spotted the fairy's shiny boots and gave a victorious coo. She crawled crookedly toward them.

"Thinking?" he asked, keeping a wary eye on the approaching child.

"Thinking a dragon baby is a *very* hungry baby."

The golden knight's eyes went wide. He took a step backward. The baby crowed again as she changed course and put on speed.

"Hungry?" the fairy asked.

"Very. And baby dragons love to eat evil."

"What are you suggesting?"

"That you take my child and wreak havoc."

The baby arrived at her destination and gently patted his golden boot before smiling at her reflection in it.

If she had many, many more sharp teeth than a human baby should have, well, she was only a few days old, and new to taking on a human shape.

"But, she's just a baby." The fairy knight looked at Bel and shook his head. "It is very dangerous in the fairy realm."

"There is nothing more dangerous, and nothing stronger than a baby dragon," RuthLess said. "The magic that surrounds her is impenetrable protection. No magic can breech it, no weapon can pierce it. A baby dragon is protected by an "egg" of magic.

"She will eat any evil you point her at. If it is made of magic, she will cancel it. If it is made of bone, she will crush it. She is mighty. A great, great warrior."

Bel hiccupped and a tail sprung out of her bottom. She spent the next several moments crawling in a circle chasing it.

"Great warrior," he said doubtfully.

"Great warrior," the king, WrecKage, said as he strode into the room. "No greater. Dragon babies have carved holes in the skies, shredded galaxies to dust, destroyed the foundations of gods."

"Why have I never heard of this?" the golden knight asked.

"Dragons know how to keep secrets." RuthLess winked.

The king chuckled. "Yes, we do. Imagine what might happen if the world discovered the power of our offspring? Precious gold would be wasted on wars."

"If you are certain…" the fairy knight said.

"We are very sure. Bel, come here my darling."

Bel crawled to her mother. RuthLess lifted her up and nuzzled her chubby neck before staring into her eyes. "That fairy knight is your mother's best friend."

"Best friend?" he asked faintly.

"Best friend," she affirmed. "He must return to the fairy world and fight an evil king to save his family. Would you like to eat an evil king and save a family?"

Bel growled happily.

"Good then. Off you go."

Ruth set her on the floor.

Bel turned into a dragon, bigger than she had been just moments before: her teeth longer, the darkness of her scales midnight. Between those scales, lightning crackled.

When Bel stalked over to the fairy knight, she wasn't a baby. She was a beast.

A hungry beast.

"Are you sure?" he asked again.

"Go," Ruth said.

He shook his head. "I can't. Someone magical must…"

Ruth snapped her fingers. "…guess your name and say it. I remember. It's Rumpelstiltskin, isn't it?"

The golden knight stood in utter shock.

A small bright spot grew in the air behind him, as if a looking glass had been mounted there. Through that looking glass could be seen a magical, wondrous land.

"How did you know my name?" he asked.

"I didn't," Ruth said. "He did."

Argentum stepped into the room. He looked just as he always looked. Perhaps there was an extra sparkle in his eyes. Perhaps there was a bit of silver glow to his skin. Perhaps his mouth looked wider, and his fingers longer.

"Argentum," the golden knight said.

"Brother," Argentum said. "I told you I would help you break your curse. Now, shall we save our families?"

Argentum shimmered, and was clad in silver armor that matched Rumpelstiltskin's.

"Yes," Rumpelstiltskin laughed. "We shall."

Argentum strode forward and patted Bel gently on the head, then stood next to his brother.

"Oh, and Argentum?" RuthLess said.

"Yes, my queen?"

"I wish you to return to us. I wish you to return with our child, and all those who would be our friends."

Argentum bowed. "As you wish, my queen."

The golden knight, the silver knight, and the black dragon jumped through the portal, which closed with a snap.

"Well," the king said. "How long do you suppose they'll be gone?"

"Long enough we could count our gold again," she said.

Queen RuthLess and King WrecKage strolled down to the cellar. Stone ceiling, stone walls, and piles and piles of gold.

They locked the door behind them before they started counting, of course. Because in the kingdom of great mountains and sprawling valleys, and rolling fields full of grain, there were dragons *everywhere.*

END

AUTHOR'S NOTE

I've always loved the Rumpelstiltskin fairy tale, especially the part where the little magical creature spins straw into gold. But I was always left with questions.

How did Rumpelstiltskin know the farmer's daughter was in trouble?

Why did he give her all those chances to guess his name?

What in the world was he gonna do with a royal baby?

Did the farmer's daughter really want to marry the king?

I'm delighted to say in WISH UPON A STRAW, I answer all those questions, plus a few more that left me giggling. Like: what happens to a kingdom when it's overrun by dragons?

ABOUT THE AUTHOR

Devon Monk is a *USA Today* Bestselling fantasy author. She writes urban fantasy, hockey fantasy, future fantasy, science fiction, humor, noir, and steampunk magical westerns (among other things). She currently has seven series, several novellas, multiple short stories, and one short story collection on the shelves.

Devon lives beneath the beautiful cloudy skies of Oregon. When not writing, she can be found drinking too much coffee, designing ridiculous knitted toys, and shouting at hockey games. For free stories, knitted whimsies, and her newsletter, please visit: www.devonmonk.com.